HIDDEN HEADGAMES

THE OUTSTRETCHED GRASPING HAND
Auctorial Preamble

****

Sometimes there isn't room for everything. That's where "Hidden Headgames" comes in. Consider it a game of 'fill-in-the-blanks'.

There certainly wasn't room for everything that wanted to be in "Goddess Gambit". (GAMBIT counted as the last full-length installment of *'The Thrice-Cursed Godly Glories'*, the inaugural trilogy released by Phantacea Publications between 2008 & 2012.) Yet, at over 350 pages, before the addition of bonus materials, it was, and remains, at least to my mind, massive.

It was so big we didn't find out, not for sure, who survived its endgame-battle for howsoever-diminished, and drenched, Dustmound until 2014's "Helios on the Moon", itself the third and final entry in the *'Launch 1980'* literary tryptich. (It began in 2009 with "The War of the Apocalyptics" and continued with "Nuclear Dragons" in 2013.)

Even that two-chapter addendum didn't finish off GAMBIT; GAMES does. It isn't a sort of sequel; it's a sort of prequel instead. One that only slightly overlaps "Janna Fangfingers", the mini-novel that led directly into GAMBIT after closing off "The Thousand Days of Disbelief", Book Two of that extraordinary epic.

"The Forgettable Fiend", the initial story sequence in the collection of novella-length vignettes you're holding in your hands, gets the long time a-coming, conclusory honours. And if you already know who the Forgettable Fiend is in terms of **Jim McPherson's Phantacea Mythos**, then Smiler's main mojo hasn't been working on you. I know it hasn't on me because I have to keep up ***pH-Webworld*** online and it contains bread baskets brimming over with Web Wheaties (information) on said Mythos; on said Smiler, dot-ditto.

Sooth as always said, at least by me, Smiler's been with us since 1978's Phantacea Three. (The original incarnation of **PHANTACEA** was as a series of six oversized comic book 'floppies' that came one issue short of completion.) Therein he was often referred to as Rhadamanthys, the same as the seemingly human piper in "Feeling Theocidal", Book One of the GLORIES trilogy. No surprise there. It was the same character.

What about Squirrelly Tethys in "The Death's Head Hellion" and Tomcat Taddletale in "Contagion Collectors", the first two mini-novels comprising 1000-DAZE? Could be. And Reilly Haddeus in FANGERS, its third composite? Almost definitely. Not that even the recurring deviant, Jordan 'Q for Quill' Tethys, also the Legendarian, can recall him at its denouement. That despite this:

"The Legendarian had a hot shower, alone. He was … towelling himself off when he chanced to look into the bathroom mirror. What was that streaked into its steaminess? No bout a-doubt-it. Undeniably, that was the letter 'D', done at an angle of 90° clockwise.

"As for why it looked like it was smiling, well, wasn't that what the letter 'D' done at that angle would do? That determined, that then instantly forgotten, he had a remarkably good night's sleep."

At least Jordy tried. Over the multiple centuries of Smiler's existence, many another has as well, with the same result. In case you haven't figured it out yet, that's his main mojo. As shall be revealed in due course it's hardly his only one. Why do his fellow devils so often address him as Judge? Is he secretly Sedon, sometimes thought of as the Devil Himself? Could he be, or have ever been, King Sodom?

Since it links all three parts of GAMES, I'll tell you this much at the outset. The 'D' stands for Daemonicus, once (as per FEEL THEO) the King of Demons. Kings have queens. King Sodom has, had, for example, Queen Gomorrah. Pyrame Silverstar reckons that was her, going back 4,000 years. She's right about that. But who else was she? Dealt with that in HELLION. Only – now it's her turn – she seems to have forgotten it.

Forgivable, perhaps. She's only just recently been decathonitized. Blame that, as mostly told in NUKE, on the launching of the Cosmic Express. Wait! Wasn't NUKE set entirely on the Outer Earth, with no mention of the Hidden Continent of Sedon's Head whatsoever? Yes and no. Some of that was made clear in HELMOON. The rest of it is herein; here in GAMES' second section, "Pyrame's Progress", to be absolutely precise.

Master Devas would be spirit beings without their power foci and debrained daemonic bodies. Pyrame's called the Pauper Priestess because she doesn't have the former; never has. Didn't need one because she'd been a solid individual for fully two thousand years prior to her devic siblings and cousins. Now, though, she's not only lost her solidifying daemon, she's forgotten her identity.

GAMES also serves as a lead up to '*Wilderwitch's Babies*', 2016's "Decimation Damnation" being the first mini-novel extracted from said open-ended saga. Might the Witch's saviour – after her near-terminal encounter with Mater Matare, the Apocalyptic of Death, at the end of WAR-POX – have been Pyrame's daemon? Let's say yes. That doesn't mean the Witch knows her identity, however. Until ...

Wilderwitch braved her best bluster. "Who's your sad excuse for a girlfriend, Sal — Murk Mist, Mad for Mud Magpies? Looks likes she could use brightening up."
"This," he said, introducing his dusky companion, "Is the lovely Lilith. She's a demon queen; make that the Demon Queen. You might have heard of her. She's the mother of Anti-Patriarch Cain, Slayer of Abel ... You're going to bear our child; whom I might name Abel simply because Lily's never had an Abel before."

Should mention that, back in WAR-POX, Wilderwitch learned from none other than Freespirit Nihila, formerly Harmony, the Unity of Balance, that she was the incarnation of selfsame none-other — at least selfsame when she was altogether the incomparable Harmony. That is to say prior to her execution, as told in FANGERS, by brood brother, Unholy Abaddon, the Unity of Chaos.

So, does the third vignette in GAMES, namely "Acquiring Nihila", tell how the Witch acquires Nihila? Not even close. The Witch doesn't even appear in the book. Not unsurprisingly given its title, Nihila does.

As do the folks, many of whom are witches, not so much behind the launching of the Cosmic Express as its destruction; one of whom is the Female Entity, aka Miracle Memory. Which in turn makes GAMES a kind of continuation of HELMOON as well as what amounts to NUKE's untold side-story.

Fear not ... BABIES will be back, full-throttle, come "Daemonic Desperation", some of which is included as a bonus vignette at the end of this very collection. You get one guess as to the identity of the desperate daemon.

Hint: it's neither Pyrame Silverstar nor Freespirit Nihila. They're devils.

Jim McPherson
Creator/Writer
The *PHANTACEA* Mythos

****

Chapter Titles

HIDDEN HEADGAMES

— 30 Maruta – 14 Tantalar 5980 —

Jim McPherson

A *PHANTACEA* Mythos Print Publication
James H McPherson, Publisher

ISBN 978-1-927844-18-2
First Published 2017

PART ONE – THE FORGETTABLE FIEND

Games 1: **Sixty Missing Stars**

========

Sedonda, 30 Maruta 5980

The Cosmic Express was launched from the Outer Earth's Centauri Island on Sunday, November 30, 1980. On the Inner Earth of Sedon's Head – possibly one of the perhaps dozens of Afterlife or Otherworld settings for myths and legends told by indigenous peoples throughout the globe – the date was much the same: Maruta the 30th, 5980 Year of the Dome.

========

Three not exactly towering, yet nonetheless distinct, not to mention extinct, volcanoes that once formed the tips of separate islets dominated the mostly man-conjoined island off the coast of Maui, Hawaii. Despite hitherto impenetrable secrecy, a comparatively minuscule Kamikaze Craft sent on its way by the recently revived WORLD (the Worldwide Order with the Right to Life and Death) intercepted the Express seconds after liftoff.

The results of the collision had to have startled all concerned. Instead of exploding, both vessels blasted into a black space. Pinpricks of light, in their dozens, approached the spacecrafts. What were they — stars, faeries, angels? None of the above. Not precisely.

Weren't gods either. Not strictly speaking; certainly not anymore. Were devils!

========

Tsishah Twilight felt antsy.

========

She should, some would say, because she was the reigning Mother Superior of the Antediluvian Sisterhood of Flowery Anthea. Reigning, she would say, in name alone. Should be, she would also say, the life-loving Antheans' comfortably retired, only ever nominal Mother Superior. Having been born in 5934, at the middling age of 46 – four years before she was even eligible to become one – there was no way she was anywhere near being a Nightingale elder, the Ants' real powers-that-be.

And the powers that be behind her throne, needs be added, albeit only one of her 'thrones'. Tsishah wasn't just an alpha Ant, though she was that. She was also an alpha Mariamnic, an alpha Athenan, an alpha Althean and an alpha Hecate-Hellion, to name just four of the Hidden Headworld's myriad other witch-sisterhoods for whom, as the non-Lemurian Aortic of Shenon, Witch Isle, she presented their public face.

Philosophically she was more anti-devil, demon-loving Hellion than anything else. She wasn't their superior, their Morrigan, however. That honour belonged to Morgianna Sarpedon, who just happened to be her mother. Undeniably mother and daughter, they nevertheless didn't look at all like each other.

Although born in the Weirdom of Cabalarkon – geographically Sedon's Devic Eye-Land – Mama Morg was actually a hybrid Utopian female. Nevertheless appeared full-blooded. That is to say she resembled a mobile, white-as-daylight, marble statue; ambulatory alabaster, as the joke went. By contrast Tsishah could and did pass for an Irache, the Inner Earth's equivalent of a North American native Indian.

That they looked so different came down to their demons. The one Morg wore was invisible, whereas the one Tsishah wore had once been pretty much just that: the altogether human child of two native North American Indians. Her name had been Shah as well; Shahiyeda as opposed to Tsishah.

They shared more than just an identical diminutive and what nowadays amounted to the same skin. They shared the same birthday, perhaps to the second. Shared the same birthplace dot-ditto: a War Witch shelter on the Cattail side of the Gypsium Wall, Sedon's Hairband, what separated the Head's ponytail of a peninsula from its occipital regions.

They didn't share the same fathers; though, like their mothers, their fathers were both Summoning Children. Nor did they share the same brain. Tsishah's Shah-demon was brainless; rather, she'd been forcibly debrained. Had to be really. At the time, most of twenty years gone now, even Ant Nightingales agreed debraining her seemed the only way to stop her insane rampages, as well as those of her daemonic followers, most of whom were proper, without the 'a', demons: man as well as devil-eaters.

Needless to say, Tsishah and Shahiyeda had quite the her-stories. So did Morgianna, who, as an Inner Earth Summoning Child, was not quite fourteen years her eldest daughter's senior. She, Mama Morg, was among those with Tsishah in Petrograd, the capital city of New Iraxas, Sedon's Blackhead, Godbad's north-easternmost province. Another was Amphitrite, Morg's fellow Summoning Child and Tsishah's fellow Aortic.

Shenon was s heart-shaped island off the Cattail Peninsula's west coast in the Hidden Headworld's Interior Ocean of Akadan. Like a heart it was divided into four distinct areas, Quarter-Queendoms to use their phraseology; unlike a heart, none of them were called atriums. Aortics were two of Shenon's appointed Quarter Queens; the other two being Ventriculars.

Long before the Great Flood of Genesis, the Hidden Headworld was known as Pacifica, the Places of Peace; not to be confused with Zealandia, the already long sunk continent in the South Pacific, what nowadays bordered on the Antarctica-lapping Southern Ocean. Then an archipelago, not a properly filled-in continent, Pacifica was Eden's Zoo, the repository for the pre Golden Age, Edenite civilization's genetic experiments.

Pre-Genesea back then, Shenon wasn't Witch Isle; wasn't even a Weirdom, occupied or abandoned; it was the Edenite zookeepers' headquarters. By howsoever-ironic contrast, these days it was the centre of one of the more successful of those experiments' aquatic heartland. These were the hence very much real Lemurians of Outer Earth fables and legend.

Amphibious, like all female Lemurians were for the first fifty to sixty years of their lives, Amphitrite was their hereditary queen. She didn't wear a demon, not technically, though they were related in that both were subterranean; subcranial, as she preferred to put it, technically. Hers was a mandroid guard-body.

Similarly composed of the subtle matter demon-stuff sometimes referred to as Stopstone or Solidium, also Godcrud, as sourced deep within the Hell Well of the World, far to the Head's north, it made her appear akin to a man-sized frog preserved in ambulant amber, albeit one with the scaly breasts of a humanoid female.

It also kept her sprayed with ordinary, as in non-vampiric, mist. Had to since, as a Summoning Child, and therefore rapidly approaching her sixtieth birthday, she'd soon have to join never-amphibious Lemurian males permanently beneath the sea. It also allowed her to appear to be almost anything she wanted to be; a useful knack to have, especially when she found her way to the Outer Earth.

Ambulant amber didn't just draw stares out there; it also drew gunfire — and, when that didn't work, bazooka blasts.

That she hadn't submerged herself already was entirely due to willpower. Her deviant daughter Lakshmi, called Arthadot, after her devic half-father, intended to marry a much older man, one Centurion Sophiscient Barson, by name and title, this coming Devauray. That'd be Saturday beyond the Dome; where she, Amphitrite, had indeed lived – and fought, as the supranormal Lady Lemurian – for a number of years, going back to the late Thirties.

An aspect of Lakshmi's deviancy rendered her noticeably Piscine rather than froglike; in other words, she cold pass for human. Until, that is, very close inspection revealed the gills behind her ears, the slightly scaly skin and the too-sharp teeth. She lived with Dand Tariqartha, Lazareme's Persian or Earth Magician, in his protectorate, the Thousand Caverns of Temporis. Which also lay far to the north, albeit not so much above the Hell Well as it made up perhaps the largest and most populated patch of it.

Hell Well's Temporis territory was mostly situated beneath Sisert, the Silent Sands of Cathune, Sedon's Cranium, which was also known as Sedon's Bald Spot. Amphitrite wanted to be there for her daughter's wedding as well as her eighteenth birthday the day before; Lazam in here, Friday out there. Assuming they weren't too preoccupied with this Panharmonium Project of theirs, Tsishah and her mother of a Morg would be attending it with her.

Assuming also they weren't bat-bit first.

========

Ferdinand Niarchos, the province's governor, had invited the three high level witches, among many another, to Petrograd in order to discuss various strategies re handling the Head's Ambulant Dead. It was a delicate matter. As if to underscore its delicacy they'd just finished a teleconference with one of them, the governor's not-entirely-late father Gomez.

Dead as he was, Gomez took a terrible risk holding a teleconference presumably originating from his exceedingly compromised base in Sanguerre, the capital of the Bloodlands, New Valhalla, Sedon's Inner Nose. He belonged to the Bloods' pro-Byronic, pro-Godbadian faction, while its currently anti-devil, pro-Hadd faction, as led by the independently intelligent Sangazur, Guardian Angel Tyrtod, was in the ascendancy.

Tyrtod and his group had become so strong of late they'd forced their supposedly only acting, but nevertheless long-serving Master Deva Dand, a Lazaremist named Badhbh Morrigu, also known as Battle Babe, to seek refuge in neighbouring Crepuscule, Sedon's Outer Nose, her sister in Thrygragos Lazareme's devic protectorate. (Her formative years there, the Land of Twilight, was why she was better known as just that, Tsishah Twilight. Her given surname, Thrae, meaning Three, derived from the three sides of her background: human, Utopian and feeorin-faerie.)

Not only was deposing a devic Dand, no matter how adoptive or usurpative he or she may have been, a nigh-on unheard of event on the Head; it wasn't very smart. Say what you will about devils – how impersonal they are; how they suck away your freewill; how they force you to worship them, body and soul, before they'll deign to do you any favours – they were effective, even occasionally beneficent, overlords.

They also didn't kill lesser beings. Weren't allowed to, sooth said. They did, they were cathonitized. Cathonitized devils were stars in the night's sky, the Sedon Sphere; hence the common term for their, with only a couple of exceptions, generally interminable fate: 'ill-starred'. (Outer Earth mythographers used a vaguely similar sounding word, 'catasterized', to describe essentially the same gods-ascribed phenomenon. Whence galaxies, stellar events or star clusters such as Andromeda, the Perseids and Pegasus.)

The proscription against killing held for their azura offspring; Sangs like Tyrtod included. Except of course they were never cathonitized because, as Spirit Beings, they couldn't physically kill anyone. Those they possessed, including Dead Things, could and often did, though. No big deal that. The Head had plenty of warriors and most of them were carnivores. In their favour, the meat New Iraxas's Dead Things ate, usually without bothering to cook it, was slaughtered and packaged for them the same as it was for anyone fully alive in modern-day Godbad.

The trouble with New Iraxas, the trouble with nearby Hadd, Sedon's Mutton Chop, was its Walking Dead, all of whom were animated by a variety of Azura Spirit Beings, were kept in line by a cadre of vampires. And many of them did feed on living men and women. Unless, of course, the animating azura decided to occupy a fresh corpse rather than keep the rotting one she or he had just used to kill his or her consequential new host.

Murder for self-preservation, as opposed to self-defense, was still murder in the eyes of the law. Things got strange when it came to sentencing. Which was why neither Godbad, nor old Iraxas, today's Hadd, had a death penalty; never had. What was the point of executing someone who was already dead?

True, in terms of the Working Dead of New Iraxas, that had been the situation for more than a hundred and fifty years, ever since the Subcontinent of Aka Godbad – Sedon's Mouth, Lower Lip, Lower Jaw and Goatee – had its equivalent of an industrial revolution. True also, New Iraxas was larger than a pimple in comparison to the rest of the subcontinent. It was called Sedon's Blackhead primarily because of what oozed out of its ground; what those on the Outer Earth often referred to as Black Gold. It quickly became so polluted only Dead Things and their vampiric overseers could work there.

There were many reasons why the status quo had changed so dramatically in recent years. The overthrow of Godbad's aristocracy in a brutal civil war that ended barely two decades ago was one. The arrival of people power, aka democracy, and the corresponding abandonment of expensive, ruling class sponsored, manpower-consuming wars of expansion down south, up north and over on the Cattail Peninsula were two others.

However, most agreed the truly telling reason was the rapid rise of Outer Earth style consumerism, as fostered by the known outsider, Alpha Centauri, and his monopolistic corporation, Centauri Enterprises. With, it had to be recorded, the ample, if belated support of Godbad's Byronic deities.

Enlightened capitalism brought with it prosperity and a burgeoning population. Young, better educated, much more skilled and far more coordinated people needed money to buy all the newfangled gewgaws and gadgets CE manufactured, mostly in New Iraxas, due to the proximity of so much petroleum and the industries derived from it .

You had to have work before you could earn money. Additionally, living men and women had to breathe healthy air if they were going to work productively. Thus the greening of New Iraxas, the gradual displacement of smelly Dead Things Working back to Hadd, and CE placing a bounty, payable by the bag, on dusted vamps.

Although Progress, as they say, was progressing, coastal Petrograd, like virtually the entirety of New Iraxas, was still so severely polluted it was a rare night you could see the stars. Not surprisingly therefore, Sanguerre being in the Head's Nostril, a fair distance north and northwest from Petrograd, it was Gomez Niarchos, during the teleconference, who first mentioned the fact that maybe sixty stars, maybe more, were missing from it, the Sedon Sphere. After an impressive windstorm cleared Petrograd's night's sky, those there were able to confirm the stars' absence, if not as yet the exact number of missing ones.

Tsishah born Thrae knew what had happened to them; had hoped there would many more than just sixty or so devils decathonitized. She further hoped her immensely powerful 'pet', the pre-Flood-constructed Gynosphinx, All of Incain, had been able to devour all of those who did escape from Cathonia. If she hadn't, there would be hell to pay. And Tsishah, unlike her mother, was tired of paying Hell, Sedon's Temple, for the demon she wore.

Was her hopefulness warranted? Waiting word on an answer to that was what was making her so antsy; what was making her, even at her relatively advanced age for a War Witch, long to go into action again. Dusting vamps was ever-so-satisfying. She didn't care that Centauri Enterprises was paying a bounty on dustbin bags full of them. Goddamned bats never should have turned her firstborn son – second born overall, of four – into one of them.

Fortunately her Shah-demon, (mostly) debrained as she was, retained the ability to bite back vampirism. That allowed mommy to sort son satisfactorily. Nonetheless, vindictive sort that she was, Tsishah would love nothing better than to sort the vamp who dared to put the bite on her boy in the first place. Would love to do so terminally.

That vamp was an ancestral relation, Janna born Somata, Fangfingers, Second Fangs. Unbeknownst to Tsishah, she too was in Petrograd.

Wasn't hungry, though. She'd feasted already.

========

"So I noticed," said her across-the-bar-table companion.

========

At Governor Niarchos's request, Shenon's two Aortics and Tsishah's Morrigan of a mother brought more than two dozen Athenan War Witches with them to Petrograd. Tsishah knew the majority of them by name; had helped train a high percentage of them. None were tiptop witches like her and her mother.

Truth told, other than they could use witch-stones to get about the Weird (the dark grey matter of Samsara, the Universal Substance between-space), they weren't very accomplished witches at all. As life's avowed defenders, however, dusting vamps was one of their specialities.

To be fair, one of them, Janna St Peche-Montressor, did have an exceptionally influential father-in-law in the Fatman, Alpha Centauri, the acknowledged outsider who, shortly after his arrival on the Inner Earth of Sedon's Head, in early August of 1945 beyond the Dome, founded the eponymous Centauri Enterprises. Of course, if the rumours were accurate, the Fatman was often devil-possessed. Not only that, the devil who often possessed him was none other than Thrygragos Byron, the last of what were once three, fully functional Great Gods left on the Hidden Headworld.

(Of the other two, Thrygragos Varuna Mithras was dead – no mean feat that, not for an until-then immortal devil – while Thrygragos Lazareme, reputedly the firstborn of the three, spent virtually all of his time asleep on Tympani, Sedon's Eardrum. And when he wasn't, asleep, he was in disguise a thousand or so miles away in the DDD {the Dinq Doinq Danq Cavern Tavern} at the far, northeast foot of the Diluvia Mountain Range, getting pissed.

(New Iraxas bordered on other side of Diluvia, in what amounted to its southwest corner whereas Tympani, Sedon's Eardrum, was also known as the Isle of the Undying One. Presumably, though perhaps not necessarily, Lazareme was the ever-undying one. He was certainly aka the Great God Everyman on account of the fact every man and every woman of every specie, human and exotic, beheld him differently; as their ideal of godliness.

(Devils sometimes referred to him as the Lackland Libertine for the simple reason he was just that, a libertine who lacked land. When he was awake, that is; which he wasn't very often. He'd been spending most of his time asleep ever since he helped abolish his Great God of a second generational brother something like 1,500 years earlier. Rumour also had it Lazareme used Mithras's severed head, shattered for pebbly softness, as his pillow.)

This was the Sixtieth Century of the Dome. Come its conclusion, in twenty years time, Bodiless Byron would celebrate the 500th anniversary of the start of his Age. Long before then though, Tsishah trusted, there would be no more Inner and Outer Earth. More importantly, she trusted that when the planet was whole again there'd be no more devils on it.

In this she was hardly alone. Male as well as female Lemurians, Iraches and demon-friendly, Mother Nature worshipping Hecate-Hellions despised devils; regarded them quite correctly as extraterrestrial invaders, as not so much fallen angels as flown devils. Utopians of Weir here on Earth hated them, too. Their equally alien ancestors, in their generational ships, had chased devils, they in their Sedonshem, across the cosmos for very nearly uncountable, multiple multi-millennia prior to landing on the planet a decade pre-Dome.

Ironically, Utopians were trapped in what became the Hidden Continent of Sedon's Head at the same time devils were, 5,980 years ago, by the same event, the Genesea or, as it was most often recalled on the Outer Earth, the Great Flood of Genesis. Ironically because Cathonia, the Cathonic Zone or Dome, what separated the Inner from the Outer Earth, was composed of exactly the same substance the Sedonshem had been — the essence of their greatest enemy, the lone member of the first generation of devazurkind, the devils' consequential All-Father, the Moloch Sedon Himself.

And not just rumour, small case, claimed Sedon was the Devil, large case.

========

Once there was a Master Deva his fellow devils addressed as '*Rumour*'. An inveterate taleteller, the devic Rumour was amongst the supposedly five hundred or so devils who survived the Genesea; who made it to the subsequent Inner Earth just before his Grandfather Sedon was forced to raise the Cathonic Dome. Rumour had it this Rumour was eaten by a wight (a feeorin, a chthonic or earthborn faerie-type), one Tom-Tiddly Taddletale by consensual name, two thousand years ago.

There was another occasionally nominal Rumour. He, however, was an acknowledged deviant, as opposed to some wight's millennia ago digested supper, or an acknowledged devic suicide like Janna Fangfingers' maternal half-uncle and forever-lover, Unholy Abaddon, the former Unity of Chaos. Currently he also was in a beer hall not far from the gubernatorial mansion. Across from him, very much against his every wish, sat a much earlier born-Somata, one who'd been a vampire for five hundred years.

He too was feeling antsy; so much so he was nervously using his Brainrock quill to tap out her first name, over and over again, in Morse code, on the bar-table between them.

========

"What do you mean none?"

"What do you think I mean, Tsishah?" answered her mother of a Morrigan. "Nada, zilch, buggery all. Nary an Eastertide petal on a Christmastime poinsettia."

(Morg was born Nauroz, but brought up by her great-grandmother Kyprian, the now thirty years dead, then Master of Weir, as a Somata, the same as Janna Fangfingers.)

"And you know this because your goddamn goddess told you?"

"Morg knows it because I told her," said the other person on the balcony with them. She was a faun.

========

Being such a tiptop witch, Tsishah had seen through the witch-glamour the faun – one of her best friends ever, whose name was Pusan Wanderlust – wore the moment she entered the ballroom where they'd gathered to participate in the tele-conference with Gomez Niarchos. Contrary to a fallacy commonly heard on the

Outer Earth, fauns were not strictly males. Couldn't be. For the most part they were entirely mortal. Ergo, fauns needed mommies as much as daddies.

For the most part didn't altogether apply to Pusan. She was a deviant, meaning at least one of her faunal parents was possessed of a devil when she was conceived. Every deviancy differed from every other deviancy, if only in its details. Hers, however, was peculiarly perverse, if not precisely unique. She died the same as any ordinary faun but she came back, invariably as a female faun — being as humourous as she was hairy, she called them fauna — and usually in the body of her daughter or granddaughter.

Another deviant had a similarly strange advantage over every other known deviant besides Pusan; had had for going on 2,000 years, roughly half as long as she did. His name was Jordan Tethys, aka the legendary 30-Year Man or variations thereof. Up until about an hour ago he'd been with them in Governor Niarchos's mansion. Right now he was out drinking. They hoped he was not the one being drunk. Tsishah's Mama Morg was about to mention him.

"Now do you understand why I was harping on Jordy to draw me to the Amateramirror this afternoon, before the sun went down and we found out about the missing stars? The Trigregos Talismans have only become more valuable now that dozens of decathonitized devils are loose upon the Head."

In skilled hands the Trigregos Talismans — a blade, a mirror and a tiara — could be used to kill devils. Chrysaor Attis, the Universal Soldier, the most renowned recurring deviant ever, used them together on Thrygragon in 4376, the day that marked the thus far unending death of his devic half-father, Thrygragos Mithras.

More than a millennium later, Chaos (Unholy Abaddon) used the Susasword alone to kill his immediate sibling, Janna born Somata's devic half-mother, Harmony (Datong Harmonia), the Lazaremists' Unity of Balance, just after that Janna became Second Fangs. The Susasword hadn't been seen since, but the other two had; both of them relatively recently.

"As if he would," said Pusan. "You know what happened to his wife, forty years and … what? Four or five lifetimes ago. Jordy was doing a family portrait and didn't realize her necklace was the Crimson Corona. It burst into flames; so did she, spontaneously combusted. It's a wonderment their triplets didn't go up with her."

"Good thing they didn't," noted Tsishah, who hadn't been there but knew the story, from every side. "Otherwise Ukemoshi wouldn't have been around for him to incarnate inside of when whichever one of the other two, Katatribe or Yomikuni, killed him during the Challenge of Weir in 5950." Like her half-sister Andaemyn, Katatribe and Yomikuni were highly effective War Witches; hence why they were still alive. In fact, chances were they were together elsewhere, searching for the same thing, at least one of the Trigregos Talismans.

"Not according to him." Morgianna had been there, in Cabalarkon, the city — the only Weirdom left on the Head that had, to a large measure, maintained its polity purity, albeit at the cost of ever-increasingly inborn idiocy amongst purebloods — tending to her dying great-grandmother when it happened. "Jordy hates coming back as a woman."

"Then he bloody well better be careful," said Pusan, yet another who'd been tending Kyprian. With just a much success. Doubly disappointingly since she had a reputation as one Headworld's most effective Altheans, deviant healers. "Last I checked his oldest eligible offspring are all girls. Not only that, with the arguable exception of Kirin, they're extremely healthy. Fit too, which isn't something Jordy's likely to keep up if one of them has an accident."

Even if he did sometimes come back female, the She-Goat loved this Tethys as a brother. Which he sort of was: Who else kept coming back in much the same way she did?

(Kirin Tethys, which wasn't the name she used, suffered from Foetal Alcohol Syndrome. Wasn't so much unhealthy as overly active, in almost every respect. Was controlled, however, albeit by medications that sometimes left her drowsy. Good thing, even her father agreed, she lived in a convent. Bad thing he might have to, too, if he came back in and as her.)

"Where is he, by the way? I woke up with a note pinned to one of my horns this morning saying he was flying here from Aka Godbad City with Al's Janna and Weird Ferd."

That was another aspect of Tethys's deviant abilities. He could send messages between-space, though not through the Cathonic Dome. He could also send people, himself included, with the same restrictions. The ability came with having a Brainrock quill, what must have once been a devil's talisman or power focus — one in truth, which he always strove to talk, albeit with some small amount of allowable embellishments, that once belonged to Rumour of Lazareme.

"Among other things it said he was having trouble with his memory."

"Aren't we all?" said Tsishah.

"His memory, not the Female Entity," Pusan corrected Shenon's non-Lemurian Aortic.

"Walrus-tusk what we're about to finny-find out," fishified a newcomer as she strode purposefully onto the balcony. "Jordan River's been gone too dugong-long the bikini thong."

Like both her fosterage, more so than step-sister, Amphitrite of Lemuria, and Treat's daughter Lakshmi, she was an anthropomorphic amphibian; albeit another who was far more humanoid than froglike. She had, for example, gills behind her ears instead of in her neck. That made her, also like Lakshmi, a Piscine.

On the other hand, she was a queen like Amphitrite. An ex-queen, make that; a queen by dint of marriage rather than hereditarily. Nowadays she was just a 'lady', Lady Achigan, but, formerly, as well as formally, until about twenty years earlier, she was Queen Scylla of Godbad, also Aka Godbad the subcontinent, not Greater Godbad, the Corporate State thereof.

(The Gulf of Aka lay just below New Iraxas. It was full of subsurface humanoids, hardly all of whom were either Piscines or Lemurian Frog Folk. Had been, rather. Pollution had driven out far too many of them into Akadan, the Headworld's vast, not quite land-locked, Interior Ocean; what, broadly speaking, separated the subcontinental landform from the Cattail Peninsula, Sedon's Ponytail.)

"About brine too," she added, then proceeded to more fay-say than fishify: "I was shoal-tired of waiting for the baiting to do its taking."

========

Yet another deviant, she was a foundling; one found shortly after her birth in the belly of a beast, an approaching impossibly huge whale, Island Leviathan, and subsequently raised by Aortic Merthetis, the current Lemurian Queen Amphitrite's natural mother. That was in 5918 Year of the Dome. Merthetis named her Scylla Nereid. Morg's paternal great-grandmother, Kyprian Somata, gave her the codename she used to this day. Said codename was Fisherwoman, though most everyone addressed her as Fish.

The then Master of Weir, then High Illuminary of Weir, then Mother Superior of the Anthean Sisterhood on both sides of the Dome and, arguably, the highest achieving Nightingale ever, did so just prior to sending her, a natural-born witch, to the Outer Earth for the fist time in 5933, 1933 out there. Not so mercifully she didn't send Fish outside alone. She sent the untried teenager out with her closest, most trusted friend and companion, Kyprian's fellow Illuminary and Fish's primary instructress, Kanin Nauroz, Granny Garuda, Morg's paternal great-aunt.

Neither did Master Kyprian have Granny take her out there strictly for training purposes. Not just rumour had it she sent Fish beyond the Dome to get her away from the faerie-bought charms of a certain, slightly younger, devil-worshipping Summoning Child who, among other things, happened to be next in line to the throne of Aka Godbad at the time.

Merthetis, Kyprian and Granny were gone now. So were most of Fish's small fry. (She was a breeder as well as a breather, as she might fay-say it. In this regard she sometimes referred to herself as a pisciculturist of rollicking roe, but almost nobody could possibly know what that meant without a dictionary and she rarely carried one with her.) Her eventually kingly husband, Achigan Auranja, wasn't; was now, however, just Lord Achigan of (note the spelling) Achigon, Sedon's Lower Lip-Tip.

Fish rarely spent any time with him anymore. Irrefutable pudding-proof lacking, she nevertheless believed he had, over the initial three decades of their ever-strained relationship, traded their small fry, one by one, by prearrangement, to the feeorin faeries of Crepuscule. He did so in order to, first, ensnare Fish, whom he'd loved since the moments he set eyes on her as a toddler; to, second, ensure his personal survival, then his survival as the King of Godbad; and, third and finally, to guarantee he survived as both alive and with his own brain.

Crepuscule, Sedon's Outer Nose, was also known as Twilight, the Land thereof. Tsishah Twilight acquired her surname because she was once subsumed within its forever Faerie Queen Godda. Not long after in effect deposing herself, as the marital Queen of Godbad; her Inner Earth Summoning Child of a husband, as its king; and his relatives, as its aristocratic ruling class; Fish helped disabuse Tsishah of suchlike inappropriateness.

Needlefish to say, Fish didn't have quite the her-story; she had bait-buckets overflowing with herring her-stories. She also looked wonderfully young, fit and fulsome for someone in her early sixties. Then again, in that regard only, deviancies usually weren't peculiarly idiosyncratic.

The majority of deviants, like the majority of Utopians bred and fed in the Weirdom of Cabalarkon – which Tsishah's Mama Morg hadn't been for thirty years – aged much less quickly than everyone save devils, demons and faeries. Unfortunately, most folks, other deviants included, felt Fish's distinctive deviancy brought with it one major disadvantage.

She tended to talk funny. To the barbed flange of a fishhook's point that she at times verged on incomprehensibility.

=========

"You're using Jordy as bat-bait!" Pusan was aghast.

"No more the seashore, mullet. This fish-head's clacking and it isn't smelt-spelling Al's Janna. We're bass-fast, we'll land us a big one."

A mullet was a goatfish; so was Pusan's devic half-mother all those millennia ago: one of Byron's Winter Zodiacals, the one representing Capricorn. Al's Janna was Janna St Peche-Montressor, Alpha Centauri's 27-year old daughter-in-law. That Janna was the same age as Tsishah's half-sister, Andaemyn, their Mama Morg's only other child, who was currently on the other side of the Hidden Headworld involved in a search for nothing less than the long lost Susasword.

The hybrid Utopian, the Hecate-Hellions' Morrigan, their legitimate Superior, not that she liked that broadcast, had been enchanted by a faerie-type, hence Tsishah, less than a year after young, barely pubescent Achigan, with his faerie-bought charms, seduced Fish, hence the first of their small fry.

Morg grasped the import of her lifelong associate, more so than friend's assertion immediately. Raising her fingernail, possibly even daemonic-lacquered hands to her face, as if to mask her astonishment – not that it could mask the astonishment eminently readable in her eyeballs – she exclaimed: "Head-aching, Jordy tapping out Janna on the inside of your skull … he's caught Second Fangs and you want us to reel her in?"

"We're not reeling in anyone, Morg. We're going to krill-kill her. For real."

Fish materialized her Brainrock-glowing, oversized fishhook, a gaffing hook, in one hand; materialized a handful witch-stones in the other. She had webbed fingers. She dropped some of these last at her feet; her toes were webbed as well. One witch-stone she stepped on; was instantly dugong-gone, the bikini thong, between-space.

Tsishah Twilight and her Morrigan of a mother, demon-decked the pair of them, followed suit. So did Aortic Amphitrite, in full Lady Lemurian mode. (Like Fish, as Fisherwoman, and Morg, as the White Witch, she'd been an active supranormal on the Outer Earth.) Back in the ballroom off the balcony, many an Athenan War Witch did a ditto.

When Fish stopped fishifying, not that she ever could for very long, someone usually died. Died a final time in the case of Janna Fangfingers.

=========

Jordan Tethys, the recurring 30-Year Man, earned one of his many nicknames, that of the Legendarian, because he made his living telling stories. He claimed he'd been doing so, incarnation after incarnation, for going on 2,000 years. And he had. It wasn't one of his stories; it was fact.

Another fact was he rarely reached his thirty years life-limit.

=========

While not prevalent, on a Hidden Headworld encased, over under sideways down, by the Devil Himself; in an Age belonging to the Moloch's lone still fully functional, second generational son, Unmoving Byron; where a great many of Dark

Sedon's third generational descendants ruled as devil-gods and, hence, were often petitioned for purposes of either paternity or maternity; deviancy was relatively commonplace.

Tethys earned another of his nicknames, 30-Beers, because (even as a she) he drank buckets of beer; up to a howsoever-indulgent, but nevertheless self-imposed limit of thirty a day. After a long flight from Aka Godbad City, and what seemed to him an endless, more importantly beer-less, morning, afternoon and early evening of discussions re the Head's Dead, he finally took a bolstering beer-break.

Over Governor Niarchos's objections, he left the well-guarded, Godbadian-government compound, with its massive, supposed air-cleansing and smog-repelling fans, strolled over to a smoky beer hall Ferd had nonetheless recommended and, as was his wont, started all but inhaling his daily allotment of suds.

With the stark-white, yet ever-enticing Janna born Somata – in a fashionable outfit as ghastly white as her alabastrine skin; a Crystal Skull containing her twin's ashes hung from a torc strung around her neck; and her fang-fingered Brainrock glove still drenched in blood from her latest kill – brazenly sitting across the bar-table from him, he was past just beginning to seriously regret his decision to leave the gubernatorial mansion.

Entertaining her was hardly his choice. Bars being public places, and bats being members of the public in not just New Iraxas, she'd sat down entirely unbidden. He never would have ventured forth if he reckoned she'd be about. Hell's Teeth, she lived – if you could use such a word to refer to an Undead vamp – in golden-walled, nowadays Necropolis.

Ancient Manoa, as Necropolis was originally known, was by far the largest, howsoever-controversially occupied metropolis in today's Hadd. Hadd – El Dorado when it was a Byronics' shared 'sphere of influence' (as opposed to devic protectorate, none of which Byronics had, not officially) – was the Land of the Ambulatory Dead. Necropolis was located hundreds of miles to the southeast, across the Gulf of Aka, from Petrograd.

Although he had bagged her, bed-wise, when she was altogether alive, that was nearly five hundred years and, for him, at a minimum, must be two dozen lifetimes ago. Furthermore, as he recalled from more than a few encounters with her over the centuries since she became Second Fangs, vampire extraordinaire, and sometime thereafter the surrogate queen of Hadd, she wasn't the sentimental sort. Unfinished beer or no unfinished beer, the time had come to draw himself safely elsewhere.

Then they had him, her vamps, demystifying out of what until then he'd mistaken for bar-smoke, as opposed to bat-smoke. Had him, arms pinned back against the chair, his Brainrock quill shaken out of his grip onto the tabletop, his garlic necklace torn off and tossed against the wall, before he could dot a ditto to any of his getaway drawings. Beer had been the death of him before. By the looks of things it wouldn't be the direct cause of his death this time, though.

Suddenly the nib of his Brainrock quill began to glow almost blindingly bright. Then, like a miniature sunburst, it ignited.

========

Whether or not she'd somehow been forewarned they were coming, Janna Fang-fingers escaped. She did so by mystifying just as the Fish-led party of Athenan War Witch-

es came through the Weird intent upon abolishing her. Many of her vamps weren't so lucky. Financially speaking the War Witches made a krill-killing — Centauri Enterprises paid by the pound for vamp-dust. But it wouldn't be complaining.

Wouldn't be inhaling, either. Not until said dust-bags were buried deep beneath the ground as if a carbon sink.

========

There were a great many successful escapes that day. By far the most notable was that made by more than sixty stars from the night's sky above the Inner Earth of Sedon's Head. For that was what the launching, and almost instantaneous interception, of the Cosmic Express became: a massive jailbreak.

Was a pre-planned jailbreak as well. Albeit, best laid plans, etc., one that was supposed to only be a matter of trading one jail cell, a self-contained star, for another, more of a storage cell in a battery designed to help an ancient She-Sphinx keep on ticking. In the name of their treasured Panharmonium Project – what Jordan Tethys called the Witch Sisterhoods' Panharmonium Pipedream – Lemurian Queen Amphitrite, other Aortic Tsishah Twilight and her Morrigan of a mother were only some of the plotters.

These last included a number of female Master Devas long ago grown intolerably weary of their genetically imposed subservience to their third generational brothers and masculine cousins. Predominant among them was the Athenan War Witches' devic goddess, Methandra Thanatos, whom ancient, far-travelled Illuminaries of Weir named after Mediterranean Athena.

Hotstuff, as Tethys sometimes referred to her, after her attribute more so than her kept-hidden looks, was married to one of the most overbearing of the locust-lot of them, her brood brother in Mithras, Tantal also Thanatos, Cold to her Heat. In something of a role-reversal, his power focus, a Labrys or double-headed war axe, looked similar to a fallopian tube whereas hers resembled an aristocrat's stick-cane or, more precisely, big-headed matchstick; a dickhead for Mrs Dickhead, as he also said, especially when he was nearing his thirty beer cut-off limit.

The mastermind was Fish's birthmother, Miracle Memory, the recurring Female Entity. Being thoroughly Gypsium-gifted, that Memory, the Mnemosyne Three-Thing, didn't need a link to the Outer Earth. Being both already part of the Weird and almost as good with Brainrock-Gypsium, Machine-Memory's mandroid-making, nonetheless at least partially alive 'organic mechanoid' from millennia earlier, All of Incain, pre-Dome formerly Ginny the Gynosphinx, provided egress to the outside for the rest of those non-devils involved.

Inhuman as she was – Mandroid Mother Machine that she also was – the borderline-intelligent She-Sphinx loved and responded to Tsishah as her master.

Tethys himself had been an unwitting co-conspirator. It was one of his Brainrock-sent, more mental than material messages that alerted the then still cathonitized devils where to rendezvous with the Express and Kamikaze spacecrafts once they were externally thrust into the Sedon Sphere. He'd been coerced into sending it upstairs, into the Dome, the day before, when he was in Aka Godbad City, by the last remaining Sedonic firstborn. The moment he did so, that devil erased his memory of it.

Although any devil could redact memories, this myrionymous, hence non Mithras Spawn had an additional, uniquely specialized talent. No one could remember he existed unless he manifested himself physically in front of you. Which, having once survived an assassination attempt by asteroid, he rarely did.

He was as circumspect as he was shy. He also smiled constantly.

========

That neither of the vessels, and none of the resultantly possessed occupants on them, reached the Prison Beach of Incain — where All could consume and thereby confine them indefinitely between-space, as was the plan — that had everything to do with the Mighty Eye-Mouth in the Sky trying to eat them first.

They didn't agree with him.

****

The complete chronicle of the launching of the Cosmic Express from the Outer Earth's Centauri Island, albeit without any mention of the Inner Earth whatsoever, occurred during "Nuclear Dragons", the second entry in the *'Launch 1980'* story cycle.

Janna Somata's stunning transformation into Janna Fangfingers appeared in the eponymously titled, third mini-novel extracted from "The 1000 Days of Disbelief", Book Two of *'The Thrice-Cursed Godly Glories'* fantasy epic.

Along with Thrygragos Lazareme and his firstborn Unities, Jordan 'Q for Quill' Tethys plays a prominent role in the first two, full-length novels comprising that trilogy. He also narrates half of "Janna Fangfingers" and (sort of) stars in the other half of that mini-novel.

Games 2: **Ahrimanic Intervention**

========

Sedonda/Mithrada, 30 Maruta/Tantalar 1, 5980 YD

Beneath the Cathonic Dome, off the southeast coast of the Hidden Continent of Sedon's Head on the Frozen Isle of Lathakra, Methandra Thanatos, all six inches of her, had been using the visual vapours of her boiling cauldron to keep tabs of events on the Outer Earth's Damnation and Centauri Islands.

It was a taxing effort given that what was happening in both places was occurring virtually simultaneously. By now though, the Damnation Brigade had vanquished the Apocalyptics and were resting while one of them, Wilderwitch, popped through between space on her Anthean Agates looking for a way to get them off the tiny Aleutian atoll.

Was nothing more the Crimson Queen could do to help them. Not yet anyhow.

========

Colonel Avatar Sol went critical just before Cosmicaptain Mikelangelo Starrus reached him. It was more an implosion than an explosion. Sol sucked in on himself and blinked out of existence. Something happened to Mik Starrus. Suddenly a being absorbed the entirety of the cosmicaptain and his pod as well. For a brief second, Thunder and Lightning Lord Yajur, once the Unity of Order, appeared in space. His hair was bolts of electricity; his brown body Apollo-perfect, muscular and dressed in a blazing chlamys.

All three of his eyes were wide open. He raised his lightning blade and pointed it at the moon. "I know you're there, entity. Wait for me. Shan't be long!"

Yajur resolved into Starrus and his pod. The cosmicaptain propelled himself back to the cosmicar. Once he was aboard and all systems were restored, he shucked his pod and removed his helmet. Wife Nidaba, one of the six other cosmicompanions aboard their cosmicar, helped her husband out of the rest of his space-suit. He helped her out of hers. They looked at each other. She gasped incredulously.

"Mik, your forehead!"

A third eye glared out of it.

========

"I'm sorry, Kadmon. I think Novadev destroyed himself – and Ti Tiecher, Avatar Sol, with him – but Starrus-Yajur escaped. Where are you going?" (Devils called Novadev Solstitial Summer. His Great God of a father Thrygragos Varuna Mithras was Solstitial Winter. His brood brothers were Mithras's Torchbearers: Tammuz and Osiraq, aka Cautes and Cautoprates on the Outer Earth, sometimes also Sunrise and Sunset, but more commonly Equinoctial Spring and Equinoctial Autumn.)

"To get my sword."

"Your sword's from the future, at least one possible future. It may not be needed. We're still not much more than ten years after your initial lifetime. The ninety-nine you've experienced betwixt and between might not be relevant. I have secured the SAG Gap, anchored it in near-space. We anticipated devils might become involved in our designs. We have prepared for it. Please let us carry on with the plan.

"To do otherwise, to do what we have so often done during your previous lifetimes, to improvise, to make things up as we go, that's the recipe for continuing failure. Do you really want another hundred lifetimes when we're so close to your first? What did you say to me less than an hour ago?"

"Let's get it right this time."

"Exactly!"

"You're right, milady. We can handle this ourselves."

========

Methandra Thanatos, King Cold's Crimson Queen and the (usually in absentia) Mistress of Mythland, hence Miss Myth, could care less about the seven who definitely weren't her children; was actually curious how Gloriel, Aires and Thalassa, the three D'Angelos who might be her offspring, would resolve their latest predicament. She hoped it wouldn't take as long as it took them to resolve their last one.

Twenty-five years earlier!

========

Even though no places had vanished, people and things disappearing, then reappearing, seemed a common occurrence that fateful day. OJ Maxwell was one who turned up again — on Centauri Island that night. Others, like Devil Wind and the Apocalyptics on Damnation Isle, didn't. Not yet, at any rate.

Adolph 'Dolph' Dulles and Loxus Abraham Ryne were right that Gypsium-Godstuff was part of the explanation; were wrong if they thought it was all of it, however. There was a Man on the Moon, a far-off planetary system called New Weir, and a continent the size of Africa hidden beneath something known as the Cathonic Zone or Dome, also the Sedon Sphere, in the North Pacific Ocean.

Devils were in all three places. Thanks largely to the Smiling Fiend they were a few other places as well. At Smiler's insistence, Miss Myth – yet another of Methandra Thanatos's many appellations – spent most of the evening focused on Centauri Island. The Unmoving One (Thrygragos Byron) and his hated spawn had been using the well-disguised, so-called Nag Gap, (for Nagasaki) to journey between the Head and the Outer Earth for getting on thirty-five years. The Cosmic Express was as much their project as it belonged to the Fatman's New Century Enterprises. (Not to be confused, though it would be easy to do, with Centauri Enterprises in here.)

In some respects, the humans aboard it were guinea pigs. Bodiless Byron, who often possessed said Fatman – born Alfredo Sentalli out there; known as Alpha Centauri in here – intended the cosmicompanions on board to find a safe haven for devils beyond the Earth. When they did, using the plentiful resources of Sedon's Head, the Great God would finance another Express and lead a mass exodus of his children, and any other devil who cared to join him, away from the planet.

Earth, the Unmoving One believed, was a prison foisted on devils by their enemies in the Celestial Sphere. All-Father Sedon, whose essence made up the Dome, was as much Byron's warden as All the Invincible was of Incain. (Although outwardly an uninhabited, nearly tropical beach fairly far south of Frozen Lathakra in the Cattail Peninsula, Incain actually held over a hundred Master Devas. Rather, All held them — within herself, within the dark grey, universal substance between-space of Samsara.)

In the process of keeping track of events on the Outer Earth's Centauri Island, they had witnessed Elephantine Ganesh and the greatest compositional aspect of Aphropsyche Morningstar attempt to kill O'Ryan Maxwell just as the Cosmic Express was launched. That was a disturbing sight. By Sedonic decree, Master Devas weren't allowed to kill lesser beings on the Head. Could they get away with it on the outside?

Then, not all that long ago, they saw what Maxwell had become. What that was, as Tantal was quick to point out, was not a lesser being. Too bad this other extraordinary mortal, the one who seemed imbued with Brainrock, one Professor Romaine Kinesis by name and title, had rescued Maxwell earlier in the day. Now he hoped the Byron Spawn had enough sense to kill both of them. To let them live would be foolhardy.

"Correct me if I'm wrong, Smiler," King Cold was saying, in the unavoidably loud voice he had when he was the giant. "But wasn't that creature a Multivoid, what Outer Earth theologians call a principality and Buddhists a Bodhisattva?"

"I'm not sure I'd go quite that far," argued the Scarlet Empress, in the near squeak she had, despite shouting, when she was the tiny one. "Principalities tend to be sentient-centred phenomena, like a fairy godmother in Crepuscule. Boddhis usually have to earn their ethereal stripes, as it were. From what little we've seen of this Maxwell mortal, he's neither saintly nor unselfish. Also, if it's a Multivoid, then it's a remarkably sane one."

Their never-remembered, unless he was physically present, visitor considered their words carefully, *"There appeared to be something of the mantel about it,"* he contributed. *"Especially the way it altered its form. Certainly it seemed to know about Solidium, but it wasn't composed entirely of the stuff. It drew substance out of the Weird and could change its constituency.*

"Formidable abilities, to be sure, but it looked to me like it was making it up as it went; didn't really know what it was doing. Then there's the obvious fact that it's this Maxwell. No, what the Byron Spawn have to deal with is a deviant, like the ones we saw in action on Damnation Isle this afternoon."

"All the same, the ease it handled Goldenrod alarms me. Mortals, even outside the Dome, shouldn't be able to humiliate our siblings and cousins like that."

"For once we agree, Thanatos. Sorceress," the Smiling Fiend turned from her, even for him, enormous brother-husband to dinky Methandra, *"I know your instincts urge you to follow the three who might be your children – and the large one wearing the Thrygragos Talismans – but I suggest you return to Maxwell and Kinesis on a regular basis. Although I realize you can only see, not hear, what's going on, there is much of value we might learn from their activities."*

"You're the one supposedly so intimate with the Outer Earth and its deviants, Smiler," Methandra – who was indeed only 6-inches tall compared to Tantal's twice-man-sized 12 feet – reminded their deliberately kept-forgettable guest. "What can you tell us about these mortals, other than our deviants are their supranormals?"

The shadowy demon-devil was a fount of knowledge. A number of the supras on Damnation Isle – what he, having no audio and therefore no way of knowing that they now called themselves the Damnation Brigade, referred to as the King Crimefighters – were born as a result of the Simultaneous Summonings of 5920. These included Jervis Murray, the Untouchable Diver, Blind Sundown, Sea Goddess and the Airealist. The Thanatoids of the same name, Thalassa and Aires, were also born late in Tantalar, December out there, in precisely the same time period one would expect of these consequential Summoning Children.

OMP (Obadiah Melvin Power) and Wilderwitch (no other name) were from the Head. So, as it turned out, was Cerebrus's mother, Eden Nightingale, an extremely high level Anthean in her day. Raven's Head was a mutated ravendeer. Gloriel was born the same day in 1933 that the Thanatoids were assaulted by Byron Spawn on Sedon's Peak. Maxwell, he said, was 'presumably' born as a result of the Summoning as was Kinesis's late mother, Roxanne, codename Slipper.

She, like her son, was gifted with Brainrock-based abilities whereas her just as late husband's supranormal talents had everything to do with Solidium. His name was Alexandros Kinesis. His codename was Pluman at least in part because he believed, somewhat correctly, that Solidium came from the Underworld, Hades, Pluto's realm in Roman mythology.

(Solidium was considered Gypsium's fixative, as well as in some respects its opposite, out there. It was Brainrock's dot-ditto on the Inner Earth of Sedon's Head, where it was more commonly known as Stopstone. The one was also called Godstuff whereas the other occasionally answered to Godcrud.

(There were those who called the dark-grey matter of the universal substance between-space Stoprock and/or Brainstone. But, as particle physicists would tell you – as they told those responsible for building the Cosmic Express – that didn't account for anywhere near the whole of it. Whichever one you chose to call it in large measure did account for whatever passed for proper magic on both sides of the Dome.)

The reason he knew these things, the fiend as was his wont further elucidated, was not that he'd physically been beyond the Dome – they all had, albeit not recently – but that he'd once aided a certain Judge Warlock invent something the outworlder called the devil-ray. (Smiler, being mostly from in here these last few millennia, tended to call it the devaray.) That device was supposed to free previously cathonitized devils from the Sedon Sphere and bring them to the Outer Earth.

It didn't quite work that way, he semi-apologized. Hadn't, he provided, mostly because of the interference of the King's Own Crimefighters and their predecessor group, the Society of Saints. A similar gadget, he confided, was Strife's Miracle Key. However, he denied having anything to do with that; even he wasn't daring – he said daft – enough to play a Trigregos Gambit. There was a reason Maenads were considered mad women.

"You should recognize the little girl."

He was referring to Alfredo Sentalli's apparently seven year old niece who had turned up, along with the Fatman (who went by Alpha Centauri in here), his son Yataghan (called Montressor on this side, Sentalli out there) and OJ Maxwell (who had no idea the Dome even existed, let alone what was beneath it), a few minutes ago in the lounge of the oldest hotel on Centauri Island.

Far beneath it, in the bowels of the largely artificial island, lay the Nagasaki Gap that went through Cathonia to connect the island and Aka Godbad City on the Head; Big Shelter, as Antheans called the hidden continent. Didn't take much of an imagination to figure how she got there, though her and associates beyond the Dome would have come up with some plausible explanation as to that. Chances were they'd have also given her a different name and a phony background story.

Tricksters were notorious liars. Devils couldn't lie. He wasn't altogether a devil. Whence why the Smiling Fiend was sometimes known as Judge Druj; Druj meaning 'the Lie'.

"She looks six or seven but she's the mother of your adherent, Morgianna Sarpedon; who, in addition to being the wife of the Deva-deadly Utopian, Demios Sarpedon, was once the Sister Superior of Flowery Anthea on the Outer Earth. Her name's generally given as Hush Mannering and/or Young Life, as opposed to Young Death, her ex-husband, whom you'll also recall, if you cared to put your mind to it.

"He's the Sraddhites' Chief Revenant, has been for many mostly inconsequential years, whereas she's caused us a great deal of inconvenience over the last six decades or so, particularly on Apple Isle in '64 and again in '68. Evidently still does; is about to again, make that. Causing trouble's her most telling talent. She also inadvertently invented – more like reinvented – the name my surrogate shells use on the Outer Earth."

"Daemonicus," said Methandra. Unlike her drunkard of a brother-husband she didn't mind bringing the past back to just that, the mind; not even the failures of the past.

"Just so. You may not my recall my involvement, but the pair of you would remember our efforts, that of the Mithras Spawn, on Ap Isle. It was our intention to secure our own way outside in order to counter Great Byron's Nag Gap and the apparent ease with which the Warlocks – the Judge and his long gone son, Wiccan – could traverse the Cathonic Dome via All the Invincible and her male equivalent, the Giza Sphinx, on the Outer Earth.

"To do that we attempted to reopen the link-way that once existed between Kore's volcano and the Aegean island of Trigon. Both those ventures failed. The first was a real fiasco. We fell into a clever trap set by Judge Warlock, become a dream man by then. He was aided by the Outer Earth supra known as the Sphinx, an acolyte of All and the Frog Queen Amphitrite, Shenon's Lemurian Aortic. As humiliating as that was, what was worse was the ignominy we had to endure of being rescued by a band of other supras as led by Hush herself.

"Two of her followers in that regard back in the mid Sixties were Pluman and Slipper, the parents of this Kinesis fellow. The second occasion resulted in the destruction of Mediterranean Trigon on the Outer Earth, though I'm not sure I can blame that entirely on Hush, whom Tralalorn devolved into a perpetually 7-year old faerie sort after she had your Morg."

"Between times," recalled Methandra, in a tone verging on condemnation. (By Sedonic decree, devils weren't allowed to kill lesser beings. However, presumably because he was fully fused with a very nearly primordial daemon – their original king, as it happened – Smiler could get away with it.) "You had the pleasure of slaying the triple daughters of the Solitary Entity, the ones Hush and her witches eugenically manipulated into what she hoped would become the new Trigregos Sisters."

"Father Sedon, in his wisdom," protested the fiend, *"Knows I cannot be held responsible for the actions of Daemonicus, even if he is, in many respects, my alter ego. An opportunity presented itself and Daemonicus seized it. Unfortunately they turned out to be one of her tricks; a ploy her and suchlike witch radicals deva-devised to draw us out into the open on the Outer Earth, where we are at our most vulnerable.*

"Besides, the Trigregos Sisters, even potential ones, are not lesser beings. In fact, as you females and your sympathizers often suggest, they are our superiors."

King Cold wiped beer foam off his shaggy, veritable icicle beard. "I have this Hush now." The massive lord of Lathakra's Fire Kings and Intuits – thick was one of the milder adjectives Smiler used to characterize him – paused to burp. "Her initial offspring was Saladin Devason, the current Master of the Weirdom of Cabalarkon."

"Well done, Thanatos," congratulated the fiend.

Like Sedon above, he had never understood why the Scarlet Sorceress, who truly was hot stuff in all senses of the phrase, bothered with her buffoon of a brood brother. Besides drinking and brawling with his cousins, including Abe Chaos and Rudra Silvercloud, and younger brothers, most of whom were as tedious as King Cold, about the only thing he was good at was having hundreds, maybe even thousands of useless azuras, all but one not by Methandra.

"When Hush bore him, she was possessed by our sometime friend, Pyrame Silverstar, the Pauper Priestess — who, much later on in mortal terms, was also involved in the devaray venture I was just relating. Hush was changed into a perpetual seven year old by Pyrame's brood sister, Tralalorn, the White Dwarf, shortly after she had Morgianna."

"Mithras's Ninth," commented Methandra admiringly, "With the exception of Cathune Bubastis, a minor Apocalyptic at best, are an impressive litter. While we will never, ever, forgive her for losing control of the Death's Head Hellion and thereby, howsoever-indirectly, causing our Thousand Year Sleep, what the priestess lacks in terms of Tralalorn's abilities, she more than makes up for in guile.

"Her coercive influence on such apparently diverse beings as Grandfather Sedon and All of Incain always amazed me. I still don't understand why she risked so much by attempting to conquer Cabalarkon thirty years ago. Even Sedon could not ignore that."

"I made quite certain of that," claimed the fiend.

"No doubt," gurgled King Cold. He finished his beer and called for another keg. A couple of ice statues immediately became mobile and went off to obey their devic lord. (When you had scores of azuras, by dozens of different devic mothers, it would be a waste not to have many of them animate his handmade snowmen and use them as servants or, less frequently, soldiers.)

"With the re-emergence of supras, there is potentially very dangerous chemistry at work on the Outer Earth," Smiler said to the Crimson Queen, ignoring, as was his wont, the besotted onetime Emperor of most of the Headworld and still

King of Lathakra. ***"Mind you, attempting to manipulate Brainrock as we have is always a risk. Of course, we may be able to turn it to our ultimate advantage but, just as likely, we may be forced to destroy Centauri Island. To do that would be to destroy the one reliable link to the Outer Earth we devils have. I am loathe to do so, but I have already made contingency plans to accomplish just that."***

"A point, Smiler," squeaked tiny Methandra. "We have seen one of our children, Earth, decathonitized. Because of him, two more, Air and Water, have presumably been rescued from a quarter century of ... what? Call it oblivion. Should we not be attempting to bring them back to the Head before, as you say, we are forced to decide the fate of Centauri's island?"

"A valid point as always, Sorceress. Necessity may dictate enacting other options. As you implied, Thanatos, the whatever it is that seems to be OJ Maxwell is an unknown factor. Although Damon Goldenrod was on the Outer Earth and occupying a human shell – and, as such, at the nadir of his power – he should not have been beaten so easily.

"If I was to make a prediction, I doubt Great Byron will jeopardize any more of his spawn by letting them outside. Not after he learns what has befallen Maelstrom and, now, Goldenrod. He may decide to destroy the link himself, saving me and mine the trouble. I'm inclined to give matters a week or so to develop before we make a final decision on how best to proceed. At the very least, we will want to know where the other cosmicars and the hub-craft have gone. The only way to do that is to keep abreast with events on Centauri's island."

"We should also discover just who got out of the Dome."

"If only all your requests were so simple. It's night. Shall we step outside and see just which stars still shine in the Sedon Sphere? Don't worry, Thanatos. We won't smooch. Given my luck and the size of your empress, I'd probably end up inhaling her."

========

Sometime later that same evening, he still enormous, she still dinky, the first-born Thanatoids were once again indoors. They had already forgotten who'd been visiting them. Could have cared less even if they had remembered him. They were elated. All their children had escaped the night's sky. Now all they had to do was discover where they got to and bring them home.

One way or another.

========

West of Lathakra, by now late Sedonda night, early Mithrada morning, the Towers of Screech, the highest range in the mountainous subcontinent of Aka Godbad, sometimes just Godbad, crackled with energy that wasn't just elemental. Thrygragos Byron had called a literal summit conference of his children. More than two dozen were in attendance. Also there, though not known to them, was another.

Invisible and entirely undetectable by even the Great God, Smiler was there not to judge but to eavesdrop. As the one-time Laird of the Laughing Lands, he – aka, among many another name, Judge Druj – had already passed judgement on the Great God and his children.

Although he could order capital punishment, he didn't have the ability to enforce it. Others could, at least so he believed. And they would come out in due course.

========

The Byronhead was as huge as a mini-sun without a concomitant body.

That had been lost centuries before Xuthros Hor unleashed the Great Flood and Dark Sedon turned his essence into the Cathonic Zone (more correctly than Dome) in order to preserve Pacifica (the Places of Peace to some; ancient Lemuria or legendary Mu to many others) from devastation. One of his human eyes was shut: at Sedon's command its usual occupant – Vayu Maelstrom to antique Illuminaries of Weir; Huracan to his long ago worshippers in the Outer Earth Americas, Devil Wind to many devazurs, including his siblings, their azuras and his – had been sent to the Outer Earth via the NAG Gap some twelve hours earlier.

Out of the other human eye flew ever-changing Chimaera Glimmenmare: just now with vaguely humanoid legs; a scales-covered, yet also humanoid torso; a long, reptilian tail; the wings of an eagle; and the head and eight arms of a three-eyed octopus. Not so much wrapped in one of those arms as extending from it was his power focus, a massive Brainrock war-mace that could have as easily been extruding from his or (almost as often) her bellybutton.

From the Byronhead's third eye billowed a visually naked woman entirely composed of smoky particulates. This was Sedona Spellbinder, through whom the Great God always spoke: the mere movement of his lips being beneath Byron's exalted status. Not for nothing was he known as the Unmoving One.

Vayu, Chimaera and Sedona made up Byron's second brood or litter of three. Also atop Screech were two members of his third litter: Aphropsyche Morningstar and Damon Goldenrod. APM, as she was better known, was a woman composed entirely of eyes, hence also All-Eyes; Damon a man whose skin was as golden as the rod he perpetually carried.

Yati, of Byron's Fourth, was a smallish oriental-looking man upon whose skin was emblazoned a coiling dragon, both his talisman and his alter ego. The Great God's consequential Dragon was often known as Byron's Brain due to the high level of his scientific acumen. His litter brothers, also there, were heroic Hektoris, the Brawn of Byron, whom his brothers and sisters tended to call Headcase, and the inarticulate poet, Babbar Ninkuray, less flatteringly referred to as Byron's Babbler.

Elephant-headed Ganesh, cow-headed Vach-Hathor and the monkey-man, Tau Hanuman, made up Byron's Fifth. Representing the Sixth was the bewitching jinni, Parsis 'Flying Carpeteer' Urartu, who kept the surname, but spelled her first name Persis when she occupied a homun being made specially for her on the Outer Earth. The remaining spawn in attendance, notably Djerrid Ruin, the Bowman of Byron, and some of the other Zodiacals, came from much later on. Like all the Great God's devic children, they were the offspring of the Trigregos Sisters, had Brainrock power foci forged by Tvasitar Smithmonger and, as a result, unique abilities.

Missing, though still free, were Bodiless Byron's eldest son, his Beast, Savage Storm, Rudra Silvercloud, and Malar Tzigame, Byron's Butterfly, Pretty Parsis's brood sister from the Sixth. The former was on guard duty in the Strait of Clouds, which lay between The Argent on the Cattail Peninsula and the Frozen Isle of Lathakra, the domain of Tantal and Methandra Thanatos, Rudra's equally highborn cousins and former friends. The latter, aka the Beauty of Byron, was a highly-skilled metamorph. She might be masquerading as one of her brothers or sisters. More likely, she was somewhere else.

"Opinions on events on the Outer Earth," requested Smoky Sedona, using Byron's voice; rather, the voice she used when speaking for their father.

"We should be out there," stated Damon.

"Agreed," said Yati, whose opinions were highly respected by the others; albeit not so much so their father. (Byron regarded his offspring by the three Sisters distrustfully, hence why he insisted they redirect most of the worship they received into him before he passed onto their Grandfather Sedon his due.) "I cannot countenance leaving our shells – even the homunculi I specifically commissioned from my homeland for this venture – in charge of matters that are best left to us."

"Disagreed," pronounced Sedona flatly. **"Forces are at work that we know nothing about. It is best we withdraw until we know more about what has truly happened."**

She paused as if to receive and digest more of Byron's words before imparting them aloud. **"Superficially what's happened is simply this: You, Yati in particular, were charged with launching the Cosmic Express into space. It was to be our first tentative reach back to the stars. It was to pave the way for us to escape this planet after nearly seven thousand years of virtual imprisonment here.**

"Success was at hand, then something intercepted the Express and it was thrust into the Cathonic Dome. Two parts of it, three if you count Cosmicommander Sol and his portion of the hub, made it beyond the Dome. The rest of it is still lost. Until all of it is located, there is no point in any of you being out there.

"Surely, your shells can handle that. I am in constant contact with mine – so should you be. It's an easy matter to go outside when we're required. More to the point, right now it may be too dangerous for you, what with this creature that so easily put paid to Goldenrod lurking thereabouts. What is it?"

Babbar blurted out his never-nonsensical, yet nonsensical-sounding two-cents worth. "Tivatimsa. Nikaya. Mellifluous Multivoids siren-singing oblivion."

"Interpretation, Sedona."

To which Spellbinder responded, eerily, in her own voice: "Tivatimsa: pristine land of perpetual summer; Nikaya: land of demons, hot but hardly summer, more like Hell; Multivoid: Bodhisattva gone bonkers but, the poet implies, forewarning us against pursuing this folly. All three terms are from the Outer Earth faith or religion known as Buddhism. There is much of their Buddha like you, father. In fact, I believe you were his inspiration."

Her voice switched. Once again, she was imparting Byron's words. **"Tivatimsa, equate with lost Elysium; Nikaya, with Satanwyck. Elucidate on Multivoid, Bodhisattva."**

"Roughly, Buddhism says that certain holy ones can transcend Samsara, the Universal Substance: this Mortal Coil, as another Outer Earthling once said. They go beyond Samsara to Nirvana, a state of perpetual bliss. These are the ascended Buddhas, but some holy ones choose not to lose themselves in Nirvana, Pure Enlightenment. They return to the Earth in order to guide others, less fortunate ones, towards Nirvana. These are Boddhis — call them angels, principalities, mini-gods, intercessors, teachers of the divine, even space ghosts.

"Theoretically they exist in a multitude of voids, heavens, paradises for sentient souls throughout the cosmos; hence the term. Multivoids are multifarious. Some are presumably more in tune with Nikaya than Tivatimsa. Although largely the stuff of legend, they're hardly creatures of Babar's imagination.

"The Sedonshem encountered them a few times on its way to the Earth's Moon and thence down here. That said, to the best of my knowledge none of us has come across one since we became solid individuals; particulate, what passes for solid, in my case. Maybe they shouldn't exist but, reputedly, they're not just irrational, they're insane. They make even less sense than the Babbler's here."

"Himalayas, Anthea, Tvasitar, Sodomy. Strong Women," contributed Ninkur-ay helpfully.

"Even I understand that," said pretty Parsis, burqa-clad Flying Carpeteer, jin-niya or genie that she was, squatting cross-legged on her hovering Brainrock carpet. "The Himalayas are an Outer Earth mountain range: if you exclude those sprouting from the ocean floor, the highest on the whole planet, even higher than the Towers of Screech. As all of you know, Flowery Anthea is, or was, a highborn daughter of Thrygragos Lazareme. You also know the state she's been in for … what? More than a few millennia by now.

"Sodomy must refer to Sodom and Gomorrah, the nowadays oft-wandering SAG Gap. It was centred on the Outer Earth's Sedon Sphere, which stood between those two great, antediluvian city-states until their destruction, along with that of the Sphere, prior to we devils gaining solidity.

"Other than erratic Tholoi, until Divine Coueranna opened her volcano from Ap Isle to Strongyne, Strong Woman, some four thousand years ago, it was about the only reliable egress to the Outer Earth we had when we were just insubstantial Spirit Beings like our azuras remain.

"Coueranna's link, what most everyone who knew about it called the Kore Gap, was closed some thirty-five hundred years ago. But the Antediluvian Sister-hood of their Anthea, the wife of Xuthros Hor, the Biblical Noah, discovered its corollary, said SAG Gap, when stationary, off Sedon's Peak and have used it to go between our inside and their outside ever since.

"Sedon's Peak," continued the bewitcher, who wore a burqa supposedly be-cause she was too beautiful to behold otherwise. "Is Anvil's protectorate, always assuming their father lets Lazaremists have protectorates these days, which he hasn't always. Thereon – make that therein – lies the caldera filled with Brainrock, the stuff Lazareme's smith used to forge our talismans.

"Nink's on about links – not the wildcat lynx – between the Head and the rest of the planet. Somehow this No Name thing has an affinity for the universal substance. It can probably go through the Dome as well. I suspect it could kill us, or at least immobilize us, if it knew what it was doing. Could it be the progenitor, the first of its kind? If so …"

"Just so, Enchanter. Which strikes me as a good reason to stay away from it. Next problem: how many stars have been lost from the real Sedon Sphere?"

Monkey-Man (Tau Hanuman, commonly called Monk-Eye) had been count-ing. "I make it approximately seventy. Some ours; some Lazareme Spawn. Perhaps tale-tellingly, the majority are Mithradites. Had I an opinion, in such illustrious company, I'd say those who intercepted the Express were Mithras Spawn. In ordin-ary terms we're talking basic jailbreak."

"Ours?"

"The entirety of the Seventh: Vanthysces Vastness, Thon Ablutter, Pump-kin-puss Samhain; the Eighth and Ninth as well: Camorva Freeflight, Myrmeister, Crinsom, Srivari, Beltane, and the gallant Gelid. The Zodiacal Pyçonja might be loose as well; the one we figured Machine-Memory stuck up there when she was trying to become the Trigregos Sisters and ended having Queen Scylla, instead. Eventual Queen, ex Queen now, nuisance anyway you look at her."

"Lazareme's?"

"By far the biggest is Thunder and Lightning Lord Yajur, the Unity of Order, but he's hardly the only one. Susal's the longest up there that I can see, mostly be-cause all three of the First Fools are out, but there are a bulbous barrel of fun others. Couldn't come close to naming all of them; got no Lazaremist expertise, me. Just know his quadrant's dimmed a bundle."

"And Varuna's?"

"Most of the heavy-hitters, I'm afraid." Hanuman plainly enjoyed playing stat-istician, a role he'd picked up from Patrick Monk, his non-homun shell on the outside's Centauri Island. (Not all the Byronics occupied specially developed, more so than bred, homunculi – false men, homun beings – like Yati's oriental-looking head of operations on Centauri Island. Despite his last name, some like Monk were actual humans.)

"Start with the first born, Phantast Thanatos, then list them down: Zuven Nergalis, Domdaniel-Pride, Pteraterror, Carcinogen, Bellona, Ramazar, Pyrame Silverstar, mass-murderous Novadev, Mater Matare, Grim Thordin, Santa Mam-mon, the Domination of Satanwyck's Grand Vizier Ibal, that envious little sprite Bobby Badboy, Mordira Faeriedust, the rest of the Crimson Conspiracy, save Marut Kanin – though I guess she technically wasn't one of them on account of her never having been ill-starred – and the entire Constellation Thanatos."

"Quite a list," grimaced Elephantine Ganesh. "Centuries of work wasted, though I grant you most of it wasn't ours."

"Make that all of it wasn't ours," said Headcase, Heroic Hektoris. "Grand-father Sedon's the cathonitizer-in-chief. We prefer our banes in Incain."

"Fortunately, thank Sedon for small blessings," added the monkey-man, whose name antique Illuminaries took from Hindu religious mythology even though they named the majority of Byronics after ancient entities worshipped, or dreaded, in the pre-Columbian Americas, where many of them dwelled for multiple centuries, "Not Bouncing Belle, Beguiling Belialma, twice-over-formerly Sinistral Lust, whom Grandfather presumably decided to keep for himself.

"Drought, Cathune Bubastis, is still there; still secreted in our quadrant, even though magnificently misled Mithradites think she's actually up north in the Lake Lands. So is her counterpart, Flood, Diluvia Ran, whom Machine-Memory stuck up there sixty-something years ago. Not Underlord Yama Nergal's brood brother and sister, Gibran Nimiki nor Shal Ereshkigal, Mines and Minerals, the Lord and Lady of the Underworld either, at least as near as I can make out, though we were never certain which stars were theirs. Shall I go on?"

"I get the picture. All the more reason we should back off the Outer Earth for now. Final question: should we proceed with our business up north?"

"You would abandon our sister?" spoke Djerrid Ruin angrily.

"Father was simply asking for viewpoints, bowman," placated Sedona, in her own voice.

Chimaera broke his silence. As the eldest son amongst them, his words bore weight. "To you, Ruin, nay! To you, father, yay!"

For even Unmoving Byron, that was enough.

========

For the Smiling Fiend, it wasn't.
He needed to know more!

****

Smiler, usually operating under the rubric of Rhadamanthys, appeared with the Parents Thanatos, King Cold and the Scarlet Empress, throughout the **PHANTACEA** comic book series. Their stories, along with that of the Byronic Nucleus and the Damnation Brigade have been collected in two trade-format graphic novels released through Phantacea Publications entitled "The Damnation Brigade" and "Cataclysm Catalyst".

Games 3: **Hellsent to a Pauper's Grave**

========

<u>Mithrada, 1 Tantalar 5980</u>

On Sedonda the Thirtieth, the Sedonic Eye-Mouth spat the Cosmic Express not just out of its craw, or its equivalent of a craw, but out of wherever they were in the first place.

(Cosmicommander, cosmicaptains and their consequential cosmicompanion crew were Outer Earthlings through and through. If they'd known to call it Cathonia, the Cathonic Zone or Dome, they would have. If they'd known to call it the Sedon Sphere they might not have. Sedon was, after all, the closest thing any of them would ever get to Satan.)

The Express broke into its various sub-vessels: its command craft, its hub craft and its six cosmicars. At least one cosmicar, Cosmicar Six, did land on the Hidden Headworld, albeit not on the Prison Beach of Incain, where it should have if all had gone according to Panharmonium Project designs as devised primarily by Shenon's witches, their rogue techno- and biomages, who were mostly of Utopian descent, and their devic allies.

It landed in Hell on Earth.

========

The next day, the first of Tantalar on the Inner Earth, a lone woman walked into the throne room of Pandemonium. Sloth, the reigning Prime Sinistral of Satanwyck, regarded her curiously. By almost any reckoning she was an unimpressive sight: a fit but haggard-looking, brown-skinned, short-haired human wearing a tight, black and white striped, hooded shirt, black pants and boots.

That the shirt and pants glistened with silver sparkles, possibly Brainrock, possibly Stopstone, probably a combination of both, along with contributions from non-Godstuff fabrics, did not particularly interest him. Despite the fact they were of a design he had never come across before, nor did the holster with its hand Gatling, the carbine slung over one shoulder, and the survival pack on her back.

He reasoned she was from the Outer Earth but, ordinarily, there would be nothing special about that. What was so special about her was her spirit, her soul, still seemed housed in an apparently healthy body. In other words, she was alive. That was the only reason he had agreed to give her an audience. She could not possibly be here. And otherwise inexplicable things intrigued even Lord Lazy, as his mostly demonic subjects often referred to him when they were just talking amongst themselves in private, rather than when they were out and about attempting to slaughter each other as painfully as possible.

Why wasn't she being digested?

"Welcome to Hell," he shrugged, obligatorily. (He didn't practice shrugs in a mirror; didn't practice much of any thing, sooth said. He was the embodiment of Indolence.) "If you've come to ask for the soul of your lover back, I don't do requests. Besides, if it is here, I wouldn't want it back if I were you. Which of course I couldn't be. I'm not remotely human."

Also too sluggish to shape-shift, Sinistral Sloth presented his usual Humpty Dumpty self: red-skinned, dwarfish, almost egg-shaped, with spindly arms and legs, no hair on his head, virtually no neck and the three eyes, one in the centre of his forehead, most devils had. Clothed in a regally purple robe, excessively flabby by any standards, Sloth slouched in the overstuffed Highchair of Satanwyck.

Which, like Hieronymus Bosch – called Bosco when he visited the Domination prior to the onset of the Thousand Days of Disbelief, in the last quarter of the Dome's 55th Century – painted it a number of years after his return to the Outer Earth, doubled as a toilet seat. (Baaloch wasn't Prime Sinistral then, Lady Lust was – Bosco's man-eating, then grossly defecating, bird-woman shown sitting on it was either her surrogate or she was just messing with him. She, Bouncing Belle, was next-to-irresistibly attractive.)

(Hellblob's mostly demonic subjects had no qualms about referring to him as Lord Lazy. They did, however, tend to do so mostly when they were just talking amongst themselves, in private, rather than when they were out and about attempting to slaughter each other as painfully as possible. They did so in front of him he might fricassee them on the spot; always assuming he could be bothered to think flames and frying pan.)

With stick-figure fingers, he held the elaborately filigreed Evil Eye, symbolic of his authority, in one hand. (Substitute a host-holding pyx for the Eye and it reminded the rare Roman Catholic outsider of a ceremonial monstrance.) Behind him, scarcely clad, ibis-headed nymphs fanned him using glowing fronds similarly moulded out of Brainrock-Gypsium, the remnant Godstuff of the Big Bang's commencing Godhead.

"I am," said the cosmicaptain. "Though not entirely."

Her skin lightened, went from brown to a greyish-white. Her weapons and backpack vanished between-space just as her clothing (seemingly) transformed into a sheath dress. It was held up by cross-straps that tied behind her neck, leaving her breasts bare. And a very nice pair they were, too.

(Although in her peculiarly decathonitized state as an otherwise bodiless Spirit Being, the consequentially insubstantial Master Deva occupying the cosmicaptain was both a practised dematerialist and a highly skilled etherealist. She knew how to fashion lovely breasts out of the ether itself, even if it was more correctly thought of as an individual's natural aura.)

Her face became triangular, pointed at the top. Her head, top, back and sides, crunched in on itself until it had only three upper sides and a flat underside. The face cleared, a single eye peered out of each upper side. That didn't answer why she wasn't being digested; did suggest an easy way to find out. He could ask her.

"Correction. Welcome to Paradise for the Damned, Pauper. Mind telling me how you managed to avoid being eaten on your way here?"

"Information has its price, Blob."

"What happened to your daemon then?"

"Still working that out, sooth said. Surprised you noticed."

"Twenty-odd years ago, while you were, um, away, an impressively devious changeling named Shah gave me more than just a spot of bother; make that a spot of Nikaya — Holy Hell to her. Turned out it was cancerous, the spot; her as well. Only, her full name was Shahiyeda, not Tsishah like I thought. In any event, out of necessity I got pretty good at telling the difference between an ordinary witch's glamour and a daemonic over-casting, as it were. That is you, isn't it?"

"It is." The (supposedly) ninth-born Pauper Priestess, whose Illuminary-given name was Pyrame Silverstar, began to dispel the splendour she'd cast about her human shell, Nehrini Purandar, Cosmicaptain of Cosmicar Six. She left her devic eye shining out of Purandar's forehead, lest Sloth forget he was dealing with his elder in Thrygragos Mithras.

"The price?"

"Nothing you'd miss," she said once she didn't look like her regular devic self anymore. "A frond and one of your Egyptian Ibises. They are demons, aren't they?"

"Feeling peckish, are you?"

"If I must."

"You must. You'll have to do without the frond. It's mine. So is the Eye."

"Well, at least I asked."

She was quick, this comparatively highborn, but decathonitized Master Deva. Rather, her superbly trained, Outer Earth shell was quick. However, before Pyrame-Purandar could yank her hand Gatling even halfway out of its holster, she was jolted unconscious. The Evil Eye packed a humongous wallop.

She should have come in shooting.

========

The day before, Sedonda-Sunday, an impressive windstorm cleared coastal Petrograd's night's sky of its clouds of moisture as well as its approaching tangible haze of pollutants. There was nothing natural about that windstorm. Nothing natural unless you considered devils forces of nature; which they largely were on the Hidden Headworld.

That was what it was, though: devil-doings, pure and simple. The Master Deva who caused it was a second-born Byronic, one of his three Primary Nucleoids.

========

The All-Father of devazurkind, as well as the 400-plus years' post-Sedonshem-landing King of Demons, was often called 'dark' because, even as by far the brightest star shining in the night's sky above his Hidden Headworld, he was usually only visible after dark. Consequently, once Star Sedon ceased shining in late Tantalar 5953, most everyone on the inside, that is to say within the Cathonic Zone, came to assume he'd somehow been killed.

Not so puzzlingly, Cathonia no more collapsed in on itself than any more stars fell out of it. He'd vanished before. Once, circa 4825, it was thanks to the Death's Head Hellion, Morgan Abyss, the demon-loving Melusine Piscine that the annoying deviant called Fisherwoman counted among her ancestors despite the fact that the then reigning Master of the Weirdom of Cabalarkon had no known children.

(Pyrame Silverstar, already occupying a demon in order to gain solidity, had been possessing Master Morgan, who had no Utopian blood, for quite some time when the Master received a bag of ringots for safekeeping. That Morg, though, turned one of them on her, Pyrame, keeping her demon for herself.

(In this Pyrame joined a number of other Master Devas who'd been captured in the Tvasitar-made, Brainrock ring-things that had been embarrassing, more so than permanently disposing of, her siblings and cousins during the Expansion of the Empire of Lathakra over the course of the previous century.)

That the Dome hadn't collapsed in 5953 – that it hadn't any other time Dark Sedon went dark even at night, including throughout the Thousand Days of Disbelief in the late 55ᵗʰ Century – indicated remnants of the two surviving Great Gods' daddy lingered. Devils, and not just devils, knew who those remnants were: Sedon's deviant, yet nonetheless mortal, half-sons by the Perpetual Presence, female, adult — half-mom Pyrame Silverstar; hence why grateful devils used to call her Providence, not Pauper, to her face.

(They and their grandsons, though their mystical Earth-Heaven binding, what allowed the Dome to remain raised, never transferred to a third generation.)

At least one Sed-son had to be alive on either side of the Dome in order to preserve it; that too was known. However, no one, not even the two remaining Thrygragos Brothers, Byron and Lazareme, knew how many were left, let alone their identities and where they lived. Clearly, with Pyrame a silver star shining out of the Sed-Sphere since 5950, and especially with Sedon Himself apparently no longer around as of almost exactly three years later, there would be no more engendered.

Ergo, given the 9-month lapse between conception and birth, the theoretical last of the Sed-sons could have been born in 5951, 1951 beyond the Dome. Be that as it may, there was no way of telling if a Sedon-possessed man had conceived anyone on a Pyrame-possessed woman in the days or months prior to him cathonitizing her for trying to conquer Cabalarkon, the territory.

(It, Sedon's Devic Eye-Land, was the eternal resting place of the Undying Utopian by the same name, whom Sedon regarded as his father and after whom the Weirdom was named.)

Ergo as well, the Dome would collapse when the last Sed-son in here or the last one out there died. Quite plausibly that could occur before the turn of the century or earlier, dependent on their individual lifestyles. The Dome collapsed, what would be the result? That was another thing no one could answer with any certainty.

Without Sedon around to either cause or countenance another one, Thrygragos Byron found himself controlling the only devil-safe link to beyond Cathonia. Called the Nag Gap, it was named after Nagasaki, the Japanese city where the American military detonated an Atomic Bomb in August of 1945. Energy released by that explosion, unless it was just between-space reverberations from it, rent the Dome hundreds of miles away, off the coast of Hawaii.

When Cathonia sundered, Great Byron was in Aka Godbad City, on the other side of the tear. While investigating what had happened, he emerged beyond the Dome. Residual radiation quickly overcame him. Had he not immediately possessed a teenage, Canadian-born outsider, one who had lied about his age when he joined the American navy, he could have become the second Great God ever to die.

Likely his fusing with the young serviceman saved them both. However, to this day, slightly more than forty-five years later, the effects of that A-Bomb exploding on the other side of the Dome, so far away from the subcontinent he considered his own, continued to adversely affect the Great God. As a result he sometimes had to repossess that selfsame boy, now every bit a man, a very big man, CE's Fatman, self-named Alpha Centauri, in order to sustain himself.

Today the Nag Gap went through the Dome between-space from somewhere beneath Aka Godbad City to an opening secured in subsea concrete during construction stretching deep beneath the Outer Earth's mostly manmade Centauri Island. As always, its exact location remained undisclosed but, on the Head anyway, its existence wasn't much of a secret.

Back in '53, once it became evident Star Sedon wouldn't be returning to the night's sky anytime soon, numerous Master Devas from the other two tribes petitioned him to share his tribes' until then exclusive access to the Nag Gap. Bodiless Byron, through his usual mouthpiece, Smoky Sedona, refused to heed their pleas.

What would be the point of devils fleeing to the Outer Earth anyway?

If the Dome collapsed, a Second Great Flood might ensue. Even if it didn't, there was no way to guarantee the planet could bear a thoroughly dried-out, then devil-terraformed, onetime archipelago the size of Africa suddenly popping, as if out of nowhere, into the mostly land-empty basin of its North Pacific. The world might break apart; become uninhabitable except for we devils. Who'd worship us then?

So get us off the planet before it collapses, Smoke. Get us back to the stars. How, cousins? Devakind arrived on the Whole Earth in the Sedonshem. Sedon's astral essence composed it and he's gone walkabout. Who knows when or even if he'll be back. Utopians of Weir came here on their generational ships, recall. Their wreckage doesn't so much surround the Weirdom of Cabalarkon as wreathe its land only borders.

Wreckage wreath, precisely. It's dead tech. No one in the Weirdom, or anywhere else, knows much in the way of anything with respect to how they worked anymore. What about Outer Earth's humanity then? They make horrific weaponry; their Atomics can crack the Dome; why couldn't they make spacecraft?

At that, a proverbial light bulb, one akin to the golden halo cast by Fisherwoman's Vesica Piscis when she activated it, went off in Bodiless Byron's Byronhead. Even though Star Sedon reappeared in the night's sky above his Hidden Headworld in 5978, a quarter century after vanishing the last time, the end-result of that light-bulb going off was Sedonda-Sunday's launching of the Cosmic Express.

Just about every one of its 60-plus crewmembers was the son, daughter, grandson or granddaughter of a Summoning Child. That made them, potentially anyhow, long-lived, supranormally-talented deviants like so many of their parents or grandparents had been. With its six cosmicars, their teleportive Gypsium fuel, they could scout nearby star systems for a planet suitable for colonization. Or, better yet, one that was already populated.

They did, they could be there and back long before the turn of the century. That happened, devils could pile onto its successor ships and get themselves safely elsewhere prior to the Dome collapsing. They didn't. It didn't, more precisely. WORLD's Kamikaze saw to that. Rather, it seemingly hadn't happened yet.

When dealing with Brainrock-Gypsium not even a Great God could state, with any degree of confidence, that some of the Express's sub-vessels – called cosmicars, not vimanas – wouldn't reach the stars. Nor that, if they did, they wouldn't be back with news of a potential new home for devakind prior to the turn of the century. Call it Brainrock, call it Gypsium, Godstuff – as in what was left of the Big Bang's Godhead, besides everything else – wasn't unknown; it was unknowable.

Such notional nonsense duly slotted within the ample capaciousness of his Byronhead, the Unmoving One remained determined to celebrate the 500th year of his Age by making the Head his Head. For starters, that required pacifying Sedon's Forehead. Generally he left the Upper Head, face-side of Sedon's occipital regions, to its prevailing Mithradites. Tomorrow, though, wouldn't be the first time he'd respond to complaints from some of the biggies that some of the other biggies were infringing on their thought-inviolable territories.

Ones whose touch could kill.

========

"Oh, my God, Jordy. When did you die again?"
"Do curtail your glee, Mel, and get me a beer."

========

Salvageable, pre-Earth, Utopian technology had indeed gone into the construction of the Cosmic Express. What passed for blueprints for some of it had been brought to Aka Godbad City, and thence the Outer Earth's Centauri Island, by Melina then still Sarpedon. She'd be the very esteemed personage whom the Legendarian was now visiting after his early morning's experience on Incain.

Visiting in the form of a woman, hence her exclamation and his response.

He hated coming back as a woman, mostly because it meant one of his daughters or granddaughters had just as good as died. Besides, giving birth hurt and he'd feel obliged to get pregnant at least once until he moved on again, hopefully to a son or grandson. Had no choice really; not when you've a procreative imperative. Worst of all, though, the prospect of nine months without beer (in order to forestall foetal alcohol syndrome like Kirin, his daughter by none-other than Alpha Centauri, suffered from) was positively terrifying

He didn't feel the same way the times he came back as a man. Felt sure his sons or grandsons would have way more fun with him in them than they would all by their lonesome. Not to mention that, without him dancing the legless limbo waiting for another body to re-inhabit mindfully, they'd be dead.

Him coming back in his offspring, boys or girls, amounted to one of the most bizarre forms of resurrection recorded.

========

Mel, the long-serving High Illuminary of Weir, and her even longer banished twin brother Demios were Utopian purebloods. Inner Earth Summoning Children born and brought up in the Weirdom of Cabalarkon, Demios married Morgianna born Nauroz raised Somata, Tsishah Twilight's mother of a Hecate-Hellions' Morrigan, shortly after his exile from Sedon's Devic Eye-Land in 5950. Mel married as well, albeit not until well beyond what was for her a very eventful decade later.

Contrary to expectations, she didn't marry her brother-in-law, the by then 13-years' ruling Master of Weir, Saladin born and still officially Nauroz. So what if, almost from the moment of her birth on the Hidden Headworld's equivalent of Christmas Day 1920, virtually everyone living in the Weirdom figured she and

Sal would hook up in due course? As far as she was concerned that only served to emphasize the tragic truth that the majority of those living in Cabalarkon were congenital idiots.

How could anyone with a lick of sense expect her to marry the serial womanizer and spiteful opportunist who'd exiled beloved brother Demios anyhow?

Instead of Sal, she chose Aristotle 'Harry' Zeross. A Gypsium-gifted outsider, he was barely 20 when they formally tied the knot some seventeen years earlier. Perfect, or 'perfecti', Utopians such as the Sarpedon twins matured much slower than non-deviant humans, so little was made of their nonetheless approaching scandalous age-difference. Even Sal, whom she pointedly always addressed as Master, was happy for her when, sixteen years ago this month, Harry and her had their first of three hybrid daughters.

Mel claimed she wasn't a witch, not even an Althean witch-healer; this despite the possibility that she may have been born with the real thing, Amal-Althea, also Althea Brand, inside her. She was, however, a largely Godbadian-educated medical doctor. So was Harry. In fact she was responsible for overseeing a good deal of his practical training, which was when love did its thing and they became an item.

Being Gypsium-gifted made Harry ever so much more useful than just as a physician. He had these amazing Brainrock rings, some of which he'd inherited from his now dozen years' dead father Angelo, that allowed him to traverse the Dome. Long ago, albeit only in mortal terms, Mel had parlayed that usefulness into becoming Cabalarkon's High Illuminary.

She was content with that. As for the Mastery of Weir, she was content with her sister-in-law's ambitions for it. So long as she still meant it for Demios, not Morg herself, it went without saying. As Kyprian had told them both on her deathbed, no Master of Weir should ever be factually known, albeit never to his face, as Saladin Devason.

And, yes, at least some of Harry's rings originated as ringots.

========

Like Savage Storm's poleaxe, the even more melodramatically named Evil Eye was a devic talisman or power focus.

========

In their beginning multiple-millennia ago — and as remained the case with their azuras — third generational, skyborn devils were simple Spirit Beings. Some four thousand years earlier, a series of fluky circumstances involving an attempted assassination by asteroid on the Outer Earth enabled a highborn Lazaremist to discover there was something about their complex, no matter how spiritual, genetic makeup that allowed them to occupy, and thereby control, earthborn, subtle-matter-composed, daemonic bodies, either spelling.

It only worked if the daemon or demon — the former moderately less dangerous than the latter in that they weren't generally considered man-eaters — was already debrained but, in that way, they could become individually solid entities. (As opposed to the collectively solid entities some of the highborn could become, to the detriment of the multitude of lesser devils they subsumed and thereafter 'coagulated', during their nearly endless migration from the Second Weirworld to Earth.)

While, thanks to the subtle matter composition of their demonic bodies, they could still possess sentient beings, about the only other thing occupying a debrained demon allowed them to do was shift shapes. Not all that long after his discovery, that same highborn Lazaremist, whom much-later-on Illuminaries of Weir named Tvasitar Smithmonger, learned devils could do much, much more than just maintain their solidity.

They could become the forces of nature many of them did become if they wielded talismans he forged for them individually out of molten Brainrock, what they'd also called Gypsium since pre-Earth times. (Vapour from a superabundance of the same miraculous Godstuff is what rendered daemons brainless in the first place. By contrast, a superabundance of its Godcrud fixative, Solidium-Stopstone, rendered devils immobile statues. Some of these last could still be found in Outer Earth museums awaiting a good hammering.)

Debrained demonic bodies or no debrained demonic bodies, power foci made devils what they were today. Pyrame Silverstar could use them – anyone could – but didn't have one of her own. Never had; never had a devic protectorate either. Appreciably therefore, devils such as Sinistral Sloth thought her the Pauper Priestess.

As the first devil to gain individual, not to mention single-minded, solidity after the three Thrygragos Brothers, who'd always had that option, she didn't need a power focus. The reason for that was because her demon – whom she'd acquired shortly after her grandfather, the Moloch Sedon, raised the Cathonic Dome out of his own essence in order to protect the then archipelago of Pacifica, his eventual Headworld, from the Genesea – already had three precursors to devic talismans. They were a sword, a mirror and a tiara.

Their destruction, after equally self-named Pyrame survived said assassination attempt by asteroid, led directly to Tvasitar making his monumental discoveries on Sedon's Peak circa the Year of the Dome 2000. The first three power foci he crafted after his own Brainrock anvil and necessary accessories were a sword, a mirror and a tiara.

They were meant to replace not-yet-Pyrame's precursors. However, three lowborn, female Master Devas, each of whom came from a different tribe, tricked him into dedicating them to his, their and, indeed, all Master Devas' three long lost, second generational mothers. These were the Trigregos Sisters. Although they never came anywhere near the Whole Earth of the Golden Age Patriarchs – Adam (2) to Noah, biblically speaking – Illuminaries of Weir had always known to call them: Demeter the Body, Devaura the Soul and Sapiendev the Mind.

Hearing their stories, these selfsame Illuminaries subsequently named the three lowborn devils: Susal, Amateram and Crinsom, after deities or characters featured in the mythology of ancient Japan, the Outer Earth's Land of the Rising Sun. In order they were the spawn of Thrygragos Varuna Mithras, Thrygragos Lazareme and Thrygragos Byron by the three Sisters.

Time and tradition further rendered the power foci they tricked Tvasitar into dedicating to their mothers: the Susasword, the Amateramirror and the Crimson Corona. The devic Smithy had deemed them differently: respectively, the Body of Demeter, the Soul of Devaura and the Mind of Sapiendev. Collectively non-devils called them the Three Sacred Objects whereas, not surprisingly, due to the fact their mothers hated their own offspring for abandoning them on New Weirworld multiple tens of millennia gone by, devils called them the Thrice-Cursed Godly Glories.

Prior to Thrygragon, which occurred in the Year of the Dome 4376, it was common knowledge that, in skilled hands, the Trigregos Talismans could be used to best, as in overpower, devils. After the events Thrygragon, which took place in what were now the Gregarian Fields, the Mole of Sedon's Cheek, the belief took hold that these three, hence thoroughly accursed objects could be used to kill devils.

(Thrygragon, which took place on Mithramas Day 4376, mostly in the Gregarian Fields, Sedon's Mole, was an Inner Earth theomachy. Another Outer Earth term, it was most commonly used out there with reference to the legendary battle between the Titans of Kronos {Saturn} and the Olympians of Zeus {Jove or Jupiter}. It literally meant 'combat among the gods'.

(Thinking he'd have no problem winning the day – it was his feast day after all – Thrygragos Varuna Mithras, the father of easily the largest of the three devic tribes, deliberately provoked it in an attempt to usurp his two brothers' worshippers. Perhaps fittingly, after the Trigregos Talismans came into play Thrygragon marked that Great God's Death Day.

(To his credit, Mithras had thus far proved irretrievable.)

The Evil Eye didn't initially belong to Sloth, a Teen, maybe even Twenties or Thirties' born Mithradite. On the contrary, recognizing his attribute was unmitigated idleness, Tvasitar crafted him a solitary frond fan for a power focus. Plainly, since the ibis-headed nymphs had a number of them, Sloth's frond suffered from a form of manifold mitosis.

The devic Smithy, whom devils generally addressed as Anvil, after his own primary talisman, crafted the Evil Eye for a moderately higher born, oddly solitary-eyed Mithradite. Appropriately enough, antique Illuminaries, who could be perversely quirky, named him Cyclopean Ibal.

Like every Tvasitar Talisman it was mutable. (The Trigregos and Thrygragos Talismans were no different.) Not quite twenty-five centuries after Anvil the Artificer forged it for him, monotheistic Christianity – in the form of the Roman Catholic Church – established itself as a major religion on the Outer Earth.

The Domination of Satanwyck thereafter becoming Hell on Earth, this Ibal sacrilegiously set his power focus in a monstrance, a candlestick chrysanthemum akin to those carried into a Christian Church at the beginning of High Mass. Lidded, like a Eucharist in an enclosed pyx, when it opened it could unleash eyefire unmatched by that which most devils could emit from their third eyeballs.

It was still Mithrada, Monday on the Outer Earth, when Pyrame-Purandar recovered from experiencing its whack firsthand.

========

"*Demonic brains, yuck!*"

"*Fresh today. Prepared by the finest sous-chefs of the underworld and hand-sautéed by its greatest chef de cuisine, yours truly, in yak, not yuck, butter. Brother Gluttony wasn't Hell's only great cook, remember. Better choke it down, Pauper. You've a human shell and, from what I recall of them, humans need nourishment.*"

"*This is nourishment?*"

"Consider it a treat. I do. The vegetables are fresh, too. I grow my own. Rather, as you might expect, they're grown for me. Vermicular demons are fabulous gardeners."
"They're also cannibals, I see."
"Not really. They're wormy; they segment. Waste not, want not."

========

The Moloch Sedon, the mighty big eye-mouth in the sky, spat Cosmicar Six out of his Sed-Sphere Head-side of the Cathonic Dome the day before. It crashed in the Domination of Satanwyck, Sedon's Temple. There were at least two, more likely three dozen protectorates in this vast, though because of that, hardly ungodly land.

Truth told, which Pyrame did since she couldn't do otherwise under the glare of the Evil Eye, there could be as many as fifty, if not more, devil-godly domains in its layered mass. Vassal states, their Master Devas were subjects of the current Prime Sinistral. He was indeed the embodiment of Sloth.

That the cosmicar ended up here may have been an accident but, in many ways, it could not be more appropriate. Although one of them, Djinn Ghoster, was a Lazaremist, the other six possessing Six's seven cosmicompanions were Mithradites. Of them, five belonged in Hell and four had ruled it.

The eldest Mithradite was Domdaniel, Pride, from Thrygragos Varuna Mithras' fourth litter of three. Pyrame Silverstar, the other devil that did not belong in Hell, besides Ghoster, who'd also spent a good – or bad – deal of time on the Outer Earth, was next. She was from the fifteen hundred years' late, Great God's Ninth.

Like Pride, who had founded the Unholy Domination, three of the rest – Grim Thordin (Wrath), Santa Mammon (Avarice), and Bobby Badboy (Envy, also Cupidity) – had preceded Sloth, whose Illuminary given name was Baaloch Hellblob, as Prime Sinistrals of Satanwyck. The last devil who belonged here, Cyclopean Ibal, had been their Grand Vizier, chief advisor and under-king.

Silverstar knew them as well as she knew Lord Lazy. Like them, as a decathonitized devil she had to hold onto her sentient shell until she found a suitable substitute. Which, as they'd noted during a preliminary scan of the area where their cosmicar crash-landed, did not seem very likely.

Evidently only demons, preferred spelling, lived in Hell these days and they couldn't transfer over to a bebrained demon because bebrained demons ate devils; Rumour of Lazareme and Byron's Capricorn Zodiacal being but two examples of same. Plus, unlike all except Ibal – who, due to Sloth having acquired it on the day he was ill-starred, didn't have one either – without a power focus she couldn't cut herself out of Sloth's Domination. Also unlike them, in this case including Ibal, she had no intention of staying in Satanwyck.

Djinn Ghoster – Djinn being more of a title than a name – was a familiar of hers from way back. Being a self-teleporting Heliodromus or Sun-Runner, he was the one who transported her directly outside the throne room of Pandemonium. That was why demons hadn't devoured her while she was making her way here. At her insistence, he didn't come in with her. It being a Mithradite realm, probably wouldn't do to be seen accompanied by a Lazaremist, no matter how accommodating he'd been in the past.

(Sun-Runners were angels, in the traditional sense; messengers of the gods. Every Great God had at least one. Mithras for example had Djinn Domitian, aka the Masochist, the lion-headed brood brother of Ibal and Cupidity, whereas Ghoster had a much higher born sister by the name of Irisiel Mercherm, aka not surprisingly Speedy, who performed much the same angelic functions he did for Lazareme. Except, that is, when he wanted a quickie.

(Heliodromi could do more than get about in the Weird pretty much at will. Unless ill-starred for crimes against humanity – read: worshippers or potential worshippers – like he'd been, they could get into, and out of, the Sedon Sphere; evidently from both sides as well. Oddly enough, they couldn't go through it, though.)

Perhaps she should have come in guns blazing. Perhaps she should have inconvenienced Sloth by shooting him first, square in his devic eye. If she had, then perhaps she'd have had enough time to employ a found-frond, or an Evil Eye, as the case presented itself, to debrain herself an Ibis-headed nymph and thereafter to acquire both a demonic body and a power focus.

Instead, she'd opted to try being duly respectful and asking for his help. Having been on the receiving end of a brain-bolt for her ill-advised courteousness; having been disarmed of Purandar's armaments as well; she figured there was only one way out now. After they finished munching the nicely sautéed, yak-buttered brains of what she anticipated would soon be her latest demonic body, she stunned Sloth by telling him her plan.

"You're serious, aren't you? You're threatening to make my life a Living Hell."

"Do you doubt me?"

"If you were still the Perpetual Presence, no. As Grandfather Sedon's favourite, I would never dare. But, without your demon, you aren't that anymore, are you?"

"You wouldn't starve my shell."

"No, of course not. She's a lesser being."

"Then?"

"You're giving me a headache, priestess."

"Precisely. And thanks for the Priestess bit. It's a lot better than Pauper."

"Pleasing is easier than displeasing. Unfortunately I had to learn that the hard way. That's why I've let Satanwyck become Paradise for the Damned of late; cuts down on rebellions."

"It does seem tamer than the last time I was here, thirty odd and mostly very, very boring years ago. What happened?" He told her, in detail this time. Talking distracted him. It was also infinitely more desirable than trying to make up his mind as to what he was going to do with her. Even if he was its god, making decisions was against his religion.

Procrastination for the nation.

========

The Moloch Sedon was killed in 5953.

Unlike their Great God of a father, Sloth said to Silverstar, he came back. It took him a quarter century to do so but, in the meantime, his absence contributed mightily to the audacious rebellion of the eldritch earthborn, not just Sloth's demons, from the authority of the skyborn, him, Sloth. After all, even though he was Satanwyck's Prime Sinistral, Dark Sedon was the King of Demons. Had been since Ragnarok, which occurred nearly 250 years pre-Dome.

"You see, priestess, as I pre-buttered-muttered in passing, pre-prandial battering, there was this human – a Mother-Earth-worshipping Hecate-Hellion – who deliberately turned herself into a chthonic demon. Her birthparents were Summoning Children born in here, but brought up out there; where they became thought of as supranormals.

"Her name turned out to be Shahiyeda …"

========

Ghoster opted to remain with the others in Sedon's Temple, Hell on Earth, mostly because the last time he got caught up in one of Pyrame's grand schemes he ended up cathonitized. It was an embarrassing turn of events. Until then, since he was the male Heliodromus or Sun-runner of Lazareme, he reckoned he was immune to cathonitization.

That was a Sun-runner speciality. They could pass into and out of the Sedon Sphere at will; at Sedon's will, make that. If he was feeling amenable to visitors.

Although she claimed she had no idea where they were hiding, Sloth appeared not to care. As he told her, he was already aware that some sixty to seventy of his siblings and cousins, including his old-time viceroy, Ibal, and his predecessors, except for Beguiling Belialma, Lady Lust, had escaped the Sedon Sphere.

The Domination of Satanwyck was his devic protectorate. He'd inherited it, as one might expect given his attribute, by default after his immediate predecessor, that spiteful little cupid – Bobby Badboy to antique Illuminaries, Cupidity to his siblings and devic cousins, Sinistral Envy to the locals – got outside during the French Revolution and couldn't resist guillotining Marie Antoinette himself.

Even beyond the Dome, Grandfather Sedon took a dim view of Master Devas killing off potential adherents and consequently gave the perverted putto a dim view of his Headworld. From above. He ill-starred him.

Even if, as she'd sooth said under the influence of the Evil Eye, albeit with the exception of Ibal, they were cathonitized then decathonitized with their power foci intact, he wasn't too worried about them. For one thing, while, like any devil, she could use the power foci of any other devil, talismans couldn't function in his protectorate if he didn't want them to work.

For another, again even if they came back still occupying their demonic bodies, it was a known fact decathonitized devils had to possess living, human, or at least thoughtful shells in order to avoid recathonitizing almost immediately. That was because, once they were outside the presence of their Grandfather Sedon, Master Devas thrived – rather than simply survived, as they'd done on stellar power for most of their evidently endless existence – on the freely given worship of other sentient beings.

No one would worship them in Satanwyck because they all worshipped him, their Prime Sinistral; at which point he passed on a good percentage of what he received to his grandfather.

(All devils were supposed to pass on a set minimum portion of the worship they received to the Mighty Moloch, usually via their fathers, the Thrygragos Brothers. Varuna Mithras having been killed on Thrygragon, Mithradites didn't have a father anymore, but Baaloch felt obliged to pass on more than just his father's share straight up to the rightful King of Hell. Called it rent on its High Chair.)

For all of the above, not just because of his attribute, he couldn't be bothered to go look for them. They'd have to come look for him, just as she had. As for whether he'd bother to feed their cosmicompanion shells when they did, he hadn't made up his mind about that yet. Time would tell. He had, however, made up his mind about what to do with her.

"As for you, Pauper, since he kept you upstairs for … what? Going on thirty years now. And since you only got out by escaping Cathonia, presumably against his will, self-evidently you only used to be Grandfather Sedon's favourite. In other words, he doesn't need you to bear his Sed-sons anymore. So why should I risk his wrath and help you any more than I already have?"

"You know the answer to that as well as I do, Blob. We Master Devas are genetically incapable of disobeying our fathers. So are our azura offspring, as far as that goes. But we're also genetically obliged to defer to our elders and I am your elder in Thrygragos Mithras by a considerable degree."

"That you are, Lost Providence. I agree. And, especially since you ate its brains, I have no objection to giving you the Vermicular Demon's body to supplement that of your shell. But I'm no more about to lend you my frond than I am my ex-vizier's talisman. Care to try to compel me, Miss Former Perpetual Presence?"

"What — in your protectorate?"

"Precisely."

In no way had Hellblob been pleased to see this commonly tetrahedral, or pyramid-headed, Panharmonium-supporting, daughter of Thrygragos Varuna Mithras from the long dead Great God's ninth brood of Master Devas by the Trigregos Sisters. Sure, no Witch Sisterhoods were named after her, but Pyrame Silverstar was nonetheless a clever cunt, as Sinistral Lust might have put it before she got on the (very) wrong side of her Lazaremist lover, Unholy Abaddon, just prior to the Thousand Days of Disbelief.

As well, he'd ruminated while he was making up his mind, for far more than 6,000 years she'd been tight to All-Father Sedon; was the first of the third generation to become solid; and was consumed by an unending ambition to be treated as Sedon's equal. She had to be back beyond the Dome for a reason. He didn't want to learn what that reason was, so, with another blink of the Evil Eye, he transported them both elsewhere.

So subtle was he, so brain-baffling was the Evil Eye's effect on her, she didn't realize she wasn't in the Domination anymore.

"See how you do in yours."

"Mine? I don't have a protectorate of my own. You know that. That's why you toadying lowborns call me the Pauper Priestess. Hold on. What's happened. Wait!"

"Precisely." He left her without another word.

Returned directly to Pandemonium.

========

A mass of darkness had congealed on the Highchair of Hell. Darkness had form, a very dark form but clearly – ha, ha – humanoid. Darkness had a pink face and three eyes. With six pink fingers, each of them too long by at least a joint, Darkness had been playing a set of panpipes. Darkness ceased playing them. Darkness smiled.

A couple of seconds passed before he realized Darkness had far more right to sit there than he ever did; that in fact the Highchair of Hell belonged to him, always had. Whereupon, in what had been his throne room for nearly three centuries, the Prime Sinistral of Satanwyck went to his knees, laid the Evil Eye on the floor between them and scuttled backwards even more cravenly until it was safely out of his reach.

"My apologies, Judge. I'd forgotten you exist."

"That is at it should be, Egg. So, shall I pick your brains or simply scramble them up with the rest of your foul body and have supper?"

The Smiling Fiend was myrionymous; had many names. Ahriman was one, Judge Druj another. Druj meant 'the Lie'. That made him the exception that proved the rule.

****

Pyrame Silverstar featured throughout **the Phantacea Mythos** webserials, as did the Smiling Fiend. They also appeared, together and separately, in "Feeling Theocidal", Book One of 'The Thrice-Cursed Godly Glories'. Her humiliation at the hands of Morgan 'Q for Aquatic' Abyss, the Melusine Master of Weir, in 4825 YD, begins "The Death's Head Hellion", the first mini-novel extracted from "The 1000 Days of Disbelief", Book Two of 'The Thrice-Cursed Godly Glories' fantasy trilogy.

Details as to how the Moloch Sedon came into being, survived Helios, in an unspecified lifetime, nuking the first Weir Star as well as weathered, as if in a bubble bath, the Genesea of 4000 BC were provided in the 1990 graphic novel "Forever & 40 Days — The Genesis of ***PHANTACEA***".

He, who does resemble – evidently intentionally – the typical image of the Devil, capitalized, was never shown in any of the original ***PHANTACEA*** comic book series. A map of his Hidden Headworld did appear in Phantacea Three and a version of it in Phantacea Five, however.

Games 4: **Hideaway Hellacious**

========

Mithrada, 1 Tantalar 5980
"If it pleases you, Milord." Darkness more like glared this time.
"Do you doubt who I am, Hellblob?"
Sloth couldn't get any lower without fusing with the floor. He tried that; tried to go straight through it, sooth said, to howsoever fleeting safety a layer – better yet, layers – lower. He couldn't go anywhere. Ergo ... now there was definitely no question of doubt. Time for even more sheer abjectness.
"No, Milord ... Ahriman."
"Judge will do for now."

========

Baaloch Hellblob was just that: a blob from Hell. Entirely red-skinned, entirely fat – so much so that his head sunk nearly neckless into his chest. His spindly arms and dinky legs seemed almost an afterthought. A devic Humpty Dumpty without an eggshell, he was the epitome of sloth (seventh and least of the vices); the seventh and least of the hereditary rulers of Satanwyck, Pandemonium, Sedon's Temple not just on a map of the Headworld.

Low as he was already, he trembled before the fiend as if an omelette frying in its own grease, which most eggs didn't have. "Yes, judge. Thank you, judge."

"Scrape yourself off the floor, little Lord Lazy. Or do you need a spatula?"

"No, judge. I mean thank you, judge, I can manage."

And he did — he, Little Lord Lazy, as opposed to Large Lord Lazy, a not just Mithradite nickname for Thrygragos Lazareme, who reputedly spent nearly all his time sleeping between-space off his home on Tympani, Sedon's Eardrum, the Isle of the Undying One. Heaved himself to his cartoonish feet theatrically, with no exaggeration of effort. Tellingly left the Evil Eye between the throne and himself.

"Beg pardon, judge."

"Where were you?"

"Wailing Souls, judge. Disposing of Egyptian, Pyrame Silverstar, no longer that last; not in the night's sky at least, not after thirty years of shining down on us."

"Disposing?"

"Granting her wish to be elsewhere. It seemed the least I could do. The Pauper Priestess was once as much a Perpetual Presence as Grandfather Sedon."

"You always were one for doing the least."

"Too true. Forgive me, milord. I had no idea you were still around."

"Forgive you, child-eater? How could I not? Even the most barbaric of societies do not execute imbeciles. All this was once mine, egg. Heaven and Hell were for me to command. I was the arbiter, the Judge. I am that no longer, but

I am still your superior. I walk through your nominal protectorate, I remorse. What has become of my dream? You? Hah! I laugh in your face. Belialma, even Domdaniel: now they were worthies; semi-worthies anyhow.

"It is with profound sadness that I witness what you have made of my lands of glory. You are not alone in your incompetence. The Nergalids are at least as culpable; as are so many others. I go away too long. It is hard for me to come back and have to refocus our three tribes. Tell me what has been happening in Sedon's Forehead since I have been otherwise occupied."

"I'll gladly tell you all I know, judge," promised Baaloch Hellblob. "It would help me if I knew where to start. I have no idea where you have been or how long you have been away."

"That is my business. Begin with Pyrame who, as you may now recall, was my consort when we co-ruled the Outer Earth cities of Sodom and Gomorrah. I object to the term Egyptian, by the way. Though I knew her real name, which I will not repeat to you, to me she was always Astraea, Queen of Courts, my Perpetual Presence, not just the planet's. Why did you leave her in Wailing Souls, Pettivisaya. She hasn't been gone that long. Who or what could she hope to find in a dead, and still toxic, city? No one can live there."

"One can. And last I heard he had a spare power focus. Besides, it was once her home. She was happiest there."

"How very considerate of you. I meant no non-devazur, but her wanting a power focus to call her own after multiple millennia without one is highly suggestive. But that's hardly all of it. You're a conniving little toad. You wanted her out of Satanwyck, yes, but you wanted her somewhere her shell would die, sooner rather than later."

"I won't deny it. She had the effrontery to demand asylum, but there is no way I am having someone in my protectorate with her kind of never-ending ambition. Wouldn't be long before she made a play for my throne." Smiler bestowed that glare on him again. "Sorry," he quickly corrected himself, "Your throne."

"Let us not mince words, Blob. I have no intention of reclaiming rulership of this mockery of a protectorate. My goals are much higher. You may have it at my sufferance. As for the perplexing Pyrame, that she's forced to possess a human shell is no surprise. That she now needs a power focus, presumably to get around, is instructive.

"Maybe she secreted an extra one there, whilst it was Grand Elysium and she shared its pyramid with Father Sedon. When the recurring deviant, Chrysaor Attis, the so-called Universal Soldier, was her sideman on either side of the Dome for far too many centuries after Fitna Marutia bore him, coming up to 4,000 solar years ago now, he used to bring her talismanic trophies as a token of his, um, affection more so than love or even admiration. But that hasn't been the case for fifteen hundred years.

"Or maybe the usurpatious Reaper – our Underlord, King Harvest above ground – will deign to donate Byronic Vanthysces' scythe, or his own pickaxe, to her. I would have thought they were irretrievably fused after all these centuries, but I'm no more omniscient than Father Sedon. He will know when her shell

dies, though, and he will know you sent her there for just that reason. Do you really have a secret star-wish, blob?"

"Of course not. And aren't you the one taking the bigger risk? How dare you presume to speak for Grandfather Sedon?"

"Getting cocky?"

"Do I look cocky? I'm no preening rooster like Domdaniel-Pride. It's a legitimate concern. I know your Demon King aspect preceded Grandfather Sedon on that throne, and that your devic aspect figures you qualify as a Great God – hence you referring to Sedon as your father, not your grandfather – but, even with such an unprecedented combination of near-deities you're no match for our All-Father.

"Besides, Silverstar can look after herself and, needs be, her shell. I just preferred it wasn't here, so I got rid of her."

The judge didn't look satisfied, though he was extremely difficult to read facially, ravelled in darkness as he forever was when he appeared before anyone.

"I'm not lying. I'm an unadulterated devil. Unlike you, I can no more lie than I can kill. Child-eater is an Outer Earth slur on my time beyond the Dome. If the Nergalid isn't there, she'll find another way out. With or without her demon, she's still an etherealist. Maybe she'll sprout lizard wings and fly out of there. Demons have tried that here, albeit without success.

"Or maybe she'll walk to Cabalarkon; even if it's dead, her shell should still be able to ambulate. Mind you, after what Grandfather did to her last time she tried that, Pyrame might be wiser going for the Mystic Mountains, to the north, or the Floods, far to the south. Then again, either/or are a very long way away from there, especially on radioactive feet.

"Like I said, I really didn't care. Seeing her shapely backside out of Satanwyck was all that mattered to me. Is any of this relevant?"

"Not immediately. I may wish to track her down in time is all."

"As opposed to in All the Invincible, on Incain."

"Just so. As for what is relevant and what is not, I shall be the judge of that. I am aware of how she was cathonitized. As you said, her ambition is never-ending. She should never have tried to take over the Weirdom of Cabalarkon. I warned her Father Sedon would not tolerate it. Would use any excuse he could find to stop her, even her killing the Male Entity, who's no lesser being. But she refused to heed me and paid the price.

"What I do not know is what interest Unmoving Byron and his sycophantic Spawn have in the Forehead. Ask me it isn't much of a prize, bordering on the Ghostlands as it does, and for most of the five hundred odd years since the Disunition of the Unities, he has been content to leave this part of the Head to us."

Hellblob couldn't hide his horror at this revelation. "So I thought he still was. Unless...."

"Unless what?"

"Are you aware that the Lake Lands are drying up? Have been for almost twenty years?"

"Tell me about it."

"You said you were aware of how Pyrame was cathonitized," began Baaloch, squatting awkwardly on the step of the dais while Smiler continued to occupy Hell's

Highchair. "You must also know who else was cathonitized with her in 5950. Ibal, my chancellor, was one, but so was Cathead, Cathune Bubastis, Pyrame's brood sister, the Apocalyptic of Drought; at least, and this is the key, so everyone thought."

"One is either cathonitized or one is not, egg. There is no in-between. You are not making sense."

"Hear me out, judge. Twenty-five years ago, shortly after the Winter Solstice, a mountain man stumbled out of the Mystics into the Ghosts. He was snow-blind, starving, and probably quite mad. Needless to say, he didn't stumble out again. Humans don't last long there, but his body was found by one of Death's Angels, who discovered something even more interesting in his backpack.

"He brought it to his master, Underlord Yama Nergal, who recognized what it was immediately: the severed head of a dried-out, famously feline woman with three eyes – that made it the severed head of none other than Pyrame and Tralalorn's ninth-born brood sister and ally, Cathune Bubastis, the Apocalyptic of Drought. Quite obviously, she'd been killed, or as killed as our unkind kind ever can be, and not cathonitized.

"As the devic Grim Reaper, our King Harvest could read the minds of the dead. He learned where it happened, who killed her – not that that matters now – and, since even five years murdered devils know such things, where the rest of her body was buried. Or at least last seen. So, employing agents in the Mystics, he had it exhumed and brought to him. At which point he rejoined head to body.

"In time, Cathune became whole again, though not wholly with it. The rest of the story is a little foggy but, as you should also know, Chameleon, Emperor of the Lake Lands, is married to Malar Tzigame, Byron's Beauty. With the connivance of Chameleon's brood brother, Klizarod Rex, Underlord Yama trained Drought to take on Malar's shape and personality. In 5960, he managed to substitute her for Tzigame. Which presumably explains why Cathead's star shines out the Byronic Quadrant. It's not hers, it's the beautiful butterfly's.

"Very slowly, very deliberately, so much so you'd hardly notice it, the real Cathead has been drying out what amounts to a north-south trench, a corridor, from the Ghosts to the Cheeks. Even as we speak Mithras's Reaper is leading Nergalazur-animated Dead Things, his Angels of Death, out of the Ghosts and across it toward the Northern Cheeklands."

"I would not have given either the Underlord or the Saurlord credit for such inventiveness. They are almost as complacent as you, though not quite with your sublime indifference to anything but your own comfort level and next meal."

If Smiler was attempting to get a rise out of the Domination's sedentary Devil-Dand, it didn't work. Nodding in silent thanks for what he took to be a compliment, Baaloch merely carried on with his story.

"It is a plot of some magnitude, not to mention ingeniousness," he agreed, howsoever-courteously. "At the expense of the Emperor Chameleon, his hated brood brother, Klizarod Rex, will conquer the Lakes. In return for his aid, Yama Nergal will be given safe passage all the way through the Lakes, Marutia, and Diluvia.

"He'll thereupon take over Hadd, the Land of the Dead, where the rest of the Nergalazurs – his and Devil Doom's azuras by the Vampire Queen, Nergal Vetala; rain-ruined spirits that solely inhabit corpses – roam freely. Along the way, the

Reaper has agreed to help Marutian devils throw off the yoke of third-born Plathon, he of Corona City and Apple Isle.

"We are talking about nothing less than a full-scale revolt, judge. Plathon is Byron's puppet; Yama our redeemer. Before this week is over, there will be a new order in the traditional territory of Thrygragos Mithras. Soon the Age of Byron will be over; that Great God and his inferior minions once again confined to Godbad. The lands of Lazareme will, in time, become ours as well. Just as they were a millennium and a half ago."

"When the Empire of Lathakra was at its height, King Cold and his followers, be they Mithradites, Byronics or Lazaremists, demonstrated virtually no regard for tribal loyalties. They were the most powerful of the powerful. Until I stopped them, they took what they wanted and left the rest of you in their wake."

"Just so," meekly accepted Sloth. "This time we will be conquering the Head on our own behalf. If Cold and his hot-tempered sister-wife join us, it will be on our terms, not theirs."

"Are the Thanatoids aware of what's going on?"

"Of course not. Haven't you realized yet who is behind all this?" As counter-intuitive, as plain preposterous, as it sounded, Baaloch meant himself.

"It has been obvious to me the moment you opened your blabbermouth, blob. There is one problem in all this, however. If Drought was killed, not cathonitized – and even if, much later on, the Tyrant Lizard and King Harvest combined to ill-star Byron's Beauty – then whose star was masquerading as Cathune's before it was supplanted by Malar Tzigame?"

"It wasn't supplanted as such, judge. But, to answer your question, it was leontocephalic Domitian, one of my most loyal acolytes and the former herald, Djinn, Angelus or Heliodromus of none other than our real father, Thrygragos Varuna Mithras. When Drought was killed, Chancellor Ibal, using his power focus, what's quaintly known as the Evil Eye, cathonitized Domitian, his own brood brother, in her stead.

"When Klizarod and Yama conspired to atomize Byron's Butterfly, her spirit appeared as just one more anonymous star in the Byronic Quadrant far to the south and west of us. That was the signal for our lion-headed herald to come out. All in all, albeit without All, it was and, so far, remains a brilliant scheme, even if I do say so myself. Unfortunately our Grand Vizier was cathonitized shortly after Domitian. Long before he could see it to fruition."

"No doubt you saw to that as well. Makes a degree of sense about Domitian, though. Wasn't his attribute masochism?"

"Just as patience and entrepreneurial spirit are as much mine as indolence." Baaloch glistened with pride. Was almost as if he was channelling one of his more esteemed predecessors. And not the one he was usually accused of copying — Arisandesam, the Conqueror Worm, better known as Sinistral Gluttony.

"Did I tell you the best part?" Smiler smiled; this time emulating his never-remembered, but much earlier, even pre-Dome precursor. "No? I get the Ghostlands to add onto Satanwyck."

"You seek to reunite my realms!" The fiend tried to keep his voice evenly modulated but (in all likelihood) had to admire the conceit of the concept. So many

carrots extended, so many fools willing to chance a bite. The Great Tempter had never been so devious. ***"Surely that's the height of lunacy. The Ghosts are a vast, radioactive wasteland, uninhabitable by anyone wholly alive."***

"Anyone worth receiving worship from, don't you mean."

"As you say."

"For now; not for much longer. I'm arranging for Trawl to free the Idiot Twins, Tammuz and Osiraq. Regardless of who put them up to it, Pyrame or the Death's Head Hellion, they're the ones who blew themselves up in the first place. Stands to reason only they can absorb the radiation that turned them into the Ghosts and make them the Elysian Fields again."

"And how will you convince All of Incain to release them, especially now that you have dismissed Pyrame? The Idiots are comparatively highborn; you're nowhere near their level. They were Solstitial Novadev's brood brothers, Equinoctial Spring and Equinoctial Autumn; unlamented Mithras's torchbearers for millennia. They provide her with tremendous power."

"By giving it Byron's first son," trumped Baaloch.

"You're not serious? Much more likely the She-Sphinx will just eat you."

========

An invitation, that's all Great Byron needed and, as planned, he'd received more than a few of late.

========

A devastating drought had been parching areas loosely identified as Sedon's Headband (not to be confused with Sedon's Hairband, between his otherwise oceans-locked ponytail, aka the Cattail Peninsula, and the backside of the Hidden Headworld's aforementioned occipital regions) for going on thirty years now.

A completely dry corridor had formed between the Floodlands, Sedon's Human Eyebrow, and the Lake Lands, the beads of Sedon's Sweaty Brow; hence also Sedon's Sweatband. Taking advantage of it, the Inglorious Dead had begun marching out of the Ghostlands, an immense territory between Cabalarkon and Satanwyck, just below the Mystic Mountains, Sedon's Crown, that had been radioactive and thus essentially uninhabitable for well over a thousand years.

(These territorial Ghosts once contained the Laughing Lands of the Glorious Dead, Valhalla and the Elysian Fields, among many other Mithradite homelands.)

As led by their devic overlord – also an Underlord, the Mithradites' Reaper, their latter day King Harvest, Yama Nergal as bygone Illuminaries had him – they were heading southwards to the Head's other two lands of the Ambulatory Dead: Hadd, the shaft of Sedon's Mutton-Chop, and the Bloodlands, aka New Valhalla, Sedon's Inner Nose.

When faced with the Inglorious Dead, aka Death's Angels, whose touch could kill, even biggies breached their bowels, filled their breeches and called on Nanny Byron to help them clean up their mess. Once he liberated, from All's digestive tract, his last surviving firstborn daughter, whose attribute was gravity, and his paladin, whose most predictable talent was an ability to stir up trouble, pacifying the Upper Head shouldn't present much of a problem.

After that, well, his paladin desired a protectorate of his own and Spellbinder, bless her, put the perfect place into his mind, limited as it was. Of course Nevair

Neverknight, as Illuminaries named him, Blackest Knight as devils sometimes did, would have to win the Bloods, New Valhalla, for himself. But now that, as anticipated, the Sangs had booted out Bellona's Battle Babe (Badhbh Morrigu), their highborn Lazaremist of a latter-day devic goddess and protector, that shouldn't present much of a problem, either.

Sangazurs, through their shells, gloriously dead that they may be, considered warfare a science that could be taught. Neverknight considered it a brawl to be won. Although Byron's only ever decathonitized offspring, until yesterday, had his disobedient moments, which necessitated him having to be disciplined, for a typically minimum sentence of fifty years, by being fed to All of Incain, Neverknight rarely lost a brawl.

Sure, there were exceptions. And one of them, Thunder and Lightning Lord Yajur, the Great God Everyman's Unity of Order, had also been decathonitized, as of yesterday. So had the fourth generational children of two other firstborns, both Mithradites, King Cold of Lathakra and his sister-wife, his Crimson Queen, once his Scarlet Empress, she also formerly Mithras's Virgin, Miss Myth of Mythland, the Jewel of Sedon's Crown, said Mystic Mountains.

Suchlike matters didn't present imponderables, but they did belong in the future-file beside whatever had happened to the rest of the Cosmic Express. One victory at a time.

Bloody Sangs deserved his paladin's imminent attention. They should never have threatened one of his most loyal adherents, Gomez Niarchos, dead as he undeniably was thanks to his foolhardy heroism on Apple Isle back in the Sixties. What possessed Gomez, the onetime Duke of Aka Godbad Province, to give up his life saving an incarnation of Lazareme's Rumour, that was beyond even Bodiless Byron's capacity for comprehension.

That he was an incarnation of Lazareme's Rumour, and not his multi-lived deviant son, only proved Byron's fallibility as far as the Legendarian was concerned.

========

Midday Mithrada, Smiler left Baaloch Hellblob to his throne in Pandemonium.

========

Until the next morning, he wandered the multiple dimensions that made up the (currently) seventeen layers of Satanwyck. Those other realms were collectively called by the Outer Earth Hebrew word Topeth or Topheth, an actual place outside ancient Jerusalem that was once sacred to the Moloch or Baal, who may or may not have been either Dark Sedon or Baaloch himself. They amounted to the Hell-Worlds of sentient beings throughout much of the planet.

Journey far enough into Topeth and one would come across Gehenna, Avernus, Tartarus, Hades, Nikaya — perhaps even the fiery inferno of Lucifer the Light Bringer, who in that respect might have been based on Methandra Thanatos, or the frozen depths of Dante's Satan, who might have been based on her brood brother Tantal, he with the icicle beard.

It was easy to become perpetually lost in Topeth; more than a few Master Devas had gone for a walk there and never emerged again. Smiler knew his way around; had even invented a few of Topeth's offshoot zones. He knew who he was looking for and, when he found him, promptly returned to Pandemonium, whereupon he went back through Samsara to Lathakra. Tremendous Tantal was passed out in an adjacent chamber – you'd think he'd had enough sleep after the time of the Death's Head Hellion until earlier this century – but diminutive Methandra was faithfully keeping her vigil.

As he had requested she do – not that she would have remembered him doing so – she was staring at images formed out of the vapours coming from her smoking cauldron. (An actual devic talisman, one once belonging to Titanic Metis, aka Metisophia, Wisdom of Lazareme, before Miss Myth 'confiscated' it, as a spoil of war, during the early years of the expansion of the Lathakran Empire in the Dome's 48th Century.)

It wasn't a very entertaining vision: Professor Romaine Kinesis and O'Ryan James Maxwell were on an airplane beyond the Dome. Both were asleep.

It was around dawn Demetray, Tuesday, out there as well.

========

"Who's that, judge? Looks like something a snow tiger would drag in after a polar bear was finished with it."
"An apt description, Sorceress."
Smiler was carrying a three-eyed, lion-headed humanoid whose skin, more like fur, had been flayed off most of its body. The only reason its internal organs weren't spilling out of its abdomen was that the creature was a devil and devils, being solidified by demons, didn't have much in the way of internal organs.
"I'm not surprised you don't remember one of your more insignificant brothers in Mithras. His injuries are self-inflicted."
"Djinn Domitian?"

****

Mainly as Mithras's Herald, the lion-headed masochist appeared in the early stages of "<u>Feeling Theocidal</u>", Book One of *'The Thrice-Cursed Godly Glories'* fantasy trilogy. His look, however, is based on an aspect of Mithra-Kronos famed in certain circles as Boundless Time, as found in Manly P Hall's "<u>The Secret Teachings of All Ages</u>".

Boundless Time, by the way, shows up in Zoroastrianism as its 'incomprehsible' single power, Zrvan Akaran. See "Magic, Supernaturalism and Religion" by Kurt Seligmann for addtional reference.

Games 5: **Calling All She-Sphinxes**

========

Demetray, 2 Tantalar 5980
"What do you want, Mithradite?"
"A trade" said the Cyclops. "To trade you, as it happens."

========

Rudra Silvercloud was bipedal, with the orange and black striped fur of a Bengal tiger. It covered his powerfully-built body from neck to toe. His humanoid face was both orange-coloured and orange-textured. With brownish-red hair stroked back, he sported a Fu Manchu moustache and had a long, goat-like beard. Often not just devils referred to him as Rufous Rudra after the colour of his hair and fur.

His power focus was a spear – more correctly a halberd – with an outwardly curved crescent moon attached like an axe blade just beneath its metallic point. (Call it a poleaxe if you must, just don't call him a polecat. Although he could be ornery, there was nothing of the weasel or ferret about him.)

He was devil-god to the Bandradin race and a weather-wizard, the Devalord of Storms, in addition to being a Beast Master — were-creatures adored him; would even die for him. He was also the only male born in Great Byron's initial litter of three. Drugs, alcohol and, unless pushed to the breaking point, violence were abhorrent to him, but sex was an addiction.

His home, though never official protectorate (since, to this day, Byronics did not have protectorates as such), was ancient Bandrad, aka the Holy Heights, a long plateau high up in the Cattail Peninsula's Whiplash Range, whose pinnacle peaks more like backed it up. Once nominally part of Greater Godbad, which today lay mostly down slope to its south and west, its most distinguishing feature was Lake Byron. In many respects the whole area was akin to the high plains, 'Altiplano' (Quechua: 'Collau') or Andean Plateau of Peru and Bolivia, making the Head's largest navigable, alpine lake analogous to the Outer Earth's Lake Titicaca.

Historically, one of the Cattail Peninsula's many indigenous peoples, the orange skinned and textured Bandradin race, considered him their god. Once the Cattail fell under the sway of Unholy Abaddon, Thrygragos Lazareme's Unity of Chaos, who was intolerant of anyone purporting to bring order to anything, its self-anointed nobility fled to the faraway Subcontinent of Aka Godbad. There, under Rudra, who'd travelled with them, and immediate sister-wife Umashakti's auspices, they eventually became its ruling class.

Being non-natives, Bandradins were never very popular in Aka Godbad. Nevertheless, though the Bandradin aristocracy's supremacy, or lack thereof, waxed and waned over the decades, that remained the status quo until its overthrow during the course of Godbad's Civil War. (Which was won by 'republican', so-called democratic forces supporting Alpha Centauri, Great Byron's still occasional shell.)

Long before its inevitable ending in 5960, both Silverclouds had abandoned the subcontinent in order to take up residence in the Strait of Clouds, which lay on the Cattail's mid-eastern coastline between the Frozen Isle of Lathakra and The Argent, the ponytail peninsula's largest metropolis. Where, as one might expect given its name and her status as a Moon Goddess, Uma (when she'd been around) had proved much more popular than him; much more popular than their Great God of Father Byron, dot-ditto. Which, she should have known, would never do.

Even though it was farther to Bandrad's north and east, the lake's namesake, Unmoving Byron, posted him to the Sea of Clouds, off the mid-eastern Cattail (more like Sedon's Ponytail) between the Thanatoids' Frozen Isle of Lathakra and the mainland metropolis of The Argent. He rarely hung out in the sea, preferring the city state where, it being an ancient satellite of Krachla, the Phoenicia of the Hidden Headworld, merchandise was as close to God as wealth and trade.

In fact, the northerly neighbourly Metal Range was where the Pani Merchants of Krachla mined and minted their silver money or 'Argents'. These coins had been in use on the Head for hundreds of years, particularly in coastal regions and occipital city states. (Today, though, Godbucks, the somewhat facetiously named currency of Greater Godbad, as instituted in the early Sixties after its Civil War ended, was more accepted in the subcontinent and along the Head's far west coast 'facial' area as far north as Apple Isle.)

Rudra had been single since 5933, when his wife and last remaining brood-sister (on the Whole Earth anyhow), Umashakti Silvercloud, had been summarily convicted of the equivalent of high treason amongst Byronics and sentenced to fifty years within All of Incain. Even though he still loved her — brothers are born loving their sisters, and vice versa; couldn't help themselves — he hadn't exactly gone into a state of abstinence while he waited for her release from the Prison Beach.

In various humanoid forms, homunculi — courtesy of Yati, the Dragon of Byron — and unwitting hosts, he had seduced just about every pretty girl in The Argent for two generations. He was now into the third; the mortal grandchildren of his initial conquests. Demetray morning, Tuesday on the Outer Earth, he was in bed with one of his former shells' granddaughter when the Brainrock cat-o'-nine-tails bit deep into his psyche. Struggling against unconsciousness, he opened all three of his eyes long enough to behold to whom it belonged.

The lowborn, but always overreaching, Mithras Spawn's Illuminary-given name was Trawl, also known as Taskmaster. Somewhat unusually for a devil, Trawl was a Cyclops: had no human eyes, just a large devic one in the centre of his forehead. Normal-sized — not that size was immutable when it came to devils — he affected medieval-style, beautifully embroidered tunics, ruffs and leggings.

His clothing totally clashed with his attribute, which was sadism, inflicting pain and punishment, particularly on the unwilling or 'unworshipful'. Trawl's reputation for cruelty was well-earned. When he was alive, Thrygragos Mithras used Trawl as his chief 'persuader' (read: torturer). Even gave him his own House of Pain in the jungles of Apple Isle, whereon Mithras had his headquarters.

(His six millennia-old Mithradium stood atop Theopolis Hill on the outskirts of Corona City, the largest as well as oldest conurbation on the Hidden Continent.)

Since Thrygragon, that Great God's death on Mithramas 4376, his own feast day, there was seldom any need for his talents anymore. Consequently, even though he maintained a protectorate within the Domination's boundaries – where he was welcomed, even worshipped, by soulless demons eager to learn at the feet of the master – he spent most of the next fifteen hundred years asleep. Once feared, the Taskmaster was now largely forgotten.

Rufous Rudra felt the complete twit. He had grown too slack, too consumed with self-satiation, let down his usually formidable defences. Not that there was much he could do about it now. Contact with the Taskmaster's whip (which did have nine weighted thongs akin to barbed tails) rendered him his servant.

There was no fighting Trawl's compulsive ability. He gave into it, not even cursing his own stupidity: "Come again?"

"Doubt there will be any need, beastie boy. All the Invincible, the mainly mandroid overseer of Incain, has a well-known proclivity for exchanging captives for better captives. A first-born of Thrygragos Byron should be more than adequate compensation for three comparatively lowborn sons of long-dead Mitravaruna.

"Things are happening in Sedon's Brow. Seventh-born Klizarod Rex, Devalord of the Floodlands, has finally got up the nerve to challenge his brother for suzerainty of the Forehead's Lake Lands. He requires raw power. Not many devils have more raw power than my liege lord and much older brother, Monstrous Ravana. You're going to join your sisterly love within Incain. Ravana's going to join our revolution."

"Ravana's madness dates back four thousand years, before any of us were independently solid beings. What make you think he yet persists inside of All."

"Oh, he does. Be assured of that."

"You said three."

"The Idiot Twins are going to do us a favour: return the Ghostlands to the Elysian Fields, the Laughing Lands of the Glorious Dead."

"Just like that?"

"Just like that."

"Sounds fair to me."

========

Other than it was well-swept to the point of being detritus-free, the Prison Beach of Incain looked like any other barren stretch of gloriously white sand on the Whole Earth.

Trawl wasn't fooled by its desolation. Having been her prisoner on a couple of occasions, he knew that All had sunk roots, her heart or soul if she could have either, deep beneath the beach itself, as well as extended her mechanoid 'hatchery' for mandroids underwater well off its coastline into Tempestuous Psychron.

Knew also the real Incain, where All kept her 'prisoners' – her 'chargers' as well as charges, as she put it, echoing Jordan Tethys, once a frequent traveller through her to her moribund male counterpart on the Outer Earth's Giza plateau – was between-space, in as good as another dimension — the universal substance of Samsara, to be precise; what devils called the Weird and witches the Grey.

(Pocket dimensions were hardly uncommon on the Head; witness Satanwyck's many Hells. Its largest one, Antagone Negaura's Land of Nothingness, was on the Akadan coast north and west of here, within sight – on a clear day – of heart-shaped Shenon, Witch Isle. It leaked, ate actual land on the Hidden Headworld; had done ever since the Demon Abaddon, once the Unity of Chaos, moved in to be with his long time lady love, who was also known as Perfection.

(Needless to say, its resultant growth, the territorial cancer it engendered, wasn't just a blotch on the landscape. It was entirely imperfect blotch on the landscape)

All's portal from the Outer Earth to the Head opened here, in the shadow of the Whiplash Range, to the north and west, and on the coast of Psychron, to the south and east. About as far south as one could go on the Hidden Headworld without having to learn how to swim, All the Invincible existed in both places, off and on, inside and outside, simultaneously.

Trawl had Rudra slung over his shoulder, still entwined by his cat-o'-nine-tails. "Hear me, Mistress Machine," he shouted unnecessarily. "I have come to barter."

A solitary eye on a periscope-like tendril poked out of the sand. Like Sedon's in the Cathonic Zone encompassing the entire Hidden Headworld, the eye developed a mouth. "All see that." The mouth in the eye changed into a nose in the eye. It sniffed the air. "Smells power. Scent familiar. Not yours. All had pleasure of your company before; weak buzz at best. His! Beast of Byron."

"Why ask when you know?"

"Purely formality."

"You may have him, for as long as you wish, if you turn loose three of my siblings – namely the Nuclear Twins, Tammuz and Osiraq, and my liege lord, the Monster of Mithras."

"All has no difficulty releasing Ravana. No Idiots. Sorry, not possible. We have special relationship."

"Then the rumours I've heard about you are true. They power you. Without them, you would cease functioning."

"All finds inference insulting. You do well ignore rumours. Entity make All to last. All has. All is Invincible. All is Forever. You leave."

"Wait!" Trawl panicked, as sadists often do when things aren't going their way. "I will accept Lord Ravana. Even trade."

"As would All, but too late. Goodbye." The periscope retracted into the sand.

Something tapped Trawl on the foot. The Taskmaster looked downward. It was difficult to see with just one eye, a devic one at that, but there was some kind of humanoid mote, no more than six inches tall, rapping on his toes with a cane or some such. Focusing on the creature, Trawl gasped. It was a woman dressed in varying shades of red, pink, and purple. Her face was hidden by a violet mask but he knew who she was instantly.

"I, I, I'm sorry, Imp … Empress," he stuttered futilely.

Something gigantic appeared behind him. Trawl commended his spirit to All just as massive Tantal Thanatos, King Cold, used his labrys, his double-bladed war axe, to chop him into so much sausage filling. Thereby freed from the cat-o'-nines, Rudra regained sensibility just in time to see her husband – one of his most common drinking buddies – slice open the air itself and step through it, presumably back to the Frozen Isle and its fine ice-beer.

Tiny Methandra, for sixty years no longer Mithras's Virgin, lingered. Standing on a platform of her own conjuring, she tapped her Brainrock cane or firebrand, her magician's wand, rose up and hovered in front of him. "All knows us, Bestial Storm. Be thankful for that at least. We refuse to bargain with the Mandroid Mother Machine, so we did not even try to trade Trawl for your Shakti, Byron's Moon. All wouldn't have released her in any case. She's too loyal to her jailers.

"Only those who put them in can get them out. Unless the Unmoving One dictates otherwise, your wife's stuck here for another three years. Still, you are a loyal friend. We protect our friends. You would do well to remember that next time we ask you to stand against your father. That day is coming, Silvercloud. Make no mistake about it. You are in our debt. Remember that as well."

With those words, the Scarlet Empress, who rarely spoke to anyone she did not judge an equal, which was almost nobody, swiped her wand into the Universal Substance; returned to Frozen Lathakra, her home away from home. (She almost never went back to Mythland, her actual protectorate, lest her drunkard mate recommence his both wanton and wandering ways.)

The periscope-like tendril went from nose to snout, complete with mouth and tongue. Slurped out, slurped in Trawl-mush, cat-o'-nines with it; chewed, savoured, swallowed. Said: "All love chopped liver."

========

Stuff happens.

And not just up in the Sedon Sphere, although stuff on the Head usually does happen as a direct result of what happens up there. The Moloch Sedon was notoriously capricious. He also tended to get bored with what was going down below, on this Africa-sized continent of his. Consequently, every two or three centuries, he tended to get inceptive.

Not all that long after causing the windstorm as he, Vayu Maelstrom, passed over Petrograd, the highborn devil's first generational grandfather and his second generational father combined to send him to the Outer Earth. He, also Devil Wind, hadn't been seen, let alone heard from since. Tough tiddlywinks for him. Third generational Master Devas were as immortal as their progenitors; that meant they were retrievable. So long as you could find and reunite their constituent bits and pieces.

Since they would have done that themselves, if they could – and Wind hadn't – that would take time. Plus, given everything else he'd set in motion besides the disaster that had become of his two decades long, pet project on the Outer Earth, the launching of the Cosmic Express, the last, not just fully functional, Great God on the Inner Earth had more immediately pressing engagements. He wouldn't have enough time to go beyond the Dome and look for his bits and pieces for at least a couple more days.

Thrygragos Byron felt no sense of urgency because he had a potential Secondary Nucleus almost as effective as his Primary Nucleus. Once he fused with their constituent Nucleoids, and they with him, both Nucleuses (Nuclei) could cathonitize Master Devas. It was just a matter of releasing the missing component of his secondary one from imprisonment within All of Incain.

Not a problem. The Great God had fed him to All. At his say-so the She-Sphinx would howsoever-happily regurgitate him.

========

The Byronhead shimmered into sight above the pristine – because it was All-swept – Prison Beach of Incain. It was as huge as a swollen barrage balloon without a concomitant body. That had been lost more than three centuries prior to Xuthros Hor unleashing the Great Flood of Genesis; the cataclysmic debacle that drove devils to the eventual Headworld.

One of Great Byron's human eyes was shut. Its regular occupant, Devil Wind (Vayu Maelstrom, as Illuminaries still residing beyond the Dome during what for the Hidden Headworld was its 4th Millennium named him) was the Nucleoid he'd sent to the Outer Earth via the Nag Gap the day before at Father Sedon's command.

(Outer Earthlings on what was now, mostly, the very much non-hidden continent of North America called him 'Huracan' – hence hurricane – when he, in the far distant past, resided out there along with many of his siblings. Byronics often became Mesoamerican deities. Indeed, a number of graven images of Unmoving Byron, accurately minus a body, have been unearthed in sites identified as belonging to Central Mexico's Olmec civilization.)

Out of his other human eye flew his ever-changing stallion: Chimaera Glimmenmare, as Antique Illuminaries named him. (His name was a generic term not to be confused with Chimera, without the 'a', which was a kind of man-eating, goatish demon found on Apple Isle, the pupil of Sedon's Human Eye. Trala-lorn, Pyrame's brood sister, the child devil, unless she was an actual demon child, often rode one. Since hers could go through the Weird, and since chimeras weren't self-psychopomps, she'd likely turned one of Kore's hellhounds into one.)

Although worshipped by traditional centaurs and only minutely intelligent, Pegasus psychopomps alike, Chimaera didn't look like either/or just now. Instead, he continued to feature the octopoid look he'd adopted late Sedonda night, early Mithrada morning, in the Towers of Screech.

(Centaurs could still be found in Krachla – the head of Sedon's Muttonchop – as well as (rarely) in Hadd and (much more commonly) well to its north, beyond the Diluvia Mountain Range in Sedon's Cheek, the vast plains of Marutia, which had always been outside the realm of Byronics. Pegasus psychopomps, who could traverse the Weird beneath the Dome, were a species of generally man-friendly daemon, with an 'a', properly known as pterippi.)

Simultaneously Sedona Spellbinder, an unmistakably female figure entirely made up of smoky particulates, billowed from the Byronhead's third or devic eye. The mere movement of his lips being beneath Byron's exalted status, the Great God always spoke through her. Not for nothing was he known as the Unmoving One; albeit obviously only physically, not spatially.

Vayu, Chimaera and Sedona made up Byron's second brood. (All Master Devas were born in litters of three because immediate siblings were born simultaneously, via the Trigregos Sisters, in the first Weir's Star System. It was consumed in a supernova caused by the Dual Entities in one of the male of the two's earliest lifetimes.) Illuminaries named the members of Byron's third brood: Aphropsyche Morningstar, Damon Goldenrod and Nevair Neverknight.

APM, as she was better known, was the lone woman. She presented herself as having a shapely, female outline filled-in entirely with blinking eyeballs; hence her other nickname, All-Eyes. Damon's first name sounded suspiciously like demon. Irony-inclined antique Illuminaries gave it to him because he invariably showed himself off as the epitome of glorious godhood; as a man whose skin was as golden as the rod or sceptre, his Tvasitar Talisman, that he perpetually carried.

As for what Neverknight looked like, that was why Illuminaries named him thus. He was never a never knight; he was always a knight, a Black Knight, even at night. Although his power focus was a shield, he used it to outfit himself with ebonite armour from tip of his head to the tips of his toes. He even used it to materialize his own warhorse or destrier. In deference to his older brother Chimaera he generally refrained from becoming it. Let Chimaera keep centaurs his exclusively; Nevair happily accepted adulation from noble-hearted warriors everywhere.

Neither All-Eyes (Byron's Venus) nor Goldenrod (Byron's Apollo) were here. Nevertheless Knight (Byron's Paladin) was, however.

He was whom they'd come to release; he and one other.

========

Incain lay about as far south as one could go on the Head without leaving land. While the Hidden Continent occupied what amounted to its own separate dimension, it was geographically contiguous to the Outer Earth's North Pacific. Even though the Winter Solstice was only three weeks away, when the Byronhead arrived it was pleasantly warm; the same as it customarily was down here in what would have been very nearly Hawaii, but for Cathonia.

Its arrival signalled a bone-chilling squall to blow in from Tempestuous Psychron. The silver cloud that blew in with it disgorged an enormous hailstone that only narrowly missed the Byronhead. Upon impact the hailstone cracked. Out of it stepped Rudra Silvercloud, Byron's Beast – more like, given how he looked, Byron's Tiger – back on Incain barely an hour after he last left it. Not that travelling tremendous distances took devils much time beneath the Dome, so long as he or she still had his or her power focus.

As befit a firstborn, he was one the Hidden Headworld's most powerful Master Devas; along with Tantal and Methandra Thanatos one of the last three firstborns left as well. Both a weather-wizard, the Devalord of Storms, and a Beast Master – though these days his favourite sort of beasts were were-beasts – he'd thoroughly earned the descriptive epithet of Savage Storm. To say the least he liked to make a dramatic entrance.

"That was rude, Beast," exclaimed Sedona Spellbinder in her own voice. "You could have hit father."

"Maybe that's why ancient Illuminaries named me Rudra, Secondary Smoke." Funny folks, devils. Regular crowd-pleasers.

========

Illuminaries named him during the course of the Hidden Headworld's Fourth Millennium beneath the Dome. (This was its Sixth). They did so, first of all, because his attributes reminded them more of those ascribed to a god worshipped in a different subcontinent, that of India, during Vedic times as Rudra. They did so, second of all, because he always travelled about in a silver cloud..

(Turned out this wasn't so quirky as it was odd. Like his siblings, he spent most of his time beyond the Dome in today's Americas; as often as not Mesoamerica, which two thousand years later Christopher Columbus still mistook for India. What was truly quirky, Illuminaries gave the more territorially appropriate, big cat nod of Balam Jaguar to a much younger brother, one of Byron's three Summer Zodiacals, their equivalent of Leo the Lion.)

He called his poleaxe power focus Cloud-Pleaser solely because it pleased him.

****

Vayu Maelstrom, as Devil Wind, first appeared in Phantacea One. Chimaera, Sedona and the Byronhead were depicted on the wraparound cover of Phantacea Four. Maelstrom, along with members of the Damnation Brigade, showed up on the covers of "The War of the Apocalyptics", the opening entry in the *'Launch 1980'* story cycle, and the graphic novel entitled "The Damnation Brigade".

GAMES 6: **Then Till Tuesday**

========

<u>**Demetray, 2 Tantalar 5980 YD**</u>

The Conurbation of Corona City, the huge, though hardly island-wide capital of Apple Isle, the pupil of the Hidden Headworld's 'Human Eye', was the most cosmopolitan of places.

========

There, in the relative peace of a largely self-policing metropolis, dwelled factions from just about every one of the myriad sentient races that populated Sedon's Head. Smiler did not pause in the city proper. Nor did he go to Mt. Maenalus, an active volcano in whose heart hid Kore of the Many Names and where there once was – and might be again someday – a between-space link to the Outer Earth accessible to devils. Instead, he went directly to the long-abandoned, but meticulously kept Mithradium atop Theopolis Hill.

Here, from roughly the middle part of the first century YD to late in the Dome's Twentieth, dwelled Thrygragos Varuna Mithras. He did so, for the most part, alongside the conglomerate female devil supposedly dominated by the personality of his second born daughter. Think of her as the original Kore, meaning both maiden and heart, hence core. Upon gaining solidity returning Illuminaries of over a thousand years later named her Divine Coueranna.

Those first couple of millennia were a time of joyful bliss, of unparalleled prosperity, in the Upper Head. Coueranna was not the miserable, spite-filled creature she would become once all the other Kore-devils essentially escaped her dominance and gained individual solidity themselves. She was the most beautiful of all Master Devas, the simultaneous embodiment of the three-in-one Great Goddess: Maiden, Mother and Crone. Corona City was then the City of Happiness and Apple Isle the centre of the Inner Earth, if perhaps not the whole world.

In or around the Year of the Dome 2000, her brood-sister, the relatively newly solidified, and possibly self-named, Fitna Marutia (later variously identified as Marut Kanin, Kore-Eris, Kore-Discord and, most enduringly, albeit never endearingly, Strife) seduced the Great God then more commonly known as Varuna.

She bore him his first and only child who wasn't an azura spirit being. The consequential deviant boy was named Chrysaor Attis. In a relatively short period of time, perhaps even as early as during his first life, he became identified as the Universal Soldier, of whom legends are told both on the Head and on the Outer Earth — where, for five hundred years, the Age of Heroes, he roamed in one incarnation or another.

Even with Marutia as its de facto reigning queen, as well as devic goddess, Happiness City carried on most cheerfully. Then, ca YD 2500, Mt. Maenalus, aka Kore's Volcano, ceased huffing and puffing petulantly. It sucked it all in for a few years then blew its by then bulging top big time.

Blame for the massive eruption was apportioned variously. Marutia, for example, pointed the finger on Divine Coueranna, her insane jealousy and the collapse of the 500-year Mediterranean Goddess Culture beyond the Dome. Others said Mithras's Torchbearers, Tammuz and Osiraq, caused it in a fit of delayed pique. According to this theory, theirs was an unprecedented deadly overreaction to the cathonitization of their litter brother, Novadev (Solstitial Summer), ostensibly for drunkenly destroying the Outer Earth island of Strongyne (Strong Women), the remnants of which today is most commonly called Santorini.

Still others said it was the completely cold-blooded, though in their case hardly unprecedented, work of the ever-recurring Dual Entities, who – lest anyone ever forget – destroyed the first Weir Star tens of thousands of years earlier in an effort to eradicate the entire devic race. Whatever the case, the eruption decimated Ap Isle, the pupil of Sedon's Human Eye, killed most of its populace and wiped out a magnificent metropolis that predated the Moloch raising the Dome out of his own essence by hundreds of years.

Although not radioactive, like the Ghostlands became when the Eleventh for sure combined their nuclear idiocy in 4825 (which suggested Mt Maenalus didn't so much detonate due to devils, or anyone else, as it did courtesy of Mother Nature), Ap Isle remained virtually uninhabited for hundreds of years.

In time Varuna Mithras, with Marutia, his Ewe for Aries, still in tow, rebuilt it. Rather, since devils rarely did anything themselves, had it rebuilt. That's what adherents are for, among other things. It never altogether regained its sheer wonderfulness, but it wasn't a bad place to live. (Still wasn't; was even Time Quake free, so it had all the modern conveniences; even if, gallingly, most of these last had to be imported from the subcontinent of Aka Godbad.)

Around 4000 YD (Year Zero Anno Domini, in a large segment of today's Outer Earth), as a kind of act of contrition for the failure of the Crimson Conspiracy, Mithras, as he was then most commonly called, was forced to get rid of Marut Kanin — supposedly by cathonitization, though the Sisterhood of Anthea and, before Chaos disposed of her at the start of the Thousand Days of Disbelief ca 5500 YD, the incomparable Harmony (Datong Harmonia) had different versions of her fate. In the absence of a Star Marutia, who could say for sure?

The city continued to prosper. Did so even after Thrygragon, when the Great God who'd virtually always ruled it met his own, this time indisputable fate in the Gregarian Fields. Indeed, Apple Isle became one of the very first devic protectorates (meaning domains thereafter deemed inviolable by the two surviving Great Gods, Byron and Lazareme). Divine Coueranna, Kore of the Many Names, who'd never altogether lost her adherents thereon, became its acknowledged Dand. At the same time, her forever post-Mithras consort, Kind, Cruel or Indifferent Plathon, the multi-horned Bull of Mithras, gained Corona City, albeit subject to her approval.

In the middle of the 58th Century, the apple of Sedon's Human Eye could boast its Corona, the City, the most prosperous of the Head's great cities; the Hidden

Headworld's equivalent of London England. Then, with the murder of her Charon, her Charioteer (what had become of Mithras and Marutia's self-evidently no longer immortal, let alone recurring, deviant son, Chrysaor Attis), and probably with Plathon's connivance, Kore-Coueranna found herself abandoned in the core of her volcano, where she remained to this day.

As Kind Plathon's nowadays prohibitive protectorate, Apple Isle yet thrived. Smiler still preferred the Mithradium atop Theopolis Hill – the seat of Mithras and, before him, Varuna's power – to Corona City proper. It brought back pleasant memories. And so it should. No one could remember he existed unless he was with them and wanted them to remember him. He didn't want that right this minute but, when he did, here is where he ruled not just Apple Isle, but the entirety of the Upper Head, always excepting the Weirdom of Cabalarkon and, eventually, the Ghostlands, which weren't worth ruling anymore anyhow.

He was, after all, the firstborn of Thrygragos Sedon; the 'A' in the VAM Entity: Varuna Ahriman Mithras.

To help relive his happiest memories of Happiness City atop Theopolis Hill, the Smiling Fiend reached – with hands that had too many digits and they with too many knuckle-joints – deep into his pocket and, instead of his syrinx or panpipes, his preferred power focus, withdrew two shrunken skulls. These he juggled between his hands, chortling mirthfully.

"Hello, V. Hello, M. How are my brothers in Sedon, Starlight and Sunlight, doing today? Not saying much as usual, I see. Not much to say, is there? Like to kiss my feet? No. Oh, good. Glad to hear it." The fiend touched the teeth of one to his left foot, then the other to his right foot. *"I do so enjoy it when you indulge my fantasies.*

"You're probably wondering what I'm going to do with you today. Well, it's like this. Things are going on up here, in our lands, and I'm trying to figure out what's what. To do that, I have to rely on your special vision. Do be still, both of you. I hope this hurts, but I doubt it will."

The polydactyl fiend reached into his pocket again. This time he pulled out two Brainrock chains; made like all power foci by Tvasitar Smithmonger, the devic smithy, with whom he had a 'special' relationship. (The molten Brainrock lava lake, from where Tvasitar forged devic talismans, formed when the Dual Entities attempted to assassinate him, thinking he was Dark Sedon, by asteroid – unless it was abandoned Utopian generational ship – circa 2000 YD.)

(At that time, as had been the case for multiple human generations, he – more so, his Daemonicus aspect – was King Sodom to Pyrame Silverstar's Queen Gomorrah on the Outer Earth. Their escape to the Inner Earth via the resulting SAG Gap, before it became stationary, may not have been miraculous, but as yet unnamed Tvasitar, who was then inside a Lava Lout demon, remembered it even when Smiler wasn't around.

(He kept it, the fullness of Smiler's identity, a secret. In return, even though he could have, and should have, shared it – albeit with Pyrame and her never-acknowledged, but partially then still bebrained daemonic aspect, Primeval Lilith – Smiler allowed Tvasitar to take all the credit for being the devic Prometheus.)

The fiend, the only inseparably fused demon-devil in existence, attached an end of each chain to the cavities where the skull's third eyes had been. Standing up he twirled the two like bolas over his head. He didn't so much fling them into Samsara as the chains elongated and sent the skulls into the Universal Substance. He thereupon attached his terminal ends to his Brainrock sash – what might have held his hooded cloak of darkness together; that is if it was an article of clothing and not obscurant, but actually insubstantial darkness – then sat back and pulled out his syrinx, a word that also referred to the vocal chords of a bird.

Making himself comfortable on what had been Varuna's, then Mithras's throne, he began chirping out a soothing tune.

The visions began to appear almost immediately.

========

One skull appeared over Pettivisaya, the City of Wailing Souls, formerly Grand Elysium, in Sedon's absence once another of his personal seats of power, but now "capital" of the Ghostlands, if such a term could be used for radioactively rendered wasteland. Finding no sign of manlike movement it returned to Samsara only to emerge elsewhere a short time later. The other skull appeared over a battlefield in the southern Lake Lands. Judging by the marshy terrain it might have been the Flood-lands or the border between the two devic protectorates.

This was obviously a crucial moment. Through the skull of Mithras – unless it was Varuna; Smiler had never been able to differentiate one brood brother from the other – the fiend recognized two warring factions. It was almost definitely the Floods, he decided, because the gigantic, scaly-skinned, yet still somehow human-oid Saurs were on the offensive. Leading the Saurs assault was none other than their ruler and greatest hero, Klizarod Rex.

They were armed with clubs, rocks, and primitive cutting implements whereas their opponents, mostly plain humans, had guns, heavy artillery, and a few heli-copters. These were the legions of Corona and Marutia. (Marutian manpower only, as Marutia was once again plagued by Time Quakes; had been since Star Sedon's return to the night's sky two years earlier after an absence of a quarter century. So the weaponry had to have come from elsewhere.) The legionnaires vastly out-num-bered the Saurs and their weapons were as modern as weapons got on Sedon's Head.

Actually, Smiler reflected, they probably were from Godbad, one of Centauri Enterprises' factories in Crepuscule, the Land of Twilight. Or maybe they'd been imported from the Bloodlands; which, being Time Quake free, did have modern manufacturing facilities. Both Twilight and what was now called New Valhalla – though often warring with each other, as they were now – were virtual satellite states of Greater Godbad today. It was a good thing the Saurs had nigh-on-impenetrable hide. They would have been wiped out otherwise.

On a hillock behind the legionnaires position stood a number of Master Devas. They included Plathon, the Bull of Mithras; the to him horrifying child-devil – un-less she was a child-demon – Tralalorn, by self-naming; Icy Miros, a rogue Lazarem-ist whose pseudo-protectorate (Thrygragos Lazareme wasn't big on his spawn having their own exclusive territories but, unlike Byron, didn't forbid it) had once been the Crystal Mountains between Wildwyck and what had long been Samarand; and the firedrake, a denizen of the Lakes, Mildoth.

(As hard as it was for outsiders to credit – as hard as it was for most insiders to do a dot-ditto – Samarand had been Sedon's Tongue; the city itself Sedon's Tongue Stud. By the same token Twilight had once been Daybreak whereas Frozen Lathakra had lain off the Gulf of Corona, Sedon's Human Eye, where it in effect formed Sedon's Lens or Monocle. In all three places their leading devic Dand or overseer {Yati, Byron's Dragon; Mariamne Dawnstar; and old King Cold} started withholding more than their fair share of reverence received, at least as far as the power that be above them was concerned.

(So one preposterous, though obviously not impossible, said power, the Moloch Sedon, uprooted all three massive, territorial landforms, inhabitants with their habitation, and stuck them where they are now. Daybreak, the Land of the Rising Sun became Sedon's Outer Nose, aka Crepuscule-Twilight, the Land of the Setting Sun. Its devic ruler, no fool she, Lazareme's Venus, changed her name accordingly. Became the Grey Lady, Miss Mist, Krepusyl Evenstar.

(Sedon's Tongue, still called Samarand, took Daybreak's place on the far east coast Occipital region, such that it saw the Hidden Headworld's first sunrise. Lathakra, as incongruously frozen as ever, ended up off the Cattail's east coast as near as the Head came to having a tropical zone.

(Wasn't the first time Sedon had moved it to punish the Thanatoids, either. Originally Lathakra was Sedon's Horn, extending from the Mystic Mountains, aka Sedon's Crown, to well out into the northern extremes of Fearsome Fobbiat. However, its root nestled in Mythland, the Jewel of Sedon's Crown. In Sedon's mind that made it too suggestively close to Methandra Thanatos, Mithras's Virgin, whom the Mighty Moloch fancied.)

It was Trala that most intrigued the Smiling Fiend (who'd also fancied the Scarlet Sorceress for thousands of years, albeit without revealing it to her; not so much out of fear of rejection as fear of having to go public). Once one of the Head's three perpetual presences (the other two being her brood sister, unless she was her mother, Pyrame Silverstar, and the Moloch Sedon himself, whom some said was her father), she almost never left Ap Isle.

In truth, over the course of coming up to six thousand years, she hardly ever went anywhere off-isle without Pyrame there to hold her hand – or lead her latest Chimera, as the case may be – and that hadn't been possible for thirty years. Her most famous off-island excursion was on Thrygragon, Mithramas Day 4376 but, as Smiler well knew, having goaded her on, her distracting Mithras just before he annihilated his two Great God 'brothers' wasn't all of why Mithras died instead. That was mostly down to Attis, the Medusa (Mater Matare), and the Unities of Lazareme, notably Unholy Abaddon.

For his part the Tyrant Lizard, Klizarod Rex, soared to a height in excess of twenty feet. Nevertheless, like his Saurs, there was something distinctly humanoid about him. His arms, for example, were more humanly proportionate to the rest of his body than a standard Tyrannosaur or an even larger Allosaurus, of which there were a few in his army. He also carried a weapon, a Brainrock talisman, a kind of halberd: two axe-heads and a spear point mounted on a long pole.

Similar weapons were relatively common power foci amongst Master Devas. Carcinogen the Leper had a pendulum-shaped blade topping a long shaft with bulbous 'disease' pod at the other end; Rudra Silvercloud had a single blade shaped like a crescent moon underneath a spear point; Tantal Thanatos wielded a double-headed war-axe or Labrys; Plathon a bident; Abaddon a trident; the Emperor Chameleon, Klizarod's brood brother, another, though differently-shaped halberd that looked like it might have been made out of chromium.

Non-devils, such as the Trinondevs with their eye-staves, Blind Sundown with his solar spear, and OMP-Akbar with his Homeworld Sceptre, were armed in much the same way. Smiler wasn't given to metaphor but the plethora of penile weaponry amongst males wasn't lost on him.

He supposed it had something to do with the fact that devils, and presumably humanoids, were conditioned to obey their fathers over their mothers. Which of course galled devic goddesses no end; hence in part many of them having Pan-harmonium aspirations.

The first skull popped back out of the Weird – as devils tended to call Samsara – over yet another battlefield, undoubtedly in the northern part of the Lake Lands. This was where Yama Nergal, its initial, intended target, was leading his Angels of Death along an incongruously dry corridor out of the Ghostlands. Unlike the other one, where Klizarod's Saurs, badly outmanned and outgunned by Plathon's legion-naires, nonetheless maintained their offensive, here had the makings of a rout.

The forces of the Emperor Chameleon and his wife, Malar Tzigame, the equal-ly colourful, butterfly-like daughter of Thrygragos Byron, his Beauty so-called, vast-ly outnumbered Death's Angels, true. They also had weaponry that was as modern as that of the Bull's legionnaires.

It was probably Godbadian as well, supplied by Pani Merchants from Krachla the long (watery) way, via the Aural Sea. By contrast Death's Angels had no arms to speak of; not that they needed any. Their touch could kill. And since they were already dead, they couldn't be killed anew — though they could be destroyed.

Two visions, of two different battlefields, competed for Smiler's attention. In one, seen through whomever's perspective, Klizarod and Plathon were guiding their respective forces towards a stalemate. In the other, seen through whoever the other one hadn't been, Varuna or Mithras, Death's Angels were routing Lizarados, the pre-dominantly lizard-like army of Chameleon and Tzigame, whom Baaloch Hellblob believed was actually Trala's brood sister in Mithras's Ninth, cat-headed Cathune Bubastis, the Apocalyptic of Drought.

Simultaneously, things happened in both visions. By rights and common sense, he should have had to concentrate on one or the other. Being Smiler however, a di-chotomous being if ever there was one, the fiend fully witnessed both. Whereupon he judged – which he was good at – if he was going to do anything about either.

Icy Miros – a treacherous Lazaremist no Mithradite should have ever turned his back on – struck Multi-Horns, as devils sometimes called him, from ... what else? Behind. He thus turned him into a four-legged, vitreous model of himself, albeit with four hooves and the horns of both a bull and a ram — the Bull as china, minus the shop.

Fiery Mildoth, intelligence-wise a low-watt bulb from the same litter as Catas-trophe's equally nearly mindless Vultyrie (this despite her having two heads), bit off its head. Swallowing it whole, the simpleton creature spread its draconic wings, rose into the air, and began to fly away from the battlefield. (Devils, with the notable exception of Varuna Mithras couldn't be killed as such. They could be as good as killed, however.)

Over the other one something began to form in the sky. Neither Underlord Yama nor either Chameleon or Cathune-Tzigame noticed it. Smiler did, quickly withdrew the skull providing his vision from the scene. Wouldn't do to let Byron and his Spawn realize that Varuna and Mithras still had an interest in the affairs of the Headworld. Especially since both, supposedly as one, had died on Thrygragon.

No, it wouldn't do to let Great Byron realize they weren't his brothers; were, instead, his nephews. In other words, they were only the first born of 'Grandfather' Sedon. Or that, as a result, Dark Sedon was not the Unmoving One's father; just his elder brother. There was a third part to Varuna Mithras; an 'A' that made them the fabled VAM Entity; that he, Smiler – call him Ahriman if you must – actually existed. Wouldn't do at all.

Now it wasn't a matter of decision. Smiler had no choice but to concentrate on what was happening in the Floods. To do otherwise was to invite detection and he liked being never-remembered. He pulled back and pocketed the skull that had been observing what was going on in the northern Lakes; unravelled his Brainrock sash and flung it through Samsara. Hooked his fish, pulled it out of Samsara.

Wasn't a real fish. Was a real dragon — Fiery Mildoth.

Like his other two simultaneous siblings, not much when it came to intelligence, the firedrake recognized the Mithradium. The Vultyrie's brood brother wasn't so much shocked as incensed that someone, something, somehow had just snagged, then dragged him through between-space to this despised, almost impossibly old, to be so well kept, temple atop Apple Isle's Delphi-like Theopolis Hill.

(The two-headed, two-conjoined bodied – one male, one female – but only two-winged Vultyrie was among the missing stars in the night's sky. His other brother, unless it was his other sister, was a worm; hence had both sexes entangled in his tubular, one-eyed physicality. Was no ordinary worm, not even for a devil. Was Arisandesam, the Conqueror Worm, Sinistral Gluttony of Satanwyck. He wasn't shining upstairs, either. Indeed, the entire Crimson Constellation, as led by Dream, Phantast Thanatos, no longer shone out of the Head's heavens.)

Mithras used to ride Mildoth like a common garuda above his home on the hill. (Uncommon in almost every other aspect, Garudas were common in Djerridam-Goatwood, Sedon's Beard, down in Godbad.) Used to ride him above the island's expansive, nowadays virtually impenetrable jungle and the surrounding gulf as well.

Even more reprehensible, when he wasn't being so sorely misused, the Great God his (thought) father's long-time enforcer, Trawl the Taskmaster, kept him in a stable out in the then less dense, almost garden-like jungle proper. There, in what was more like the House rather than the City of Pain, the unconscionably cruel Cyclops indulged his sadistic tendencies.

Kept him going, but only by force-feeding him on horses, donkeys, and dogs – none of whom were sentient enough to offer worship to anyone meaningfully – instead of allowing him to hunt, and kill, as was his birthright. (Mildoth was so stupid he might have roasted a sentient, and got himself ill-starred, otherwise.)

From his nostrils he belched smoke and flames. His unknown foe became akin to Miros, ambulatory crystal, immune to fire. The obscurant, transitory manling opened his third eye. Mildoth was engulfed in a blaze not of his own making. Having no choice, he flapped to the ground and, furling his wings, bowed abjectly.

Smiler released the dragon from his eyefire, reverted to his normal form: a figure shrouded in darkness whose pink, grinning face and hands, with their abnormally excessive, long, spindly fingers, were the only parts of his skin visible. Making himself larger than the dragon, he calmly patted his distant brother in Sedon on the snout. Mildoth almost purred.

"Quiet down, mindless beast. I mean you no harm. On the contrary, I'm here to help you. You've been eating things not on your regular diet and I wouldn't want you to get indigestion." He yanked on his sash; hauled the multi-horned, glassine head that properly belonged to Cruel Plathon's debrained daemonic body out of Mildoth's gut. ***"Return to whomever you call master these days. Perhaps he will be as merciful as I am and not fillet you for your failure to dispose of the Bull's head as directed."***

The firedrake unfurled his wings, rose into the sky, and headed north-north-east, back towards the Floodlands across the Gulf of Corona. Smiler still had a skull over that battlefield. Through the chain attached to it he sent his command. The skull opened its jaws and inhaled the vitreous statue of Cruel Plathon that was standing near Tralalorn into its mass, then vanished.

The skull came to the Mithradium; disgorged the Bull's remains, which promptly shattered into a thousand shards. Smiler shrank the skull and placed it his pocket with the other one. With a wave of one of his strangely elongated hands, he swept the shards into a huge pile then placed Plathon's glassine head atop it. (Psychokinesis, also telekinesis, was second nature to devils; something they could do, like releasing eyefire or hardening close by ether, without having to occupy debrained daemons or be in possession of a power focus.)

He began to play his panpipes. The shards started to vibrate, then to dance grotesquely. In a matter of minutes, a semblance of the Bull of Mithras had pulled itself back together again. Smiler kept on playing, reversing the effect of Miros's surprise attack and Mildoth's even more inexcusable double-cross. (They were Mithradites whereas Icy Miros was only a cousin, a typically anarchic Lazaremist.)

Soon, but for a few minor details – a couple of his two sets of horns in rude and probably painful places, his head attached to an armpit whilst one of his forearms connected to his left knee and the corresponding lower leg stuck out of his neck – Plathon was mostly normal again. Normal enough to focus on benefactor at least, if not identify him as yet.

"Sort yourself out, Bull. I can't do everything for you!"

========

Trala wasn't just Tralalorn's diminutive.

It was what she tended to call herself, especially when she was talking about herself in the third person during one of those nonsensical rhyming sessions she was so fond of improvising while playing with her dolls — some of whom were alive, if 'devolved' or, often more applicably, 'de-matured'. Ostensibly she was the brood sister, from Mithras's Ninth, of Pyrame Silverstar and Cathune Bubastis, both of whom had been worshipped in Pharaonic and, in the former's case, pre-Pharaonic Egypt. Equally likely, especially since records of her predated 2000 YD by a considerable measure, she was Pyrame's daemonic daughter by the Moloch Sedon.

The White Dwarf, as Trala was nicknamed, mostly amongst devakind, after her talisman, which appeared to be a glowing meteorite, was a perpetual child. Seemingly never more than six or seven years old, like all devils and most demons she was a shape-shifter. Today, as she commonly did, she sported black and white striped hair and three-toned eyeballs: blue, red and yellow, or variations thereof.

Tralalorn and Plathon had been concentrating on the battle progressing before them. Icy Miros – a Lazaremist who had attached himself to the high devic muck-a-mucks that, having nowhere else to go due to too often disappointing their would-be-worshippers, frequented Corona City after the Grey Lady, Krepusyl Evenstar, kicked him out of Twilight (aka Crepuscule, Sedon's Outer Nose, her protectorate) – chose that moment to sneak up behind the Bull and turn him into glass.

Mildoth, who like Miros had obviously been bought off by Klizarod, snapped off his head and rose into the sky just as she reacted. Undoubtedly, she was Miros's next target, but it took him a couple of seconds to re-energize himself. At the same time, having rampaged his way through the legionnaire-bulwark as if no more than toy soldiers, Klizarod was pounding up the hill towards them.

The child-devil had been prepared to deal with the Tyrant Lizard; that was why Kind Plathon had brought her along, promising fun and games and at least one new dolly, if she really thought she could handle a devic dolly. She dealt with Miros first – devolving him almost instantly into an infantile, bowling pin shaped, ampoule the likes of which she'd seen in local pharmacies on Apple Isle. By then Klizarod was upon her.

Fortunately she didn't need to recharge herself. Her power focus looked like a chunk of fallen meteorite and was called, like her, though she wasn't one, the White Dwarf. It had rarely been used in the thirty years since Pyrame Silverstar, whom she herself regarded more as her mother than her brood sister, was cathonitized. She turned it on the enormous Tyrant Lizard. It took a little longer but, in the space of a minute, Klizarod was reduced to something akin to a squirming tadpole without a puddle in sight.

"That'll teach you to double-cross my daddy." Like the Anthean usually known as Hush or Young Life – a onetime 'dolly play-pal' of hers, one whom she both deliberately resembled, unless it was the other way around, and whom she'd turned into a perennial seven year old, on Pyrame's instructions, nearly sixty years ago – Tralalorn had a succession of daddies.

The Bull had been her favourite false father since the middle of the last century when the fickle, but endlessly ambitious Pauper Priestess took a fancy to Plathon and decided to get rid of Coueranna, the Bull's paramour for most of four thousand years. (Even since Mithras dumped that Kore, Kore-Concord, his Boss Cow for Taurus, in favour of her ruthless, endlessly flattering brood sister, Fitna Marutia, Kore-Discord, who became his Ewe for Aries.)

The Saurs weren't impressed with what she had done to their devic master and warrior-king. Bursting through a picket-line of legionnaires, two dozen of the things rumbled towards her. She turned the rays of her white dwarf on them. Devolving devils, one at a time, hadn't taken much time, but two dozen Saurs at once was a bit extreme for a little girl who had been a little girl for going on six thousand years.

Her smart dress was torn, her intricate braids all a mess. She slipped in a pool of blood and skinned a knee; nevertheless finished the last one just in time to see a huge skull in the sky suck in what was left of Glassy Plathy, as she'd already dubbed porcelain Plathon. Crying in frustration she hurled her talisman, once the size of a basketball, now the size of a softball — two games popular on Ap Isle — at the skull.

The Dwarf missed as the skull vanished into the air, but it boomeranged back to her. Seeing the skull take in the statue then vanish was almost too much for Trala, whose fondness for spouting nonsensical rhymes was matched by her unsavoury reputation for damaging her dolls. She wasn't used to thinking on her own: Plathon or her litter sisters, Pyrame and Cathead (Cathune Bubastis, who did indeed usually appear to have a cat's head) always did that for her.

Suddenly she received a psychic call for help. Its florid coloratura timbre identified it as coming from the Emperor Chameleon, a lesser daddy married to Byron's Beauty, who wouldn't make a bad mummy if she was from the same tribe. Underlord Yama's Angels were overwhelming his forces but, he imparted, there was a new factor on the scene. He demanded their immediate assistance. She shot back that Bull Daddy was gone. She was tired, dirty, and more than a little fed-up. She was going to go home for a nice hot bath then play with her toys until bully came back.

Another psychic cry came to her. This one she recognized from three decades ago, and a lot more than merely three thousand years before that. She didn't need her daemonic chimera — the latest in a long line of self-converted hellhounds — to get about the Weird; hadn't even brought it with her this time as Daddy Bull warned her he might need a snack if things didn't go well. Wasn't teasing either.

When it came to demons, Multi-Horns was of the eat-before-getting-eaten school of demon-devil relations.

========

Trala blipped through Samsara; arrived at the Emperor's side on the battlefield in the Northern Lakes with next to the speed of thought.

"Get him away from me, you little witch!"

It was her immediate sister in Mithras, the Apocalyptic of Drought!

========

"I used to think you were one of the four or five of our kind left that was worth speaking to on equal terms, Bull. Has Loquileptic come out of the Sedon Sphere and turned you into a complete imbecile in the years I've been otherwise occupied?" (Plathon's brood brother Loquileptic epitomized Divine Madness. His was not among the missing stars. Then again he'd been so unpredictably crazy even Sedon couldn't trust him to stay put. So who knew if he was even still up there?)

As befit such a highborn, the third-born Bull of Mithras was one of the most successful of all devazurs, not just Mithradites. In the multi-millennia before Master Devas became solid, his had been a highly individualized and industrious spirit; one whose personalities dominated all his brother and sister Mithradites whenever he hardened a form for himself-themselves to get about.

Upon arriving on the then Whole Earth, one of his first assignments was to make himself into the God of Cain, son of Adam (2), aka Alorus Ptah, and the Trishtar Thrae Eve (or Primeval Lilith, dependent on who you believed). Yes that Cain, brother-murderer of Abel then, long thereafter, the Anti-Patriarch who opposed that of his blood brother, Pseth Ra, the second Patriarch of Golden Age Humankind.

Because of Plathon, in what amounted to 4661 BC (661 pre-Dome), Cain destroyed the original Tree of Life. The Golden Apples produced by its offshoot trees were what gave the so-called Rainbow Class of antediluvian humanity the incredibly long lives they enjoyed before the Genesea (Great Flood of Genesis); not to mention, albeit their class alone, immunity from devic possession. (Notwithstanding the subsequent and perhaps not at all surprisingly ancient legend of Johnny Appleseed, they did not reseed successfully on the Outer Earth. Did in here, for a time. Hence Ap Isle's enduring nomenclature.)

After he became independently solid, the Bull briefly acted as Varuna Mithras's right-hand monster; make that devil, even though he was left-handed, as in left-pawed. Then, ca YD 2000, the recurring deviant Chrysaor Attis came along and, upon achieving manhood, promptly took his place in the Great God's affections.

For the next five hundred years, Plathon joined with Mithras's estranged queen, Divine Coueranna, the Great God's discarded Boss Cow for Taurus, in trying to destroy Attis — who often came to lead the Mithrant Legionnaires as, howsoever-ironically, their Taurus, a position Plathon filled originally; one that was in fact named after him, not the zodiacal sign.

(Mithrant legionnaires were entirely male. Their female equivalent, their mostly stay-at-home mothers, wives and daughters, were called Korants. Both Mithrants and Korants remained the main powers-that-be on Apple Isle. Also ironically, their duties included retaining Theopolis Hill as a spot sacred to all the Hidden Headworld's devil-gods, no mater which tribe, and maintaining both the Mithradium and Corona City's nevertheless nearby Kore Dome.)

Just as incarnations of Attis became some of the greatest heroes of Outer Earth mythology, as well as some historical or quasi-historical figures, Plathon became some of the most memorable monsters he/they vanquished. What generally wasn't reflected in those mishmash myths is that he was more often successful than the hero. It was just that the Attis had an uncanny knack of getting reborn whereas his monsters didn't; at least not in the form Attis or his fellow 'heroes' killed.

When the Xuthrodites destroyed their Outer Earth portal, Strongyne, the Isle of Strong Women, in 1500 BC and (arguably) Kore, with the help of the Idiot Twins, reciprocated by blowing Mt. Maenalus, Head-side of the same portal in 2500 YD, Plathon's stature deteriorated to the point that he became nothing more than Coueranna's charioteer, her Charon.

That ignoble state of affairs lasted until Thrygragon, when he helped kill Mithras and, after carefully crippling – not killing – him, forced the Attis to take over as Charon. That was in the Year of the Dome 4376. For the next nearly fifteen hundred years, he was Kore's consort, her regent on Apple Isle.

Tiring of that subservient role, he fell in with Pyrame Silverstar and isolated Coueranna in her volcano. The whole island, not just Corona City, became his de facto protectorate. It remained so, despite the loss of the Pauper Priestess in 5950, until some seventeen years ago when, on an archaeological expedition to the ruined, so-called City of Pain in the thickness of Ap Isle's jungle, he became the thrall of

Trawl the Taskmaster, long an indentured servant of Baaloch Hellblob, Lord Lazy of Satanwyck. Since then, he hadn't been his own man or devil or monster.

Suddenly feeling free of Trawl, he knew he could become a full-fledged puppeteer again — not an impotent, mind-controlled puppet. Furthermore, once he pulled his body parts back into the right places, his brain cleared and he at last recognized his benefactor. If the known world's only true demon-devil could ever do anything of benefit to anyone other than himself.

In some respects he wished he wasn't back in his right mind. The Smiling Fiend, for that's how he thought of this Ahrimanic abomination, wholly devil yet wholly demon, was the one-time Judge of Grand Elysium, the Laird (Liege Lord) of the Laughing Lands, of Hell on Earth, Pyrame's thought-long-gone mate. And, if the two of them, whole or only in part, were earthborn demons, as had often been bruited about, and not devils, quite likely Tralalorn's legitimate, albeit chthonic or earthborn, father.

"Your faith in me was well-placed, Judge, though I have not been myself since '63. Hellblob shall pay for what he and his minions did to me and mine."

Smiler regarded the Bull cautiously. He looked his usual self: double set of horns, one like a ram's, the other like a standard bull's; distinctive, somewhat bovine face with nastily sharp teeth (a flesh-eater, no cud-chewer this one); hairy, muscular, humanoid arms and the body to go with it, hoofed feet, and a two-pronged pitchfork or bident, his power focus. Still, was he worthy to be treated as an equal? Not yet, the fiend determined.

"Why do you blame Sloth of Satanwyck for your misfortunes? Is Apple Isle not your protectorate, bequeathed to you by Kore of the Many Names? Why didn't you just overpower the Cyclops?" (Trawl, Ibal and Arisandesam were not the only devic Cyclopes; just the best known. Then again, their daemonic bodies being protean, any one of them could appear one-eyed. Probably couldn't become all eyes; not for any length of time anyhow. That was pretty much the private preserve of Aphropsyche Morningstar, Byron's Venus, another third-born like Loquileptic, Plathon and whoever filled out Mithras's threesome.)

"Corona City is my domain, judge. Apple Isle I usurped from Kore and have since ruled the whole area by what amounts to acclamation. Pain was Taskmaster's protectorate in the old days. He went away, apparently to indulge his extremes in the Domination of Satanwyck. There, as I now realize, in your absence, he fell under little Lord Lazy's sway, but Kore never revoked his suzerainty. Trawl took me over when I ventured there, thinking it decades abandoned. Once I was under his control I couldn't break free."

"Remiss of her and clumsy of you. What would the Play Prince of Pandemonium want with Apple Isle? Satanwyck is one of the largest protectorates on the whole Head; might even be the largest if you discount the Byronics' Godbadian subcontinent. When it comes to Lord Lazy, ambition seems anathema."

"I believe he wanted to reopen the gap in the Dome between Kore's volcano and the Outer Earth island of Strongyne or what's left of it." All three of Smiler's eyes narrowed. No longer feeling the fool, Plathon quickly added: "You're right, of course. You always are. Hellblob wouldn't have had the wit let alone the drive for such a plot. There must have been another hand at work. Seeing you suggests whose it was."

"That effort was most embarrassing. Lemurians under their formidable queen Amphitrite and a mutated mantel then called Steltsar, with the considerable help of All of Incain and another judge – one named Warlock, I should add – laid a clever trap for us. I was up to the challenge of course, but it was a narrow thing.

"Taskmaster, mostly on his own, tried something very similar in '68 but only succeeded in destroying the Outer Earth side of the gap we were trying to reopen. Something I anticipated since, otherwise, there likely would be no such things as devazurs anymore. In a roundabout, but very real way, you owe your very existence to me."

"But not your own?" Plathon was getting uncomfortably close to the truth, so Smiler switched to the present day and gave the Bull the acting Prime Sinistral's version of the story.

"How long have you known that Cathune wasn't cathonitized in 5960; that Trawl's brood brother, Djinn Domitian, just made it appear she had until they finally managed to cathonitize Byron's beautiful butterfly in her stead? That Drought's been masquerading as her, as Malar Tzigame, as the wife of the Emperor Chameleon, since 5960? That the whole masterful plot was dreamed up decades earlier by Ibal, the grand vizier of Satanwyck, in order for him to take Sloth's place and eventually rule the entire Forehead?"

"Impossible," protested the Bull, thinking clearly for the first time in almost as long. "I was there when Cathune, Pyrame and Ibal were ill-starred. I even know how Saladin Devason, not that it was altogether him, managed it. Malar Tzigame is Malar Tzigame. If there is duplicity, it's on the part of Tzigame and her father."

"Bravo, Bull. You have just gone up a notch in my estimation. The transparency of the plot astonishes me. That the to-my-mind always ridiculous Emperor Chameleon was fooled by it, if he was, remains a moot point. How could Yama Nergal, the devils of Marutia, even Sloth – no bright light, I grant you – be so thoroughly suckered by the Unmoving One?"

"You may have just answered your own question, judge. Bodiless Byron making a move on the Upper Head is almost a contradiction in terms. Consider first whom he is not manipulating. Thanks to Spellbinder's curse of Disproportionment, the Thanatoids are too embarrassed to leave Lathakra. Add to that, even though I have doubts about it, to the best of my knowledge Kore's still shut up in her volcano.

"I'm robbed of my wits by Trawl. Underlord Yama's been inundated with radiation since the Idiot Twins blasted the Elysian Fields unto the Ghostlands; not that legitimate ghosts, as opposed to devils and azuras, could survive there for long. Of the remaining Sixth, Neargon and Typhon are content in their protectorates and, of the Seventh, Klizarod Rex's clearly in league with the Byron Spawn.

"Chroma Chameleon, like myself, our Reaper, Trala, and our siblings up here are obviously Byron's immediate targets. Sometime in the not too distant future, Baaloch will also fall victim to his machinations. That'll leave only the Neuter's Androgynia, Dandset Typhon's Moorset, the Forbidden Forest of Kala Tal and eventually, should he ever relocate the balls he was born with, Lathakra for Great Byron to subjugate, at least among the major protectorates of our kind.

"It's a power grab, pure and simple. If you hadn't been back in time to prevent it, he would have succeeded. Leave the rest to me, judge. I'll lead the counter-strike."

"And be killed or cathonitized the moment you step out of Corona? You're not competent to tangle with the Byronics; not when they're in ascendency. It's obvious to me what they're doing. Luring Mithradites out of their protectorates, setting them at each other's throats, and then cutting down those of you left.

"The pauper, Devil Doom and the Undergods tried a similar tactic around eleven hundred years ago when they opened a link-way between Temporis and Absudyl, then tempted Dand Tariqartha to take it over. Fortunately for the Chronocollector, Lord Order was there to thwart them. He even cathonitized Mines and Minerals in the process."

"Chameleon shares the Lakes with Byron's Beauty. Once Klizarod crosses the border, he'll be nailed — Chimaera's good buddy or not. Where's Trawl?"

"Forget Taskmaster, Bull. The Thanatoids dumped him into Incain yesterday. Forget your legions as well. They're as good as forfeit. About the only thing we can still salvage is the White Dwarf. I shall attend to her as soon as I take you safely to the capital. Be vigilant. By the end of the day, Corona may be the only protectorate our kind has left north of the Forbidden Forest or west of Satanwyck, Androgynia and Moorset.

"We, you, dare not lose it!"

Moments later the Mithradium once again lay splendid to behold but empty.

=========

Although huge as well as hue-suffused, the Emperor Chameleon was shorter than Klizarod at perhaps fifteen feet high, nowhere near as powerfully-built, nor even half as fearsome-looking. His chromium-glinting halberd was similar to his brother's, though its axe-blades were rounder and not as sharp.

Also unlike Klizarod, he was clothed, although his toga-like garment changed colous as readily and he did. His tail was long and curly, perhaps even prehensile. Facially, he resembled a bulbous-headed, wide-mouthed, mild-mannered lizard, like the chameleon to whom he gave his name.

He was still an impressive figure. One of his massive humanoid hands – they with their opposable thumbs, but seemingly mittened or conjoined fingers – clutched Drought by her scrawny neck. Not too much more pressure and he would snap off her feline, yet all but furless, dessicated head.

It certainly looked like catty Cathune, too. The Apocalyptic of Drought – who had indeed been worshipped in ancient Egypt with a cat's head (as Bast or, as bygone Illuminaries correctly had it, Bubastis) during the era of the Mediterranean Goddess Culture – had brown, dried-up skin the consistency of antique leather rather than fur. Her hair, such as it was, thin and white, grew out of her head in patches. Great hunks of it were missing or pulled out, along with snatches of her scalp.

That she was here was self-evident, but it wasn't possible. Tralalorn had seen her litter sister cathonitized thirty years ago, along with other sister Pyrame, Viceroy Ibal, the Chancellor or Grand Vizier of Pandemonium, the Domination's capital city, awhile later, and most of the others who risked Demon King Sedon's wrath by threatening the Weirdom of Cabalarkon and his life's energy, vampiric progenitor, his partial father, Cabalarkon himself.

"Do as I say, little one," demanded the lesser Apocalyptic. "Devolve him or something just as odious."

"What's gamely going on? Where's beautiful butterfly doll?"

For a change the devil child, unless she was a demon child, wasn't singing a nonsense song. She tended to do that when she didn't feel threatened or confused. She felt both right now.

"In the night's sky," croaked Drought, "Where I should have been thirty-odd years ago."

Even if she'd convinced herself that was the case – devils were incapable of lying – Trala, who as of 5950 became even more of a perpetual presence on the Hidden Headworld than sister-mom Silverstar, couldn't accept her statement. (Other brood sister Pyrame often spent years on the Outer Earth; plus, in addition to after 5950, she had been a star shining out of the night's sky from roughly 5916 until the Simultaneous Summonings of 5920.)

"Make sense. How you get back? Granddad never release anyone. Kind Bull told me."

"Kind Bull kept a big secret for us."

"Ignore her, dwarf," commanded Chameleon, nervously looking at the sky. A hairless, three-eyed, moon-white head hovered over the battlefield.

"Great Byron duped us with a doppelganger. Made it seem to our foes that this creature was Cathune masquerading as my wife. Except she is my wife, loyal not to her husband, but to her father. See for yourself. Use the Dwarf, change her back to what she really is, a loathsome caterpillar with as many guises as she has legs. Change her back so that I may eat her!"

Something smoky came out of the air; went up Chameleon's nostrils as if they were inverse chimneys. Without releasing his grip on the changeling-thing, the would-be Emperor snorted. The same smoke-shape came out of him. It was Sedona Spellbinder, an evidently never fully solid, always naked, female shape composed of particulate dust; possibly even faeriedust. She was one of Great Byron's second born, Primary Nucleoids.

"No use, stallion. I can't control him."

A mote of dirt transmogrified itself in front of the self-proclaimed Lord-Master of the Lakes. This was a creature of nightmare, a praying mantis with arms and hands holding a Brainrock mace. This was Chimaera Glimmenmare, the centaurs' devil-god, Byron's Stallion even though he changed sexes almost as often as he changed shapes. It, he, she whacked at Chameleon's halberd, also without much effect. Could be they hadn't lured him far enough into the borderlands between the Lakes and the Floods.

The Emperor, only now realizing he wasn't in his protectorate anymore, tightened his grip on Cathune-Tzigame's neck. "One more squeeze, donkey dear, she's headless and I start cutting you into very colourful ribbons."

"Give it up, chroma-creep," spoke Sedona, calling him by a very much disrespectful variation of his howsoever boring, though hardly dull-as-dishwater attribute, Colour. "The day's lost."

"Do something, Trala," demanded Chameleon, in that oddly husky, anything but flutey, coloratura voice of his. The enormous, bipedal, yet nonetheless reptilian Emperor of the Lake Lands was on a hill overlooking the battlefield where his army of Lizarados was in the process of suffering a stunning defeat at the (mostly skeletal) hands of Death's Angels.

"Do something now, Trala," he repeated, his voice becoming shrill and he became even more desperate. "Infantilize them!"

Suddenly a shadow-thing appeared behind Chameleon. It wielded a glowing scythe. Two swipes and it had cut off the Emperor's arms at the elbows. A third swipe and it took off his head. Resolving itself more fully, the shadow became Underlord Yama Nergal, King Harvest, the Mithradites' Grim Reaper since the days of the Expansion of the Empire of Lathakra circa the Head's 48th century.

Initially it was a skeleton in a hood and long robes; then it began to develop skin and girth. Fifth-born Yama had once been the devic god of miners. His natural power focus – what Tvasitar Smithmonger forged for him in the very late 20th Century of the Dome – was a pickaxe which, as he gained substance, materialized strapped to his back. He contemptuously kicked away the pieces of Chameleon's body, caused his hood and robes to fly off his body, wrap up the scythe, and vanish into the Weird, as devils often called Samsara.

He stood before Chimaera and Sedona his muscle-bound, but ghastly pale, sun-deprived, ancient self. His brood-older, fellow Nergalid, Zuvem Nergalis, called Gravedigger and the Planter, as well as Devil Doom, was coal-black; Yama was more like coal-smeared. Bare-chested, wearing only a pair of tattered denims, short-haired, scarred but sort of handsome, in a rugged way, he emanated strength.

He ripped the pickaxe off his back and challenged the other devils. "You wanted me, Byron Spawn, here I am — in a land that has always belonged to Mithradites and with five thousand of my worshipful followers backing me up. I cathonitized Vanthysces Vastness in his realm over a millennia ago. I should be able to handle you two in my father's territory."

Chimaera Glimmenmare smiled as best a preying mantis could smile. Sedona did her imitation of a smoking grin. In a flash over a dozen more Byron Spawn were surrounding the Underlord and the panic-stricken, forever child that the Moloch Sedon may have foisted on Pyrame Silverstar and (maybe) her still bebrained hardener, Primeval Lilith, the Demon Queen of the Night, sometime in the earliest decades of the Dome in order to maintain it.

Tzigame morphed; turned back into the butterfly woman she always had been. Beside her stood Djerrid Ruin, Byron's Bowman, a comparatively lowborn Zodiacal (Sagittarius) but who, as a kind of arboreal Green Man, had an impressively large following in the subcontinent of Aka Godbad's Goatwood, hence why aka Sedon's Beard was also called Djerridam.

Hovering above them was the Butterfly's burqa-cloaked, but nevertheless bewitching litter sister, Parsis Urartu, she on her flying carpet and with only her three dramatically highlighted eyes showing through all that cloth. Elephantine Ganesh, Vach-Hathor, Heroic Hektoris, Tau Hanuman, who'd first dubbed Chameleon chroma-creeep and Ticci-Zamma, a bird-winged serpent, another who was as often male as she was female, were some of the others Yama immediately recognized.

"Correction," he bluffed. "Tralalorn and I should be able to handle a dozen of you in our father's territory."

A silver cloud darkened the sky above the Lake Lands. It began to hail, sleet, snow and rain. Rufous Rudra, the bestial Storm God, had arrived. Yama's Angels of Death began to drop and rot, more so than melt or dissolve, where they stood. And stood they did, unable to flee. Gravity had just increased to the point where not even Angels could tread.

Freshly released from All of Incain, Rudra's wife and fellow firstborn Umashakti Silvercloud, Byronic Goddess of the Moon, had arrived as well.

Chimaera, defiant of gravity – Uma having made sure that her attribute-applied didn't affect her fellow Byronics – stepped forward and, with his mace, knocked the pickaxe out of the Underlord's hands and picked it up. Picked up Chameleon's halberd as well; not that he needed any more talismans. Still, better him than them. The Byronics didn't want subjugation or even prisoners. All was full enough already.

"I remember how you and Chaos cathonitized our Scarecrow, Nergalid. The Unity beat him to the ground then you snatched up his scythe and drove it into his stupid, straw-filled head."

(At the time in question, most of twelve hundred years in the past, this Scarecrow, called Vanthysces Vastness by Illuminaries of Weir from even earlier times, overruled much of Iraxas, the shaft of the Penile Peninsula, Sedon's Mutton Chop. Known as Hadd, the Land of the Ambulatory Dead, since the 1000 Days of Disbelief, more like 500 years ago, nowadays it was a rain- as well as devil-free zone.

(Probably wouldn't be for much longer, though. Bodiless Byron, his roughly hundred-strong tribe of still extant Master Devas and their mostly, but hardly exclusively, Godbadian adherents, had their eye on it as well.)

"The only way someone as comparatively weak as you could atomize someone like Vanthysces in his vast realm was with his own power focus."

(Actually, to this day individual Byronics did not have realms or territories to call their own. Their lands, virtually all of which were in the subcontinent of Aka-Godbad these days, were held in common for them by their autocratic father. He did allow his offspring to have worshippers, however; provided most of said worship was redirected into him.

(Whereupon he redirected a due percentage of it into the Moloch Sedon, in order to help maintain Cathonia. Which was better known as Sedon's Heavens or the Sedon Sphere amongst devils.)

Spellbinder contributed what she clearly believed was Death's epitaph. "With a power focus like yours, you should have realized our father doesn't 'pick' fights he cannot win."

Yama blinked all three of his eyes. His shadowy hood and robes draped him. The scythe reformed in his hands. (Anyone, even a human or Edenite exotica like Klizarod's Saurs or Chameleon's Lizarados, could use any devil's power focus. They just preferred their own.) Once again a skeleton armed with a talisman that had belonged to a son of Byron, the deathly, if no longer deadly, Reaper smirked.

"Then I won't fight."

He tore through Samsara and (presumably) returned to Pettivisaya, the City of Wailing Souls, now nearly as empty as it was lifeless, emphasis on 'nearly'. The Byronics turned as one on the apparent little girl. Tralalorn cuddled herself in the foetal position and defecated in terror. Wallowing in her own stench, she began to cry.

"Father," pleaded Sedona, "I am inclined to show leniency to this one."

Like every other female Master Deva save Methandra Thanatos, the one-time Virgin of Mithras, she was childless in terms of fourth generation devils. Unlike the Sorceress, who had one, and her oldest sister, Umashakti, who had many, she was also azura-free.

Lunar Gravity also had had many mortal children, inseminated when she was possessing a multitude of mothers over the multiple centuries she'd been individually solid. Since she hadn't been around for something like forty-five years not many of Uma's would still be alive, but Sedona couldn't even claim that distinction.

The Byronhead hovered above them. It didn't have to have any other devils inside it, but it did today: the entirety of the Third being still available for ill-starring purposes. The Great God's fourth daughter, APM, Aphropsyche Morningstar, she composed entirely of eyes, wafted out of its third eye. As Spellbinder often did, she spoke with Byron's voice.

(There was some debate as to what all APM's eyes were ... not fully born azuras being the odds-on favourite, though she called them her 'Little Angels'. Was no debate that Byron's other firstborn daughter, Rudra and Umashakti's brood sister, never made it as far as the Whole Earth. That didn't stop bygone Illuminaries naming her Serathrone Hallow, however.)

"But I am disinclined. We have always had our suspicions that this never-maturing child was more demon than devil; more chthonic than Cathonic. Have you not looked into the Sedonic Sky, Smoke? Her sister, the one she thinks her mother, the fabulous Pyrame Silverstar, source of millennial mysteries and inexplicable abilities, is loose again. Together they were a formidable pair. Do you want to give them a chance to reunite? No, now is not the time for foolish sentiment."

All three eyes of the Byronhead shot forth eyefire. Miraculously, Tralalorn wasn't cathonitized. Instead, what was left of her white dwarf expanded, sealing her within it. The Byronic Nucleus tried again but perhaps it wasn't as strong with APM, Goldenrod and Neverknight as it had been with Sedona, Chimaera and Maelstrom composing it.

She was now encased in another layer. Again ... and now a third layer. She was becoming akin to a Chinese egg, a humanoid onion. The first layer amalgamated with the second. Which took on the shape of a skull; which grew into and melded with the third layer. Which took on the shape of an even larger skull. This one grew a beard.

Could it be Varuna Mithras as he last appeared on Thrygragon? Couldn't be. Unholy Abaddon cut off his head, but he'd already been turned to stone and pulverized. Hardly a Master Deva there hadn't pocketed a piece of him. He couldn't have come back together; not even as just a head. Didn't Thrygragos Lazareme use it as a pillow on Tympani?

Whatever, whomever, rose into the sky; an anomalous asteroid given rising impetus, it streaked south and far westward. The Byronhead harried it/her/him back to Apple Isle, to its capital, Corona City. No, not quite — to its outskirts, Theopolis

Hill, where by inviolable agreement amongst all three tribes no Shining One, grandfather, father and offspring, no devil of any description, dare seek to harm another.

There, between head and skull, intervened Cruel Plathon, the Bull of Mithras, grown massive; clearly no longer Trawl's thrall. "This is my protectorate, Unmoving One. You will come no farther. Under the terms of the Thrygragon Compact, Great God or not, you have no choice but to leave this area immediately."

Morningstar came out of Byron's third eye. Her millions of eyes scanned Apple Isle to no gain. Tralalorn had vanished, along with the layer of meteoritic stuff and two layers of bearded skulls – Sunshine and Starshine if they were Mithras and Varuna – that shielded her. Without indicating the collective frustrations or suspicions of her father and her fellow Nucleoids, Primary or Secondary, she acknowledged his rights and authority.

"Consider yourself fortunate, charioteer. Perhaps we should also congratulate you for your curiously timely release from Taskmaster's control but, somehow, we doubt you had anything to do with it. Nevertheless, we are mildly impressed. You have preserved your place in the scheme of things, Bull."

"For now!" added Byron, through the eye-woman, his Venus; reputedly his favourite daughter even though she wasn't born until his third litter of three.

"Corona City is a comparatively tiny section of Apple Isle," APM concluded, again in her own voice. "This is not just the Age of Father Byron. It has come the time for Deva Dominance — and our escape into the cosmos, where we have always belonged. Don't go on any more long, scholarly walks, Multi-Horns. Archaeology doesn't suit you. Remember ... upstairs, the Sedon Sphere, does. We're always ready to send you there."

How she knew Plathon had fallen under Trawl's thrall while visiting the one-time City of Pain, in the midst of Ap Isle's thickest stretch of jungle, who could say? Rather, who would say? Not the Bull. And probably not APM, who sometimes referred to her eyes as Little Angels and said that one was as much her as the whole of her. In other words, that she didn't have multiple personalities; she had multiple selves, all identical.

(During their thousands of millennia travelling the cosmos within and without the Sedonshem, devic females in particular occasionally 'congealed': became relatively solid individuals with therefore multiple personalities. So, were APM's Little Angels not azuras; were they mini-devils, albeit with only her personality? Did she detach one or more of them to keep tabs on him or Ap Isle in general? Was certainly food for thought.)

Were all those years as Trawl's thrall part of the Great God's long time a-coming, very slow to fructify, plot to assert control of the entire Hidden Continent?

To make Sedon's Head effectively Byron's Head?

========

"Tralalorn and I are forever in your debt, Judge." Plathon acknowledged, once the three of them gathered together, out of sight, out of mind, in the Mithradium.
"You always have been, Bull."
"Any way we can get rid of the Unmoving One?"
"This is his Age but, within a week, you'll have an answer."

"Then we'll drink soma and toast the demise of Thrygragos Byron together," promised Plathon, anything but indifferently.

"Do I still have to have namby-pamby shandy, daddy? You're always telling me I'm too young to drink the sink."

"We'll have to see about that, little one," said Plathon, thinking she was referring to him.

"That I cannot say," *pronounced Smiler prophetically.* **"Not for certain!"**

****

Plathon and Tralalorn have often been mentioned during the course of **the Phantacea Mythos**, both online and in print. Like Klizarod Rex and Chroma-Chameleon they featured most prominently in "Feeling Theocidal", Book One of 'The Thrice-Cursed Godly Glories'.

Plathon's role in bringing the Golden Calf, with its atomic heart, to Anti-Patriarch Cain such that he could use it to blow up the Gates of Eden was depicted in 1990's "Forever & 40 Days — the Genesis of *PHANTACEA*" graphic novel.

The conurbation of Corona City, the pupil of the Hidden Headworld's 'Human Eye', was possibly the oldest constantly inhabited metropolis on the Whole Earth. It provided the location for most of "The Volsung Variations", a **Phantacea Mythos** web serial, part of the 'Heliodyssey' story sequences set in 19/5938.

Ap Isle got its name from the Golden Apples of Juvenescence that grew there both before and for the first few hundred years of Sedon's Head. As such it probably inspired the widely disseminated myth of the Blessed Isle of the Hesperides.

PART TWO – PYRAME'S PROGRESS

Games 7: **Theomachies**

========

Demetray, 2 Tantalar 5980
The effect the Evil Eye was having on her vanished as soon as Sinistral Sloth did.

========

The Pauper Priestess realized instantly where he'd abandoned her: Pettivisaya; the City of Sorrow – of the Wailing Souls, as she thought of it, howsoever more romantically – since the time of the Death's Head Hellion. Until then, Year of the Dome 4825, it had been Grand Elysium, the capital of the Laughing Lands, the Elysian Fields, Old Valhalla (when there was no need for the 'Old').

Her palace – *their* palace when Sedon deigned to pop down from the night's sky to sit by her side during the day and lie by it at night – still stood. It was, and probably remained, the largest pyramid on the Whole Earth. Even the ones on the Qin Chuan Plains, in the Chinese Province of Shaanxi, or the Outer Earth's gigantic Tlachihualtepetl complex located in Cholula, Mexico, both areas familiar to her from centuries long gone by, paled by comparison.

When last she'd been here, howsoever-briefly, and that more than thirty years ago, it was the only occupied, less so than properly populated, metropolis in the Ghostlands. She prayed someone who actually had to breathe lived here now but, from the looks of it, that didn't seem too likely.

The Ghosts were radioactive and so were the spooks who once somehow subsisted here. She didn't get out right smartly Cosmicaptain Nehrini Purandar would die within a day or two; maybe less, maybe tonight. Purandar died, she would recathonitize. All of which was proof positive that irony bites back.

If it weren't for her – if she hadn't been so stupid as to allow the Death's Head Hellion to trap her in a ringot – the Atomic Twins would never have gone nuclear.

========

Centauri Enterprises made movies as well as television shows.

======

A few years ago, Tsishah Twilight took a break from her duties on Shenon, Witch Isle, and came to visit her four children at their home in Ire, the Free Iraches' stronghold on the Akadan coast of the Northern Cattail. At their request she took her two eldest, Makhta, whose name meat Brave Woman, and Teotihuacan, Teoti for short, whose name was a mouthful in translation as well (it meant 'the Place Where Gods Born'), to see a horror flick CE produced in Godbad. Afterwards

Makhta proved herself a brave girl just by getting through it, when she told her mom the film was so scary she was afraid her skin was going to crawl off and hide.

Although she refrained from mentioning it to her daughter, that was why Tsishah never took off her Shah-demon anymore. For fear it'd do just that, crawl off and get away. Again. Indeed, their skin being so inseparably one and the same these days, she didn't shuck her Shah-demon even when she was having a shower.

For somewhat different reasons Tsishah rarely looked into a mirror after she finished showering. Or having a bath. The major reason for her non-vanity greeted her as she emerged, still briskly rubbing herself off with a towel, from her Tepidarium. That reason was an ambulatory body mirror; make that an ambulating body, in the shape of a naked woman, whose icy skin reflected like a mirror.

Regardless of the name she went by, she wasn't a Klannit demon. Was an Azura Spirit Being, the first azura born anywhere in the cosmos, let alone on the then still whole Earth, during the course of Ragnarok two or three hundred years pre-Dome. As such Klannit Thanatos couldn't make even a debrained demon mobile.

(In Sanskrit azura or 'asura' meant non-hero or non-god in the same way 'zura' or 'sura' meant hero, god, deus, dev or deva in some Outer Earth faiths, notably Hinduism. Hindus considered them demonic deities whereas Buddhists had them as lesser gods. By contrast Iranian faiths such as Zoroastrianism had asuras as gods and devas as demons. The Indo-Iranian {Aryan} Rig Veda often used asura and deva interchangeably.)

Skin, icy or otherwise, when azuras were at best spectral in their natural state, gave away her body's origins. Tsishah both knew what they were and wasn't at all surprised by them. This Klannit's body began as a never-bebrained ice statue chipped out of one of the many glaciers marking her Master Deva father's protectorate. Her parents were a pair of firstborn Mithradites with opposing attributes, cold and hot. Illuminaries of Weir named them, respectively, Tantal and Methandra Thanatos.

Their nowadays shared protectorate of Lathakra lay off the eastern coast of the Cattail Peninsula, Sedon's Ponytail. For the longest time, ever since the Hidden Headworld began in fact, it had been Sedon's Horn. Multiple centuries later, it became – albeit not for long – Sedon's Lens or, said some, Sedon's Monocle.

The northern part of today's Lathakra, in place since the Head's 48th Century, was actually on the same parallel of latitude as southern Shenon. Their weather patterns, however, couldn't be more different. In Outer Earth terms, with its close to landlocked Akadan advantage, Shenon bordered on Caribbean, Lathakra on Icelandic; though in the latter case that had more to do with King Cold's attribute than its ocean, Tempestuous Psychron.

While its glacial climate, coupled with the string of active volcanoes collectively known as the Labrys Range running up and down its spine, once again provided proof of the weather-wizardly supremacy devils exerted over their protectorates, that from the air it resembled a north-south version of Aegean Crete, where Methandra was once worshipped as its Mother Goddess, was probably just coincidental.

Although there had been a short-lived Athenan Sisterhood on the Outer Earth in the first two decades of this, nominally its 20th Century, in here the Mistress of Mythland – hence (sometimes, mostly when she was still considered Mithras's

Virgin) Miss Myth – had always been the occasionally devil-despising War Witches' devic goddess.

In the absence, until Sedonda, of the 30-years' cathonitized Pauper Priestess (Pyrame Silverstar), Hotstuff – as some of Tsishah's less respectful acquaintances sometimes referred to Miss Myth – had become the primary devic motivator behind the various Witch Sisterhoods' Panharmonium Project.

Klannit was to her mother what Smoky Sedona was to Thrygragos Byron: Methandra's mouthpiece, her messenger, her angel. Tsishah Twilight had been expecting her. Despite her morning's extensive ablutions, the imminent arrival of an angel, no matter how devilish she may be, always made her Shah-skin itchy.

Funnily enough, they had the same effect on the least respectful of Tsishah's acquaintances, Jordan 'Q for Quill' Tethys, the Legendarian.

========

Athena (more correctly Athene, after whom the Athenan War Witch Sisterhood was named)) was, howsoever-contrarily, the Olympian Goddess of Wisdom and War. During the so-called Goddess Culture, which flourished beyond the Dome, especially in the Mediterranean Basin, from around 2,000 years before the Christian Era began until the assertion of patriarchal religions about 500 years later, after the decimation of Strongyne, the Island of Strong Women, Athene was one of the Outer Earth's truly Great Goddesses.

Like the much later on Mary, Mother of the Christian God-Man, Classical Greeks considered Olympian Athene a virgin. Significantly, before it became a total misnomer earlier this century, Master Devas called Methandra Mithras's Virgin to her, at all times, publicly masked face. At least in part because of that, bygone Illuminaries presumed they were one and the same deity; might have been right as well. Whimsically scrabbling letters, they combined Athena with Med, for Mediterranean, and came up with Methandra.

As a mother of four, Tsishah had always found the virginity bit interesting. What was Klannit then? A product of her parents fevered imaginations?

Not exactly, the azura explained to her at length one cold day in the Whiplash Range. It boiled down to the difference between them being inside the subtle matter bodies of bebrained devils when they conceived her; as opposed to them controlling the identically composed bodies of debrained demons when they possessed the Dual Entities and subsequently began having fourth generational devils starting in 5919.

Whatever the case, Methandra was definitely hot stuff. Her immediate brother in Mithras was anything except that. He was King Cold of Lathakra, the Frozen Isle thereof. Perversely, Illuminaries named him Tantal, as in tantalizing. Since their surname, Thanatos, referred to the Greek, though non-Olympian, God of Death, she was death by fire whilst he was death by freezing. Her skin was red; his blue.

That he was called Tantal – as opposed to patch-eyed Odin or Woden, the Hanging God of Norse Valhalla, whom he resembled – was additionally a reference to the fact that some of their mainly warrior followers found death so tantalizing. For bygone Illuminaries, that he wielded a double-headed waraxe even he called a Labrys, clinched his identity as the otherwise nameless Cretan Goddess's brother-protector during the five centuries of the Mediterranean Goddess Culture.

(Actual Labryses could be found in Cretan museums to this day; Santorini ones as well. That they resembled fallopian tubes was only incidentally interesting. Just as much so, incidentally interesting, Crete was home to a branch of the Utopian race that lived beyond the Dome for hundreds of years, having come through when it was much thinner. Circular, beehive-shaped Tholoi, Ghost or Guest Houses for the Gods, worked for mortals as well as devils.

(The ones on Crete – there were others all over the place out there, including the Greek Mainland, nearby Anatolia, far afield India and what were now the even farther afield Americas, North, Central and South – were the Sarpedons. The oddball twins, black-as-midnight Demios and white-as-light Melina, respectively the Ace of Spades and Illuminatus during the Outer Earth's long-concluded Suprawar, were two of today's most prominent descendants thereof.)

Lathakra was his inviolable domain; hers was nearly eponymous Mythland, the jewel of Sedon's Crown, aka the Mystic Mountains, which lay due north of the Weirdom of Cabalarkon beyond the Ghostlands. Perhaps out of petty jealousy, Methandra rarely left her equally volatile husband-brother's side anymore.

Unlike his sister-wife, Tantal had hundreds of azuras, by dozens of different devils from all three tribes. (By some accounts only his presumed father, Thrygragos Varuna Mithras, had more. Indeed, being immortal, if not particularly consciously so, Mithras's azuras might still be the most numerous extant-offspring of all the Great Gods or Master Devas.) If Tantal's azuras weren't possessing Intuits or Fire Kings, the humanoid races who populated either longitudinal half of the Frozen Isle, they were animating ice statuary or snowmen.

In the Lathakran army Frosty Manazur was the name of a general.

========

"What news, Klannit?" asked Tsishah.
"Nothing good, Aortic," the ambulatory ice statue responded.

========

"Not much more than you'll have previously heard from the She-Sphinx, either. No part of the Cosmic Express landed on Incain Sedonda; no part of it has yet to land anywhere near Incain. Yesterday, though, not all that long after All chased that nosy taleteller Jordan Tethys away for fear he'd discover what we were doing there, the Unmoving One had her regurgitate Lunar Gravity and his paladin. What with her already having had to release one of the Atomic Twins in order to power the Outer Earth aspect of our project, All's feeling severely energy-depleted."

"Like you figured, we've far-spoken. Pusan and I plan to head over to Incain later on today to comfort her. Maybe we'll take her for a walk. You said 'not much more'. Yet your devic siblings no longer shine in the night's sky and your mother still has Titanic Metis's talisman, her Brainrock cauldron. Has she been able to spot any of them?"

(Bygone Illuminaries named the Lazaremist highborn Metisophia, Wisdom of Lazareme, after the Titan Metis, who was the earlier equivalent of the Olympian Athena. Metisophia had a well-earned reputation as something of a rebel, hence the real reason for the 'Titanic' sobriquet. She was also long-gone Rumour's main squeeze and the devic half-mom of the Legendarian.

(Almost ever since the expansion of the Empire of Lathakra began in the Dome's 48th Century, Titanic Metis had been without a power focus. Methandra claimed it, a cauldron that provided astonishing far-sight, albeit without any audio, as a spoil of war once she captured Metis in a ringot; one of the first devils, though hardly the last, she ever did.)

"As it happens, that's why I'm here."

"Why aren't I surprised?" Pessimism was not Tsishah's natural state. It was just the perhaps inevitable result of the too-often-disappointing life she'd led. "They ended up on the outside, didn't they? And you want me to go through All to bring them in here. Also, I don't doubt, to make sure the She-Sphinx doesn't eat any of them on our return journey."

(The only reason All never ate Pyrame Silverstar when she journeyed to the Outer Earth was because the Pauper often humanized the Mnemosyne Machine, All's maker hundreds of years before the Genesea. Once, early on in the Head's history, when she was doing just that, Pyrame made certain to immunize herself against being eaten. Again. For the same reason, she was the lone devil who couldn't be taken out, as in taken in, by Trinondev eyeorbs, another of Miracle Memory's devices, albeit from her time on the first Weirworld.)

"I wish it were that simple. Maybe you better sit down."

"Maybe I will. But not here. You're, um, looking sort of slushy. Not to be confused with slutty, I shouldn't have to add."

Tepidariums could do that to ice statuary, even the ambulatory variety.

========

As advised, Tsishah Twilight took the news Klannit Thanatos came to Shenon to deliver sitting down. She took it on a balcony outside her morning room. Shenon's appointed Aortic was wrapped in furs when she did so. Klannit Thanatos wasn't; was as shapely naked as she had been when she came out of the Quarter-Queen's body mirror from wherever, presumably her father's protectorate off the Cattail Peninsula's other coast, that of Tempestuous Psychron.

Lacking firestone-topped obelisks, Tsishah's designated domicile on Witch Isle had a wood-fired variety of central heating. The last thing the ice-statuary-animating Spirit Being needed, even three weeks prior to the Winter Solstice, and on a heart-shaped island in the Head's comparatively warmish Interior Ocean of Akadan, was any sort of central heating.

It was no wonder Lathakran General Frosty never left the Frozen Isle. No wonder its ever-so-hardy Fire Kings and Intuits considered him a desk-bound jerk, one who was too big to be a jockey. No wonder the desk binding him was a slab of ice, an ice-oblong more so that an ice-cube. He was a giant, but didn't have wings. Had he had, Frosty Manazur might have been the model for Gustave Dore's 1861 illustration of Hell's King.

Klannit's message delivered, they agreed to meet later. Elsewhere. High up a mountain, specifically in her mother's home, the Zebranid Leper colony above the Prison Beach of Incain.

Its inhabitants didn't have leprosy per se; they were striped just like a zebra.

========

Shortly after the ever-astonishing azura left her, Shenon's non-Lemurian Aortic took herself through the Weird via witch-stones to Incain.

========

As prearranged, Pusan Wanderlust joined her. (Pusan was a self-psychopomp: one who didn't need witch-stones to get about between-space, or to bring others along through it. Of course it helped that she had a devil's power focus, none other than that of Byron's Capricorn, a {presumed} devic suicide who hadn't been seen in 3,500 years at the minimum.)

There they did in deed take All for a walk on the pristine, She-Sphinx-swept beach. While they did so, Tsishah caught herself scratching even more than the doggish form the being they were walking, the form the shape-shifting, manticore-like, appreciably energy-depleted Gynosphinx had taken, scratched herself.

An anthropomorphic She-Goat, the deviant fauna was hairier than either of them. As a matter of personal pride, however, Pusan kept herself sand-flea-free. Nevertheless, she found it extremely difficult to refrain from reflexively following their lead. To distract herself, she ruminated on the Aortic's words before re-enumerating them.

"Spotted on the Outer Earth's Damnation Isle: one fourth generational Thanatoid devil; their earthen demigod, Demon Land. Subsequently re-solidifying there also: three others, who are more likely Heavenly Celestials, with Thanatoid abilities and Thanatoid talismans, than Thanatoids themselves. Possessively re-forming there as well: the entirety of Mithras's Eighth, namely the Primary Apocalyptics, all of whom are male, War, Disease and Disaster.

"Revealing herself alongside them: the missing Gorgon, the Poxes' 4-armed Medusa, Mother Murder. Who thinks she's a twelfth-born, but isn't, and who looked bursting-at-the-seams pregnant. At least so you say Klannit said her mother Methandra saw via the scarlet fumes of her purloined cauldron. Which can't be good, especially if she's not carrying azuras, who shouldn't make her look physically pregnant anyhow.

"Finally, lawn chew-back the yawn: the firedrake Mildoth's equally just as lowbrow brood sister-brother, the Vultyrie, is back from the Heaven-Earth, Cathonic crap-trap."

"That about sums it up," Tsishah concurred.

Fisherwoman may not be able to prevent herself from fishifying for long. Similarly, as also Fish would say, Pusan was prawn-prone to fay-saying; comes with being Mariamnic-trained, she supposed. As a matter of her own personal pride, the Aortic made a point of doing neither; this despite the fact she spent most of her early years in Crepuscule-Twilight, home to most of the Head's natural-born fay-sayers, the fay feeorin themselves.

"Grave news, Shah; both of you Shahs. Sounds to me like the azura was bangon the Billy Goat's billabong, as our fishy friend would fishify. At least their shells overcame them."

"Did they, traveller? If they did then the devils' stars should be back upstairs lighting up our nightlife. They aren't. That tells me the devils weren't recathonitized."

(Traveller was one of the appellations commonly applied to Wanderlust. Trailblazer was another. Pusan boasted she could track anyone through the Weird, as she called the witches' Grey; at least so long as she stayed on the inside, beneath Cathonia. She could probably do so on the outside, too. She just rarely ventured out there. Fauns were considered myths, not just missing, beyond the Dome.)

"And Mirrors mentioning who one of their shells was, Disaster's, is what's making you so itchy." Klannit Thanatos was called Mirrors, the Mirror Mentalist, because she could coerce people merely by looking at them, out of a mirror, as they were looking at themselves, in that selfsame mirror. Something else that virtually no other azura could do.

"Not me that's itchy. Shahiyeda is the one who's itchy."

"Then you'll pardon me for exclaiming the obligatory expletive."

"Which is?"

"Damnation!"

========

On the Outer Earth it was Tuesday, the 2nd of December 1980. On the Inner Earth it was Demetray, the 2nd of Tantalar 5980. Only two days into it and Thrygragos Byron was already having a bad week. Perhaps he should never have got out of bed Sedonda morning. Rather, since he no more had a bed than he had a body, perhaps he should never have got out of the Fatman when Alpha Centauri got out of bed Sunday.

Of course that presupposed Centauri was having a good week. Which he probably wasn't — not on the other side of the Nag Gap, where Sedonda was known as Sunday.

========

It being less than three weeks until the Winter Solstice, daylight ended early in the Upper Head; not so dramatically so in its southern lands. Nevertheless, dusk was approaching when the Great God returned to the subcontinent with those of his spawn he hadn't left up north to mop up. Or, in the case of his Neverknight-paladin, to commence conquering the Bloodlands, Sedon's Inner Nose, betwixt and between, west-southwest of the Cheeklands.

He'd already resigned himself to the fact there would be no new stars shining out of the night's sky once the sun went down. Especially considering how close they'd come on a number of occasions, he found their absence exceedingly frustrating. He shouldn't be feeling so inconsolable, but he couldn't help himself. The day hadn't been anywhere near the debacle that the launching of the Cosmic Express proved to be.

Still, he couldn't be happy with how it'd gone. True, thanks to one of Mithras's Ninth – the impressively powerful, perpetual child-devil who called herself Tralalorn – Icy Miros, the dissolute Lazaremist whose unofficial protectorate was once the Crystal Mountains in the Head's occipital regions, now had the mentality of the body he occupied; that of a humanoid infant. Thanks to Trala as well, her older brother by two broods, Klizarod Rex, Saurlord (Tyrant Lizard) of the Flood Lands, had last been seen in the form of something akin to a squirming tadpole with nary a puddle in sight.

Equally true, though, she'd made it back to the safety of Theopolis Hill, on Apple Isle, before he, fused with his Secondary Nucleoids, could cathonitize her. How she got away, in what looked like a bearded version of his own long gone brother in Sedon, disturbed him deeply. (Thrygragos Mithras's Varuna aspect, Starshine to Mithras's Sunshine, tended to be clean-shaven when he was last dominant, over four thousand years ago now.)

The manifestation had started out as a huge skull; he was fairly sure about that. And there was something unsettlingly familiar about that, something about the way it seemed to be grinning, but he couldn't figuratively place any of his non-existent fingers on it. Made a mental note to ask his Babbler, Babbar Ninkuray. Have to make sure Smoky Sedona was around to interpret the nonsense he usually spouted, because he found his son almost as incomprehensible as nearly everyone but Spell-binder did.

He also couldn't do anything about Tralalorn once she reached Ap Isle, Sedon's Human Eye-Land of an island, since its devic overlord, Cruel Plathon, the Bull of Mithras, had managed to precede her there. Which was doubly — no, trebly — remarkable due to the facts that: one, Miros had turned the Bull into glass in the Floods; two, Klizarod promptly chopped off his head before shattering his thereby rendered-vitreous, demonic body into shards, flakes and splinters; and, three, Klizarod's brotherly pet, that lowborn Mithradite of a firedrake Mildoth, swallowed Plathon's severed head before flying off (supposedly) to dispose of it in Fearsome Fobbiat, the Headworld's western ocean.

Corona City was the Bull's protectorate and, after Divine Coueranna's withdrawal into her volcano, his guardianship extended over the entire island. Even he who's Age this was on the Head was forbidden to act, on pain of instant cathonitization, in a devil's domain without said devil's express permission. The Bull expressed many a thing when Byron and his Secondary Nucleus showed up over Theopolis Hill; absolutely none of it was permission.

At least Klizarod's Saurs had accepted his Stallion, Chimaera Glimmenmare, as their replacement overlord. As well, the Emperor Chameleon's Lizarados, they of the Lakelands, agreed to keep Byron's Butterfly, Malar Tzigame, on as their Empress. Of course they didn't have much choice in the matter. She held her husband, their Emperor's bits and bobs in a variety of Stopstone jars, whereas he'd entrusted the latter's power focus, plus those Klizarod Rex and Yama Nergal's pickaxe, to APM to dispose of as she saw fit.

(Miros was one of those clever devils who incorporated his Tvasitar Talisman within his body, as his body, so he still had his. So did Plathon and Tralalorn, while the Nergalid got away with Vanthysces' Brainrock scythe. So it didn't much matter that APM All-Eyes kept his. Maybe he'll come and see it at Aka Godbad City's spanking new Headworld museum, once it's cleaned up and reopened. He did, especially without an invitation, they'd likely ill-star him on the spot.)

Perhaps best of all, the Silverclouds, Savage Storm with his unrelenting rain more so than his Moon, Umashakti, with her gravitational pull, had decomposed unto irretrievable putrescence thousands of Death's Angels. Even that was a hollow victory because King Harvest — that Death, their Death, the Mithradites' Reaper, onetime Underlord Yama Nergal — not only didn't put up a fight, he cut himself safely away from the, by then, not just blood, guts and rot-sodden battlefield.

The Nergalid not shining out of the night's sky had to be what galled him the most. Over a millennia ago, during the expansion of the Empire of Lathakra, he'd cathonitized Byron's own Reaper, the Straw Man or Scarecrow, Vanthysces Vastness as Illuminaries named him. The fifth-born Mithradite had done so with Scarecrow's own power focus, a scythe. He then had the temerity to keep it in addition to his own, a miner's pickaxe.

To compound the criminal cruelty, the Nergalid Underlord proceeded to fuse the two together, presumably rendering them inseparable thereafter. Even if that proved something of what humans called an old lady's tale, Byron's Reaper decathonitized yesterday and, without a Tvasitar Talisman, wherever he was he'd have to stay in his human, or at least sentient, shell until he came across another devic power focus. Which if they didn't find out what had become of him soon might be never … never until the next time he decathonitized, that is.

No, not a good day at all. Dusk was worse.

========

In the Crystal Mountains, which lay on the other side of the Hidden Headworld from Aka Godbad City, the Zebranid Leper, Andaemyn Sarpedon, ducked reflexively. With a resounding crack, a bolt of snap-zap-lightning struck a mountaintop precipice many miles away from where they were standing.

There, inside where it hit, someone blinked.

========

"Where the fuck did that come from?" cursed Sabreur Somata — a Cheeklands' Somata more so than a Cabalarkon Somata, though they stemmed from the same Marutian family tree.

Andaemyn, Tsishah Twilight's half-sister, meant *without a demon*. Sabreur, one of her fellow Good Companions in the mercenary band led by Susano Mikoto, a onetime Kronokronos of Temporis, was her latest in a long line of lovers. That he was as midnight-black as Andy, who was actually striped, was daylight-white when she was glamourized, suggested his heritage. His last name confirmed it.

When the then Master of Weir adopted Morgianna – Andy and Tsishah's mother of a Morrigan – shortly after the child-devil Tralalorn turned Morg's teenage parents into perpetual faeries, Kyprian gave Morg the same last name she had; the same last name Sabreur acquired by virtue of his birth, albeit in Dukkha, Sedon's Upper Lip-Tip, not Cabalarkon or even the comparatively distant Cheeklands (officially Marutia) themselves.

No surprise there. The Family Somata didn't arrive in the Weirdom of Cabalarkon until circa 5492. Before that they ruled a different Weirdom, now ruined, that of Kanin City, in Sedon's Cheek bordering on the Gregarian Fields, Sedon's Mole. There was more, though. According to research performed by Andy's paternal aunt – Melina nowadays Zeross, Weir's current High Illuminary – Andy and Sabreur shared the same Utopian bloodline.

She was none too concerned about that. A familial separation in excess of five centuries negated the inadvisability of having that sort of relationship in terms of having children. And Andy, at 27, the same age as Sabreur, desperately wanted children. Unfortunately they'd chosen the wrong profession for having much of a future. Highly skilled as they were, that they'd lasted as long as they had was testament to their good fortune more so than to their good sense.

Frustration, as well as the company she kept, salted her tongue: "Where the fuck do you think? The sky!"

"What ... with nary a cloud in it all day? Not even a cloud from Hadd."

"Look out! There's another one."

========

Sedon's perpetually cloud-covered, ever-rainless Mutton Chop (semi-officially, for most of five hundred years, Hadd) had two sorts of clouds. Living Vultyrie, the oversized, deviated devotees of Disaster's most common mount, the two-headed, two-bodied, devic Vultyrie, constituted the non-natural Cloud of Hadd. As often as not when Vultyrie — who only ever had one head, the same as their much smaller, but equally vulturous cousins — were spotted in their vicinity, Rakshas demons, the Bloodlands' Gatherers of the Dead, were riding them.

(Rakshasas, the plural of Rakshas, hailed from the Pristine Isles, Carcinogen Plague's onetime protectorate. Which were called, howsoever-appropriately, Sedon's Snot Splotches due to their proximity to Sedon's Inner Nose on the mainland just north of them. Rakshas demons were more mindful than most of their earthborn ilk, but nevertheless still thicker, more one-track-minded, than the majority of other sentient beings, including their fay or feeorin cousins, who mostly lived in neighbouring Crepuscule-Twilight, Sedon's Outer Nose.)

Good Companions left their fatalities where they dropped. They didn't stay dropped for long. Rakshasas carried Crystal Skulls. Reverse soul sinks, among other things, Crystal Skulls contained Sangazur Spirit Beings. For nearly thirty years, ever since Trinondev troops loyal to Saladin born Nauroz, whom they referred to as Devason, the then newly anointed Master of Weir, drove them away from the Gates of Cabalarkon, Warlord Mikoto's Two Thousand and their mercenary successors proved themselves ideal recruits for New Valhalla's Glorious Dead.

Yomikuni and Katatribe Tethys, in their 50th years; Alastor Molorchus, a one-armed, Brainrock-blessed outsider who owed his life, such as it was, to Andy's mother of a Morrigan; and Mikoto himself — notwithstanding thirty-plus years of exile, once a Kronokronos, always a Kronokronos — were some of the other Good Companions with Sabreur and her in the Crystals.

As the Warlord — no one ever called him Susano anymore, not even in bed — and the two remaining Tethys triplets had been since there were a couple thousand of them, they were searching for the Trigregos Talismans. One would do since, being composed of teleportive Gypsium-Godstuff, just one of the three Sacred Objects would lead to the other two.

They were also, as Good Companions always said, awaiting recruitment.

========

The legendary 30-Year Man — or woman, as the case may be — knew all about the witches and not just the witches' Panharmonium Project. He called it the Panharmonium Pipedream. It was named after Harmony (aka Datong Harmonia, both of which words meant harmony on the Outer Earth), the Great God Everyman's onetime Unity of Balance.

Maddened by the Susasword, her brother Unity, that of Chaos (Unholy Abaddon), used it to kill her at the start of the Thousand Days of Disbelief some 500 years earlier. Harmony was Janna Fangfingers' devic half-mother and her corpse was still there, exactly where Abe Chaos left her pinned, by the sometimes-called Body of Demeter, to a slab of Brainrock in a cave coated with Stopstone.

Killing was a misnomer. It still hurt.

========

Standing atop the Great God Byron's destination, a skyscraper that doubled as Centauri Enterprises' Aka Godbad City headquarters as well as the primary residence of CE's Fatman, when he was in town, which he probably wasn't, were two women. One was Janna St Peche-Montressor, Alpha Centauri's 27-year old, Dukkhan born and raised daughter-in-law.

Nothing unusual about that; Lovely Lady Janna, the occasional shell of his APM of an all-eyes Venus, lived there. The other didn't; not in Godbad, not officially, and then only if she was staying in the nominally independent Sovereignty of Achigon (note the spelling, Janna often reminded people), the pout of Sedon's Lower Lip-Tip.

Likely the best witch still alive, if not necessarily the best witch ever, she hailed the Byronhead as it came out of the Weird above the skyscraper. "Yoho the rowboat, Cod God. Been watery waiting for you. What's all this about the fin-fucking Primary Apocalyptics moving in on Time-Space's Thousand Caverns?"

Even Thrygragos Byron hated it when Fish didn't fishify overly much.

========

Almost directly north, way north, and at about the same time, albeit 'in' as opposed to 'on' a different skyscraper, the Master of Weir's Outer Earth modern Skyrise in Cabalarkon — the city, not the territory — Melina nee Sarpedon Zeross was enjoying herself guiltily. Despite her guest's decided discomfort, she could scarcely suppress the delight she was taking as she supervised the outfitting of her friend and oft-times ally, in a number of incarnations, with more circumstantially suitable attire.

They were trying to settle on whether to go with a patterned smock or a cream-coloured pantsuit similar to what she had on when Mel's privately detested, publicly treasured, brother-in-law walked in on them. (Melina's floor of Skyrise, the Master's abomination as she sometimes described it {very} privately, which she and her family occupied by themselves, was accessible by stairs and elevators. It also had a matter transducer, which only one person could access even farther upstairs without permission.)

"Go with the dress, Jordy," Saladin Devason advised them.

========

Sal himself, after reaching the mandatory minimum age of 30, issued a Challenge of Weir in 5950. As both the Master of Weir here on Earth, and as the Weirdom's acting High Illuminary of the day, Kyprian Somata could have dismissed it out of hand. That she didn't had little to do with the fact she had been sickly for so long. Rather, it had almost everything to do with the fact things weren't working the way they should do in Sedon's Devic Eye-Land.

The will of the populace, as funnelled through their Master, that was how virtually anything that did work up there worked. Consequently, imbeciles that the majority were, and are, Saladin and Morgianna's paternal great-grandmother, who was well over a hundred and fifty years old at the time, nowhere near an extraordinary age for long-lived Utopians, may have felt she'd lost her peoples' confidence.

And maybe she had. Even so, she could have saved everyone the bother of a Challenge simply by retiring then, though not necessarily, moving elsewhere. However, incomprehensibly to most Idiots of Weir purebloods, Kyprian remained defiant to the inevitably bitter end. As was her right as the reigning Master, she selected a champion to represent her against Saladin. That champion was none other than the by then marital Queen of Godbad, Scylla Nereid, whom Kyprian herself had codenamed Fisherwoman.

Fish was an outsider. Worse, she was a non-Utopian. Even worse, she was an evident Piscine, maybe even a Melusine Piscine, though apparently she couldn't turn into a mermaid like many female Melusine Piscines could. (Like garudas from, mostly, Djerridam-Goatwood, Sedon's Beard, did their feathers, 'proper' Melusine Piscines, who hailed from the nowadays still highly polluted Gulf of Aka, kept their tails between-space when they were on dry land.)

Did have greenish, slightly scaly skin, gills behind her ears and two sets of shark-sharp teeth, among other indicators of her innate human fishiness. Worst of all, while her parents were reputedly the time-tumbling Dual Entities, the closest thing Utopians had to deities (the city of Cabalarkon's tri-towered Grand Cathedral of Light was dedicated to them), she was a deviant.

Not at all reputedly, at least one Master Deva possessed at least one of the Male and Female Entities when they conceived her. A Byronic Zodiacal Illuminaries named Pyçonja Volant definitely possessed Miracle Memory when she had her. She might well have been holding onto two other comparatively midlevel devils simultaneously, perhaps (speculatively) in an effort to emulate the Trigregos Sisters, thereby helping to balance the scales since devils were genetically programmed to be exclusively patriarchal.

The other two almost certainly were Mandorla Auricaura, an eighth-born, Lazaremist bright light sometimes called Enlightenment by her fellow devils, and a tenth-born Mithradite Diluvia Ran, one of the famously female Apocalyptics, that of Flood. (Due to the fact that by far the vast majority of Master Devas ever to exist were lost pre-Dome, nearly all of them pre-Earth, no one could be absolutely certain which devil was born in which brood threesome or even – except by a kind of unconscious, devazur-wide, pooled consensus – in what order.)

Speculation as to her triply-shared, half-devic parentage, albeit solely on her mother's side of the bed, derived from the fact Aortic Merthetis found newly born, future Fish in the Belly of the Beast (Island Leviathan), with their power foci – respectively a fisher's gaffe, a Vesica Piscis and a fishnet – beside her. (Mandorla's Vesica Piscis was actually attached to the newborn's navel; still was, hence her calling it her bellybutton bauble. Continued to have the other two as well, though she usually kept them between-space unless she needed them.)

What, probably, determined Master Kyprian's defiance, her decision to appoint Fish as her champion, was Sal was a deviant, too. That was why, back then, 30 years ago, as now, he was often referred to (very quietly) as Saladin Devason. Bad cess that. Utopians, born and bred, hated devils.

Their ancestors, in their dozens of subsequently abandoned generational ships, had come to the then Whole Earth, a decade before the Genesea, intent upon abolishing devils from the Complex Cosmos. The Male of the two recurring Entities, Heliosophos, Helios called Sophos the Wise, led them. He proved not to be, wise; ended up being killed by Oriartes Ma, whom the Outer Earth's Bible has as Lamech.

Oriartes-Lamech was the Ninth Patriarch of Golden Age Humanity, the Whole Earth's successor civilization to Atlantis, Old Eden.

Because, as they believed – and as every shred of many multiple-millennia's worth of evidence confirmed – pureblood Utopians could not be possessed by Master Devas, almost by definition Sal had to be a hybrid. In that respect his year-younger sister Morgianna nowadays Sarpedon had to be as well. They had the same birth parents after all.

Like every Utopian male living in the Weirdom Sal was black-as-midnight. He wore or carried, as part of his Masterly regalia, Brainrock replicas of the Trigregos Talismans; a real one of which was currently on the Outer Earth in the only recently christened Hideaway Damnation (formerly Crimefighter Central).

Not that that meant it'd necessarily stay there. Or that a witchy someone hadn't already tried it on.

========

Mostly non-fishifying, Fish relayed what stepsister Amphitrite had passed onto her after far-speaking with Lakshmi Arthadot, via witch-stones, from Subcranial Temporis.

========

Treat, as Fish and a few of their friends called her, sometimes sarcastically, had gone back to Shenon in order to get ready for her next giant step. (Witches characterized their use of Anthean agates or their equivalent, Hellstones, Afrite Bulbs and suchlike, as stepping stones to traverse the Grey.) Her ultimate destination lay far to the north, in the Thousand Caverns of Subcranial Temporis. There she'd be attending deviant-daughter Lakshmi's 18th birthday party, scheduled for Lazam (Friday), as well as her wedding to Centurion Sophiscient, called Barson, the day after, Devauray (Saturday).

Even though she'd often been back there over the intervening nearly two decades, it was a homecoming of sorts. Temporis was the protectorate of perhaps Treat's greatest conquest ever, none other than the highborn Master Deva, Dand Tariqartha. Lazareme's Persian, his Earth Magician, aka the Chronocollector, aka the Time-Space Displacer, was Lakshmi's devic half-father; hence her surname, Arthadot.

After hearing Fish out, the Great God was tempted to sigh in exasperation. Being the Unmoving One he instead had Sedona Spellbinder sigh for him. Whereupon, night having fully fallen in the time it took to hear her out, the Sedon Sphere erupted in such a blaze of pyrotechnics he very nearly blinked.

It was almost as if war had been declared up there in Sedon's Heavens.

========

It had and it hadn't. Thunder and Lightning Lord Yajur had just returned … feeling betrayed, visibly angry, and not at all intimidated by whom he was challenging.

========

Tsishah Twilight had also heard from her fellow Aortic and through her, her protégé, Lakshmi Arthadot.

According to the extraordinarily capable, not to mention ambitious, teenager via Amphitrite, Plague (Carcinogen the Leper), the Apocalyptic of Disease, had appeared briefly in Centurium, Replicated Versailles, late yesterday afternoon whereas War (Mars Bellona) had only just left it, when she contacted her mother via their witch-stones. Details were understandably sketchy but Treat claimed, howsoever secondhand, that Time-Space had gifted them each with a cavern to do with as they pleased until Devauray evening.

That two of the three Primary Apocalyptics – the other being Catastrophe or Disaster (Nakba Ramazar, as eccentric Illuminaries had him), the Headless Apocalyptic of Sudden Destruction – were hunkered down somewhere in the Thousand Caverns explained why their stars weren't back upstairs brightening up everyone else's nightlife. (With the mooted exception of APM All-Eyes, Byron's Venus, even devils couldn't be in two places at once.)

In no way did it explain how they'd got there, however.

Packed and ready for her upcoming end-week, motherly duties in Temporis, Amphitrite came through for their prescheduled meeting re the witches', and not just the witches', Panharmonium Project shortly thereafter. Was a good thing she did because, just as darkness descended over the southern whole of the Hidden Headworld, yet another, potentially far more catastrophic perplexity presented itself.

Provided it wasn't overcast, as it always was in Hadd (the shaft of Sedon's Mutton Chop, also known as the Penile Peninsula) and Diluvia (the mountain range thereof, where it never stopped raining), and as it usually was in the badly polluted Godbadian province of New Iraxas (Sedon's Blackhead or Blotch); provided you weren't underground, as everyone in Temporis was; everyone on the Head with eyes to see realized one of the formerly most brilliant stars in Cathonia had returned to it.

It didn't light up their nightlife all by itself. It had company. Together they seemed intent upon rendering darkness daylight. Because of where it first reappeared, in the Great God Everyman's south-easternmost quarter section of the night's sky, Tsishah recognized whose star had come back: that of Thunder and Lord Yajur.

Due to whose star promptly exploded into it, the Lazaremist Quadrant, they further apprehended whose star it was almost immediately fighting against: the one-time Unity of Order's Grandfather. Tiptop witch that she was, Tsishah knew a term for what appeared to be going on up there: Theomachy, combat between gods, devils that they were.

Excellent, she said to Treat. Star Sedon should be having as bad a week as her and seemingly everyone else in her acquaintance seemed to be having.

========

The shaving of legs not appealing, Jordan Tethys had just opted for the pant-suit when Mel's minder, Thobruk Grudal, a Utopian Summoning Child like the Sarpedon twins burst in on them. (Not a pureblood, though; the beard gave that away.) Seeing Saladin Devason with Tethys and the High Illuminary, he pulled up short and tapped the tip of his eye-stave against his forehead in a kind of half-hearted salute.

"Master. I didn't realize you were here."

"Now you do," said Saladin, who considered Grudal his only true friend in the Weirdom; maybe even the whole world. "What is it?"

"Come out on the balcony and see for yourself."

"What the fuck!" cursed Tethys, entirely unladylike.

Mel had already realized what was wrong. "Jordy, your quill. It isn't glowing."

========

Most topnotch witches rode psychopomps when they traversed the Weird.

Status symbols more than anything else, they came in varying shapes and states. Some were alive, some were demonic; many were revenants re-enlivened by their soul-selves; most were even borderline-intelligent. Having gone through all sorts of them over the decades, Fish stuck religiously to mutable mandroids, ones without a whisper of wit, let alone breath.

Currently hers was a bicycle. She called it her psycho-bicycle. She kept it be-tween-space off her Vesica Piscis; her bellybutton bauble, as she sometimes referred to her navel accessory. As soon as the Byronhead vanished, Sedona Spellbinder back within it after promising they'd look into whatever was going on in Temporis, she sought to ma-terialize it.

It didn't materialize. She couldn't materialize any witch-stones either. It was a long swim back to Petrograd, provincial Blackhead's capital city.

****

Janna St Peche-Montressor, Sabreur Somata, Andaemyn Sarpedon and Kirin (sort of) Centauri-Tethys are hardly the only 27-year-olds in **the Phantacea Mythos** sequences starting out in 19/5980. Two others, Estrella 'Star' Dark and Adolph 'Dolph' Dulles, played significant roles in the first two entries of the *'Launch 1980'* story cycle: respectively, "The War of the Apocalyptics" and "Nuclear Dragons".

Yet another, the Athenan War Witch Garcia Dis L'Orca, showed up a few times during both "Goddess Gambit" and its surprise addendum near the middle of "Helios on the Moon". That they and a number of others were born on or about the Summer Solstice of 19/5953 gains increasing import-ance as the open-ended saga of *'Wilderwitch's Babies'* continues.

As for the Theomachy in the Sky, its causes and short-term resolution are detailed in "Helios on the Moon", the concluding entry in the *'Launch 1980'* story cycle. It's also a perhaps not quite so pivotal event in "Goddess Gambit", Book Three of *'The Thrice-Cursed Godly Glories'* epic fantasy, where-in Fish's psycho-bicycle crashes for a final time.

It's not on a cycle path either, though a definite psychopath has a lot to do with why Fish ends up having to 'recruit' Ronnie Ray-Bum (Eagle Ray Revenant) in time for events recounted toward the end of "Decimation Damnation".

Games 8: **Sorrowful City**

=======

Demetray, 2 Tantalar 5980

"Then I won't fight." With that he, King Harvest, tore through the Weird; returned to the largest remaining, remarkably still mostly intact edifice in Pettivisaya.

The City of Wailing Souls, which — not 'Sorrow' — was what Pettivisaya actually meant, was a once populous metropolis as much as a religious centre; no less than the fabled Grand Elysium itself. Now, though, it was as essentially empty as it had been virtually uninhabitable by anyone fully alive for the last eleven and a half centuries.

Essentially ... with one exception.

========

Pyrame Silverstar spent a night and most of a day in Pettivisaya searching for someone to possess — anyone, any thing even, so long as it was alive and semi-sentient. She feared it was a day too long. Rampant radioactivity wasn't the pressing problem. Without food or rest her human shell, Cosmicaptain Nehrini Purandar, would drop dead long before it killed her.

Nevertheless, when she returned to what had once been the Heavenly Hall of Grand Elysium, within the remains of what had been the largest pyramid on the Whole Earth 1500 years ago, and spotted a couch that retained some measure of its cushiony upholstery, she couldn't resist lying down. She hoped it wouldn't prove to be Purandar's deathbed but, if it was, so be it. It wouldn't be the first time she recathonitized.

What must have been hours later, she sensed a presence, opened Purandar's two human eyes and beheld the Grim Reaper. Must be time to do her witch-glamour trick again.

"About time you showed up, Nergalid. Where've you been: Sowing the seeds of your own destruction as usual?"

"Priestess?" he queried, seemingly recognizing her voice and sounding shocked, though being skinless, not showing it.

He'd never seen a well-held-together, albeit more handsome than pretty, native of Ophir-Moorset do what she was doing. (Apropos of nothing, Nehrini was from the Outer Earth's Indian subcontinent. Her parents had both been supranormals, proud citizens of Imperial India, which is to say the Raj. They, like she came to in time, considered the separation of India and Pakistan into two separate nations the singly most disastrous botch-up ever made by the British Crown.)

"Know anyone else with three eyes," she responded once she completed her transformation, "One on each triangular side of her uppermost head? I definitely don't know anyone else who looks like you. What's with all the blood? Don't tell me Devil Deaths have lowered themselves to death-dealing while I've been away?"

"And risk instant cathonitization? Not a chance. Shall we say I've just reaped a bitter harvest indeed."

"I always said you should have stuck to mining, Underlord. Unless they're your sibs, or someone like Qosgod, Saqsaywaman or Antaeor Thanatos, rocks rarely strike back." (Yama's immediate siblings, his fellow devic Earthlings, Gibran Nimiki and Shal Ereshkigal, another Underlord and an Underlady, respectively Mines and Minerals, often manifested themselves as rocklike as the two Byronics and the fourth generational Thanatoid she'd just mentioned.)

Pyrame had gone to sleep vowing that someday, should she only recathonitize, she'd get Baaloch Hellblob back for leaving her here without even the body of the demon whose brains he made her eat to occupy. Now that she was awake again, she was beginning to wonder if him leaving her here might prove a blessing disguised as Death in a shroud.

Fused together as they were, King Harvest (Yama Nergal: his first name was Vedic; his last name Sumerian) had two power foci the last time she'd seen him: his and that of the Byronic Reaper, Vanthysces Vastness (after the size of his designated domain in what he and his Byronic siblings, notably Damon Goldenrod, then referred to as El Dorado).

What could be fused once could presumably be defused; unless the word was unfused. He separated then lent her one, Purandar had enough strength left to wield it, well, Hell on Earth was hardly the only place on the Head where demons proliferated. Another was the Forbidden Forest of Kala Tal, Sedon's Moustache.

(Bygone Illuminaries named Kala after Kali, a Hindu goddess of life's ruination, though the arachnid devil was more a wrecker of sanity than anything else. Kala was both Pyrame's junior in Mithras by three broods and her sister. That last in particular might make her more obliging than her similarly lower born brother of a Hellblob. Grandfather Sedon never cathonitized – recathonitized in her case – anyone for debraining a demon. Being devil-eaters, they didn't come close to classifying as lesser beings.)

The Nergalid could cut her to Tal using either of his power foci. However, he was not only her elder by a considerable margin, he was male. First things first … and the first thing on her agenda was to secure his cooperation. Nehrini Purandar might not be much to look at facially, but she was fit and had a great body. Did have, anyhow. After her ordeal in Satanwyck, then a day and a bit in Pettivisaya, Pyrame doubted she, two-in-one they, still did.

Regardless …

Purandar didn't have to like it. She didn't have be a love-loving Afrite – the Godbadian-based Witch Sisterhood that recognized APM All-Eyes, Byron's Venus, as its goddess – in order to seduce anyone, either. Demonic or no demonic body, Pyrame was an illusionist; more, a materialist. Make that an etherealist; as in 'make ether real'. Was all the seductress they, all of three of them, would need.

She'd loved a reoccurring deviant for a couple thousand years; loved the Devil himself for a lot longer than that. What was so special about boning a bag of bones?

========

Reacquainting themselves after over three decades took mere minutes. That process, for devils, wasn't much different than for any human brother and sister who hadn't seen each other for a while: a peck on the cheek and a brief hug. The preliminaries were somewhat more convoluted.

She insisted he revert to the flesh and blood musculature of his Devil-God of Miners' self before she would touch, let alone kiss or hug him. As she put to him, her embracing Death might provoke an explosive effusion from her shell's midrange orifices and he really didn't want her to have to change her sheath dress. Her breasts were brilliant. Were all the better uncovered, wouldn't he agree?

Not to be left out, he demanded they go with the lips, not the cheek. Since she didn't have lips in her current, howsoever non-illusionary form, she cast about herself an alternate glamour; though, when it came to devils, they weren't really glamours. Were rearrangements of physical bodies: etheric substance, in her case. Not trusting Purandar's looks, she put on those the Moloch Sedon had always found favourable over the course of nearly sixty centuries: that of a darkish-skinned, Mediterranean woman with lengthy, straight and stunningly silver hair.

She opened her third eye in her latest semblance's forehead. He did the same, by now in his handsomely humanoid Underlord's form; not even particularly coalsmeared this time. After the obligatory kiss on the lips, they eyefire-glared into each other's devic eyeballs. That didn't constitute any perversion of devilishly peculiar sex; though she anticipated regular rutting in the radioactivity was imminent. All the same, them laying bare their souls, their minds more like, for each other to probe, was a mutually pleasurable sensation.

When you had a distinctly disagreeable history like these two did, like so many devils did, it was about the only way they could ensure a modicum of trust.

"How can you live in a place where nothing else does?" she asked him, once they'd completed their re-acquaintanceship process and he'd reverted to his bag-of-bones self.

"I don't," the hooded skull dithered. "I persist here. Where I intended to live, my azura adherents with me, was anywhere except here. Bodiless Byron apprehended that; suckered me accordingly. That's why I came back, to what's for all intents and purposes my protectorate, where even he doesn't dare follow.

"Had I stayed where I was I'd be a star shining out of the night's sky by now. And from what I gather it isn't an, um, stellar experience. Sorry about the pun."

"No apologies necessary. I spent most of my time upstairs dormant. Plus, considering where I came from last night, Pundemonium's better than Pandemonium."

Death dutifully groaned. He'd be doing a fair bit more of that in the next little while, if she had her way.

========

She did.

Even Purandar perked up, howsoever-briefly, not to mention internally — the Pauper Priestess keep most of the pleasure for herself. Sleep reclaimed her shortly after-

wards. The need for it even afflicted Devil Deaths. For her part, having no way out, Pyrame simply rested within her shell.

As she did so she reminisced.

========

What had once been the Heavenly Hall of Grand Elysium was situated within the most massive pyramid ever constructed on either side of Cathonia. Most of its brightly star-tiled ceiling remained in one piece. It bore the stylized, but deliberate, likeness of the underside of the Cathonic Dome as it appeared 5,000 years earlier.

As Sinistral Sloth implied while, as she now appreciated, he was simultaneously using his own frond or the Evil Eye to transport them both to Pettivisaya, it was hardly the first time she'd been here. This Heavenly Hall was the closest she ever came to having a home to call her own on the Inner Earth. Too bad it hadn't been all hers. Still ...

She didn't have a devic protectorate. Yama Nergal did but, despite what he said, it was east of here, somewhere in the now uninhabitable, former Laughing Lands — the whole of which, the Ghostlands, he could safely claim since no one capable of worship, other than desperate devazurs, could live in them for very long. The fact of the matter was, until devils from all three tribes conspired to slay Thrygragos Varuna Mithras on his own Mithramas feast day in 4376, the term had no real import.

Even though many protectorates had been proclaimed prior to Thrygragon – as not just Weir's Illuminaries recorded that singular event in their annals of the Head's history – they were akin to a kid's space in a shared bedroom. In other words, were more like recognized spheres of influence with, for practical purposes, unenforceable boundaries. Indeed, that remained the case for Byronics, who held their lands in common with their Great God of an unmoving father.

Lazaremists did have protectorates; at least some of them did, particularly in the Head's northeast, within the Mystic Mountains below Sisert (the Silent Sands of Drought, Cathune Bubastis) and beyond them, farther to the south in the upper parts of its occipital region. However, as a tribal whole, they were nowhere near as insecure, let alone as numerous, as Mithradites; hence, not so set on having exclusive, very much individualized domains.

As the only (adult) female Master Deva to achieve solid individuality until circa two thousand years after Sedon raised the Cathonic Dome out of his own essence – in order to protect the archipelago of Pacifica, the Places of Peace, from the Genesea – and as the Moloch's preferred consort from long pre-Earth, the necessary half-mother of his Sed-sons, she had no need for one. No need for the reverential populace that lived in such places, either.

From the time she retained control of her daemon (according to many, albeit not to her, the therefore always unacknowledged Primeval Lilith, the original Demon Queen of the Night), after finally getting shot of All, by then of Incain, until the Idiot Twins went atomic in 4825, this was where Grandfather Sedon came to hold court whenever he physically walked upon his, over time, thoroughly terraformed Headworld.

It was here, and in adjacent chambers, they occupying mostly normal men and women preselected for their strength and attractiveness, that they conceived hundreds of mortal, if not necessarily short-lived, Inner Earth sedons, small case.

Being immensely fond of massive monuments, especially ones built to honour him, Sedon must have wanted a dot-ditto for the Outer Earth. At least in part that must be why he eventually came to oversee the construction of a much smaller, but similar, edifice on the Outer Earth, Egypt's so-called Great Pyramid.

The builders weren't Angelycs, supplemented by his Satanwyck subjects glad for the opportunity to serve their howsoever-usurpatory Demon King, like those who built the one she was currently in here in Elysium-Pettivisaya. They were his very own, nearly eponymously named Shedim or Shedds, who had the advantage of being dust-to-dust, eldritch earthborn; therefore didn't leave skeletons behind like Angelycs did.

Biblical apocrypha mentions these Shedds. They supposedly helped King Solomon build the First Temple in Jerusalem circa 3000 YD, much more than a millennium after Sedon completed the Great Pyramid on the Giza Plateau. The Bible also states Shedds were demons, as opposed to celestial angels.

The Headworld's Angelycs weren't and aren't that. They're were, and are, yet another product of Old Eden's genetic 'manipulations' from hundreds of years prior to the emergence of Golden Age Humanity and the sinking of Atlantis, the Edenites' home continent during the planetary Ice Ages.

(Faeries, their demonic cousins, Lemurians and Iraches argued they weren't that – and they might be right – but Saurs, Lizarados, scorpionid Ophidians, ant-like Myrmidons, Cattail's Barring Bear-Men, Godbad's Garudas, the Gulf of Aka's Melusine Piscines, and so many more of the Head's exotica undeniably owed their existence to discredited Edenite experiments into the building blocks of life.)

It wasn't like Pyrame and her assertive grandfather needed another pyramid in which to make their bed but, also being a – surprise, surprise – perverse sort, Dark Sedon probably couldn't resist soiling the spot once he discovered it was very near the Biblical On, later Heliopolis. That Heliopolitan priests practised a ritual they called the Sed Ceremony, in order to test the reigning ruler's suitability for continued Kingship or Queenship, tended to confirm his involvement in Pharaonic affairs long before and long after he finished erecting the Great Pyramid of Egypt.

(Never to be the confused with the immaterial Sedon Sphere, better known as Cathonia, the Cathonic Zone or Dome, their first and longest serving, post-Flood domicile beyond the Dome, the material Sedon Sphere, was larger than either pyramid. Similar in appearance to Buckminster Fuller's geodesic dome, aka the Biosphere, in Montreal Canada, it stood near, perhaps even in, today's Dead Sea until an asteroid – unless, as both Sedon and Pyrame believed, it was an abandoned Utopian generational ship deliberately targeting them – destroyed it, along with their twin cities, Sodom and Gomorrah, circa 2000 BC.)

Whatever his reason for having it built, the Egyptian Great Pyramid was never anywhere near as glorious as this one, here in what was now the City of Sorrow. Fact is Pyrame never felt comfortable laying within the Outer Earth version. Mainly that was due to its proximity to the no matter how moribund Androsphinx, who had – millennia earlier – quickly come to be called, as one might expect, Andy.

That being the case, bygone Illuminaries could be forgiven if they thought she was named – presumably by herself since, properly speaking, Master Devas didn't have names per se – after this one, not the one on the Giza Plateau. Which they did

… except they were wrong. Her name meant 'in the middle of the fire', which she often was. Sort of comes with the territory: taking the Devil himself to bed off and on for multiple millennia.

Dating back to around the Whole Earth equivalent of 5000 BC, Heliosophos – the golden-apple-eating Male Entity – as Alorus Ptah, the First Patriarch of hence Golden Age Humankind, had the Mnemosyne Machine build Andy the Androsphinx. Did so in order to to capture and hold onto pestiferous daemons, especially the man-eating variety correctly spelled 'demons'. Centuries later it turned out that, like its just as mandroid-making mate, Ginny the Gynosphinx, nowadays All of Incain, it worked as well holding onto devils.

Not long after the intertribal, Lazareme-led, devic Expeditionary Party popped down from the Sedonshem's perch on the Moon, slightly more than seven hundred years before Xuthros Hor, the Biblical Noah, caused the Genesea, Andy got hold of her, Pyrame. Until someone, presumably Sed himself, got her out of it within a few years, maybe even a decade or two post-Dome, she remained imprisoned within the Male Sphinx.

She must have acquired her daemon during this extraordinary length of time. Must have because she emerged already individually solid; this fully two thousand years before any other Master Deva. Was also strange, but true, that All and Andy still shared interdimensional 'digestive tracts'. Which was how non-devils All favoured could traverse the Dome — from one sphinx to another.

(Devils, All ate; demons, too. Eating those last, the eldritch earthborn as Miracle Memory was wont to call them, was what the twin sphinxes were programmed to do from their Day One.)

Much to Sed's personal annoyance, Pyrame eventually refused to even enter the Great Pyramid. His irritation didn't last long. As magnificent as it was, there was nothing essential about either pyramid, whereas there was everything essential about her and her solidifying demon, whomsoever it was. Plus, he could and did come to her anywhere on the Outer Earth as easily as he could and did come to her anywhere on the Head.

Still, she couldn't have been happier when monotheistic followers of the sun-worshipping, declared heretic, pharaoh Akhenaton, arguably the Biblical Moses, sealed it shut a couple of hundred years after the collapse – due to the eruption of Strongyne, today's Santorini – of the female devils' so-called Goddess Culture in the Mediterranean Basin.

Since he needed her to have healthy sedons in order to maintain the Dome, they avoided Grand Elysium once it became Pettivisaya. As dire as her situation was now, revisiting it after all these centuries reminded her how much she favoured it compared to anywhere else they met. All the more so after the destruction of the material Sedon Sphere between his Sodom and her Gomorrah, a couple of millennia prior to the Atomic Twins – Tammuz and Osiraq, as Illuminaries had them; Cautes and Cautoprates, as Outer Earth Mithrants did – putting paid to the Laughing Lands.

While it lasted, their time here approached the true Elysium, as in the truly paradisiacal. Despite its sorry state of dilapidation, her heart – even if was Purandar's heart – all but swelled with delight that this place, its stonework and many of its mosaics anyhow, lasted still. What better place was there to recathonitize, even to die, than here, where she'd been happiest?

And where she hoped the Moloch Sedon had been happiest as well.

========

Pyrame did more than reminisce. She mused.

========

In retrospect, perhaps she should have cast about herself the likeness the big eye-mouth in the sky found so appealing prior to the Nergalid returning to Pettivisaya. If Sed was looking for her from his starry perch, seeing her that way might have rekindled his desire for her. He then might have felt a twinge of pity and got her out of here.

Erase that thought. Retrospection was for the weak and hopeless. Determination, that was for the strong and resourceful.

Grandfather Sedon had had thirty years to release her from Cathonia. She'd make him regret he hadn't ... briefly. She knew how; always had. Grandfathers had fathers. Even if it required her taking a lesser being's life, she'd hit him where it would do him terminal harm. Except, after the 5950 fiasco, there had to be a way to do so unstoppably, long before he realized what she was up to, let alone realized it was her behind it.

Recollection: Long ago, probably within a few decades of the Elysian Fields becoming the Ghostlands, the Underlord-Harvester's Accursed Dead developed a talent to slay with a finger. Reduction: Exposure to the radioactivity engendered by the Idiot Twins — also referred to as Equinoctial Spring and Equinoctial Autumn — going ballistic, atomically as well as anatomically, bequeathed them said talent.

Distinction: Make it between the mobile corpses themselves, the Accursed or Inglorious Dead, and the Nergalid's azuras reanimating them. Call them Death's Angels. Consideration: Unless it's the other way around, which it might not be, the former renders the latter meltdown-vulnerable to elementary forces of nature: excessive wetness, and not just meteorological wetness either, being the most obvious agent of ineffectualness.

Postulation: Death's Angels have the touchy-feely killing ability; not the conjugal combination of accursed-possessed with azura-possessor. Query: Is that true; does it hold water? Rephrase that: Can Death's Angels possess non-corpses while at the same time retaining said touchy-feely killing ability? If their shells were alive, then wetness wouldn't spot-rot them, would it.

Should that last be a question or a statement? She was a terrible grandma, but she was a much worse grammarian.

Further cogitation: Why am I thinking so much like the Mnemosyne Machine? Hmm ...

========

Nehrini Purandar began coughing involuntarily of the Pauper Priestess.

The one inside the other, her coughing jolted Pyrame, the onetime Perpetual Presence, also Providence, out of her reverie. It woke the Nergalid up as well. Although she quickly found the mental wherewithal to suppress her shell's incessant sputtering, the second time wasn't anywhere near as perky.

It was more like rape.

========

Birhym, 3 Tantalar 5980

Afterwards, settled comfortably on stone benches outside the Heavenly Hall, they gazed up at the heavenly Theomachy.

They knew who'd come back to the night's sky because Lord Yajur's star was distinctively lightning-like even to the naked eye. Or empty eye-hole, in the Death's Head Harvester's case. However, other than not-at-all-dark-anymore Sedon seemed to be objecting to his return to Cathonia rather strenuously, neither of them had much of an idea as to what was going on up there.

It was down here that mattered to her anyhow. She didn't get that sorted out she'd soon be back upstairs with a starry, front row seat.

Would there be enough left of Nehrini Purandar for a Death's Angel to animate?

========

Thunder and Lightning Lord Yajur was the Unity of Order until his brood-brother, the Unity of Chaos, unsheathed his black blade of same, and cathonitized him, thus ending the Thousand Days of Disbelief, in 5495.

Bygone Illuminaries belatedly named the Chaos Unity (who still existed somewhere, albeit as a devic suicide, a consequential demon who nevertheless yet retained his own brain and power focus, said once again sheathed Chaos Blade), Unholy Abaddon. They did so after the Angel of the Bottomless Pit (Apollyon), as described in the New Testament Book of Revelations, as written by John of Patmos, whomever he was.

(Belatedly because they couldn't decide what to call him the previous millennium, when they named virtually every other Master Deva save Pyrame and Tralalorn, who'd named themselves thousands of years earlier. Knowing that his trident wasn't his power focus so much as its sheathe eliminated Shiva-Shankar or Poseidon-Neptune. Knowing also that if he ever withdrew it, the Chaos Blade, that might be it for the world ... Well, maybe it'd been best they pretended he didn't exist. Simply wouldn't do to give him a name he hated.)

Three years prior to ending it, Chaos began those selfsame Thousand Days when he plunged the Susasword through their immediate sibling's heart, thereby presumably killing her (Datong Harmonia, the Unity of Balance or Harmony, also of Panharmonium) every bit as dead as the, to date, never resurrected Great God, Thrygragos Varuna Mithras.

Illuminaries of yore, as well as lore, garbled the Aryan word 'vajra', for lightning bolt, when they came up with Order's name. His power focus was the Lightning Blade. Even though it was shaped more like a standard thunderbolt than a traditional vajra, either the Buddhist or the Classical European variety, that accounted for his star's distinctiveness. There were so many of these vajras rocking Pettivisaya they were speaking more by telepathy than voice.

The Nergalid was a skeleton in a shroud again. Sated as well as seated, he no longer seemed to care how she appeared. Silverstar nonetheless kept her etheric self solidly silver-haired and looking enticingly shapely in her white, sheathe dress. Despite whatever was actually happening upstairs, she still hadn't erased weak and hopeless from her thought-processes.

Consequently, she couldn't altogether prevent herself from thinking that the ungodly, yet undeniably godly, not-at-all fabulous, eye-mouth in the sky might get around to looking for her in due course. Although the only devil known to practise monogamy was Methandra Thanatos – and then only after immediate brother, but not yet husband, Tantal 'devirginated' her circa 5908/9 – Sed was the jealous sort and she hadn't always been such a whore.

"War's Sangs were hardly the only azuras who animated the Elysian Fields' Glorious Dead," the Nergalid elaborated, following the conversational thread she'd fed him, despite her displeasure at her recent rough treatment the second time around. "Some of mine did as well. Only, mostly because my protectorate was on the outskirts of the former Fields, and I didn't want to leave it, mine stayed behind after the Idiot Twins blew themselves apart at your behest."

"Not mine, never mine. Truth told, hardly for the first, I was out of the picture by then. The blame for that abomination lies squarely with the Death's Head Hellion, Morgan Abyss, the then Master of Weir on Earth." She could have said more, in her own defense. Could have said she was stuck in a ringot at the time, put there by a Cabalarkon-outsider from the Gulf of Aka, off Godbad or thereabouts.

The then Master had been her unwitting host, until she turned the tables on her, Pyrame, and the Twins were devoted to her, also Pyrame; had been since Thrygragon. Being actual dim-bulb twits like remarkably many highborn of any devic tribe in her estimation, they doubtless didn't realize the so-called Melusine Master of Weir was the one pulling their strings. Neither, to this day, did the Nergalid Reaper. And she didn't feel like correcting him right this minute.

Getting trapped in a Tvasitar-made ringot was one of the most embarrassing events of her manifestly not impossibly long, thus far immortal existence. After all, thanks to adjustments made on her behalf while she was humanizing Miracle Memory centuries earlier, she was immune to Trinondev eyeorbs.

She therefore felt admitting her fallibility with regard to their devic near-equivalence too shaming. That Lazaremists, notably the incomparable Harmony, came to her rescue, albeit only after the Death's Head Hellion's demise, was something else she didn't feel the need to remind her broods-older brother in Mithras.

(Anvil the Artificer had made ringots on behalf the Thanatoids of Lathakra during the expansion of their eventually almost Headworld-wide Empire during the Dome's 48th and early 49th Century. They used them to hold onto Master Devas whose forces theirs had defeated on the battlefield, but whom they didn't want to cathonitize for fear Grandfather Sedon might just release them again.

(Which he might have, if only to annoy Hot Stuff. The Scarlet Sorceress – King Cold's Crimson Queen. Mythland's Methandra, the lone female Thanatoid – in her approaching three millennia as Mithras's Virgin, should never have rejected him. He wasn't the only devil, capitalized or otherwise, she'd rejected; her own Great God of a father, Thrygragos Varuna Mithras, was another. But only Grandfather Sedon really mattered in terms of devic hierarchy. She wasn't going to bow to any male, save her own brood brother, Tantal, not Phantast. Whom she eventually did, albeit not until waking up from their Thousand Year Sleep.)

"So you say; so you've always said. No matter, the deed was done. You see, unlike the various Apocalyptics, and so many of our fellow siblings whose domains, even if they weren't called protectorates then, were once up here, I didn't believe Grandfather Sedon would let them become what they became, namely the Ghostlands. After all, Grand Elysium had always been his home when he walked his world. I figured, like Bodiless Byron in Godbad, that made the Elysian Fields, the first Valhalla if you prefer, more his protectorate than any of ours."

"Yet his star no longer shone in the night's sky."

(As of Mithramas Day 4824, that was true enough. What wasn't so well known was how Morgan Abyss pulled that off — she'd shredded him into dozens, perhaps even hundreds, of previously filled, long pre-Earth eyeorbs until then kept sealed within the Weirdom's still existent Solidium vault. Until, additionally, the three Unities and their father, Thrygragos Lazareme, found a way to release him. Which, soon thereafter, spelled the end of the line for the Death's Head Hellion, as opposed to her current companion, the Death's Head Harvester.)

"That, too. Yet I still reckoned he was having us on. At any rate, by the time I realized Grandfather had no intention of reversing the Twins' atomic idiocy, it was too late. My Glorious Dead, and not just them, had irrevocably become Accursed Dead. As if it could make up for what they'd lost, I promised to lead them to a new homeland. I came close to fulfilling that promise during the Thousand Days of Disbelief. That was more than five centuries ago, though, and we've been wasting away here, more inactive than active, ever since."

"You're wide awake now, full of beans to boot, as well as bones, not to mention some awfully hale and hearty flesh. What changed?"

"Not long after Sedon cathonitized you, I found Cathead, Drought, your litter sister in Mithras's Ninth, whom old-time Illuminaries named Cathune Bubastis, in much the same condition I found you today. I took her north, to Mythland, up in the Mystic Mountains. There I quietly procured a series of healthy shells for her. At their expense, I have to admit, she eventually regained her strength and, with it, her apocalyptic abilities.

"Together we hit upon a plan whereby she could repay me for my kindness. With her assistance I reckoned I could finally do as I'd promised my azura adherents so long ago."

"Great Byron played you for a bonehead," Pyrame couldn't resist interrupting.

The Nergalid nodded said Death's Head. Given the raw material he had to work with, just that, how he got it to look so sad was quite an accomplishment. "As near as I can figure it, Grandfather Sedon must have cathonitized Drought at the same time he did you. Sometime after that, Byron's Butterfly, the one Illuminaries of Weir named Malar Tzigame, began masquerading as her even as she kept Chameleon's bed warm. And it was her father – the Butterfly's, not Drought, as I believed – who began to dry up the Lakes.

"Cathead specialized in that sort of thing back when you were Egyptian and a Great God shouldn't have any difficulty matching her expertise in drying things up; painstakingly slowly, too, presumably to add to the believability. The process took nearly three decades. It nevertheless finally got to the point not all that long ago where I felt it safe enough to march my army of Accursed Dead south, towards Hadd and/or New Valhalla.

"Since the vast majority of my forces lack the ability to traverse the Weird, the Byronics waited until we were too faraway from the Ghosts to mount a successful retreat. Whereupon they struck en masse." Yama Nergal continued to explain at some length, too much length given the desperateness of her plight, what he had been doing, where he had been, and how Unmoving Byron had not only set him up, set up his people, such as they were, he'd set up just about every reigning Mithradite on the Upper Head.

"I failed. Likely we all failed, though I didn't hang around to discover how any of our siblings fared. The day was lost. What did it matter anymore? I cut myself back here, minus my own power focus and most of my army. If I didn't relish the worship of the azuras I left behind, because their shells were too ruined to walk, or those few whose bodies can access between-space and will have made it back here by themselves, I would take myself elsewhere."

"Oh, please," Pyrame broke in, running out of patience with the way this particular devic Death droned on and on. That he only had the one Tvasitar Talisman left, and that it belonged to Byron's Reaper, exasperated her. She'd come this far, done all that, for nothing. "You'd cut yourself to Hadd is where you'd go. First of all, it never rains there. And, second of all, at least half of its presumably still absent Blood Queen's Nergalazurs are yours to command."

There were only the three Nergalids. Illuminaries named the brood-older, other male, Zuvem Nergalis. (Zuvem was Zoroastrian; as was Yima, a variation of Yama. Nergal was a Sumerian, become Babylonian, god of the netherworld.) Devils called him either Planter or Gravedigger, in part because his power focus was a wicked-looking spade, more of a body-dicing weapon than a sodding garden tool. Although she neither knew nor cared what had become of him, Zuvem's star no longer shone in the night's sky.

The lone female of the three was Nergal Vetala. (Vetala's name was doubly Indo-European, both Greek and East Indian, the same as vajra for thunderbolt.) Devils called her Fecundity. They did so because, before she voluntarily become a vampire in order to cease being so expectantly – pun intended – fruitful just prior to the commencement of the Thousand Days of Disbelief, Vetala was the Mithradites' most prolific moon goddess.

As such, waxing and waning with it on a stunningly predictable monthly basis, she churned out many more Azura Spirit Beings, often simultaneously, than any other female Master Deva in the entire history of the Head. Not even Mithras's original mate, Divine Coueranna, his Boss Cow for Taurus, was so prolific. And Vetala kept at it long after Coueranna, Kore of the Many Names, started restricting her pregnancies to once a year, and then only ritualistically, through Korant (after her) Corn Queen surrogates.

During the 48th Century of the Dome Yama cathonitized Vanthysces Vastness, the Byronic Reaper, with his own power focus, a scythe. He carried on with the Thanatoids of Lathakra as they sought to expand their empire into the Cheeklands and beyond, all the way north to Methandra's devic protectorate in Mythland. Vetala stayed behind; claimed Hadd, what the Byronics called El Dorado for its abundance of placer gold, as her own protectorate.

Its Irache natives, who still call nowadays-Hadd Iraxas, worshipped her whole-heartedly. Barrenness was for her a mixed boon since, as a vampire, she had far more vulnerabilities than any other Master Deva. Even so, it never rained in Hadd because she no more allowed it to rain there than she ever allowed the clouds in the sky above it to clear.

A lack of direct sunlight made Hadd a 24/7 haven for vamps. A lack of rain made Living Iraches happy, too. Mostly underground runoff from the Diluvian Mountain Range, on its northern extremes, where it never stopping raining, preserved plenty of arable patches for growing and foraging everything they needed to survive, so that proved no drawback. The big plus for them, though, was they enjoyed having their Haddit ancestors over for tea and crumpets. Or bannock and beavertail, as was more usual.

Needless to say, strange as it was, their ancestors were largely animated by Nergalazurs. No one really understood what it was about Nergalids that rendered the corpses their azuras animated defenceless against something as mundane as rainfall. It wasn't the price they paid for being good at keeping Dead Things ambulatory. Like their devic parents, any azura could reanimate a corpse.

It was just that, with the exception of Sangazurs, whose devic father was Mars Bellona, the bearded, usually otherwise skull-faced Apocalyptic of War, and who animated the admittedly mostly male Valhallan militants of the Bloodlands, Sedon's Inner Nose, most preferred to occupy living beings. (Presumably because they were more nourishing.)

Possession by devils, possession by azuras other than Nergalazurs, never rendered the corpses they reanimated susceptible to not just rainfall, but running water of any description. Tie a Nergalazur-mobilized cadaver to a stake in a standard bathtub, turn on the shower, he or she would rot away in maybe fifteen minutes tops. All in all, like everyone understanding what everyone else was saying no matter what language they were using, it was just one of the Head's many inexplicable oddities.

One thing was certain, now that the Nergalid had finally arrived where she'd been steering him, she wasn't about to fritter away any more precious time attempting to solve the Nergalids' 4,000 year dilemma. She had a far more pressing one of her own. Decathonitized devils needed to occupy a shell with at least a spark of intelligent life to it in order to stay decathonitized, and she could feel Purandar fading fast.

"Vetala hasn't made one of her astonishing comebacks, has she? Last I heard the Sraddhites' High Priest, whatever his name was, finally put paid to her – again – when he pulled her into the Jaag Whirlpool back in '45. That should have left the rest of her followers up for grabs. With Gravedigger upstairs you could have gone for them already."

"As you should know better than most, priestess, it's irrelevant whether she's made a comeback or not. Devic offspring are genetically incapable of disobeying their fathers. As it happens, though, she hasn't. Howsoever she stopped it raining there, with the Gulf of Aka to its west, Akadan to its south and east and the Diluvia Mountain Range, the rainiest spot on the whole continent to its immediate north … well, there or not, that hasn't changed. It still doesn't rain in Hadd."

"Take from that what you will. Point being, like you said, as many as half, if not more of her Nergalazurs, are just waiting there for me to reclaim. But that too is irrelevant. She had plenty of other azuras, by plenty of other devils, before she vamped out. Had them every full moon for thousands of years and they didn't always come out one at a time, either. Plus, since they're as immortal as us, her azuras were and are hardly the only ones populating Hadd.

"What we still think of as the shaft of Sedon's Mutton Chop's hotly contested. Life's reasserting itself there. The Byronics want it back and they aren't alone."

"Don't tell me Xibalba has come back. Now that would be astonishing. He may be a Summoning Child but, to the best of my knowledge, Summoning Children are mortal."

The Molech Xibalba was one of a set of twins born to Irache chief Lamechlan and his wife (who died having them and thereafter became a Lamia or Night Hag), nine months after the Simultaneous Summonings of 19/5920 ended. Lamechlan was one of a number of presumably ordinary men and women who became vampires during the Summonings. When last Pyrame came across him he was calling himself Night Owl to his wife's Night Hag.

"I wouldn't know. But if Xibalba was a Cattail Irache — and his name sounds like he might have been — then I can tell you that the Free Iraches and the Brown-Robes they consider invaders of their land have agreed to bury the hatchet. They've joined forces with the Godbadians to oust Janna Fangfingers and her cadre of vamps from their position atop Hadd's food-chain."

"Now that is a change. If you'll pardon the bleeding obvious, usually Free Iraches and Sraddhite Warrior Monks only bury hatchets in each other's heads."

For the most part originally from Marutia, Sedon's Cheek, the brown-robed, shaven-headed priests and priestesses of Diluvia and Lake Sedona worshipped a supposedly Living God, not a devil. That he, Sraddha Somata, a mixed-blood Cheeklands' Utopian, had been dead and dust since the tail end of the Thousand Days of Disbelief hardly dulled their messianic fervour. They knew what had become of Sraddha's soul. His still extant twin sister, Janna Fangfingers, kept it in a Crystal Skull attached to the bloodstone torc she habitually wore around her neck.

Reputedly he'd be back as soon as she found a worthy receptacle for his soul. And when he came back the Sraddhites fully expected it would be in a body very nearly identical to his own. They had copies of a painting done of him by his contemporary, Jordan Tethys the Elder (albeit only one of a number of 'Elders' since he kept coming back; kept painting too), so they knew what he looked like. Sraddhites chose their High Priests solely because, no matter how light or at least lighter skinned they may appear these days, they resembled him.

He wouldn't be back in their current high priest; that was pretty much for sure. True, they both shaved their heads as if they were, or had been, some sort of Islamic mullah on the Outer Earth. True as well, even though he did have dusky skin, Thartarre Holgatson was nowhere near as black as Sraddha had been in life. But that didn't matter so much as the fact Thartarre only had one arm. Sraddha Somata, naturally, had been perfect.

"Seems I missed my calling. Should have gone on to become a straight man, not a Deva Death."

Pyrame shrugged. Rather, Nehrini Purandar shrugged and Pyrame's plastic externality shrugged with her. (Witch-glamours worked much the same; their everyday body auras given diverse shape and tactile sensibility simultaneously.) "Maybe you should have at that. Except there's nothing funny about death. Let's hurry it up. You were saying?"

"Hadd isn't the only land of the Ambulatory Dead the Byronics are threatening. As I learned the hard way today, in what Janna Fangfingers calls Sedon's Sweat Glands, the Great God seems intent upon making the whole of the Head his Head, not Grandfather's. For all I know the Unmoving One's responsible for what's going on upstairs right this minute."

"So, Harmony's half-daughter, Janna born Somata's still around. I'm impressed. I knew she was a deviant, one with the unheard of ability to hold onto devils seeking to possess her, not the other way around; an ability she shared with her twin brother and no one else I ever heard of, at least in here. I also knew Order cathonitized Lady Luck and Chaos did a ditto for Lady Lust while first one then the other was occupying her centuries ago.

"By rights, in both cases, she should have died instead of the devils possessing her ending up stars in the night's sky. Even afterwards, once First Fangs turned her into a vamp, Janna's proven remarkably, um, persistent, to use your word. I gather she's still Hadd's surrogate queen to boot. Not only that, she's formed an alliance with the Sangazur hierarchy of New Valhalla."

"And Mother Earth's Hecate-Hellions."

"Ah, that's what I'm missing. I knew there had to be something else. Hellions hate we-devils and you're a wee devil, wit-wise anyhow. So that's why you set out for Hadd with an entire army of Accursed Dead at your back. You get through the ever-damp climes of the Lakes and the Floods, which was tantalizingly easy given the non-Drought-caused drought corridor between them, you'd conquer the rest of your way to Hadd."

"Wouldn't have to, priestess. It rains in Sedon's Cheek; wouldn't be the Head's breadbasket if it didn't. And it hasn't stopped raining in the Diluvia Mountain Range since before the Genesea. Diluvia's between the Cheeks and Hadd, in case cathonitization has robbed you of your sense of geography. On top of that, an army the size of mine couldn't have avoided every devic protectorate between them. Devils causing rainstorms is second nature to us."

"I was just coming to that. How could you possibly hope to get yours anywhere near where you were heading? You must have realized the effort was futile."

"I'm not the nitwit you think I am. Janna has a ringer; an off-the-shoulder-cuff, one-armed ringer. Put better, she had a ringer. The Hellions' latest Morrigan lured him away from her a few years ago, but Janna knows how to deal with craven mortals. She hired him back. All things considered, when you can chip gold dust off the city walls of where you're living, if vamps live, it didn't cost much."

Thirty years ago Janna Fangfingers, Second Fangs, resided in Necropolis; clearly she still did. (When it came to vamps, residing was a more accurate word than living.) Like Pettivisaya, ex-Elysium, the City of Sorrow as Pyrame thought of it despite it meaning the City of Wailing Souls, Necropolis had an earlier name: Manoa, the Gleaming City. It was built by, or at least on behalf of, Damon Goldenrod,

Byron's Apollo, when Byronics, who called old Iraxas El Dorado, didn't so much rule it as were its devic gods. Its walls were indeed made of reinforced gold.

Pyrame caught that. What she didn't catch was why the Nergalid would trust Hellions. So she asked him.

"Their Morrigan likes him the way he is, non-radioactive. She likes him as a day-walker as well. But, as much as Hellions like crows, she particularly likes him as other than crow food."

"He's dead."

"Animated by a symbiotic Sang, one she kept in a Crystal Skull slung round her neck like a Rakshas demon from Plague's old Pristine Isles. So I understand. And it's his body that makes him a ringer. Grandfather Sedon has nothing against devils destroying things that are already dead and neither do I." Devils, so long as they wielded a Tvasitar Talisman, were self-psychopomps. Pyrame caught that as well. Was her penance for not asking him if he still had two before taking him to bed, even if it was a cot.

"And a ringer is?'

"Ringers are Brainrock-blessed; they can teleport masses of things, even armies. I know of only two beneath the Dome, but they must be more common on the Outer Earth because that's where they both came from initially. The other one married the Sarpedon girl, so he spends most of his time in Cabalarkon, which makes him out of reach, at least for me.

"You're the only devil I know of who's immune to Trinondev eye-staves outside their protectorates. Why is that, by the way?"

"Wait a minute. Melina Sarpedon didn't marry my Sed-son?"

"I keep forgetting how long you've been gone."

The Nergalid was about to say more, but stopped himself. Pyrame's howsoever-illusionary jaw had just dropped. Someone was behind him.

========

"Judge?" she queried, uncertainly.

****

Pyrame isn't any more alone in favouring long silvery hair than Dark Sedon is at liking women who sport it. Most female Utopians have whitish hair to match their white-as-light skin. However, truly silvery hair isn't popular in the Weirdom of Cabalarkon, mostly because it's known both Pyrame and Sedon favour it.

This caused Gloriella D'Angelo Dark a degree of trouble there before she vanished, as yet never to be seen again, during "<u>Decimation Damnation</u>". As also mentioned therein, it did a ditto to her aunt, Celeste Mannering (Celestine D'Angelo on the Outer Earth), the Celestial Superior, when she was around decades earlier.

Games 9: **Silverstar's Twilight Moments**

========

<u>Birhym, 3 Tantalar 5980</u>

"Mistress?"

Pyrame Silverstar, still in the semblance of a silver-haired humanoid, opened all three of her eyes with tremendous difficulty. Dawn was approaching. The sky remained ever-electric.

"All supposed to eat you. All not eat you smelling so bad."

========

The thing speaking was about the size of a dog. It had a dog's head, that of a terrier or near enough, and a dog's collar as well. It wasn't the ugliest dog in the history of ugly dogs only because it wasn't just a dog. It was a composite creature; one seemingly stitched together by an insane and very twisted taxidermist; the sort who would construct a wolf in sheep's clothing, or vice versa, just because he or she could. If Frankenstein's monster had a pet, this was it.

In addition to its dogface, it also featured the torso of a scrawny human hag with pendulous teats that rubbed against the sandy ground, the stumpy legs of a crocodile, the oversized wings of a house fly and, perhaps most grotesquely, a corkscrewed salamander's tail. It wagged this last — more like sprang it in and out than side-to-side — as if the creature attached to it was genuinely happy to see her.

Creature? She-Sphinx! Clearly All was having a bad period.

The two of them were alone in the lush, pristinely white sand of this deserted, not just windswept beach. Had to be Incain. Where'd she been? Right, Sorrow, Wailing Souls, Pettivisaya. How'd she get here? Reaper must have cut her here. Wasn't someone else there with them — a mass of darkness like King Harvest, albeit with a pink face instead of bone and an actual third eye instead of an extra eyehole?

She couldn't be sure. No matter. Because the next minute she couldn't remember even that much. She could feel her shell's pain, shared it.

"A sentient, All. Find me another sentient. Now!"

========

Dawn may be imminent but the extraordinarily bright, Gypsium-negating Theomachy in the night's sky showed no signs of abating.

========

Virtually from the moment they'd noticed something amiss upstairs, if perhaps not from the moment it actually started, Tsishah Thrae — more commonly known as Twilight, after her longest time dwelling place — had been watching it alongside her fellow, if possible even more bundled-up Aortic, Amphitrite of Lemuria, their friend and ally, the goatish, between-space trailblazer, Pusan Wanderlust, and some of the local Zebranids.

They only went back inside the half-built, but chimneyed and at least partially roofed, longhouse they'd already resigned themselves to making their guest home until it ended because it was time for their appointment. That and the fact their witch-stones no longer worked, though how something so high in the sky could affect Brainrock Godstuff … most distressing.

(There were plenty of well-insulated cabins nestled nearby; were even a few proper houses, ones with fairly modern conveniences, including toilets that flushed. Tsishah could easily stay in mother Morgianna and step-father Demios's should she so desire. However, having lived on Shenon for so long, she didn't have a place of her own. Neither did either Pusan or Amphitrite, but they were only visitors.)

That they'd have to have beds and bedding brought over from the other buildings if this kept up, well, that was Sedon up there. Wasn't much he couldn't do on his Hidden Headworld. That in turn brought into question whether there would even be an appointment to keep. If the Grey was denied them, would the Weird be denied their icy contact with the devic mainstay of the Panharmonium Project.

Geographically speaking, the longhouse was being put up in a mountain meadow high atop the Whiplash Range, the Hidden Headworld's equivalent of Tibet or the Incan Andes. More specifically it was being built in the Zebranid 'leper' colony founded by her mother and stepfather over a decade after Mama Morg finally realized her Shah of a Tsishah hadn't died of Crib Death back in '34; had in fact been stolen by fucking faeries from Twilight, on the other side of the world.

Speaking even more geographically specifically, the Prison Beach of Incain lay over the nearest summit and way, way, down below. Be that as it may, as the Aortics and equally mortal allies had prearranged, the absolutely amazing azura, Klannit Thanatos, in her usual state as an ambulatory ice statue, awaited them at the appointed hour inside it. Perhaps counter-intuitively, she was actually bundled up, lightly, in furs the same as everyone else there. Perhaps Klannit didn't want to seem so comparatively alien or otherworldly when out in public.

"What's going on, Mirrors?" Pusan immediately demanded of the much more than merely mentally accomplished Spirit Being.

"You tell me, witches."

Yet another bolt of lightning crackled out of the cloudless sky above Whiplash. This one went straight through the longhouse's only partially finished roof. It hit the Thanatoid squarely in her reflective skull. Whereupon she began to fracture. "Ouch!" Klannit managed to mutter. Or a word to that effect.

"Where's a Shedd or an Angelyc when you need one?" wondered the fauna, looking up. Then she sighed, though it was more of a bleat, and got to work.

========

Somehow or other the Theomachy in the sky denied witches, psychopomps and All of Incain access to the Weird, the Grey, Samsara, the dark-grey universal substance of between-space. Evidently not so devils. Klannit's mother, Methandra Thanatos, had managed to send her hither from Frozen Lathakra when her usual transportation, from mirror to mirror, failed.

Fortunately for Klannit it was so cold, even this far south in the Whiplash Range, high above the Prison Beach, that the fauna, Pusan Wanderlust, who was a highly skilled healer, had no problem icing her back together again. (Hey, you could ski on the Outer Earth's Big Island of Hawaii, not all that far from Centauri Island as the firefly flew.)

Pusan was not <u>the</u> Amalthea, the goat who nursed Zeus when he was just baby in the mountains of Crete. Her devic mother wasn't ether-either, as fays might say. She was a Byronic Zodiacal. By contrast, the goat who raised infant Zeus was a Lazarem-ist, Amal-Althea (Althea Brand, according to Illuminaries of Weir), Lazareme's female healer. And Zeus wasn't Zeus. He was Thrygragos Varuna Mithras reduced to infancy by Tralalorn on ... someone's behalf.

Maybe even his own.

========

Tsishah Twilight left Pusan to her artistry.

She, Treat – who, as an almost precise contemporary of her mother, was four-teen years her senior – and a number of Zebranids, some of whom carried eye-staves produced by the Weirdom of Cabalarkon's replication units, went back outside. There they stood watching the lightshow until the arrival of dawn threatened to over-illuminate it. She was about to go back into the sparse, unfinished longhouse when she spotted the She-Sphinx, on the ragged wings of an approximate eagle, laboriously flying towards the mountain meadow.

When she landed, All laid a Stopstone egg. It cracked, albeit not quite in the same way Klannit had hours earlier. A rough-looking woman wearing a black and white striped uniform crawled out of it. Her skin colour indicated she was from up north in Ophir-Moorset, on the occipital side of the Aural Sea, Sedon's Ear. The etching of a third eye appeared dimly in her forehead.

Third Eye? Uniform? Cosmic Express? If so, thought Tsishah, better make that the Outer Earth's vast Indian subcontinent.

Almost inaudibly the woman said: "Please, help me."

Eye-staves had eyeorbs atop them. In Cabalarkon, Tsishah knew, they were supposed to open automatically in the presence of a devilish intruder. The colony not being a devic protectorate, they should have done so here as well. And once they did, what looked like a solitary eyeball would suck the devil out of whomever he or she was possessing.

Would do so together with his or her subtle matter daemonic body and mutable power focus; composed as it was of much same miraculous substance as their bodies. Would thereupon hold him or her in the Shadow or Nebuland be-tween-space forevermore. Or until their captors willed them released, which Weir's Trinondev Warrior Elite would never permit.

Another almost exact, to the day, contemporary of her mother of a Morg, Melina nowadays Zeross, its current High Illuminary, as well as one of the most effective Althean healers she'd ever come across – possibly, according to essentially unprovable scuttlebutt, because she was born with Amal-Althea insider her – once told her there was a constantly guarded, Stopstone-lined vault in Cabalarkon City's Citadel of the Thinkers stacked to overflowing with full-up eyeorbs.

In fact, during the final months of the reign of Morgan Abyss, the Death's Head Hellion, as Master of Weir, dozens of the oldest, pre-Earth prison pods once held the Moloch Sedon himself until someone, perhaps Pyrame Silverstar, though she denied it, willed him released. None of that happened here and now. Unless the

Theomachy up top affected eye-staves the same as it did witches far-speaking and traversing the Grey, there could only be one explanation.

"Pusan," yelled Tsishah. "Get your hairy ass out here, goat. I think Uncle Sal's half-mommy's come calling."

========

Theomachy or no Theomachy, devils were not the only ones who could still travel between-space. Indeed, devils were hardly the only ones who could send others of their devazur-ilk through the universal substance. Even more impressively, something in combination with someone somehow or other could and did do it from the Outer Earth.

Thusly thrust through Cathonia, Headless Ramazar and the monstrous Vultyrie arrived in Centurium on what therefore could no longer properly be considered Wednesday.

========

Sapienda, 4 Tantalar 5980

Escaping the Sedon Sphere, howsoever-unwittingly, was one thing. Altogether regaining said wits was proving to be a bundle more problematic.

========

When Pyrame Silverstar next opened her eyes she found herself in a large log cabin; a community hall or longhouse, to go by its size. Judging from the smell of freshly milled wood, the hall's lack of furniture, and an incomplete roof that looked as if it had been damaged by a flash fire or, more likely, lightning, it was still under construction. From the frigid temperature she reckoned it was high in the mountains, though which mountains she had no idea.

(The Hidden Headworld was extremely mountainous; this as one would expect from what was once, both pre-Flood and pre-Dome, a vast archipelago spanning what today appeared to be the Outer Earth's largely empty North Pacific Ocean. For what else were islands except the tops of otherwise altogether undersea mountains?)

Also in the longhouse – which did not lack for either chimneys or the fireplaces that went with them; though, the fireplaces being as unfinished as the roof, did lack for fires – were a number of others. Almost all were bundled in wool caps or toques, scarves, gloves or mittens, and thick coats. Most were standing or leaning against the walls. Because they were so well covered it was difficult to tell where they came from, let alone to which race they belonged.

A couple had obvious orange-coloured, orange-textured skin, which made them Bandradins. Their home territory, their Holy Heights, lay in the high plains of south-central Cattail below Sedon's Peak. A few more were so black or so white they had to be Utopians. A good percentage, perhaps even the majority, had black and white striped faces; Zebranid Lepers, she realized.

Theirs wasn't really a form of leprosy. Nor was it vitiligo in that they didn't lose pigment in patches. Zebranids actually were striped; the males having lost their black pigmentation in strips and the females having gained it, as if in charioscuro ribbons. Although rare, they were, almost exclusively, pureblood Utopians born or at least raised beyond the confines of the Weirdom of Cabalarkon and the mishmash mush spewed out of its food replicator units that so many non-Utopians found inedible, even in small quantities.

One of the most thoroughly covered had the distinctive, jutting-out, froglike eyes of a Lemurian female; Lemurian males being strictly water-breathers. Eyes were all Pyrame could see of her face. That made sense. Being cold-blooded, Lemurians would freeze more quickly than Zebranids or representatives of most any of the Head's other sentient races. The frogwoman was standing beside the lone chair in the otherwise cleared-out wooden hall.

It was occupied by another heavily-garbed woman. Although she had incongruously blue eyes, this one appeared to be a middle-aged Irache or half-breed. She certainly dressed like one. Sported dozens of evidently handmade ornaments or fetishes, some of which glowed; even had on the beaded, toque-like headdress, complete with a couple of eagle feathers, many Iraches favoured. Also had the reddish brown, well-lined skin and braided, dark hair turning to grey typical of them.

Mind you, Pyrame reminded herself, as always when it came to upper-level witches her looks might have been a splendour or aural glamour.

Three others caught her three eyes. Like many, though by no means all the rest, these three were female. The first was statuesque. Well-built – well-constructed, she fancied, albeit in a strangely colourless way – with chiselled features and seemed, while not completely naked, close enough in a light-looking furry top, skirt and boots. Which, given the chill air, definitely had to be an illusion.

The second was an actual statue. Appeared to be one anyhow, though it wasn't mounted upright on a pedestal. It was lying on a worktable against one side of the longhouse. Was very lifelike. Was of herself, her shell rather, Nehrini Purandar. Was, in fact, so lifelike it very likely was her. Pyrame reckoned the Cosmicaptain was cocooned inside it. Reckoned who had done it as well. The one she recognized was a thoroughly-trained Mariamnic fauna, a female faun or satyr; a faintly hairy, dual-horned and lightly be-bearded, scantily clad anthropomorphic goat.

The middle-aged, blue-eyed Irache or half-Irache, who still looked something of a stunner, was manifestly their leader. Was the only one sitting — they'd have taken the posted planning boards, workbenches, sawhorses, tools and suchlike out in order to present an impressive hearing space for such a notorious devil. At least the floor was finished; quality workmanship, too, if Pyrame was any judge. (*Judge?*)

Blue-eyes was petting the conglomerate, mismatched shape All had assumed, likely because she was feeling the part. (For a machine with only a modicum of hence artificial intelligence, All was remarkably whimsical. Always had been — and the Pauper Priestess had known her, literally inside and out, since not long after she'd arrived on the then Whole Earth something like seven hundred years pre-Dome as a member of Thrygragos Lazareme's expeditionary force.)

As potentially disturbing as all that was, Pyrame was far more concerned about her own predicament. She felt lethargic, as if her new shell had been drugged and the drugs had somehow affected her, a Master Deva, which was exceedingly improbable. The odds favoured an even more distressing scenario. Although she was possessing someone, she was not in control of that someone. Rather, whomever it was, unless it was a whatever, swas in control of her.

He, she or it was at best only borderline-sentient. Nonetheless, whomever or whatever seemed perfectly capable of keeping her deadened; paralyzed physically as well as mentally. It was almost as if whomever or whatever had been designed to neutralize devils. Something of a poser, to be sure.

Having lost Purandar, not to mention her solidifying demon, albeit 30 years earlier, Pyrame was just a Spirit Being. While her shell was incapacitated, if not already dead, and therefore useless to her, there were lots of fully sentient beings in the hall. Spirit Beings were mobile over short distances; they could get about nearby between-space as well as perceptible regular space with little more than a thought.

She should have no problem going from here, in whomever or whatever she was in, to there, into one of the non-Utopian women or men, since purebloods could not be possessed. Yet she couldn't. She attempted to speak. Nothing came out. Her lips – rather, her shell's lips – did not move. With the exception of her three eyeballs nothing of her moved. She tried telepathy, a standard way of communication for Master Devas. Her brain refused to respond.

Would she have to resort to eyefire-burning those in front of her?

Eyefire's effect was mostly psychological. It only felt like your body was burning up, but those hit with it usually became very cooperative very quickly. She tried it, aiming for the Irache. She was scorched instead. Was as if her eyefire had been reflected back at her; that she'd acted against her own self. The Irache stroking the All-thing like some kind of docile gargoyle half-smiled in what Pyrame took to be grim satisfaction.

"Let her talk, baby," she instructed the conglomerate creature.

The Pauper felt a relaxation of sorts. "What have you done to me?" she demanded in a voice so weak it came out as more of a plea than a demand.

"Explain her situation, traveller," requested the seated Irache.

The female faun, the only one Pyrame Silverstar for sure recalled from years gone by, stepped forward. Traveller was a Trailblazer, capitalized; also a trail-finder and trail-trailer, a kind of between-space scout not so much on a horse as on a goat; as a goat, more accurately. Officially she was a deviant, the half-daughter of a pair of Master Devas who were possessing her real parents when she was conceived. (Master Devas? Not if her deviant father was possessed by his own devic half-father, none other than the Great God, Thrygragos Varuna Mithras.)

Her arguably even more curious talent was the ability to spiritually recur, over and over again, with her identity and consequential memories completely intact. She did so almost invariably within her own daughter or granddaughter, all of whom were faunas; had been doing so for going on four thousand years now.

Her name was Pusan Wanderlust and, although she denied it, Pyrame was all but certain she was a devic suicide. Was – had been, make that – a Byronic Master Deva, one of his three Winter Zodiacals, she knew best as Goat or, far less regularly, Goatfish. This last because that was how she regularly disported herself when she was around, which she hadn't been for a long time and that a very long time ago.

(Illuminaries had her as Deneb Makara but, like more than a few of their names, it hadn't caught on. As for her looks, it wasn't as if she went around as a kind of 3-eyed mullet. On the contrary, she liked to look as iconography for the Zodiacal sign for Capricorn often did to this day: namely, as a sea-goat with a she-goat's head, chest and forelegs fronting a decidedly fishy midsection and tail-end. Such an awkward choice of semblance made her comical on land, so Makara usually swam or, when out of water, flew, albeit winglessly — called it sky-swimming.)

As unlikely as it seemed, if Pyrame was right and she was a devic suicide, then Pusan was effectively her own deviant self's devic half-mother. Nevertheless, that she carried around a proper pedum – an illustrative motif for fairy godmothers on both sides of the Dome – or shepherd's crook made of Brainrock, an obvious devic talisman, one identical to the Byronic Goat's talisman as it happened, tended more so than less so to verify that near-certitude.

Oddly for a devic suicide, albeit not for a deviant, Pusan could be possessed. Silverstar had as yet no way of detecting if she was so right this minute. However, when she was, Pusan was usually occupied by a non-devic-suicide, the other devilish goat: one Amal-Althea Brand by Illuminary-determined name (which had caught on), Thrygragos Lazareme's nurse, who was also goatish, though not goat-fishy.

A Byronic suicide who kept her own power focus, yet was commonly possessed by a Lazaremist, whose power focus was a caduceus? Regardless of the fact Tvasitar talismans were nothing if not mutable, that had to be one of the weirdest, if not the weirdest, relationships amongst all the weird relationships found upon the Hidden Continent of Sedon's Head. (The weirdest relationship was undoubtedly her, Pyrame, a comparatively lowborn Mithradite, and her grandfather, the Moloch Sedon himself.)

"Not much to explain, is there, Aortic?" said the fauna. She turned to address Pyrame directly. "As you may or may not realize, pauper, today is Sapienda, the 4th of Tantalar, in the Year of the Dome 5980. You were decathonitized last Sedonda and we've had the dubious pleasure of your company since early Birhym.

"You are in a Zebranid Leper Colony, one not established until after your cathonitization near enough to thirty years ago as to make no never mind. It's situated high up on a mountain meadow in the Cattail's Whiplash Range just above the Prison Beach of Incain. And, yes, it is snowing outside. It usually is this time of year, Mithramas being only three weeks away."

(Mithramas was one of the most common names used on Sedon's Head to mark Yule. It was named after Thrygragos Varuna Mithras, the Great God who celebrated the equivalent of his birthday on the winter solstice and was slain on Thrygragon, which howsoever-ironically occurred on a Mithramas in the Year 4376. A heckuva day to die, your own feast day, most devils would agree — even if they didn't agree they could actually die.)

(Of some interest Mithramas was still celebrated on the 25th of Tantalar, the same day Christmas was on the Outer Earth as well as in parts of the Headworld where Christianity had taken a still very much shallow root over the centuries. It did not celebrate the birth of a saviour, as Mithras would have had it. It celebrated the death of an inconsistently arbitrary autocrat.)

"You are inside a mandroid guard-body belonging to one of our distinguished visitors from Shenon, Witch Isle. As you can appreciate, none of us were lining up to become a devil's shell, especially one with your reputation. However, once we decided to respond to All's cry for help on your behalf, it was all we had immediately available."

"All not cry," the hotchpotch conglomeration protested. "All inform friends. All can help priestess. All like priestess. All can give priestess home, not prison."

"All did help her," soothed the Irache. "Without All we could never have extracted the priestess from her shell. And All helped her shell, too. Because of All she may have a chance of living out the fullness of her years. But All is very busy right now and the priestess is no ordinary devil. As All knows, she can be very distracting. We need All to continue to concentrate on helping us, All's friends, not her."

"All happy if Aortic happy."

"Aortic very happy with All," the Irache assured the haphazard horror.

"We all are, All," Pusan reiterated, before returning her attention to Pyrame. "Aortic Tsishah is correct. Without All we could never have separated you from this cosmicaptain you possessed in Cathonia. Unfortunately, while I've purged her of what radioactivity I could without seriously afflicting anyone else, her survival is by no means assured."

Althean-healers, especially deviants with the gift, had a literal hands-on way of purging, more like transferring, degrees of illnesses from sick people to healthy people; albeit only in small measure before moving their hands to the next healthy volunteer. (Alts may not a hundred percent subscribe to Ahimsa, the do-no-harm Jain, Buddhist or Hindu principle of non-injury to living beings, but came close.)

"Truth told, I was forced to plaster her in tellurian crap in order to suspend her deterioration until we can get her to someone with talents superior to mine when it comes to healing." Goat was fond of using off-colour language. Were no excremental expletives deleted in her vocabulary.

"Even though, when it comes to devils, the notion of survival does not necessarily include something as mundane as life and death, make no mistake, neither is yours guaranteed. The way I see it you are on the cusp of going one of two ways. First, as you might recall, mandroids are mostly shit themselves; akin to eldritch earthborn or chthonic creatures such as droopy demons and fucking faeries.

"We could have Amphitrite's guard-body thoroughly harden around you. We do that, it finishes sealing you inside it, we shut it down, you become our permanent guest, our prisoner if you prefer, a statue to display in an art gallery we're considering building on Witch Isle. This is my recommendation."

"It isn't ours," objected one of the older females there, a white-as-light Utopian who could have been anywhere in her seventies or eighties on up, since pureblood Utopians aged much slower than full humans or members of the vast majority of the Headworld's other sentient races. Came with their extraterrestrial ancestry, Pyrame supposed. As well as slop they ingested growing up in Cabalarkon, which this one might have done if she was as old as she looked.

"As any of us who trained as Illuminaries under Master Kyprian know, the Greek Solution never works for long, not when it comes to devils. Statues break."

"They can also be broken," provided the Lemurian helpfully.

"Too true, Aortic," Pusan agreed. "But my argument remains valid. So long as we maintain due vigilance over it, having the Pauper Priestess inactivated within mandroid statuary means we have the option of releasing her anytime we please. Even if we risk her coming out cranky, it's preferable to the second alternative.

"We let her recathonitize, the miserable Moloch can release her anytime he pleases. The difference should be palpable pith to anyone here."

"Except Dark Sedon's had her for thirty years," this sitting Tsishah, the Irache Aortic, reminded the fauna, as if for the umpteenth time, "And he never did. That must mean he regards her as insignificant; that she's no longer needed in order to have his sedons. Which is curious, in and of itself, and a mystery that begs further investigation, I'll allow.

"Be that as it may, trying to keep her immobilized inside Amphitrite's guard-body is a greater one. Although all of us normals here, even the men, wear menstrual stones ensorcelled to prevent devils possessing us, so long as we leave her down here, no matter how hardened she might be, any idiot with a hammer can break her out. Whereupon she could possess anyone not so protected.

"She's decathonitized. She can't be trusted. Even if it looks as if there was some sort of ferocious battle, now quietened down, going on in Cathonia, I say let her go back upstairs."

"Wait a minute," Pyrame managed to protest. "I'm a devil, yes; a decathonitized one, true too. But our oaths are inviolable. There must be a third alternative."

Nobody offered one. Shenon's other Aortic, the Lemurians' Queen Amphitrite, expressed a reason for their reticence: "Inviolable, you say? Then why are the Primary Apocalyptics, decathonitized devils the lot of them, killing my daughter's half-brothers and half-sisters every time one of them is sent to Temporis from wherever by whomever?"

(Treat's daughter, Lakshmi Arthadot, was a deviant. Her devic half-father was the Chronocollector, also the Time-Space Displacer, in the guise of Neptune or Poseidon, after whose mythological mate Queen Merthetis named her daughter Amphitrite. Like her half-brothers and half-sisters, that made Lakshmi not just an Artha; it made her a Kronokronos – or Kronakrona, according to sexist-some – and in line for the 'throne' of Temporis, such as it is.)

"Temporis?" mulled Pyrame. "Dand Tariqartha, the Lazaremist Earth Magician's Thousand Caverns? It's full of replicates, mantel half-lifers. Killing mantels hardly constitutes killing truly sentient beings." (Tariqartha, Lakshmi's half-father, was an immortal Master Deva. As such, it was unlikely he'd vacate his throne at any time during Lakshmi's life.)

"Maybe it doesn't," the Irache put to her before Aortic Amphitrite could argue, yet again, against her position. "But the Apocalyptics trying to kill my demon's father does. As yet another unanticipated result of diverting the Cosmic Express into the Cathonic Zone, John Sundown, Raven's Head and a number of their supranormal companions seem to have come back unaged, alive and wholly active again."

(Tsishah, like Pusan, knew this from Mirrors, Klannit Thanatos, who in turn knew it from Hotstuff, her mother Methandra Thanatos. Aka Heat to her brood brother-husband's Cold, the eternal Mistress of Mythland had observed the action on the Outer Earth's Damnation Isle the previous Sedonda-Sunday via revelatory fumes emitting from Metisophia's purloined power focus, her Brainrock cauldron.)

"And devils even trying to kill fully alive beings does constitute violating their Sedonic oaths not to kill. The Mighty Eye-Mouth-in-the-Sky should have recathonitized them last Sedonda. Yet he either didn't, for his own reasons, or couldn't, for reasons beyond his control, possibly because he's under siege himself upstairs. In any event, it's evident decathonitized devils no longer have any meaningful strictures placed on them."

Pyrame had trouble believing what her ears, such as they were, were hearing. For starters she focused on only one of them. "You're wearing an Irache demon?"

"Yes."

"And your demon's father was Blind Johnny Sundown?"

"Blind Sundown, yes again. It was after your time, pauper, 5953 if my information's correct, on an Outer Earth island known, appropriately or otherwise, as Salvation. But, other than the Dual Entities – and them only arguably – my demon's father came closer to killing the Moloch Sedon than anyone has before or since."

"Now why doesn't that surprise me?" muttered Pyrame Silverstar. Sundown, she recalled, wielded celestial weaponry, a Solar Spear no less, and rode an equally, originally celestial, mono-horned ravendeer.

Someone else had. Actually a goodly, if not necessarily godly, number of Whole Earthlings over the intervening millennia had — but she was thinking of one in particular. That would be Xuthros Hor, the Biblical Noah, the tenth Golden Aged Patriarch, he who caused the Great Flood of Genesis.

========

Past precedents suggested devils only avoided killing lesser beings whilst the Moloch Sedon was around to enforce said strictures. He hadn't been during the 1000 Days of Disbelief, when the two Male Unities, Chaos and Order, howsoever-inadvertently wiped out something like half of the Inner Earth's living beings while trying to do in each other.

That he wasn't around then, some said, was because he'd been very nearly wiped out himself most of a couple of decades earlier, circa 5475 YD. Who had that kind of power? None other than Lord Order — the very devil he'd been battling upstairs.

****

Thrygragos Lazareme and his three firstborn Unities, Harmony, Chaos and Order, were the main devic 'protagonists' during the three books comprising 'The Thrice-Cursed Godly Glories'. Pyrame appeared in the first two, albeit as a pivotal character only in Book One: "Feeling Theocidal", which told of Thrygragon – Mithramas 4376, one of the most fateful days in the Hidden Headworld's very long history.

In chronological terms it was followed by "The War of the Apocalyptics", the opening full length novel in the 'Launch 1980' story cycle. It in turn was based in large measure on the **PHANTACEA** comic book series, specifically the storyline captured in "The Damnation Brigade" graphic novel.

As for Tsishah's demon, Shahiyeda either Sunrise or Sundown, she was introduced during the 'Heliodyssey' web-serials, all of which were set in early 1938, late 5937. Her most significant role came during "The Vampire Variations". How Tsishah 'acquired' her Shah demon – indeed, how that Shah became a demon and challenged Baaloch Hellblob for control over the demons of Satanwyck – has as yet never been fully told.

Games 10: **End Problem Pyrame, Twice**

========

<u>Sapienda, 4 Tantalar 5980</u>

Pyrame Silverstar had a lot to digest. Too much, really.

On the second of Tantalar Underlord Yama Nergal tells her that, from roughly late 5953 until sometime in 5978, Star Sedon did not shine out of the night's sky above his own Headworld. Might have, upon quick reflection, been true, too. Silverstar's silver star shone out of the Mithradites' northwest quadrant whereas Sedon's star was prone to roam wherever it pleased.

The significant thing of it was, she couldn't recall it roaming anywhere near her for most of her thirty years upstairs.

========

First, she finds herself decathonitized in Satanwyck, more specifically Pandemonium, Paradise for the Damned, what was quite literally Hell on Earth. Next, within a few hours, if that, of making herself known to its devic ruler, Baaloch Hellblob, aka Sinistral Sloth, aka also Lord Lazy, he sends her to Pettivisaya, the City of Wailing Souls, probably just to get rid of her.

There, after its devic ruler, the Nergalid Grim Reaper, finally shows up, she makes a very much belated pitch to help him undo her doing-in of the Ghostlands via the Atomic Twins – which, not that he cared, she had nothing to with, other than losing control of her shell of the time, let alone her own demon – in return for her release.

The Underlord, nowadays the even emptier Ghosts' Overlord, not-so-promptly sends her to Incain in order to have her use her influence with All and thereby make good on her promise. Except, as a result of exposure to the Ghost's radiation, her shell's already dying within her. In retrospect she should have evacuated Cosmicaptain Purandar, leaving her for crab food, and gone into All right away.

Would have as well, but she was terrified that in her diminished state she might have been unable to resist All's built-in inclination to imprison her as a rogue devil and instantly forget she even had her inside her. So, instead, the Pauper Priestess gets downright abject and, humiliatingly, pleads with the She-Sphinx to get her a new shell.

Only All has a covetous coven of new, witchy masters these days; for the most part Panharmonium Project proponents from the sound of things. Whether or not the Mandroid Monster Maker was acting in good faith, after two days without consciousness, Pyrame awakens to find herself immobilized inside a mandroid guardbody; a devil-hating Lemurian Aortic's mandroid guard-body, no less.

Turns out one of All's new masters is another Aortic of Shenon, Witch Isle. Baaloch had said something about a Shah leading a rebellion of demons against his authority something like twenty years earlier. It wasn't named Tsishah; was named Shahiyeda, he'd said, but he mentioned a Tsishah in passing, hadn't he? She couldn't quite recall. Wasn't thinking too straight, was she.

Be that as it may, what are Shenon's two Aortics (and, for all Pyrame knew, its two Ventriculars) doing in a Zebranid Leper Colony that not only did not exist prior to her cathonitization, but had to be a good thousand miles from Witch Isle? Were they all Panharmonium project-pushers?

Were there no devils in their number? No way to be sure, but it was hard to imagine them getting anywhere without devic assistance; female devic assistance, in all likelihood. And how can a woman who, by her own admission, is wearing a presumably debrained Irache demon become the colony's apparent leader? Had to be the same Tsishah; the same masquerade-Morrigan who'd got little Lord Lazy so twisted round, so upset, he turned Satanwyck into Paradise for the Damned just to salve his demon subjects and thereby save his own, ha-ha, bacon.

Despite their striped skin, Zebranids were Utopians; were descended from pureblood or near-pureblood exiles from the Weirdom of Cabalarkon; ones who were denied – or had never tried – the life-extending crud churned out by the Weirdom's Mother Machine units. While Utopian hatred for devils was all but genetic, that was just as true for demon-loving Hecate-Hellions.

She loved to watch the game of baseball when she visited the Outer Earth's United States of America, as well as many of the Latin American countries where it rivalled proper football in popularity, this between the two times this century she'd been cathonitized. To use an analogy that probably wouldn't make sense to anyone else here – not unless Greater Godbad had baseball leagues now, which they may have – she had two strikes against her already. Worse than that, she considered, chances were these Utopians hated her most especial.

Only the Master of Weir had the authority to exile anyone from Cabalarkon. And, if everything had continued to go as it looked to be going before she was cathonitized, the man who succeeded to the Mastery of Weir after she was ill-starred was Saladin Devason; so-called in part because he was her half-son. That he achieved the Mastery anyhow mostly had to do with his other half-parent, none other than Dark Sedon himself.

To compound her problems, this devious, demon-wearing Tsishah Twilight informs her Blind Sundown came as close to killing the mighty Moloch as anyone, even the Dual Entities, ever had. And what was with that strange turn of phrase she'd used: 'Wholly active again'? Had Sundown and his fellow whatchamacallit, Wakinyah Creature of the Cosmos, his mount, a solitary just that, Raven's Head, not been active for a time? Were the two related, besides by blood? How long a time? Since almost putting away the Hidden Headworld's lone male, perpetual presence for good, in both meanings of the term?

Coyotes of a conundrum, to use one of Sundown's favourite phrases, all of the above. A pack of them and at least one had to be rabid. Not only that, had to have managed to bite the Primary Apocalyptics: War, Disease and Disaster, plus their Death, Mundane Death, Mother Murder Death, the Medusa who'd done so much to put paid to Father Mithras on Thrygragon.

Fanciful as it was, how else could you explain the foaming-at-the-mouth madness reputedly afflicting them? Only recently decathonitized, yet wilfully killing off Dand Tariqartha's mantel half-lifers? That sounded to her like a devic death wish. Was a direct contradiction of Sedon's inviolable command that devils never kill lesser beings. Disobeying their grandfather was akin to killing themselves; a ticket to instant recathonitization.

Unless Tsishah was right and decathonitized Master Devas were no longer bound by either Sedonic dictates or their own oaths; in which case no one could trust the word of someone like her ever again. The Apocalyptics doing what they were doing meant she was at the mercy of these ensorcelled witches, Zebranids, their parents and their deviant ally, the Traveller, the Trailblazer, Pusan Wanderlust.

At best, if they were to go with the fauna's recommendation, they were on the verge of condemning her to potentially interminable containment within a mandroid guard-body. At worst, they were about to sentence her to recathonitization, to a return reliance on the mercy of the Demon as well as Devil King, her grandfather, now her ex-lover, to release her. Which, as Aortic Tsishah had just put to the goatish traveller, he might never do.

After the better part of six thousand years, had she become that irrelevant, that non-essential, to the maintenance of the Cathonic Zone?

========

"Do tell," Pyrame muttered, seeking additional information if only to prolong their dialogue and, consequently, her longevity as other than a star in that selfsame night's sky.

"Even though they spent most of their time on the Outer Earth," she elaborated, "I had plenty of dealings with this Sundown fellow over the years. His father was one of mine, a Sed-son. I had even more dealings with his mount, Raven's Head, and his wife, Solace Sunrise, Sorciere, particularly in the late Thirties and early Forties. Sundown and Sorciere had three sons around that time. Their names were John, James and Joseph, weren't they?"

"I believe so," Tsishah Twilight as good as confirmed. "Something like that anyhow. All I really know is each of them was killed on his seventh birthday."

"In the late Forties out there, too true. Strangely coincidental tragedies that; though I am surprised to hear you say they were killed. Weren't their deaths deemed natural? The two I remember hearing about were." (Although Joseph, who was known to his parents as Autumn Sunshine due to his birth date, died in September 1950, it was out there. At that time, in here, Pyrame Silverstar was preoccupied seeking to overthrow Master Kyprian and retake the Weirdom of Cabalarkon for herself less so than for half-son Saladin.)

"As I'm beginning to suspect you're already well-aware, their deaths were just that; too strangely coincidental to be natural. Turned out they were killed; turned out their killer was the Conqueror; turned out the Conqueror was Jesus Mandam and it turned out Jesus Mandam went by the name of Wiccan Warlock when he was in here. He was one of yours too, wasn't he?"

Pyrame knew who the Conqueror was; knew who both Jesus Mandam and Wiccan Warlock were as well. She didn't know if Jesse/Wiccan was hers. Not that that mattered if his father was Judge Warlock. He, Sedon St Synne, out there, definitely was hers and Sed-sons could be grandsons. Didn't admit as much; for her, bargaining chips were hard to come by.

"I'll keep that to myself, if you don't mind. Unless of course you find me a fully sentient shell to occupy and thereafter let me go my own way. You do that I'll send you an answer by mail, unless you're back to using carrier pigeon: Aortic Tsishah, care of Shenon, Witch Isle, Quadrant Whatever, should do the trick, right?"

"Guess we girls will have to keep our secrets then." Tsishah had had enough bantering. It was time to make a decision. She made it.

"Seal her up, baby," she instructed All. "Then shut down the guard-body and sprout your She-Sphinx's wings. I'll ride you out into the middle of Psychron and we'll dump them both, one in the other. When we come back I'll have you detonate the mandroid from afar. Whereupon, with nothing even remotely sentient anywhere near her to possess, your priestess will instantly recathonitize. End of problem."

"Beginning of problem," persisted Pusan Wanderlust.

"No more, Goat." Tsishah was angry now. "You said you'd abide by my decision. Well, I've made it. It isn't the one you'd have made, but it's the one most everyone else here would. Myself, I've always preferred to go with the consensus wisdom of the many rather than the self-serving wisdom of the few, let alone the one. Go with your wisdom especially, suicide," she threw in nastily. Wanderlust hated it when folks thought her a onetime devil.

"I've said it before and will say it again now, for all to hear and for the final time. Other than you, Pusan, I'm no different than anyone here. I'm, we're, much more comfortable having Pyrame Silverstar a silver star shining out of the night's sky than I, we, would be with her immobilized in some hypothetical art gallery on Shenon that you just made up. All the more so since that crook of yours would make a passable shatter-hammer.

"Seal her up and let's fly her away, baby," she instructed All of Incain. "If Neptune has an art gallery out in Psychron then you can visit her there, Goatfish."

========

End-problem Pyrame Silverstar. Until …

========

Although there was considerable debate with respect to degree of intelligence, virtually everyone, on both sides of the Dome, agreed whales were sentient beings. There was no debate, on this side of the Dome, about one whale in particular. If he was a whale; could have been a bebrained cetacean demon or daemon, albeit obviously one more sea-born than earthborn. He not only had a name, he knew his name. It was Island Leviathan.

Most whales simply opened their maws and inhumed everything, including humans and any other sentient or non-sentient beings that thereupon found his, her or its way into their bellies. Island Leviathan was no different in that respect. Was as omnivorous as he was voracious. Didn't enjoy eating mandroids. Being entirely artificial, they weren't exactly loaded with nutrients and, besides, they tended to give him indigestion.

There were times you couldn't avoid them, especially down here, near the tip of the Cattail Peninsula, due to its proximity to All of Incain. Sapienda, the 4th of Tantalar 5980, Year of the Dome, was one of those. Talk about indigestion, Island

Leviathan felt as if his insides had exploded. Which of course they hadn't; something triggered from afar had, however, inside him.

Guard-bodies weren't usually booby-trapped, but they could easily be made so. Especially if you're a She-Sphinx and you rebuilt them to order.

========

Lazam, 5 Tantalar 5980

That night the only fourth generational Thanatoid anyone knew for sure had been decathonitized the previous Sedonda-Sunday ended up in Temporis. The next morning the Medusa, Mater Matare, the self-proclaimed Apocalyptic of Death, appeared in Centurium, replicated Versailles, the central cavern and capital of Temporis.

Dand Tariqartha knew the routine by then. He quickly assigned her a prearranged cavern; one called Calvary and accessible via only four others, which he'd previously given over to Demon Land (Antaeor Thanatos) and the three Primary Apocalyptics: War, Catastrophe and Plague, their acknowledged leader.

She was still pregnant; albeit not for much longer. And, no, she didn't give birth to any more next-to-useless azuras.

========

Not too much later on that same day, Friday the 5th of December 1980 on the Outer Earth, the person who'd sent the Apocalyptics and their allies (Antaeor 'Demon Land' Thanatos and the monstrous, double-sexed, double-headed and sort of double-bodied Vultyrie, whom Catastrophe {Nakba Ramazar, the headless Apocalyptic of Disaster or Sudden Destruction} rode standing on his/her backs) from out there's Vancouver Canada to in here's Subcranial Temporis showed up himself.

He spotted his half-sister cavorting in the nude with three other half-sisters. He had no idea they were his, and their own, half-sisters — since they only shared the same devic half-father, best consider them quarter-sisters. They were playing at 'make Actaeon a stag again, then kill him'. Being literate, if a mite more than mildly pixilated, he knew the story. Didn't know who he was, though. Not really. Not yet.

Lakshmi Arthadot, whose eighteenth birthday they were celebrating howsoever-innocently (their Actaeon was 'only' a mantel half-life fashioned by her indulgent Earth Magician of a devic half-father for the 'game' they were playing), had chosen the part of Diana the Huntress. Looked it, too.

Wasn't wearing a witch glamour. Wasn't nude either; just looked it, equally also. Had on an externally transformative prophylactic that could shift shapes as easily as her mother's had when she lived beyond the Dome, at times assuming the identity of SOS: the Society of Saints' submersible supra-stalwart Lady Lemurian.

She spotted him, recognized him by his renowned Homeworld Sceptre — something he himself didn't realize – and promptly croaked. Couldn't help herself.

Beneath her guard-body she really was a half-bred Lemurian Frogwoman.

========

Devauray, 6 Tantalar 5980

By Friday night Obadiah Melvin Power, once the Outer Earth supranormal codenamed Old Man Power, aka OMP, knew himself born Akbarartha, the seemingly ageless, fairy son of Temporis's immortal Devalord. By then also, thanks to the Apocalyptics and their allies, he was the eldest surviving Kronokronos on the Whole Earth.

On top of that, he was the father of the groom-to-be, Senator Sophiscient Barson. Until, that is, Lakshmi decided she'd rather marry the father than the son.

=========

The Theomachy in the sky actually ended Sapienda morning, prior to the prime, non-devic movers of the Panharmonium Project dealing with Pyrame Silver-star. So it was witch-stones started working again. So it also was the two Aortics — Amphitrite, having commandeered a replacement guard-body as if another suit of armour, and Tsishah Thrae, better known as Twilight — were able to make it as far as Centurium.

Fisherwoman, whom Lakshmi next door to worshipped, didn't join them, having been caught up in the latest and hopefully, to many, culminating chapter in the battle for the control of Hadd. Was just as well. Saved her encountering OMP and his fellow members of the self-proclaimed Damnation Brigade then and there.

One was her sister in more than just Flowery Anthea, who happily went by the only name she acknowledged with any regularity: her codename, Wilderwitch. The other was Aires D'Angelo (Airealist), whose twin Thalassa (Sea Goddess), who'd stayed on the Outer Earth, once believed that she, Sea, had killed her, Fish.

Tsishah hadn't stayed for the wedding; left the moment OMP-Akbar appeared in front of the replicated palace of Versailles with his devic father and the rest of these Dand-advertised supra-saviours. Had to really. Her Shah-demon started itching like crazy-eight-chrysanthemums the moment she perceived her (its?) resurrected father, Blind Sundown, and Raven's Head amongst this D-Brig of theirs.

So it was she, thankfully non-itchy again, was back in the Zebranid Leper Colony when Pusan Wanderlust rushed into her borrowed cottage-cum-cabin-cum-manor house — what mommy's hubby and onetime bodyguard, Demios Sarpedon, had built, albeit not by himself, and expanded over the decades.

Goat demanded she get up, get dressed and come outside immediately. And, no, the Theomachy hadn't resumed. Nor had Star Pyrame finally shown up upstairs two days late. Nor was her exhilaration entirely due to the fact that Constellation Apocalypse was four-fifths visible again, counting the Vultyrie.

Or, from the looks of things, it had added four new stars. Or even that Dark Star Sedon was seemingly hunkering down, alone and comparatively dull, in the northeast quadrant. Pusan was all but pissing herself, pointing due west, into the southwest quadrant of the night's sky.

Exclaimed: "That'll teach him for masterminding the Cosmic Express."

The brightest star in the Sedon Sphere that night was no longer Dark Sedon.

=========

Sedonda, 7 Tantalar 5980

Days after those in the Zebranid Leper Colony — as they realized almost immediately, due to the entirely unexpected absence of a returned star — prematurely celebrated end-problem-Pyrame high up in the Whiplash Range's mountain meadow, Island Leviathan was still suffering from intense intestinal discomfort.

Wasn't doing very well brain-wise, either. Had, for a whale, a concomitantly even more throbbing, whale of a headache. Found himself drifting dangerously close to shore. Beaching not being on his barnacle-bucket-list, as friend Fish might fishify, he spout-spewed. Felt immensely better, physically and especially mentally.

Spume wafted westward, toward the Prison Beach of Incain.

========

There, on the All, as well as windswept beach, Tsishah Twilight and Pusan Wanderlust were jointly walking the hodgepodge, doggish thing who had unilaterally decided, millennia earlier, to reject Ginny the Gynosphinx and name itself All the Invincible. It was, the Aortic and the proclaimed deviant (not a devic suicide) knew, because it was one of a number things they were talking about, the morning of Sunday, the 7th of December 1980 beyond the Dome.

They truly did have much to discuss, too. The lack of Pyrame's star finding its way back upstairs being one of the least important. Events had overtaken them. Much more than that, actually. The consequences of their comparatively moderate, personal involvement in the diversion of the Cosmic Express, immediately after its launch, into the Cathonic Zone exactly a week previously were threatening to overwhelm them.

So much had gone right at first, then everything suddenly started to go wrong, very wrong. Crystallion, Sharkczar, Hell's Horsemen, their atomic firedrakes, whatever had happened to Sheba-Strife and Solomon-Daemonicus, absolute madness had set in out there, and now it looked like they were all – along with All – about to become complicitous in the slaughter of everyone still alive on the Outer Earth's Centauri Island, launch site of the Cosmic Express.

(Turned out Strife was indeed a long bodiless, devic Spirit Being, one without a power focus. In that she was like Pyrame; was additionally a {very} much higher born but, equally so, myrionymous Mithradite: Fitna Marutia, Kanin Marut, Kore-Eris, Kore-Discord, she of the Golden Apples of same. Unlike Pyrame, she dare not return to the Inner Earth; would be ill-starred the instant Dark Sedon detected her presence. He hated her that much.)

This was supposed to be the Age of Byron; had been since the Disunition of the Unities, which ended the Age of Lazareme as the 55th Century of the Dome ran down. Yet Star Byron now shone out of the night's sky. They'd witnessed it bursting out ever so brightly the night before from their vantage high up in the Whiplash Range, from the Zebranid Leper Colony established there in the early Fifties.

It wasn't until well after dark that Treat (Aortic Amphitrite) far-spoke them with an explanation as to why that was. She was still in Subcranial Temporis, beneath Sedon's Scalp, his bald spot, tippy-top of the Hidden Headworld. The Bright Battle upstairs having ended Sapienda (Thursday) morning with the extinguishment or expulsion of Star Yajur from the night's sky, she and her fellow Aortic – Lakshmi Arthadot's equivalent of a godmother, if not an idol – had gone there via witch-stones. Which was also how she far-spoke them.

Tsishah beat a hasty retreat in order to avoid losing her skin more so than her mind, whereas Pusan stayed behind down here due to the need to keep All company and on track to do what she had to do, but Treat didn't dare. While a mother wasn't required to attend the party for a daughter's 18th birthday on the 5th; a mother was expected to be there for her anticipated wedding the next day, the 6th.

The one, the birthday, happened. So long as you were alive that long you turned 18 regardless of whether there was a party. The other, the wedding, albeit not to Senator Sophiscient Barson, didn't. But so much else did. Now, thanks primarily to Treat, they also knew the reason Constellation Apocalypse was all but full again, even had four never before seen stars in it.

The reason called themselves the Damnation Brigade. The members of this D-Brig were Outer Earth supranormals, apparently back in action again after 25 years in Limbo. One of them, Blind Sundown, was the father of Tsishah Twilight's demon. Another was his mount, a very special ravendoe; one who could actually fly on talarial wings just like ravendeer of Inner and Outer Earth legend, be they bucks, does or fawns, supposedly could thousands of years gone now.

Plus, mere moments earlier, Tsishah's Morrigan of a mother (Morgianna long Sarpedon) had far-spoken them, via witch-stones, that Sundown and four members of this D-Brig of his, including Raven, had suddenly shown up in Hadd in order to fight alongside friend Fisherwoman and the forces of the Living against those of (yes, she was back again, after 35 years) Nergal Vetala's Dead Things.

Neither mother – not Lakshmi's, nor Tsishah's – had formulated much in the way of a firm conviction as to why the night's sky, the Sedon Sphere, had been blazing so brilliantly throughout the nights of Demetray and Birhym last. However, both Tsishah and Pusan already had more than just a notion it had something to do with who and what was on the Moon. That was why Pusan in particular had been sticking to All since Sapienda.

Long distance radio transmitters built into the She-Sphinx millennia ago were their lone method of contacting Moon's Angel, arguably the singly most powerful ally they had in the furtherance of this unfortunately very long term, potentially even futile, Panharmonium Project of theirs. Despite all their efforts – despite all of All's efforts, better make that – she remained as annoyingly non-communicative as she had been all week. Something else to blame on the launching of the Cosmic Express, no doubt.

On top of that, and so much more, Aortic said to deviant, there was a squall blowing in from Tempestuous Psychron. What to do?

"Find shelter," responded the Traveller, who was holding onto the doggish thing's leash. "And I don't mean in your personal Shelter."

That was something else witches could do with their once again fully function-al witch-stones: conjure otherwise exclusive hideouts for themselves in the Weird. Truly skilled witches – and as the lone non-Lemurian Aortic of Shenon, in effect the president of all the Whole Earth's Sisterhoods, Tsishah was a truly skilled witch – could even hide stuff on and about themselves, for example in their bottomless bags, that they could then materialize at will.

"Wait a minute," pointed Tsishah. "Out there, there's a whale. He's huge. He's what's spewing the squall. That's Fish's Island Leviathan!"

Suddenly a lightning-bolt-whip, the leash the Traveller, the between-space Trailblazer, was holding, crackled electric. Pusan dropped it. The leash filled up like a fireman's hose and drained itself, albeit not with water. All, the mismatched thing, suddenly transmogrified, reared up on its evidently extendable, crocodile hind legs; became a wings-sprouting, leontocephalic approximation of her original manifesta-tion from going on 7,000 years gone by.

She-Sphinx, most of that time no longer Ginny the Gynosphinx, said: "Isn't it past time you two start soothsaying? You don't, I'll have All eat you."

"Pyrame!" cried Pusan. Her shepherd's crook was aglow with Brainrock luminescence. She was about to take herself elsewhere, anywhere elsewhere, through the Grey, the Weird, the dark grey matter of between-space. Typical of her. Typically of Tsishah, despite her age, 46, and hybrid-humanity, she wasn't going anywhere. Unless it was into All.

Subtle-matter demon-coating made flesh-and-blood humans, or humanoids, just as much shape-shifters as devils; they with their solidifying daemonic bodies. The shape Tsishah took was ophidian, serpentine — she was also a trained Ophirant witch. (Ophirants were mainly snake-suckling, occasionally scorpion-tailed natives of Ophir/Moorset, the devic protectorate of Dandset Typhon, a sixth-born Mithradite, on the eastern shore of the Aural Sea, Sedon's Ear, in the mid-range of the Head's occipital region.)

It wasn't of a cowl-headed cobra or Egyptian asp, one of Pyrame's favourite forms. Rather, it was of a rattlesnake. Had a rattle at one end, her butt-end. Didn't a devil have a rattle for a power focus, Pyrame had time to wonder. Then Tsishah had the equivalent of a suction cup at the other end, her face-end. Was there a devil with a plumber's plunger for a Tvasitar-talisman, also had time to wonder Pyrame just as Tsishah clamped, face-to-face, onto her lioness-head.

Whereupon Tsishah's demon, and Tsishah herself, revealed yet another ability. Tsishah wasn't attempting to suck Pyrame out of All; she was sucking herself, her soul-self, into All. Top-drawer witches were good with soul-selves. Wasn't just how they made their between-space psychopomps. That was just the start of it.

All held devils, dozens of devils. That wasn't what the Dual Entities built her to do much more than sixty-five hundred years previously. Wasn't what they'd built her male equivalent, the Outer Earth's wingless, but enormous, albeit millennia-moribund, Osiris or Giza sphinx, to do either. Was, however, what both sphinxes became good at once the Entities realized devils had come to the then Whole Earth, this more than seven hundred years pre-Dome.

Pyrame had been stuck inside it, Andy the Androsphinx, for hundreds of years. Until years, probably not decades, after the Genesea, the Great Flood of Genesis, sooth to think if not to say. She wasn't going to let that happen again. Might not be able to do anything about it. Matters were complicating exponentially.

As suicidal as it could be for someone her unfit age, the astonishing assault of Tsishah's soul-self on All's front-brain was enabling the devils All held onto, first of all, to awaken and, second of all, to stream forward from All's back-brain. The Aortic seemed prepared to do whatever she could to ensure Pyrame didn't take over All.

To counter the threat coming from the non-Vanthysces, virtual vastness of All's between-space back-brain, Pyrame brought to bear the full force of her very impressive will-to-win on All's front-brain. Her determination, her resolve to prevail, proved too much for the Aortic. Tsishah was repelled; was, in her altogether human form again, back beyond her, bum skidding on the sand, in the merest of moments.

Pyrame allowed herself a figurative pat on All's back. Her self-congratulatory mental gesture was premature. The fauna (Goat, Traveller, Trailblazer) wasn't bending over Tsishah because she'd lost their clash of wills. Was bending over her because the Aortic was hurt; from the looks of things hurt badly, perhaps terminally.

Maybe Tsishah had been suicidal. She was obviously well past her prime. Plus, the thrust of her assault was daemonic, not witchy. Even the highest level Hecate-Hellion hardcases like her mother Morg paid a severe price for dealing with demons, either spelling. Tsishah might have been a Morrigan once; not anymore. Might she die in front of her, in front of All, thereby disgustingly dirtying All's pristine beach? Might Pyrame proceed to ill-star automatically for howsoever-inadvertently killing a lesser being?

Crabs burrowed out of the sand; dozens of them, more like hundreds. Of course they would. That was how Pusan Wanderlust worked her healing hoodoo. She laid on hands: a hand in the case of Tsishah Twilight; fingers in the case of the little crabs. The fauna thereby divvied up and fractionally expunged Tsishah's affliction into the crabs. It wouldn't be enough to affect them overly negatively, but they'd be feeling a mite poorly for a few days.

As for Tsishah, she was visibly feeling better almost instantly. With only a glance back at her, them, which Pyrame took to be more of a warning than resignation, and a baton-swing of her shepherd's crook, Pusan took them both away. Pauper let them go; had no real interest in trying to stop them anymore. She had her victory. Had control of All as well.

Next question was, what was she to do with her? Besides reassert All's containment of the dopey devils within her, that is. Which didn't prove too difficult a task. All was superb at what she did and Pyrame was superb at controlling All. Always had been. Well, not always. When you're an undying, physically unaging, shape-shifting immortal, always was a very long time. Still, most of six thousand years often felt like always.

That said – that thought, rather – she was at her best when she was controlling All's creator, the Female Entity. Which she had been, with a few absolutely unintentional, and far too lengthy blips, from 5908 until she was cathonitized, for a final time, in 5950. Which in turn, and hardly for the first time since her escape from the Sedon Sphere, reminded her of another thing Baaloch Hellblob told her in Pandemonium. The time-tumbling Dual Entities were back on the Whole Earth for what was apparently his hundredth lifetime.

Lord Lazy claimed he didn't know where they were and neither did the She-Sphinx; not that Pyrame could glean anyhow. All did know a whole lot of other things and, by that afternoon, so too did Pyrame Silverstar. As she had already assumed, they – that idealistic band of entirely mortal witches and mostly female, thought-immortal Master Devas – were back at it, this interminable Panharmonium Project of theirs. Probably never hadn't been at it.

The term stemmed from a 500-year period between roughly 5000 and 5500 YD. It was the height of the freewheeling Age of Lazareme; a time when his Unities and their lord laziest, as well as totally laissez-faire, father oversaw an unheard of era of peace, love and comparative good fellowship on the Hidden Headworld.

It then, and the witches' – and not just the witches' – reinvention of it now, was called Panharmonium mostly in honour of Harmony (Datong Harmonia), reputedly the first born of the firstborn. (Thrygragos Lazareme, aka Thrygragos Everyman, was himself the first of the six Great Gods generated by the Moloch Sedon at, since it was so long ago, what might as well have been the dawn of time.) The lone female Unity's soothing influence on her father and brothers was such that it should have been ascribed her Age, not anyone else's.

Today's version of Panharmonium-yet-to-come differed from the Lazaremists' Panharmonium that had come, and gone, in that it didn't rely on even the highest born Master Devas for enforcement. They had no intention of seeking to revive or replace the Unities. Nor did they wish to reverse the consequential decrepitude of their sunshiny father Lazareme, who never recovered from Harmony's murder by Chaos (while under the sway of the Susasword, one of the Trigregos Talismans).

Pyrame no longer had anything against their plan. After him having treated her like any ordinary devic killer for thirty years, bringing the Moloch Sedon down to earth, as it were, appealed to her. Even the manner in which they intended to do it – by in effect balancing off the three domineering, male Great Gods with incarnations of the Trigregos Sisters, the three, long pre-Earth-lost, simultaneous mothers of Master Devas like her – made a degree of sense.

It had just never struck her as too likely. Even if, after yesterday's events in Temporis and, according to All, above it in Sisert, only one of the Thrygragos Brothers was alive and (presumably) on the Head, it still didn't. Nevertheless, back during Master Kyprian's long reign, when her pre-Fish protégé, the so-called Celestial Superior (Celeste Mannering in here, Celestine D'Angelo out there), was at the pinnacle of her abilities, she'd somehow sensed them getting very close — twice.

The first time, in April 1916, she substituted Tralalorn (her brood-sister, whom some claimed was her devic and/or daemonic daughter by Sedon Himself) for one of the three possible Great Goddesses Reborn. Trala made it seem that the girl – on her 7th birthday, the same as the other two – she replaced had died; meaning the witches' Panharmonium Project failed before they could confirm the goddesses had been reborn. The subterfuge was so successful the Moloch Sedon cathonitized her for killing the real little girl even though she'd done nothing of the sort.

The second time, in 5919, with the Mnemosyne 3-Thing by then being humanized by none other than Methandra Thanatos on Frozen Lathakra, the mighty Eye-Mouth mostly in the Sky released her for a shot at atonement. On his instructions, Pyrame promptly took herself and her demon, who'd been ill-starred with her, into the witches' centuries-bred, intended mom Pandora Mannering, who'd been called Hush since birth. (Mostly because she'd never shut up.)

At the same time Granddaddy Sedon went into their intended dad, Augustus Nauroz, Kyprian's grandson via daughter Chryseis and son-in-law Ubris. Instead of Triplet Goddesses, the result was a new Sed-son, Saladin Devason, the current Master of Weir and just possibly the last sedon, small case, residing on the Inner Earth.

Undaunted, early the very next year – though still late 5919 in most of the Hidden Headworld – Master Kyprian, the Celestial Superior (Hush's likeliest mom) and her 'Nubian', Kyprian's selfsame son-in-law, Ubris Nauroz, issued the Summoning of 19/5920. Pandora and Ubris's son Augustus (Chryseis died having him, the future Black Death) had a girl this time: Morgianna nowadays Sarpedon.

Counting their lucky stars – so to speak – that it was only the one, Pyrame and Trala made certain neither of them would ever have another child. By sprinkling transmogrifying faeriedust sprayed out of Trala's power focus, the White Dwarf, over them both, they rendered them the thus far perpetual, seven year old faerie tricksters, Young Life and Young Death.

The witches learned from the error, not to mention the naïveté, of their ways the year before. There was no more eggs in one basket, Pandora's, for them. Instead, they baked their Trigregos buns in more than one oven; many more than one oven: hence the dozens, perhaps even hundreds, of Summoning Children.

Just to frustrate patriarchal devazurs to the point of madness trying to find the ones most dangerous to the status quo, they went so far as to mix up some of the likeliest girl babies born as a result of the Simultaneous Summonings such that Pyrame and her pals, Sedonic deputies the lot, couldn't locate enough of them to prevent three becoming Trigregos. Not that their extraordinary efforts seemed to matter much. By the time she was cathonitized the last time, in 5950, there was no sign of any Triplet Goddesses being reborn, let alone being re-empowered.

(Sedon brought Pyrame, with her daemonic body, upstairs the first time as potentially interminable punishment after he mistakenly thought she'd killed the little girl in the substitution-subterfuge of 1916 beyond the Dome. He only released her when she showed him that the actual child was safe. It meant revealing her greatest secret of the time, but she was an earthy kind of gal. She loved the firmament; hated being a star in the fundament.

(That secret? The 7-year-old, potential Trigregos Sister Reborn was her own half-daughter, via the Memory Entity, whom she was humanizing at the time of both conception and birth. So were the other two. Memory had split the newborns up amongst three exceptional witches to be raised as their own.

(Said witches were Leonora D'Angelo {Celestine and Dolores's probable mother}, Louise born Riel become St Synne {natural mother of Sophia St Synne, eventually D'Angelo and, speculatively, Solace Sunrise, eventually Sorciere & surname Sundown}, and the notorious Hellion Rhea Sangati, she always of the Ararats {Barsine nominally Mandam's grandmother, although that wasn't confirmed until the late Thirties in here}. The children themselves, collectively known as the Trigon Triplets, grew up to become, respectively, Mnemosyne D'Angelo, Cybele St Synne and Eden Nightingale Ryne.)

There was a much better way to humble, moderate or maybe even abolish the devils' grandfather. Her onetime shell, Master Morgan Abyss (the Death's Head Hellion), had figured it out all by her lonesome going on 1200 years earlier, but she'd hardly been the first. The Lazaremists thwarted the Melusine Master's designs on Grandfather because they too had recognized his weakness. Whereupon, once Star Sedon went AWOL way back then – on Mithramas Day 4825, as it happened – they took steps deemed appropriate to turning it to their advantage.

Pyrame going for the same goal in 5950 was at least partially what angered Sedon; what got her cathonitized not so much as punishment as a preventative measure. (So what if she'd been forced to slay the Male Entity. Not that she'd pulled the trigger as such, but that had never been a crime before.) However, as far as she was concerned her consequently losing control of Miracle Memory, while she was in the midst of going for it, was what had left her vulnerable to cathonitization in the first place.

Through All's connection to said Female Entity, one way that it was, she was bound and determined to get a second chance at going for it. And this time, once she had her, the Mnemosyne 3-Thing, wherever she was, even if it was the Moon, she wouldn't lose her. After all, the way she had it figured, Memory had stolen her demon in 5950 and it was long past time she got both of them back.

Got back Miracle Memory and hope she still had her demon, rather; even if it/she was Primeval Lilith, the Demon Queen of the Night, something Pyrame heartily denied.

========

There were two Entities, a male and a female: Helios called Sophos the Wise and the truly miraculous Mnemosyne Machine. What made Machine-Memory so truly miraculous was she could be humanized; could thereupon become Miracle Memory. Demons, debrained or not, mandroids and even homun beings (homunculi), made for and by her, could make her ambulatory. She nonetheless needed devils to occupy in order to wholly humanize herself body, soul and mind.

That did not mean she supported them. Quite the contrary. She, it, one-third of her, was the computerized insides of Trans-Time Trigon. As such she was based on the devil-despising, wannabe devil-destroying, onetime planet-wide Mother Machine of Old Weir System. All of Incain was a ditto to that dot.

So were all the mini machine-moms in the asteroid-sized generational ships that Utopian Trinondevs of, by then, New Weir System, New Weirworld with it, used to chase the Sedonshem, on a find and destroy mission, across the cosmos for multiple millennia. (Some of these last, at least partially stripped before abandonment, formed the land-only perimeter around the Weirdom of Cabalarkon, Sedon's Devic Eye-Land.)

One of Dark Sedon's first acts after his creation, as opposed to procreation – by none other than the Dual Entities themselves, using some situationally significant 'raw material' – was to destroy First Weir's Mother Machine. As much for revenge as anything else, the Female Entity, regardless of whether she was in Machine-Memory or Miracle Memory mode, desired his eradication and the subjugation, if not outright elimination, of the Moloch's nowhere near as mighty devic descendants.

In that, according to memories Pyrame scoured from All anyhow, the Female Entity agreed with Tsishah Twilight's Hellion more so than Athenan inclinations. Then again the Mnemosyne Machine was pretty much subservient herself. Was slave to the whims of Heliosophos, the equally time-tumbling Male Entity, he who had her built in his Third Lifetime and, in large measure, had created Sedon out of said raw material (read: cells; an entire eyeball in fact) taken from a Utopian Scientocrat named Cabalarkon – yes, that Cabalarkon, the Weirdom's as-yet-undying Utopian – in his Fifth.

Which, in terms of cosmic chronology, actually occurred a few decades, maybe even a few centuries, before his third one. Time-tumblers could do that sort of thing. (Couldn't time-travel non-randomly, though. That was impossible.) Too bad Heliosophos was as reckless, and as arguably mortal, as any human. Thus it was the Female Entity was his subordinate in a far more significant way than just in terms of her having to obey his every whim.

Both were as much Brainrock-blessed as they were Gypsium-cursed. The God-stuff – remnants of the Big Bang's Godhead – was as ineffable as it was unknowable, even inconceivable. When he died, it somehow made him go back into the time stream. When he did so, he went randomly, not linearly. And so did she; she carrying Trans-Time Trigon with them.

The Pauper Priestess knew how Heliosophos died that 11th time. She was there. Was even complicit in him being killed — by a boy, a no more than 10-year-old, then wholly human boy. His name was Kadmon Heliopolis. And she, initially occupying what had become of the boy's surrogate mother, dared do nothing to stop him. In truth, should have bent every effort to get the kid out of there before he put himself at risk.

There was a simple reason for that. Simple, albeit only in terms of immediate cause; immensely, bordering on impossibly, complicated in terms of resultant effect(s). She needed him to grow up such that he could be blasted backwards into the time stream for the first time. She would thus ensure her and hers, the devazur race, came into existence many multiple millennia earlier, in the original Weir System.

Destiny, whom she felt certain was finally on her side after a miserable week, would give her a choice this time. Initially, though, she'd have to find the time-tumbling Dual Entities. Then she'd have to somehow prevent him dying a 100th time. But where were they? The two who just left might know and All could fly her to them between-space.

Question was, could she chase them down, Tsishah Twilight and Pusan Wanderlust, through the Weird, the Grey, the universal substance of Samsara? She had to because, as soon as she did, an even more challenging task awaited her. She had to find a way to neutralize him such that he couldn't subjugate Machine-Memory any longer.

That, subjugating Memory, to her will this time, would be her, Pyrame's, job.

=========

'What being, with only one voice, has sometimes two feet, sometimes three, sometimes four, and is weakest when it has the most?' That was the riddle a winged, female sphinx once put to Oedipus Rex, a direct descendant of King Cadmus of Thebes, as the remarkably extensive Cadmean cycle of apocryphal, Ancient Greek story sequences wound down at last.

In legend, less so than myth, Cadmus brought the Phoenician alphabet to Europe, which was named after his sister, Europa, whom mythological Zeus had absconded with in the form of a white bull and swam to Crete, thus instigating the Minoan cycle of same. This time wholly in myth, Cadmus married Harmonia in a ceremony reputedly attended by all the gods, devils that they were.

In reality, Pyrame knew because she was among those there, Datong Harmonia was a devil, the Unity of Balance. And King Cadmus was Heliosophos in his second lifetime.

Apocryphal Oedipus answered: 'A man.'

=========

"Riddle me this," perhaps the same winged, female sphinx queried Tsishah Twilight after she finally tracked the Aortic down late that night. She was in a typically tipi-shaped shelter located in her personal Shelter off the Irache Nation's post-exilic homeland on the northwest coast of the Cattail Peninsula.

"'If boy is father to man, what boy could kill what man and not call it suicide?'"

Like many a witch over a certain age, and with a capacious bottomless bag, Tsishah traveled relatively well. She was lying not just in a small tipi, but on a double bed-sized camp cot that came equipped with blankets as well as, height of decadence, two pillows. She'd taken the braids out of her dark, moderately greying hair, brushed it out and looked to have applied some sort of moisturizer to her skin before she went to sleep.

Might have ladled it on a mite thick because it glistened perceptibly, as if a faint, shiny facemask, the kind used in cosmetic, skin-cleansing treatment. Might also have taken a soporific because it took her a few too many seconds to realize she was no longer alone; something most witches not anywhere near her reputed calibre would have done almost instantly.

Nevertheless, she finally opened her eyes, glassy as they were. Her vision was cloudy, bordering on glaucomatous. She couldn't focus. More evidence of drugs? She blinked, once, twice, thrice. Her mind cleared as soon as her vision did. She regarded the comparatively tiny She-Sphinx squatting on the footstool beside her cot and bedroll.

She responded: "Fuck off, pauper!"

"Wrong. The correct answer for that is *'the boy who wouldn't become the man for another ten lifetimes'*. Let's try a different one, shall we? Where the fuck are they?"

For a high-level witch – and in order to be Shenon's non-Lemurian Aortic Tsishah had to be a very high-level witch, indeed – no place was safer than her between-space Shelter. Should have been safer, make that. Yet Pyrame, through All, had tracked her down. It shouldn't have been possible. She thought she'd thoroughly covered her trail. Had All taken her scent when she tried to take her over; had her soul-self try to take her over, more like?

Must have, because there it was; there both of them were, one in the other: a decathonitized and, consequently, presumably killer-devil in control of a three-eyed, winged, bipedal and leontocephalic She-Sphinx instead of the other way around. A She-Sphinx who, were it any other devil, would have, should have, eaten her.

As for Pyrame it seemed to her that, as soon as Tsishah overcame her shock, she must have mentally mulled over her situation and realized it was time to talk true. Which she did. Spoke forthrightly. Claimed she was not privy to everything Machine-Memory did, let alone intended to do, but did warn her, in another peculiarly enigmatic turn of phrase, that the Female Entity could finally become human without occupying an extant devil. Perhaps even more remarkably, her male counterpart was now supposed to be unkillable.

(The Dual Entities seemingly believed they not only possessed devils they took over in his most recent lifetime, in what amounted to today's future, but were in control of them. That they weren't extant therefore meant only that they were yet to be. This despite the fact the future devils had current selves, albeit ones shining out of the night's sky above the Hidden Headworld upon their return in 5975.)

With respect to where the Entities were and what they were doing there, the Aortic said they were on the Moon attempting to render humanity, at least humanity beyond Cathonia, immune to devic possession. Once that was accomplished they would return their attention to the Head and renew their ages-old efforts to correct the mistakes they made in his fifth lifetime. Miracle Memory – Moon's Angel, as Tsishah and her witch pals in the Panharmonium Project were calling her these days – had merely jumped the gun somewhat.

Now would Pyrame kindly fuck off? How was that for a polite request? She really wasn't up to the kind of exertions she'd tried to put her body through today.

Wasn't up to much at all, sooth said; other than to stay lying down.

The Cosmic Express was the Female Entity's idea? Hardly, the apparent Irache told her. That was mostly Great Byron's doing. He sent it into the Cathonic Dome? No, that was the Thanatoids of Lathakra's idea. And they had accomplished it largely thanks to All of Incain, whose link to the Outer Earth was well-known to devils and non-devils alike.

Except, other than me, Pyrame said, no devil dare use All as a gateway through the Dome. She'd just imprison them. So the Thanatoids had to rely on human allies. Who were they? Us, said Tsishah. And it wasn't like we and ours had to go to the Egyptian Sphinx first. All found and raised a Krachlan shipwreck sunk with a cargo hold loaded full of Brainrock mined up at Sedon's Peak, in the middle of the peninsula, Sedon's Ponytail; got it to go through the Dome, ship and all, back and forth, and all this in the last year.

True, one of our agents did have to go to Egypt in order to start setting things up a few years ago. That'd be Sheba Faerieflight, who wasn't even born when you were last around, but is currently both the Korant and the Mariamnic Ventricular of Shenon. Her twin brother, Solomon Taurson, who's taken to calling himself Daemonicus of late, is another involved in coordinating our activities on the outside. At the same time, Moon's Angel charged me and my fellow Athenan War Witches with keeping All in line, in here, during her absence out there.

Daemonicus, Silverstar wondered aloud, my Daemonicus, Judge Warlock? Primeval Lilith's Daemonicus, said Tsishah, the original Demon King. Remember him? Probably not. You were stuck in Andy the Androsphinx, the Giza or Osiris Sphinx, the one on the outside before there was an outside, for most of that time, weren't you? You'd definitely remember lethal Lily, wouldn't you? If it was meant as a jibe, Pyrame via All didn't seem at all fazed.

Taurson's Daemonicus is the Demon King Dark Sedon, who took his place, debrained during Ragnarok a couple of hundred years before Xuthros Hor unleashed the Genesea. Whereupon, out of necessity, the Moloch raised the Cathonic Zone out of his own essence in order to preserve what was to become his Headworld, the archipelago of Pacifica, the Places of Peace, as well as Eden's Zoo. What was left of Lilith's Daemonicus anyhow; an essentially hollow shell of a man-demon anyone who knew how could put on.

One and the same, said Tsishah, thus confirming in Pyrame's mind what she had been suspecting since Baaloch Hellblob told her the Dual Entities had time-tumbled back to the planet for their 100th Lifetime together a few years earlier. Machine-Memory was indeed unoccupied by any currently extant devil. Fact of the matter was – had to be – Memory wasn't occupied by any devil whatsoever.

She'd taken Pyrame's demon – whom everyone else seemed to believe was none other than pre-Ragnarok's King Daemonicus's distaff side, Primeval Lilith, the Demon Queen of the Night – with her into the time stream the moment Heliosophos was killed for the 11th time; the time that began in 19/5908.

(Apparently these selfsame every ones, clearly including Tsishah Thrae, reckoned she'd lied so often about never having Lethal Lily she'd convinced herself that was the truth. And maybe she had; made a Big Lie factual, to herself anyhow. Maybe upwards to six thousand years of personal pride, her own supreme sense of self-worth, had persuaded her the Moloch Sedon kept returning for her, not her demon.)

Killed, irony upon irony, by his first self. Whom Pyrame had been forced to instantly take over in order to get them both safely out of Trans-Time Trigon as it too went into the time stream. Had to, if only to preserve their immediate and future existences. Presumably Memory still had hold of Lilith, if it really was her, and was using her to humanize herself.

And that was yet another reason for Pyrame to get to Machine-Memory. So she could get hold of her demon and thereby became independently solid again.

"Think demon-devious to the extreme," advised the Aortic who, unlike Sinistral Sloth, could not read Pyrame's mind. "First, the Unmoving One and his thoroughly kept clandestine spawn, be they possessive or homun-hidden, help a bunch of the Outer Earth's genius-calibre scientists and mega-billionaires construct the Cosmic Express."

(Samarand, even before the Mighty Moloch moved it, until then Sedon's Tongue, to the other side of the Head, was a hotbed of homun beings, deliberately-made homunculi once used as expendable soldiers. Not surprisingly since its scientific practitioners were mostly descended from star-trekking, Trinondev techno- and biomages.)

"Its mission, from Bodiless Byron's perspective anyhow, is to scout the stars looking for another world suitable for devazurs. The Thanatoids find out about it; the Great God may even have told them. Or had his Beast, Rufous Rudra Silvercloud, a drinking buddy of old King Cold, or his sexually dichotomous Stallion, Chimaera Glimmenmare, likewise, at least up until the early Thirties, do it for him. In any event they determine to divert the Express into the Dome.

"Their intent is to free their nearly fifty years' cathonitized, fourth generational devic children — the ones they started having after you were confined to the night's sky in the mid-Teens and Miss Myth got hold of the Female Entity, whilst Tantal did a ditto with Heliosophos. And not for the first time either; not even for the first time this century. They intended to bring them back to the Head, at least for the short term in possession of cosmicompanions like your Nehrini Purandar."

(Pyrame knew that Trans-Time Trigon landing on Lathakra in 5908, after causing what came to be known as the Tunguska Incident on the Outer Earth, was what woke the Thanatoids from their Thousand Year Sleep. She got Miracle Memory on the rebound, as it were, from Methandra Thanatos after the latter realized she was no longer Mithras's Virgin, at least in part because Tantal woke up moments before her and got cuddly.

(As for who got Herr Hel Helios, because of what ensued immediately thereafter, she'd always assumed it was Grandfather Sedon. Whoever it was didn't hang around after Pyrame-Memory got pregnant almost immediately and they quickly gleaned it was with three deviant females – the Trigon Triplets – and not a new generation of Master Devas … yet.)

"And for the long term?"

"Haven't the foggiest," the Aortic informed the untrustworthy, not particularly highborn Master Deva, warming to the topic. (Her protestations in the Cattail's Zebranid Leper Colony to the contrary, Pyrame was notoriously unreliable. Did she really believe anyone else found her denial of the identity of her demon as Lilith convincing? Or that Tralalorn wasn't her demon child, not her devic brood sister? Both stretched credibility.)

"And Klannit, our go-between with her parents, who would never deign to speak to lowlife mortals like us, hasn't been forthcoming."

"Klannit, the Thanatoids' mutual azura, their Haunted Angel, of course," said Pyrame, through All. "She was the nearly naked one in the Zebranids' longhouse, wasn't she; the one I figured had to be wearing an illusion because it was so cold up there. I never made the connection because every time I've come across her in the past she was occupying a low-watt sentient. Or one of those otherwise brainless homos they manufactured over in Samarand for Byronic azuras to be-brain."

"You're showing how long you've been gone, Pyrame. First, in your absence Samarandin biomages learned to manufacture homos for humans as well as azuras. Second, homos are more correctly referred to by their proper name, homunculi, these days, though I like what Jordy calls them." Jordy – Jordan 'Q for Quill' Tethys, the Legendarian – was a recurring deviant whom Pyrame counted among her best, perhaps even only, friends.

"Which is?"

"Homun beings. Kind of cute, wouldn't you say. Homos, I've been given to understand, is a degrading term for homosexuals in Godbad and beyond the Dome."

"And the correct term for homosexuals is?"

"Gays and lesbians; gays being the male variety, I think."

"Hmm," Pyrame-All considered, resisting the temptation to make a socially incorrect, not to mention sidetracking, comment. Had another question, instead: "You gave me a 'first' and a 'second'. Let's try for a 'third' shall we. Was she or wasn't she wearing an illusion, one of those glamours you witches are so fond of casting?"

"You're anticipating me. I hope that doesn't mean you're reading my mind. But, hey, you're a duplicitous devil, so you probably are. That being the case, why bother with a conversation at all? Even if it's through All." (One the most despicable traits devils had was their mind-over-mind mastery of most mortals. While witches' were supposedly protected against possession, for someone like Tsishah, with all her training, having her mind read without the courtesy of a warning was, well, galling.)

"Do not tempt fate, Aortic. I'm in All, not some specialized, brain-boggling mandroid I can't get out of this time. I'll admit you're unexpectedly skilled when it comes to hiding your thoughts, but I realized the moment I found you so readily, you in your own between-space Shelter of all places, that there was a reason for that.

"You're a living trap, a human trap, maybe even deviant trap, though I doubt that. Only, I've got news for you. The trap you set is for you, not me. Might be different had you any ringots about you, but you don't. I checked. Third eyes are ever so useful, I'm sure you'd agree, and I always check for them after what the Death's Head Hellion did to me all those centuries ago.

"Ensorcelled witch-stones, like the ones you and your minions wear, like the one you're trying so artlessly to suck me into, are just variations on Utopian eye-orbs. They have no effect on me. Sedon's Teeth, girl, when I was possessing Machine-Memory, long before we devils arrived on the Whole Earth, I invented the damn things. So I can go directly into your mind anytime I please; take possession of you, dot-ditto.

"And why wouldn't I? You're wearing a debrained demon, that's my temptation. It would make me solid again. I overrode a bebrained demon once, the Demon Queen of the Night, you might recall from your witchcraft's textbooks, even if they're wrong. I go into you, your thoughts, all of your thoughts, become mine. As does your demon. As does you.

"Another thing you might want to keep in mind, Aortic, is that devil-possession is a whole lot more healthful than azura-possession. You let me in, you discard or, better yet, you subsume Klannit Thanatos, which you should have no problem doing if you are such a high-grade hag, I'll make you as unkillable as you say Heliosophos is nowadays, up there on the Moon with, you seem to think, a future Lightning Lord inside him.

"Take that message back to your Miss Myth of mother, azura. Now let me speak to Tsishah Thrae directly."

"Who do you think you have been, priestess?" said Tsishah, in someone else's voice. "It just took me a while to get back with my instructions." Whereupon she, the Aortic, went all glassy-eyed again. Whereupon Pyrame Silverstar saw herself, saw All, reflected in those selfsame glassine – make that mirrored – eyeballs of hers.

Whereupon she – only a spirit being herself when without a debrained daemonic body – was sucked into not so much Tsishah Twilight as her demon. Who, in life, had once been Shahiyeda either Sunrise or Sundown, daughter of barely pubescent Solace and John. Who as well, like a serpent its skin, promptly shed herself off her previous husk and, Pyrame inside her, went through between-space on one of Tsishah's witch-stones to somewhere else.

Evidently Destiny, capitalized, if not personified, still wasn't on Silverstar's side. As for All and Tsishah, the latter, Klannit still in her, rode the former back to Shenon, where she took to her bed immediately, in hopes of the Thanatoids' Haunted Angel continuing to work her own version of a healing hoodoo on her internally.

Hopes that Klannit might or might not have shared had her mother Methandra not required her back on Lathakra to help resume the search for her missing sibs, the ones beside Demon Land and Aires, who were already back on the Frozen Isle. Klannit's mirrors may yet prove more effective in that regard than Metisophia's purloined cauldron. (Lazareme's Wisdom, in addition to being a full time Spirit Being these days, was Jordan Tethys's devic half-mother.)

Pyrame had been right about one thing. Master Devas were much better at that sort of thing than their azuras.

========

Tsishah's demon wasn't altogether debrained.

She had enough, call them residual, be-brains left to contest against the Pauper Priestess for dominance over their now forcibly shared being.

=========

The Pauper Priestess had won one of those struggles before, much more than six millennia earlier. Then, after hundreds of years of trying, she finally asserted her will over that of the Demon Queen Lilith, or whomever she had hold of and wanted again. At that time they were both confined within the absolutely capacious Osiris Sphinx, the by then already moribund, hence seemingly all-stone same that still stood on the Giza plateau not far from Egyptian Heliopolis, the Biblical City of On.

(After which – unless it was Baalbek, the Lebanese Heliopolis – the Crete-based Heliopolis family took its surname, howsoever many centuries later. After which also, combined with the much more ancient, Egyptian On-specific, Sed Ceremony, Sedon himself may have intuited the name he gave himself in Heliosophos's fifth lifetime.)

The Headworld's former Perpetual Presence (adult, female) won the battle this time, too; a whole lot quicker as well. Managed to open her three eyes. Realized where she was: Absudyl, once Minius, but always the subterranean Land of the Mandroids, where All got its raw material. Spotted, in the distance, the onetime tiny, tri-peaked islet of Aegean Trigon.

What was now Trans-Time Trigon – had been for a dozen years; plus a hundred lifetimes for Heliosophos and the multiple millennia they encompassed – glowed with the luminescence of Brainrock-Gypsium. It resolved itself into a visage; one that was sort of hers, except it had dark instead of silver hair. Was that of Miracle Memory, Machine-Memory humanized. It spoke.

"Afraid I can't afford to let you twiddle your thumbs literally, old timer. But I can let you twiddle them figuratively. Bide your time, I may have use of you later."

"And until then?" thought but couldn't say Pyrame Silverstar.

Humanized Memory, her tremendous visage simultaneously blanking as it reddened both alarmingly and indicatively, hesitated; didn't answer. Something was happening to her, Moon's Angel, on the Moon. Must mean someone, perhaps a devil, was trying to take her over; to displace the Demon Queen – if it was her – as she did so.

Was that her, walking over her grave, she and Shah's, two in one, their final resting place, moments later? Had to be. Or so it seemed.

=========

Here in Absudyl, Stopstone shit, the stuff of mandroids, Godcrud to many devils, most commonly called Solidium on the other side of the Dome, rose up to engulf her, en-case her: Pyrame Silverstar, she being inside Tsishah's demon. Hardened her, two-in-one her, them, within itself.

The Pauper Priestess, once Providence, had enough time to additionally think to herself, to think to Tsishah's demon as well, just how tired she was of it being end-prob-lem-Pyrame.

Then it was, yet again.

****

Who or what was striving to take over Machine-Memory wasn't so much told as implied during "<u>Nuclear Dragons</u>". Who or what it was wasn't implied at all in "Helios on the Moon". Was made explicit. Not so in the comic books. That aspect of *Phantacea Phase One* had just started to wind down in Phantacea Four. It was supposed to end conclusively in Phantacea Seven.

Unfortunately, only six of its 32-page script ever got drawn. They were printed for the first time in the 2013 *'Phantacea Revisited'* graphic novel entitled "Cataclysm Catalyst".

PART THREE – ACQUIRING NIHILA

Games 11: **Noticing Nothing**

========

<u>Mithrada, 8 Tantalar 5980</u>

Even in an unheard-for-Hadd deluge of near-biblical proportions, facially Fisher-woman (born Scylla Nereid) looked good in a glowingly golden, chainmail fishnet.

========

Plus, there was nothing better against incoming, oversized vultures ridden by Sangazur-animated Dead Things firing modern ordnance, helicopter gunships lower down, Godbadian warplanes higher up and, yes, even a few missiles, no matter what they were tipped with, than teleportive Brainrock-Gypsium chains transmuted into an acreage-covering umbrella composed of said Godstuff, one that shimmered as if akin to multi-coloured Northern Lights.

Of course, being impossibly huge, so much so that her webbed feet straddled either side of Diminished Dustmound, there was no way that could just be Fish (officially Lady Achigan, onetime Queen Scylla of Godbad). For another, she ordinarily didn't have, let alone display, a third eye.

And while it was true she'd managed to acquire, and keep hold of, no less than three devic power foci in her sixty-odd – very odd – years of deviant life, one of them was not, and never had been, a Borealis Brolly. Evidently lost was Scylla Nereid; evidently found was Nihila Nereid.

========

Far below her, below even shockingly diminished Dustmound, UD, Yehudi Cohen, the Untouchable Diver, an Outer Earth supranormal in effect reconstituted after most of twenty-five years in what he'd still thought of as Limbo, reached out of the sodden, collapsing ground, grabbed what he had to and kept on soil-swimming away from the pursuing Indescribables, some of whom had to be daemonic moles.

Make that demonic moles; being a quick study he would have been able to spell it properly, too. Didn't doubt they were man-eaters. Above and behind them, the severed skull's until then not-so-miraculously-extended tongue muscling itself/himself toward those selfsame targets finally gave up the ghost; animating Sangazur that it was in proper terminology.

The lights went out in his eyes. Endgame evermore, Susano Mikoto.

========

"God curse all Antheans. Their illusions and their spells!"

========

That was Wildman Dervish Furie.

Blind Sundown couldn't believe his ears. He'd never heard Furie shriek before, but he recognized the voice. No, wait, it wasn't so much Furie, the Dervish, as the Murray, maybe even the Jervis. And neither of the latter had a next-to-impervious hide, nor an exclusion zone such as he and Raven's Head; Wakinyah Thundercloud Creatures of the Cosmos that they were. Hence their continuing existence amidst all this mad death and mayhem. And not just here on the Head, but far too often throughout their lives.

He was truly blind without Raven to see through. (She'd tossed him when they thought he had better than decent shot at finishing off what had become of Cyborg Cerebrus's probable slayer, Mars Bellona, War, the Apocalyptic thereof.) Having missed Bellona due to the latter's teleportive talent for getting out of the way of incoming human missiles, he stood all but abandoned on the flats over which Dustmound once towered; though beneath today's thus far unending drenching it more like pimpled.

The cry of frustration, as much as anything else, came from up what was left of the hummock: an enormous, centuries old, open air cemetery piled high with remarkably never decomposing dead bodies. Until the rains hit not much more than an hour earlier, that is. As such it was too far away for him to do anything in time to prevent anything grievous befalling his longtime comrade in not just the Damnation Brigade. Or was it?

He could envisage, in his mind's eye, precisely what Furie was doing just after he, OMP, Raven and he himself, Sundown, extracted themselves from the concreting efforts of the hellish Indescribables. Had the where down just as much so. He'd been going after Morgianna Sarpedon. (Who, along with her one-armed 'ringer', Alastor Molorchus, had brought the eldritch earthborn to Dustmound in the first place, presumably from Satanwyck itself, Hell on Earth.)

And he had the wherewithal — in his hands even a power-drained Solar Spear could become a guided missile; albeit one hurled rather than fired per se.

Holding onto his upright, noticeably pointy ears, the slow-to-age Morrigan, Superior Sarpedon, an Inner Earth Summoning Child, white-as-light like all pureblood or almost-pureblood Utopian women, was doing something to her former friend, now furious foeman. Ordinarily a nearly indestructible juggernaut of untamed physical might, the black-skinned supranormal, an Outer Earth Summoning Child like he and the Diver, was going from the Dervish to the Murray to the Jervis in short order. As Jervis he would be completely normal.

Sundown may be sightless without anyone to hold onto, but his other senses were so heightened – he wouldn't be a supra if they weren't – he didn't need to see them in order to as good as launch his missile not just at her. It caught the former White Witch in the upper back, just below her neck. It stuck into her only shallowly; ergo, she must have taken in just enough of Furie's hard hide to save her own, howsoever-momentarily.

Still, it did stick and it being a spear flung with supranormal force, even a blunted blow should have killed her instantly. That it didn't was extra testament to the tremendous power she claimed as both the Hecate-Hellions' latest Morrigan as well as the Athenan War Witches' Superior. Of course it helped that her now shredded pantsuit was a debrained demon. That the Cheyenne's devastating weapon inevitably would kill her, very soon, indicated just how much in the way of vestigial power his Solar Spear yet retained.

Eyes bulging, her immediately impending death being all they beheld, she released the Murray on the cusp of becoming the Jervis. Falling to her knees, she grasped futilely for the spear grotesquely sticking out of her upper back. Obligingly Gentleman Jervis Murray yanked it out of her, no doubt considered driving it through her treacherous skull, thereby ending her menace once and for all time, then perhaps unthinkingly, dropped it beside her.

The Inner and the Outer Earth Summoning Children exchanged glances. It was almost as if Morgianna, whom he'd known since the late Thirties, was attempting to apologize to him; to say sorry, to beg his forgiveness, for her trying to kill him. No words came forth; wasn't much point in words by then. Besides, he wasn't the forgiving sort.

As she pitched forward into the ominously bubbling crypto-crust of Diminished Dustmound, he turned his back on her. Gentleman became Wildman again; went from the Murray to the Dervish. Looked around for some other Dead Thing to rip apart. There were plenty available down-slope and on the plain off-slope, so that settled that.

D-Brig weren't supposed to kill and, other than Blind Sundown and Raven's Head on their Vengeance Quest, never knowingly did; not even in self-defense. Still, you can't kill what's already dead. He, especially his never-seen Full Furie aspect, was beginning to like this place. He'd leave Morg for the buzzards — the regular, normal-sized ones, not the gigantic Vultyrie that made up the living Cloud of Hadd.

So preoccupied was he, the Wildman failed to notice that hardly all the awfulness accumulated atop Dustmound during today's latest battle between the Living and the Dead was blood, bone and chunks of already rotting flesh; Haddit zombies previously animated by Vetalazurs that couldn't hold together anything in the torrential downpour. Much of it was the demonic remains of hers and Molorchus's Indescribables, deformed splats of Subtle Matter akin, if not precisely kin, to Morg's pantsuit-demon.

As if she, the Morrigan, was calling to it, the chthonic crud oozed about her. In the pelting rain, with freshly slain and not yet altogether ruined corpses being reanimated by Sangazurs lately fled from their former home turf, the Bloodlands, New Valhalla, no one paid any attention as her body started adding to itself, layer by layer, hardening.

She continued to ameliorate herself; was forming a cocoon, a chrysalis, about her being, when Dustmound finally finished collapsing in on itself, all but burying her in a resultant pit.

========

Superior Sarpedon was born Morgianna Nauroz nearly sixty years ago in 5920 Year of the Dome. Upon her adoption by Kyprian Somata she was declared a Somata. At the time Kyprian — called Copperhead by some for her, by them, deemed treasonous dealings with mostly female Master Devas on the Panharmonium Project – was the Master of the Weirdom of Cabalarkon. (Sometimes thought of as Weir on Earth, it was a devil-free zone making up the entirety of Sedon's Devic Eye-Land on a map of the Headworld.)

Kyprian's children were all dead by then, but Morg's father was Augustus Nauroz. His mother Chryseis died having him. Chryseis's mother was none other than the selfsame Master of Weir. Decades later, when Morg finally married her long-serving bodyguard, Demios Sarpedon, who, like her, was an Inner Earth Summoning Child, she took his last name.

(Sarpedons as a group were once the so-called Utopia's underclass. That hadn't been the case since they were 'emancipated' by Zalman Somata shortly after he became the Master of Weir in Kamor {July} YD 5476. Zalman and his wife Melina born Tethys, aka the Trigregos Titaness, were the then devil-possessed parents of the Terrible Twins, Janna and Sraddha, both of whom directly or indirectly continued to affect events on the Inner Earth to this day.)

Master Kyprian died, under the usual mysterious circumstances, thirty years ago, in late 5950 YD. She couldn't have picked a worse time. Just as she breathed her last, forces loyal to Pyrame Silverstar were laying siege to Cabalarkon. (Howsoever-ironically, they included both Kronokronos Mikoto and his two thousand, rebellious samurai from Temporis, alongside Tyrtod von Blut and his Lost Legion, whose equally dead, onetime Nazi German fighters, they and their remarkably still running Panzer tanks, were also losing the battle for continuing persistence, more so than survival, on Diminished Dustmound right this minute.)

Her successor, Morg's year older brother, Saladin Devason, broke the siege by turning against his devic half-mother, thus earning the Mastery for himself. (Pyrame ended up ill-starred, cathonitized; ergo he somehow got his devic half-father, the Moloch Sedon, to turn against her, too.) One of Sal's first acts upon acquiring Call-Me-Cabby's throne was to banish his chief rival, her husband, from the Weirdom.

Rather than stay behind, which she could have done, Morg stuck with Dem. She was hardly alone. Like many another Utopian exiled at the same time or shortly thereafter – the survivors of whom eventually helped the Sarpedons found the Zebranid Leper Colony in the Cattail's Whiplash Range – she disapproved of having a devil's half-son as the last fully functional Weirdom's Master.

Morg was just one of many who died that day, presumably never to rise again. Virtually no one shed any tears for her. Not even, once they found out about it, her husband or the youngest of her two children, Andaemyn, 27, both of whom were laid up on Sraddha Isle. Truth was, although it was too early to be sure, Andy might never walk again. As a result, not that they likely would have been so inclined anyways, neither of them were able to participate in the Living's great victory celebration that evening on Sraddha Isle.

If the Morrigan had died, never to rise again, it had not been heroically. In not just her penultimate minutes she was fighting against the Living.

========

The fifth member of the once 10-strong D-Brig on drenched Dustmound that day was Raven's Head.

========

Absolutely inhuman, if not inhumane, she was far beyond a semi-sentient psychopomp with a crow's head, a stag-sized doe's body covered with feathers, not hide, and talarial wings on both sides of the upper part of her four hooves. (Although the terms 'ravendeer', 'ravenbuck' and 'ravendoe' sounded a little like reindeer, other than size-wise she looked more deer-like than reindeer-like. Also had something of the horse about her, particularly in the legs.)

Could speak as well, although Sundown was one of the few who could translate what she said, in that peculiarly chittering, neigh-caw way of hers. The other thing about Johnny's Beauty, as he called her, was that ever since D-Brig encountered their first devils on the Aleutian archipelago's Damnation Isle, hence their name, just over a week earlier (after wasting a quarter century in Limbo, bodies separated from minds), she'd been sprouting a single, unicorn-like, telescoping horn.

As Dustmound collapsing in on itself destabilized the flatlands abutting it on every side, she located her usual rider, Blind Sundown, alone and spear-free some distance away from where she dealt with the dead Field Marshal, Tyrtod von Blut, his surviving crew, also dead, and their panzer, one of dozens the Sangs of the Bloodlands had kept operational over the decades.

Leapt into the air, talarial wings flapping powerfully. Went for him, her Johnny; he having just missed skewering the mostly mindless, yet nevertheless still teleportive Apocalyptic she'd catapulted him towards minutes earlier. Rescued him before he had to battle off any more Dead Things Fighting, now with just his bare hands, legs, no matter how strong, and an ordinary, albeit very sharp, hunting knife.

They, he on her back, spotted OMP-Akbar in the clutches of the Trinondevs' Wyvern of Weir. (Not the Weird, it was no between-space-travelling psychopomp.) This just after they took out what was left of Mars Bellona – the by then imbecilic, Sangazur-animated Apocalyptic of War Sundown had tried to skewer – and he'd thrown off the last of his attackers, most of whom had been Warlord Mikoto's similarly Sangazur-reanimated samurai.

(Remarkably the near-giant remembered very little of his time on the Head. He did recall, almost viscerally, how much he hated his half-brother in Dand Tariqartha; more like quarter-brother, since they only shared the same devic half-father. Did so despite the fact that he was once married to Mikoto's daughter Takeda, who came to be known as Corona Power on the Outer Earth, the supranormal once codenamed Crimson Corona after her talisman.

(Turned out it was one of the {presumably} now destroyed Thrice-Cursed Godly Glories, the pursuit of which had just come to a head, on the Head, here on not yet drenched Dustmound.)

The oversized faerie proved too heavy for the composite Wyvern – a collective casting similar to the way Trinondevs' manifested gargoyles (grotesques) off their individual eye-staves – to carry and fly simultaneously. The Cheyenne Summoning Child hauled him onto and across her back, laying him unceremoniously belly down in front him. Fortunately, Raven was up to the burdensome task of keeping airborne despite their combined weight.

They quickly found the Solar Spear sticking out of the sinkhole subsuming Morg inside her yet-forming cocoon; whereupon it shot up into his hand as if a well-trained dog called to come by its master. Then, despite the cascading rainfall and her own dwindling energy reserves, Raven, following in the wake of the massive Utopian collective, flew them both towards comparative safety on Sraddha Isle, a couple of hundred miles east of Dustmound.

Also fortunately, for devil-slayers and devil-detainers both, Nihila Nereid made no effort to stop them.

(Deva-detesting Trinondev Warriors of Weir, led by Black Skull-Face, the 80-year-old clone whose actual name was Golgotha Nauroz, had joined the fight against the Dead on Master Saladin's behest. The Wyvern of Weir was their latest, collective gargoyle. They'd shredded War with their eye-staves; said shreds were now sucked inescapably into their eyeorbs. Endgame evermore for him too, the last of the Apocalyptics the Byronic Nucleus brought D-Brig to the Head to deal with late Lazam, early Devauray, the previous week.)

As they were leaving the area, the three of them, Sundown seeing through Raven's eyes, spotted Furie rushing along the fracturing plain. He was carrying someone. They assumed it was the Diver. It wasn't. It was Alastor Molorchus, Morg's onetime ringer, her one-armed man. He was a Dead Thing ordinarily animated by a symbiotic Sang. He wasn't that anymore.

He was occupied by Morg's Young Daddy Death, Auguste Moirnoir, as they knew him beyond the Dome from the late Thirties on. Then as now a perpetually 7-year old faerie trickster he called Furie 'son'. Didn't matter that he wasn't; couldn't be — Jerry knew who his parents were, just wasn't sure how he caught the Furie as if a never-ending cold. Young Death believed he had once been Morg's birthfather, Augustus Nauroz. In this he was probably correct.

(The Weirdom's biomages 'developed' Golgotha, the clone leading Utopian forces in Hadd, from genetic material taken from Augustus's undeniable father Ubris, ca 5900 YD. Ubris, in turn, was the 'Nubian' who co-called the Simultaneous Summonings of 19/5920. That he didn't survive it himself had a lot to do with Janna Fangfingers, the remarkably resilient vampire born Janna Somata in the then Weirdom of Kanin City back in 5456 YD.)

Be that as it may, and as useful as an animate Molorchus could be – assuming he could start attracting teleportive Gypsium-Godstuff into himself again, which he might once he was far away from Nihila Nereid – that was the main reason D-Brig 4 weren't celebrating with anywhere near as much gusto as everyone else who'd made it back to the monastery on Sraddha Isle in one piece that night. Which, particularly for OMP-Akbar, was a damn shame.

The brown-robed, shaven-headed Sraddhite Warrior Monks, almost as many of whom were warrior women, made an especially fine pilsner.

=========

"I told you they wouldn't needle-nose-need us," said Fisherwoman, to herself.
"Oh, do stop making things up, child."
"I tuna-belly will, as soon as you release me. And stop calling me child. I'm over sixty years of tears. Besides, I told you, Miracle Memory's my mom; half-mom, I mean."
"And who do you think I am ... minced meat?"
"I'd have said fishmeal."
"Fine. Into which fishing hole should I dump you?"
"I'd have said fucking fish-hole."

"Fucking fish-hole then."
"My fish-lair will do finny fine."
And so she did, separately.
Endgame Nihila Nereid.

========

Today's survivors vastly outnumbered those killed in action, though nowhere near those already dead put permanently out of dot-ditto, action. They, the altogether alive, were already calling their victory D-Day Dustmound. D-Brig-4, once they regrouped on Sraddha Isle and discovered he hadn't preceded them there, just hoped it didn't turn out to be D-Day Diver.

They didn't believe he'd been careless enough to get himself killed. Still, even if they'd turned around and gone back straight away to look for him, they realized there wasn't much hope of finding him, not without Cyborg Cerebrus or Wilderwitch, who had their uses that way. (Not knowing, or remembering, anything about her, Pusan Wanderlust didn't enter their minds in that regard. Jordan Tethys did, but he hadn't hung around Sraddha Isle after the forces of Living had clearly won a famous victory.)

That it was only raining cats and dogs was, admittedly, better than it raining arrows, bullets, shot-apart Vultyrie, falling Dead Things, Godbadian gunships and Outer-Earth-bought or purloined ballistic missiles; all of which, Transformed Fish's Borealis Brolly notwithstanding, it had been a comparatively short while earlier.

Realistically, say he was laying injured somewhere deep beneath caved-in Dustmound, what could they do about it? Nothing; not in the dark; not with the skies above Hadd spilling forth like a burst-open hydroelectric dam and with all that consequential slop underfoot. Sooth said, a lack of lightness and deluge-like weather aside, it wasn't just Raven who had run out of gas. It was all four of them.

What bolstered them, in addition to their knowing he could render himself either untouchable or supra-hard, was their awareness that, included among the Diver's many other ancillary abilities, he didn't need to breathe. Apparently as well, they were informed by the Sraddhites' High Priest, Thartarre Holgatson, another one-armed man, UD had learned how to ingest Brainrock-Gypsium.

Meaning, not at all counter-intuitively, he could also teleport these days; had therefore become as much of a self-psychopomp as Raven had since Limbo. In other words, the Diver could look after himself. Aside from getting themselves all-but-irretrievably stuck in Limbo for a quarter century, they all could.

(The always unofficial Secret War of Supranormals lasted seventeen years, from early 1938 until late 1955. Excepting Limbo, Furie, Sundown and Raven, along with the Diver, survived all of it. As Old Man Power, Akbar only made it through the last ten but, prior to arriving in Hiroshima, unscathed from its A-Bomb, he'd made it through most of perhaps 150 years under one name or another, none of which he recalled. One thing about faeries, no matter how oversized, once they survive birth they can last a very long time, wittingly or not.)

Nevertheless, if the Diver didn't show up overnight, they, D-Brig 4, determined to find a way to go back to Dustmound come morning in order to search for him. He didn't. Despite their best intentions, they didn't go back to Dustmound either. Instead D-Brig 4 found themselves in the Weirdom of Cabalarkon. Which for them was about as happy an ending as they were ever likely to get.

Endgame them … albeit, like Freespirit Nihila, only for the time being.

========

Meanwhile, on the Outer Earth someone who should have swallowed the barrel himself, and then pulled the trigger, murdered John Lennon.

****

Freespirit Nihila, as resurrected Harmony had started calling herself the previous week, broke through Fisherwoman's formidable defenses, her Vesica Piscis foremost, during the course of "Goddess Gambit". That she managed to do so mostly had to do with the ravenous Diver, who had been feeding on Brainrock-Gypsium since "The War of the Apocalyptics".

He'd tried to do the same, ingest her bellybutton bauble, on Sedonda. Only succeeded in weakening its protectiveness. Fish remained possessed of nowadays Nihila, hence Nihila Nereid, during her brief appearance in "Helios on the Moon", wherein the final, howsoever anti-climactic acts in the 5980 War between the Living and the Dead were recounted in detail.

Games 12: **The Diver's Talismans**

========

<u>Demetray, 9 Tantalar 5980</u>

If the Hecate-Hellion's most recent Morrigan (the White Witch, Morgianna born Nauroz, become Somata, then Superior Sarpedon) had died, never to rise again, shortly after midnight that night — ergo into the following day, the 9th — something that looked a lot like her, an exceptionally enormous her, certainly did.

It gurgled, more like belched, out of the fissure into which Morg sank while still cocooning herself.

========

Torrential rain fell incessantly; was a downpour so intense it approximated a skyborn tsunami. Fish couldn't swim in it, not legless ones, but one could and did. Could also stand in it, once she came off a leftover Hellstone dropped by one of ex-Superior's, now Janna St Peche-Montressor's War Witches, one long since re-treated to Sraddha Isle or elsewhere.

Unless she was lying dead or dying nearby. Or it was by Morg herself.

(That Janna, Alpha Centauri's 27-year old, Dukkhan born and raised daughter-in-law, not Janna Fangfingers — dust since the weekend; now likely mingled in the muck irretrievably — had only taken over the Athenan leadership when both Morg and her deputy, an identically-aged Outer Earthling born Garcia Dis L'Orca, couldn't carry on in that capacity. For Morg it was for reasons of daemonic duplicity preceding death. For Garcia it was due entirely to why Morg's Daddy Death, Augustus born Nauroz, only just recently renamed her Dead Dis L'Orca.)

"Humping humpbacked whales!" exclaimed that someone, steadying herself with webbed feet. (Actually only webbed-toes — Nihila hadn't bothered to resupply her with footwear after releasing her late that afternoon.) She gazed up at the enormity that looked so much like her oldest 'friend' in the entire world, both sides of it. "Watery-what have you done now, Morg?"

The enormity dropped a teardrop her direction. Didn't matter Fish was amphibious. Teardrop was spongy solid. She dodged it. It didn't crack. Was a chrysalis.

========

Fish, more correctly Fisherwoman, was the codename Kyprian Somata bestowed on her prior to dispatching then teenage her to the Outer Earth for the first time in the early to mid Thirties. That was where she began her association with the Master's long ago ally on both sides of the Dome: Magister Joseph Mandam, Jesus and Barsine's father of record.

A foundling, her real name, Scylla Nereid, was given to her by Aortic Merthetis, the Lemurian Quarter Queen who came across her newborn self in the belly of the beast, Island Leviathan, before they were both rescued by none other than Pusan Wanderlust, as then. (Which wasn't as now due to regular death of one, recurrence in another; possibly two or three others by now.)

A couple of years older than the Summoning Children, she was a deviant like OMP-Akbar, albeit one without the additional advantage of faerie half-parents to go along with devic ones. Although every deviancy was different than every other deviancy, most deviants lived long, healthy lives; aging very slowly.

While, to the five members of the by then dubbed Damnation Brigade she reencountered in Hadd on Devauray night, she had visibly aged in the nearly three decades since they'd last seen her in 1952, all agreed it wasn't by a great deal. (Of course, since all ten members of D-Brig emerged after twenty-five years in Limbo altogether unaged, they looked to her eyes even less changed than she did to herself.)

For many a man, and the occasional woman, she was almost as much of a stunner at 60-plus as she had been in early adulthood. Truly striking to behold, as a Piscine, an amphibious humanoid, she had gills well-hidden beneath her tangle of hair, such as it was, and behind her ears. Had webbed toes and fingers. Her toenails and fingernails were long, curved and spear-tipped, though nowhere near as piercingly pointed as her two rows of shark-sharp teeth.

Her skin pigmentation had a faintly greenish tinge to it. Her skin was also slightly scaly. Her eyes and mouth were somewhat larger than most normal humans while her hair, well, flowing seaweed, often with stuff in it, was perhaps the best way to describe that. Freespirit Nihila having kept the glowingly golden hauberk when they separated, she was back to wearing what amounted to a half-wetsuit. It had no sleeves, no legs below mid-thigh and a midriff gap cut in its front in order to display her so-called bellybutton bauble, her Vesica Piscis.

This last, her navel accessory, howsoever much diminished, was one of three Brainrock power foci Pusan and the late Aortic Merthetis found on or beside her infantile self in 5918, after Fish's real mother, whoever that was in reality, abandoned her inside Island Leviathan. The other two were a fishhook or landing gaffe and a fishnet or soul-net, as she sometimes referred to it.

These she kept dematerialized between-space, only a shake away from being solidly in her hands. Like most top of the food-chain witches, as she often characterized herself, Fish was a materialist. Especially given Morg's current condition, or lack thereof, she may well be the best witch still alive. Given whose side Morg had been fighting on at the end, she'd probably been that for a while.

(Fish and her aquatic Athenans, some of whom, like her, were veterans of the Godbadian civil war of 20-plus years earlier, were in Hadd fighting the watery Dead – onetime men, more often Piscines, and even more often creatures, reanimated by non-Vetalazurs whose loyalty belonged to Janna Fangfingers, thence Nergal Vetala, Janna's predecessor as well as successor, again. Had to not be Vetalazurs for reasons drippingly, make that that soakingly, obvious.)

They had known each other for going on fifty years, from the time they were young teens and met at then Faerie Queen Godda's travelling court in Twilight's Venusberg. (Godda was a faerie type. When she died, or was killed, her body was reduced to ash and sprinkled over her designated successor. As Tsishah Thrae could testify, since faeries stole her from Mama Morgianna, death was hardly the only way to get shot of daemonic overlays.)

Because both had Mariamnic training to go with their Athenan, Afrite and, due to the loss of their baby girls within a few years of each other, foreshortened Anthean upbringing, Fish recognized what Morg was doing even when she was still half of Borealis Brolly-projecting Nihila Nereid. She didn't make the former Unity aware of it mostly because she wasn't sure how kindly Nowadays Nihila would react.

(Utopians and Hellions – and Morg was both – were adversative to devils. Which was one reason she found it so surprising her Northern Lights Nihila-side let the Trinondevs' Wyvern of Weir get away despite what it had collectively done to the severely brain-damaged Mithradite, Mars Bellona; his humiliating condition due to D-Brig's leader Cyborg Cerebrus, David Ryne, Eden's son and Saul-Psycho's twin, who fared even worse.

(Plus, Harmony-Nihila, also (rarely) Harmony-Nemesis, albeit most commonly Datong Harmonia back then, had been Janna Somata's half-mom; still was, as she may or may have realized or even cared. Would have certainly recalled that it was those selfsame Somatas, Kyprian and Morg's ancestors, Zalman, that Melina and their Janna, who as good as cost her her life for damn near 500 years.)

Cocooning was a feeorin ploy designed to preserve the lives of those inside the resultant, sort of self-generated coverall. Although the chrysalis trick worked best for fays – duh-the-dogfish that – there remained a decent chance Morg remained borderline alive inside it. If she was then she would need the help of a major league healer to ease her out of it.

As good as Fisherwoman was in that regard, she knew of many better in the Althean Sisterhood. Because of who was possessing her the last time she saw her, no one could be better than Telepassa of Godbad. Although currently Witch Isle's resident Althean as well as Afrite Ventricular, she was also a life-loving Anthean.

Had, not long after having her triplet daughters in early '61, gone through the second seven years of training that higher-ups in the Anthean Sisterhood, alone of all the Head's Witch Sisterhoods, demanded of those who wished to become thoroughly educated in their much more advanced version of the craft. More problem-significantly, that made her a highly trained, restorative, life-loving Ant.

As such, come the New Year, which was celebrated on the Spring Equinox throughout most of the Head, Telepassa was scheduled to take over as the Ants' primary representative on Shenon. As for who was possessing her, that was Amal-Al-thea (Althea Brand) herself; according to some – though not to her – the devic half-mother of Pusan Wanderlust, yet another of Fish's many deviant acquaintances.

(In fishy fact the recurring, trail-blazing self-psychopomp hauled Aortic Mer-thetis out of the Belly of the Beast, where she found future Fish in 5918.)

A goatish fauna like Pusan – whose devic half-mom was more likely the wintry Byronic Goatfish (the Capricorn Zodiacal Deneb Makara, according to Illuminaries of yore) and hence Fish's half-mother's immediate sister (the devic half of Fish-mom being the Pisces Zodiacal Pyçonja) – she was a seventh-born Lazaremist. Was also among the most life-supportive devils of any of the three devic tribes.

(In what amounted to a quadruple life-saving transference, Telepassa got Amal-Althea as good as bequeathed her by Melina then still Sarpedon, who kept her power focus, a Brainrock caduceus, as a kind of trade-off. That was in 1965 beyond the Dome; 5965 in here. The other three thus saved were her triplet daughters, Autonoe, Ino and Agave, then barely four. As not everyone realized, the little trickster Hush Mannering's expertise with fairy-stocks also contributed to their survival.)

Consequently, in Telepassa's case anyway, being possessed by a Master Deva could be considered benevolent bedevilment. Having herself just been dispossessed, as it happened by Amal-Althea's lone firstborn sister in Lazareme – Freespirit Nihila, as Harmony, the onetime Unity of Balance, had decided to rename herself – Fish wasn't sure that was a good thing.

(Also wasn't too sure how much damage the ravenous Diver did to her Vesica Piscis, which she was as good as born with, bauble be-stitched to bellybutton, earlier on Sedonda-Sunday. Although Gypsium-Godstuff tended to replenish itself; although it was still there, still glowed when she put her mind to it; it was supposed to prevent devic possession. Notwithstanding any of that, she couldn't help worrying her navel accessory had finally worn out, sixty very odd years after its insertion, presumably for prophylactic purposes.)

Nevertheless, Telepassa was Fish's prescription for what ailed Morgianna.

========

Leaving the oversized, but spookily lifelike, fabrication it squirted out of where it stood, she hefted the cocoon onto her shoulders easily; began to walk through the Weird via a series of witch-stones. Decided, not quite on a whim, to take a slight detour. A few steps later she emerged from between-space in the heart-shaped island's non-Lemurian Aorta instead of its Afrite-Althean Ventricle.

(Fish had never understood why Aortas weren't Atriums. Reckoned against logic that it was just another one of the quirks of the Universal Tongue spoken, or at least comprehended, on the Hidden Headworld since its inception coming up to 6,000 years ago.)

The Aorta's soon-to-retire Quarter Queen, who for reasons Fish did understand was called an Aortic, wasn't too hard to locate. (Couldn't very easily call an Aorta's quarter queen an Atriumic.) Tsishah Twilight was in bed. Looked rough too, really rough, as if she could do with more than just a topnotch healer herself. Far worse, not just her eyes were bluish.

Fish had known Tsishah virtually since the day of her birth. Knew just about all there was to know about her. Knew she was a Mariamnic – as Queen Godda, the highest possible Mariamnic there could be save their devic goddess, Althea's broods-older sister, Mariamne Dawnstar originally; long Krepusyl Evenstar these days – years before she received advanced Anthean training. Knew she'd gone on to receive Athenan War Witch training as well; knew that because it was Fish and Tsishah's mother Morg who'd provided most of it.

Illusions were second nature to her, but Fish was almost as skilled in that regard as Tsishah. She could easily see through these glamours and realized immediately the Aortic's appearance was no Ant-artifice. (The best illusionist she ever met was Sorciere, John Sundown's tragic beloved and possibly, along with Barsine Mandam, who turned out to be Nergal Vetala re-engendered during the Summoning, her best friend ever. Illusionist, though, was something of a misnomer, since what they did was more like aural manipulation, of the non-ear variety.)

She was wasted, emaciated. Was much like an already scrawny kid suffering from both anorexia and cyanosis. Except she had an old woman's face; had as well long-ago-white, but only now radically thinning hair. More than anything else, Tsishah reminded Fish of a barely fleshy wraith; an apparition that appeared just before the person herself died somewhere else. What had happened to her Shah-demon? How long could she survive without it?

Howsoever paler it was today, Tsishah's skin colouration was now as it had been at birth: light, celestial or sky blue. Fish took it as a hopeful sign that her eyes remained a richer blue, a royal blue, just as her father's had been once he, Tammuz Rhymer of Dukkha, human troubadour, was sprinkled with Tom-Tiddly Taddletale's ash and became the latest faerie troubadour, aka – and not just to teenage Morg, either – that ash-hole.

(Of course, being therefore half-fay, or half-feeorin, that both Tsishah and her mother survived her birth was a minor miracle in and of itself. There was a reason Twilight's feeorin, fays, faeries or fairies, also the Sidhe or Shee, so often stole human babies — reproduction among their own kind was not just difficult. It was far too often fatal for the mother.)

While fays were not blue-bloods in the royal sense, blue was a faerie colour. Even though her father, an Inner Earth Summoning Child, wasn't born a faerie, he had become one by the time he impregnated her mother. Blue was also a devic colour. Tantal Thanatos, Lathakra's King Cold, had blue skin. Two Outer Earth supras did as well, Aires and Thalassa D'Angelo, albeit only when they went into action.

The Elemental Twins, Fish knew from speaking with the Diver more so than the other four on Sraddha Isle, were the only unaccounted for members of this Damnation Brigade of theirs. She had a horrible idea she knew why as well. Tsishah as good as confirmed Fish's fears when she explained how she'd lost her demon.

It was mostly down to Mirrors, Klannit Thanatos, the Thanatoids' Haunted Angel, their only jointly co-conceived azura; and a confounding one at that, a rival to the Sangs' Guardian Angel Tyrtod in terms of human-level self-possession. (Klannit was actually way beyond that Tyrtod, whom the Trinondevs had shredded and sucked into their eyeorbs hours earlier along with his Apocalyptic shell. She could do things on her own; compulsion being but one.)

Two mornings ago on Incain, with everyone's eyes on what was going on in Hadd and up in Sisert the day before, Pyrame Silverstar – who'd been decathonitized the previous Sedonda, the 30th of Maruta, and whom they'd thought disposed of in the Zebranid Leper Colony on Sapienda-Thursday – reasserted her past control over All the Invincible. In trying to prevent it, Tsishah was badly hurt.

In a moment of inspired desperation, Pusan Wanderlust, who was with her, took her to the Frozen Island. There Tsishah willingly let Mirrors inside her. Their purpose was two-fold, primarily because azura possession was restorative, if not necessarily healthful long term, but also in order to set a trap for Pyrame. Last night, in the Aortic's personal Shelter over in Ire, Free Iraxas, on the Cattail's mainland well to the north and slightly to the east of her current resting place on Shenon, they sprang it.

They did so to get her out of All, such that the She-Sphinx could complete her work on the Outer Earth unimpaired. Did so, as well, mostly on Klannit's say so.

As Fish already knew, due to entirely involuntary, not to mention far too intimate, contact with Freespirit Nihila of late, Mirrors' mother Methandra, the Athenan War Witches' nominal goddess, succumbed to the lure of the Trigregos Talismans (the Crimson Corona, the Susasword and the Amateramirror).

Had done with Nowadays Nihila and Umashakti Silvercloud, Thrygragos Byron's last surviving firstborn daughter. Had done, moreover, very nearly terminally for all three highborn Master Devas. Being there, hours afterward, in support of old pal Demios Sarpedon, who sought one for himself, was how Fish – Diver-damaged Vesica Piscis unable to prevent it – very much inadvertently caught Nihila. Unless it was the other way around.

Being between Nihila, pinned to the back of Vetala's Brainrock throne by the Susasword as she was, and Fish's no longer prophylactic bellybutton bauble – which was also made out of the Godstuff known as Gypsium to the Dual Entities and, (presumably) via them, the Outer Earthlings – he became the conduit through which the devil went into the deviant when he tried to yank the so-called Body of Demeter out of both her and the throne.

That misfortune explained how Sarpedon ended up in critical care on Sraddha Isle alongside natural daughter Andaemyn. That'd be the same Andy whose back, on Sedonda-Sunday, her uncle Sal might have broken when he thought she was attacking him and not the samurai Morg's ringer, Alastor Molorchus, had just sent through the Weird behind him in order to kill him — this because he'd just (very briefly) acquired the real Trigregos Talismans.

The Thrice-Cursed Godly Glories, as the terrible talismans were also known, weren't just poisonous to devils; they did no one any good.

As for the rest of Tsishah's story:

Klannit's devic father Tantal – who barely acknowledged her existence, and not just because he had godly gobs of other azuras, by just as godly gobs of devic goddesses – kidnapping old friend Melina born Sarpedon and her hybrid daughters from supposedly inviolable Cabalarkon, amongst devils all-but-contrarily considered the Moloch Sedon's protectorate …

King Cold then forcing Morg's Young Daddy Death, inside of Alastor Molorchus, Morg's one-armed dead man, to send a different ringer, Ringleader himself (Mel-Illuminatus's husband, the father of her darlings, Aristotle Zeross, he with his teleportive Gypsium rings) to Lathakra either just before or during Vetala's Soldier attack on Sraddha Isle …

D-Brig's Air and Sea missing; the Elemental Twins being Summoning Children no one on the Outer Earth seemingly knew anything about until they, a pair of ragamuffin twelve year olds, showed up in Rome, Italy in April 1933; this sometime shortly after the Byronic Nucleus cathonitized the Thanatoids' fourth generational devils, two of whom were named Aires and Thalassa, coming down from Sedon's Peak in here …

Morg herself, having gulled Mama Methandra into believing she worshipped her as the Athenan War Witches' devic goddess, showing her true Hellion colours and turning on her; what was probably Miss Myth's lowest moment since the Atomic Twins blew up in her face thanks to the Death Head Hellion, who was a Piscine like Fish, though one supposedly of the Melusine mermaid strain, coming up to 1200 years ago …

All this and so much more, it all fit.

Served them right in a way. You deal with devils sooner or later you get burned; heat being Methandra's attribute. Or frozen nigh unto death, Tantal being aka King Cold. Her, Morg, Tsishah, Amphitrite, Pusan Wanderlust, Melina Zeross, every other altruistically minded deviant and witchcraft practitioner who shared the Panharmonium Pipedream, as Jordan Tethys often characterized it; every one of them should have known better. And not just for dealing with devils, either; for dealing with the terrible talismans, too, howsoever-tangentially.

Shame on Nergal Vetala (formerly Barsine Mandam become Holgat-wife) first off, Methandra Thanatos, Umashakti Silvercloud and especially on the one highborn female devil who for sure should have known better, self-named Freespirit Nihila. (Vetala and her soldier, her Trigregos Titan, were the ones who foiled the firstborn females on Dustmound yesterday, make that the day before yesterday, though they paid a much heavier price for it much earlier today, make that yesterday.)

Hell's trolling bells, Nowadays Nihila had been immobilized for nearly 500 years in a Stopstone-lined cave with the Susasword pinning her to a slab of Brainrock. Yet, immediately after the two or three times late – and to both Fish and Tsishah ever unlamented – Kronokronos Mikoto pulled it out of her on Devaura-Saturday, immediately after she declared herself Freespirit Nihila as well as the renewed Unity of Panharmonium, she went after them again.

Initially, at least ostensibly, it was to destroy them. But that would never do. No, no, no. She had to conscript Miss Myth (Methandra Thanatos) and Lunar Gravity (Umashakti Silvercloud) then go after them jointly. Had to play a Goddess Gambit; had to in (very) vain hopes of becoming their own mothers, for whom Anvil the Artificer (Tvasitar Smithmonger) forged the accursed things in absentia.

Had to become the Trigregos Sisters re-embodied here on Earth; had to thusly become the equal to their fathers and thereby also the superiors to any male Master Deva, their firstborn brothers most especial. Maenad-madness as much as mass murder and unmitigated mayhem, that was the legacy of pursuing, let alone acquiring, the Trigregos Talismans.

Suicidal desperation, giving up her Shah-demon, who was much more than just a bordering-on yet-bebrained self-psychopomp, in aid of the Panharmonium Pipedream, that was nothing more than trickledown idiocy. She needed her to stay alive; more, she needed to hold onto her mindfully. Otherwise Shah might recover enough to raise holy hell again, just as she had in 5960, when she almost replaced Baaloch Hellblob on the Highchair of Hell.

"I'm going to cuttlefish-get Telepassa," she told the Aortic, in her inimitable way, after they finished trading recent her-stories with each other.

"Don't bother. Like I told Pusan, who came by here a while ago, when I wasn't where she left me anymore, I've had years of Shahiyeda Sunrise holding me together. If I can't get by without her, so be it. The important thing is we got Pyrame out of All. We're so close to achieving Panharmonium, we can't afford the meddling of a decathonitized devil who's as good as the Moloch's perpetual playmate."

"Sky-guy-Sed star-fished her, Sea-Saw. Chances are better than good-eating she'd be on our side the wide seas over nowadays in the bays."

In other words – not that Tsishah needed a translator after all these years listening to Fish spouting her famous fishisms – her days as a Perpetual Presence were over the moment the Moloch Sedon ill-starred her thirty years ago. Pyrame bore grudges. Why couldn't they have reasoned with her, tried to work with her, rather than seeking to get rid of her?

"We can't be sure of that, Fish. We needed All as she was; needed all of All ours, not whatever Pyrame may or may not have allowed us to have of her."

"Scald All, you're what boiling-water spatter-matters. Why didn't the meandering Mullet take you to her already?"

'Sea-Saw' was Fish's pet-goldfish name for Tsishah. She called Pusan Wanderlust 'Mullet' because a red mullet was a tropical goatfish. She used to call her Auntie Goat, but that was when she was a whole lot younger and thought it was funny. That she didn't anymore was mostly due to it not being very fishy, as in fishifying.

(It was funny, too; appropriate as well, doubly so. If Pusan had been Byron's Goatfish, Deneb Makara, prior to committing devic suicide, and Pyçonja Volant, his Pisces Zodiacal, was Fish's devic half-mom, then she was indeed her goatish aunt. Even funnier, the between-space Trailblazer was a healer and who'd know more about antidotes than an Auntie Goat?)

"Sedonda, after Pyrame, through All, knocked me on my ass, she said it was because she was afraid Pyrame would use All to come after me and she didn't want to take the chance she'd spot the triplets and figure out who they were, are." (Telepassa was no more her given name than she was originally from Godbad.)

"Maybe are the sandbar; maybe aren't the lake's char."

"No matter. The Frozen Isle was the nearest protectorate she could get me to where neither Pyrame nor All would dare follow. Today, well, I think she went looking for Shah."

"She driftwood-would, wouldn't she? Ocean swell better her than me I support-hose. Scum along, bluenose, we're off to seashore-see the heliozoan healer."

"You go ahead, Fish. I'll be all right here. My mother needs her more than me."

"Then I'll leave her here and get Shelly Pasta to do a hose-call. Human Memory's medicinal miracle-worker can treat you both simultaneously."

(Shelly Pasta was a dot-ditto in terms of Fish's pet-goldfish names; albeit for Telepassa of Godbad. It was nonsensical; not so her further characterization of her as 'Human Memory's medicinal miracle-worker'. As for 'hose' instead of 'house', fishisms included allusions to water words as much as eating and fishy bits. For her part Tsishah resolutely avoided fishifying as much as she did standard fay-saying. Too easy to end up tangling one's tongue.)

"Ask me," said Tsishah, sounding far too resigned to her fate for Fish's taste, "She'll refuse to treat either of us. Telepassa's a devil-worshipper. She owes her life to Bodiless Byron and APM's shape-shifting cohort; probably blames us, all of us, you included, for what happened to him and his Nucleoids on Devauray. I don't know how accurate that is, things just got out of hand is my take on that, but it's certainly more right than it's wrong."

It occurred to Fish she hadn't been anywhere the sky was clear enough to see the stars shining out of the Sedon Sphere since Sapienda night in Petrograd. She'd heard that Great Byron and his three second-born, Vayu Maelstrom, Sedona Spellbinder and Chimaera Glimmenmare, had been cathonitized Devauray-Saturday, however. Good riddance to bad cesspools.

(She and Tsishah, along with Auntie Goat Pusan, Janna St Peche-Montressor, the Fatman's daughter-in-law, whom APM All-Eyes often at least partially occupied, and Morg herself, had been in Petrograd as part of the Living Leadership. They were awaiting delivery of the Outer Earth armaments Harry Zeross, in the Morg-set guise of Meherr agent and Armenian freedom fighter Amos Annulis, purloined from US armed forces that morning on the other side; in Death Valley California, to be precise.)

If the Byronics, their All-Father in particular, hadn't turned on her self-purchased and administered, love-potioned (poisoned?), therefore devoutly loyal, Summoning Child of a husband, Achigan Auranja, in the late Fifties, she might still be the marital queen of Godbad and her actual homeland (home-water?), the Gulf of Aka, wouldn't still be so horribly polluted by petro-dreck spewing out of New Iraxas.

"Shelly Pasta's no Hippocratic hypocrite. No harpy hippo, either. She'll kelp-help you. It'd go against her seining-training not to."

"You're not listening, Fish. Her Ant and Alt training are just that, training. No fervour required. A devil occupies her. Amal-Althea's a Lazaremist and so is her eldest surviving and fully functional sister, Mariamne Dawnstar, Krepusyl Evenstar, who used to occupy me. But she worships your pal All-Eyes, APM, Byron's goddess of love and love-making, while Athenans nominally worship a Mithradite, Methandra Thanatos, long ago's Mediterranean Athena ..."

"APM's is no pal of mine-the-slime; SPM's only the war-watery-witchery's nominal lead-bleeder dew to predecessor decession."

SPM was Janna St Peche-Montressor — Montressor being her married name. (Yataghan Sentalli, on the Outer Earth, was brought up in Dukkha by the Montressor Family. Suffering from Foetal Alcohol Syndrome as she did, and always would, Centauri-Sentalli's only other offspring, Kirin, also now 27, the same as Janna, had had a much more difficult life. Still lived in the same Godbadian convent where she was born.)

After the defection of Tsishah's mother to the forces of the daemonic Dead, her second-in-command, Garcia Dis L'Orca, assumed leadership of the War Witches in Hadd. When that didn't stick, due to Garcia getting struck dead, then having her heart ripped out and eaten by a berserker bat, Janna took control of the Athenan War Witch contingent for the Living's final assault on Dustmound on the Eighth.

(Garcia did rise from the Dead; still was in all likelihood, albeit not animated by a Haddazur; by a symbiotic Sangazur. She was last seen on Drenched Dustmound burying Vetala's Brainrock talisman, her moon-sickle, in the deadhead of Alastor Molorchus, Morg's Outer Earth born, one-armed man; her ringer, as he came to be called.

(As it turned out, especially for D-Brig, this was a good thing because Molorchus had run out of Brainrock by then. Absorbing the moon-sickle's Godstuff recharged his teleportive talents. Since he was now animated by Morg's Young Daddy

Death, Auguste Moirnoir, who called Dervish Furie son, he/they was/were able to use that ability to send D-Brig 4 back to the Weirdom of Cabalarkon, where they were now in all likelihood.)

"And you don't even do that, warship-worship Miss Myth. Which is a large bilge bucket full of how-the-scow the Ants let you get where you got. So I fish-net-catch where you're shoal-going. You're more Hellion than anything else. You watery-warship anyone, and you probably dugong-don't, it's Mother Earth."

Devils were highly intelligent, skyborn, Cathonic. If she possessed any semblance of sentience whatsoever, Mother Earth self-generated it. Which would make her earthborn, chthonic. Hellions, sometimes called Hecate-Hellions after an adversary of the (Second) Adam & Eve version of the Dual Entities (Heliosophos's 61ˢᵗ lifetime according to the Annals of Anthea, as well as Melina Zeross's Illuminaries of Weir), claimed they were by far the oldest Sisterhood on the Whole Earth.

Probably were, too; may well have predated, by thousands of years, the Superior Sisterhood, that of Anthea, which was named after the Golden-Age-wife of Xuthros Hor, the Biblical Noah, and not the flowery Lazaremist over whom Catastrophe (Nakba Ramazar, the Headless Apocalyptic of Disaster), lost his head close to four millennia ago; not long after Master Devas became individually solid beings.

Fish had learned a lot more about Hellions over the course of the previous twenty-four hours. Much of it she hadn't as yet shared with Tsishah because, well, the waves do swell and the Aortic had a mother in Morg and a half-sister in Ancaemyn who had proven themselves entirely untrustworthy over somewhat more than just the last twenty-four hours.

"I baleen that way myself, Sea-saw. But, if I admiral-ask her, she'll commodore-come. And you know why, small fry. In a confluence-contorting cantaloupe, she's my Hellespont-half-sister. So are her Dardanelles-daughters, the other way roustabout." (A roustabout worked on docks. Cantaloupes weren't at all fishy, probably didn't even float, but you could eat them. Plus, sea cucumbers were fishy and sometimes in her enthusiasm to exercise her expressiveness Fish confused herself.)

Even Tsishah – who had known Fish for over forty years; owed the fact Miss Mist (Krepusyl of Crepuscule) no longer possessed her, primarily to her and her mother of a Morg – once in awhile had trouble deciphering Fish's interminable fishisms. Too bad she was too tired to tell her to clam up; to tell her to start making sense instead of her even more tense. Or to bring her a recuperative daemon to replace Shah and take Klannit's place. (Mirrors having gone back to Lathakra at least in part in order to prevent Tsishah altogether subsuming her.)

Had Fish been encouraging her to make sense, she'd have used the word 'flense', as in stripping blubber off a whale's carcass, and thereby confused her all the more.

========

The day before, on Drenched Dustmound, the decapitated Dead Thing who'd once been OMP's implacable enemy – his head mobilized by an absurdly long and very muscular tongue – could not be allowed to get hold of the Trigregos Talismans. Not even if it was just tongue in cheek, Yehudi Cohen, D-Brig's Untouchable Diver, couldn't help thinking as he kicked upwards after them himself.

Being prawn-prone to punning, would have said it, too. Except he was soil-swimming at the time and even he would have found it difficult with a mouthful of dirt.

========

How they – the Crimson Corona and its sister objects, the Susasword and the Amateramirror – even came to be out there atop Diminished Dustmound, free for the grabbing, the Diver could only speculate. The last he'd seen of any of them was when he took the Amateramirror off Morg, via the expedient of rendering her shield arm intangible, thereby denying its purchase on her, and tossed it onto the other two.

Whereupon OMP-Akbar blew all three of them out of existence with the exploding Dand-head of his Homeworld Sceptre. Or so he thought. Or, and here was another thought, so he was meant to think. Meant for Morgianna to think, too, as well as anyone else who wanted the damn things.

(Once, back in December 1955, only a couple of weeks before Limbo, OMP disposed of the Olympian Tantalus the same way. Which is say he blew it – the source of the three Etocretan Extremist-Olympians' supra-talents as well as, to hear her tell it all those years ago, Melina 'Mel-Illuminatus' Sarpedon's caduceus – not so much up as into his Homeworld Sceptre between-space. Might still be there, the Tantalus, for all he knew.)

As for where he was now, well, he'd never blipped while in motion before, not consciously. (Was it only yesterday Fish's aquatic Athenans found him in an untouchable stasis state after they slew anew, then cut open, an already dead crocodile in Lake Sedona?) Yet he must have done precisely that, blipped propulsively, while fleeing from the demonic moles, terrible talismans in hand.

He had absorbed a whack of Gypsium from the Trigregos Titan, Vetala's Soldier, and, as he'd learned over the course of his last two days, on Dustmound first, then on Sraddha Isle, he blipped when he tried to metabolize too much of the miraculous Godstuff, what was called Brainrock here on the Head.

Blipping meant he went unconscious as well as, thankfully, self-protectively untouchable; simultaneously went between-space, the same as one of those self-psychopomps Sundown believed his Beauty had become since emerging from Limbo, the psycho-bicycle Fish was riding yesterday, or Morg's self-made Night Mare of a hobbyhorse from (as he'd only recently started to accept) decades ago.

He'd just de-blipped, so to speak. Found himself somewhere interspatial. Wasn't soil-swimming anymore. Was more like treading water in the nowhere that was the everywhere externally — treading ether, put better. Was still holding onto the Susasword, but could feel the Crimson Corona strung around his dumb-skull. Did it really have a mind of its own?

(OMP's Corona, whose given name turned out to be Takeda, thought so, when she had it all those years earlier in everyone's – even his – past.)

As far as the Diver was concerned that would be fine, so long as it left his alone. And where was the third one, the mirror? He didn't need to touch the Corona to realize it was around his head, albeit overtop his wetsuit's hood. He'd had it on before. Most recently … well, who could say for sure? When he blipped he lost track of time; obviously lost track of space, too. Must have blipped in mid-kick, as it were, and kept right on going.

Had the Corona commandeered him? Could it do that? Of course not. Despite what Corona-really-Takeda Power believed, the Crimson Corona (also her codename) wasn't sentient. Someone had to have controlled it from afar. Who? No, again. That was too dreadful to think about; much better to believe it was at least semi-sentient and programmed for self-preservation.

As if through a hazy veil — no wonder witches called it the Grey — he caught himself, Peeping Tom-like, looking into a large room in what might have been a palace or great house made entirely of wood. Was quite a scene happening out there in front of him, he with his gorgon goggles not needing to do anything tricky to see what was going on. Nor to hear it, even more surprisingly.

(Although he may or may not realize that Etzel Sangati, Count Molech's Djinn in 1938 was a devil, he definitely wouldn't have realized the one who came back in Pyrame-Purandar's cosmicar, was that Djinn, also Ghoster, the Heliodromus of Lazareme. Ophiomedea's Lamiae, who also served Sangati, were at least connected to Mater Matare's reputed sisters, the therefore equally lowborn Gorgons, Euryale or Stheno. His goggles, which he'd found in the Roman Colosseum that year, belonged to one or the other.)

None of the three there — a tanned, athletic and, to his mind, very pretty woman in her early to late thirties, one who looked vaguely familiar, and two others, neither of whom appeared to be altogether human, though one was much more than vaguely familiar — seemed to realize he was spying on them. (When they get to a certain age, he remarked to himself, well held together women ceased being pretty and start being handsome. This one definitely retained the pretty.)

The room was lit with kerosene lamps. He could see through its windows. It was night; evening at the earliest, given how close it was to the Winter Solstice — if it was still close to the Solstice, if months hadn't passed since the last time he was conscious. So much for not losing any time. It had been drenched daylight on Dustmound when he hauled the terrible talismans underground and kick-started himself off again.

The other thing that told him he had lost pecks, if not bushels, of awareness was the identity of one of the non-humans there. It was Fisherwoman. The last time he'd seen Fish, what was sort of her anyhow, if she was a humanoid skyscraper dressed in what had to be golden chainmail-fishnet ... Well, when was it? Earlier today or weeks ago?

"I told you, Scylla," said the Pretty. "Told the lot of you, you included, traveller, I wasn't going to get into any part of this goat-shit. Sorry, Goat. Yet only a few days ago Pusan here brings me an Outer Earthling and tells me to sort her out. This so-called cosmicaptain, whatever her real name is, is dying of radiation poisoning, for Celestial Christ's sake. Radiation poisoning directly attributable to the lot of yours goat-shit.

"Now you want me to go over to Tsishah's Aorta, what'll be mine in a few months, and sort out not just her but her mother as well; sort out a pair of killer witches, the Morrigan and her Hecate-Hellion of a daughter. Even if they're not fully trained in the traditional sense, Morg and Tsishah are meant to be Antheans. Ants are vivacious, positive people; restorative, not recidivist. Yet their loyalties have been more Athenan, war witch, than anything life-affirming for almost as long as I've been on Witch Isle. Ask me Superior Sarpedon got what she deserved."

"Listen to me-of-the-sea, Telepassa." The name meant zip to the Diver, but Pretty's face was head-butting at the dim recesses of his memory. If she was a bit older, and from the outside, then maybe he knew her as a youngster; maybe he knew her mother or grandmother. "I'm not potty-pot-part of it either, not to the extent Morg and your fellow Quarter Queens abalone-are anyhow. All I'm saying is my frothy friend, probably my oldest non-fishy chum on the Whole Earth, may be dying inside that cockamamie cockleshell cocoon of hers."

The one Fisherwoman addressed as Telepassa tried not to smile. Didn't succeed. Despite the undeniable seriousness of her message there was something about Fish's famous 'fishisms' that made it all but impossible for the Pretty not to do so; making her look even more so, pretty, in the process. Between-space the Diver made no similar effort. He was grinning as wide as he had since returning from Limbo.

"And if you dogfish-don't owe it to her," Fish persevered. "Or to me. You Orca-owe it to her little Mako-mother. You and your Dungeness-precious daughters, the older three anyhow, wouldn't be alluvial-alive, let alone splake-safe and so crab-cake comparatively anonymous, without Young Life intervening on your behalf with Bodiless Byron twenty years ago. That's how you bended up with Althea Brand, recall the squall."

"Hush wasn't the only one," the third person there reminded this Quarter Queen of somewhere, presumably right here, wherever right here was.

To the Diver she, 'traveller', looked to be a goat-woman, a satyr, a faun. Had seen paintings of them in Venice once upon a long time ago, pre-Limbo. Which was how he knew they existed, at least in legend. Then again if satyrs did, they had to, too. Notwithstanding patriarchal religions everywhere, you couldn't have daddy fauns without mommy fauns. God being the exception of course.

Had goatish horns, this one; hooves rather than feet, a face covered with silken hair and a thin goatee. Was dressed in hides, not very many of them, so no question of gender. Or of near-human more so than near-goat. Carried a shepherd's crook akin to what a fairy godmother would in an Arthur Rackam painting or some such. Since there must be faun females, did that make her a fauna? More than likely, he similarly supposed.

This being the Headworld, what didn't surprise him was that there were satyrs or fauns period. That she could talk didn't surprise him, either. What she said did: "And just to assuage any Alt-qualms you might yet harbour about helping a wannabe devil-slayer, from what Lady Achigan tells us the Trigregos Talismans were lost on Dustmound yesterday morning. That means it's over, Ventricular. Without them Superior Sarp-sharp couldn't kill the munificent Moloch, let alone her own bastard brother, even if she got the opportunity."

Yesterday morning, thought the Diver. That must make it the Ninth, albeit not of December. What did they call it in here? What did it matter? What time was it? Did that matter? Was it morning again … afternoon … evening? Even if it was later, full night, it sounded like he hadn't lost that much time. Comparatively not that much time anyhow. Nothing like Limbo, that was for sure. But who, or what, was the Moloch?

Etzel Sangati, purported vampire-making Black King, that he and few others encountered back when they were pre-supra teenagers in Rome, his gold, silver and bronze Volsung 'cousins' (except Valfreja, horrid Hulga's grey baby, had stayed at home, hadn't she; or had she?), Virginia Mannering, the D'Angelo twins, Furie and Sundown among them, had called himself a Molech, with an 'e'.

But that had been a stage name: Count Molech, the something or other Magician — wasn't Melancholy, but something like it. Led them on a mighty long and winding goose chase, that one did, the night he found his Gorgon Goggles in the Roman Colosseum's onetime gladiatorial pit no less. Might have got silver-haired cousin Tanith pregnant, too, if not so later on rumours had any validity. But, from the sounds of this goat-woman's voice, her Moloch was spelled with an 'o'.

Surely it could not be the one from the Bible, especially if he really was munificent and she wasn't being sarcastic. Which wasn't how he'd read her. That Moloch's followers baptized their babies by running them through flames. Unless, as was also said, said babies were instead sacrificed to him by fire.

Then again there had been a Vedic Vayu who claimed he was once called Huracan in pre-Columbian Mesoamerica out there, a Mars, a Varuna, a Mithras, a Golgotha, who said he was married to a Gethsemane, and a Vetala on the Head. Had been a Calvary Cavern too, albeit under the Head, in Subcranial Temporis. Why not a Moloch?

Melanchlaeni, that was it. Something out of Herodotus, meant 'black coats' but referred to an ancient tribe from Scythia, southern Russia. Knew it sounded a little like Melancholy.

Next truly pertinent question remained … where was the Amateramirror?

If he understood how these things worked – had worked possibly since Wilderwitch brought the Crimson Corona in here over the strongest objections of Sedona Spellbinder and the other two Nucleoids – he would not be here if it had not arrived before him. They attracted each other, didn't they, these ungodly talismans? Maybe he should try to ingest the ones he had. Then again, given what he'd seen of them, that way lay madness and he was crazy enough already.

This Quarter Queen Telepassa, of wherever, appeared to be considering her response when he, they, heard a rap on the door. Two other women entered the room. Women? Girls more like. The youngest was maybe eleven or twelve, into puberty but barely budding, while the older one was in her late teens; was even more striking to behold than the (very) pretty Ventricular, whatever that was. Something else suggestive of a heart, he didn't doubt.

Were they sisters? Surely this Telepassa couldn't be their mother. Fish had been talking about healing and Antheans – even if they were as frequently calling themselves Altheans in '55; had been, he'd heard, calling themselves thus for decades by then – were far more commonly considered healers beyond the Dome; next to never illusionists, let alone actual, supernaturally talented witches. No need to put into practice remedies prescribed by the Malleus Maleficarum around Antsy Alts out there back then.

(Thanks at least in some measure to the invention of the printing press around thirty years prior to its publication, 'The Hammer of Witches' was the second best selling book besides the Bible in the late Fifteenth and early Sixteenth centuries. The Diver read a version in his native German while growing up in Hamburg as a secret ward of the 'old' Baron, Tyrtod von Alptraum, who may have been his ever-unacknowledged father. Which, if so, would have made Brunhild, the bronze Volsung, who definitely was in Rome with them in January 1938, his half-sister, not his very much non-Jewish cousin.)

Indeed, only a few Ants back then were even capable of wearing illusive castings, glamours, splendours, aural manipulations, to use Wilderwitch's term. Still, in here, it was hardly out of the question that the Very Pretty was a whole lot older than she looked. What was certain was what the Even Prettier was carrying — the missing mirror's frame.

"Semen and I were practising our chords when this thing popped into my lap out of nowhere. What is it, mother?"

Telepassa seemed to draw a blank. Fish and the humanoid she-goat didn't. "By the Triplet Goddess," the latter exclaimed, "That's Ama-Tera's talisman, the Soul of Devaura. What's left of it anyhow. But where are the other two?" (Each of the Thrice-Cursed, Godly Glories, usually capitalized, was named after a Master Deva from a different tribe: Ama-Tera or Amateram, Susal and Crinsom. The three devils were their first victims.)

The Ventricular visibly paled. Recovered quickly and – masking her shock rather well, the Diver fancied – attempted to maintain her outward calm. Did so, many moms typically, by castigating, howsoever-mildly, her daughters: "Stop calling your baby sister Semen, Autonoe. Where are Ino and Agave?"

Agave, snapped the Diver, apropos of nothing. That's what Susal reminded him of: sisal, a kind of Mexican or Central American agave with sword-shaped leaves. Ama-Tera probably had something to do with being dirty, as in loving the earth, whereas, he'd been reliably informed while in the Sraddhite Monastery, Crinsom most commonly took the form of a blood-drinking, prick-nosed mosquito-woman.

Regular charmer, that one must have been. The Diver hated skeeters.

"I don't know," answered the older of the two. "Up in the hills with their boyfriends maybe. Semele and I were waiting for them."

Fish must have noticed Telepassa's discomposure and, unlike the Diver, realized what she was so concerned about. "You think the otter-other two," she said to the Ventricular, "The Kraken-Crown and the bass-ass-Susasword, have gone tuna them? Can't be. Hissy Huffy thought the Mollusc Sedon doorknob-dead in '68. Wouldn't let us deep-fry-dip, tipple-triple-them in Kore's codswallop Cauldron on their seventh bidets. Ino-Ichthyosaur and Agave-Abalone are no more Geoduck-Demeter and seaweed-Sapiendev than Auto-Octopus is debacle-Devaura."

"Weren't confirmed," agreed Telepassa. "And it was me who wouldn't let Hush test them. What was the point if Sedon wasn't around anymore?"

(The Diver recollected a Hissy Huffy Hush – General Huff 'n' Puff Jollity – from the same, anything but a Roman Holiday in the late Thirties. Also recalled a Joli Blon from Castle Nightmare, von Alptraum, where he sometimes visited with its owner, his patron and probable father, the selfsame old Baron. Had forgotten all about her until he came across another perpetual child, the Black Death, Auguste Moirnoir, apparently born Augustus Nauroz, at the Sraddhite Monastery on Devauray night, and got himself thoroughly re-educated.)

"How do you explain that then?" demanded the female satyr, motioning her shepherd's crook at what had become of the Soul of Devaura. (The Susasword was also called the Body of Demeter while the Crimson Corona was called the Mind of Sapiendev. That much else, along with a list of local locos searching for them, the Diver had heard on Sraddha Isle.)

"All I see is a barnacle-Brainrock frame, Mullet," protested Fish, no doubt mindful of what Freespirit Nihila had come to Dustmound to find after she took her over. Mindful, more importantly, of what she intended to do with them once she did – assuming she didn't change her mind again and dare to put them on herself – and what she'd do to anyone who tried to prevent her doing so. The word 'destroy' answering both postulates.

"That doesn't mean it's the albacore-Amateramirror."

"There's only one way to be sure," insisted Telepassa. "Find my other two daughters, Wanderlust," she as-much-as-ordered the fauna. "If they have the Crimson Corona and the Susasword, take them to Sedon's Peak and dispose of them." The Diver took it as a geoduck-given Very Pretty was referring to the three Sacred Objects, not her Dungeness-daughters.

"I'll do no such thing."

"You will. If you want me to try and save your Superior Sarp-Sharp."

"Oh, I'll find your daughters, outsider. And, if they have them, I'll take all three talismans to Sedon's Peak straightaway. But not to get rid of them. To dip them into the crater and renew them. Superior Sarpedon, as we both still have her, was right on the billy-goat button. He who is above us all needs to be abolished with extreme prejudice. And not just because he's the Devil, capitalized, if he is." (Definitely sarcastic, confirmed the Diver.)

"He's all that stops us from bringing down his sodding Sed Sphere on our shoulders; all that stops us from getting ass-kicking-loose upon the Whole Earth the way we were, should be, gods and monsters regardless. From everything I've seen and heard, whenever All lets me out there, Outer Earthlings need the likes of us to whoop their butts right smartly, for the good of us all, not to mention the planet herself, and we can't do it from in here."

Moloch, Sedon, the Devil Himself, hmm. Not hard to reckon which camp, malefic not munificent, the faun fell into: the one whose members would ally with the Dead and their demons against the forces of the altogether alive. That was enough for the Diver. He tumbled out of between-space, ripped the mirror frame out of this Autonoe's hands, and tumbled back into it.

Now all he had to do was find out where on the damn Head was this bloody Sedon's Peak. Or was it this bloody Head and that damn Peak?

========

Once she caught their scent, and no matter where they went – so long as it was in here – Pusan Wanderlust, the capric traveller, the trailblazing fauna, could follow most anyone between-space, through the whatever you wanted to call the dark-grey matter of the universal substance of Samsara, of mundane reality, today.

She was about to chase the Diver to wherever he was going when they, the three of them, Fish, Telepassa of Godbad, who wasn't just Telepassa of Godbad, and the fauna herself, heard a far-spoken cry of alarm from their faltering friend and Panharmonium point-person, Tsishah Thrae called Twilight.

"Holy fuck! Toothy's back. And I mean back. Only I've no Shah-demon to put the bite on him this time."

****

The Diver's identically-aged (presumed) cousins, the gold, silver and bronze Volsungs, had names: respectively, Valfreja Faust always Volsung, whose hair was akin to spun gold; silver-haired Tanith von Blut always Volsung, whose already dead father, yet anotherTyrtod, Raven's Head finished off – once again – on by then Drenched Dustmound; and his maybe half-sister Brunhild von Alptraum always Volsung, who got tagged with the bronze medal since her hair was reddish-brown.

They definitely were cousins because Freya's mother, Hulga born Mannering, become Faust, always Volsung, whom the Diver considered a horrid old harridan mostly because she was just that, was Tanith and Brunhild's grandmother. They were the titular characters in **the Phantacea Mythos** web-serial: "<u>Heliodyssey IV — The Volsung Variations</u>".

The two-part opening of these story sequences, "<u>Heliodyssey I — The Moloch Manoeuvres</u>", was set entirely on the Outer Earth in January 1938. Amongst the first-time supras General 'Huff 'n' Puff' Jollity led into action against Count Molech and his manservant, whose name was Djinn, during Manoeuvres were the Elemental Twins (Sea Stuff & Airhead), Werewolf in Shorts, Torches for Arms and Ginny Gemstone, all of whom the Diver recalls by their given names in Games 12.

Games 13: **Twilight Bites First**

========

<u>**Demetray, 9 Tantalar 5980**</u>

Tsishah Twilight did not call her eldest son 'Toothy' just because that's what she called him when she was a nursing mother and he was teething. She'd called her first-born, Makhta, a daughter, that for an identical reason. Had, when they were nipping at her nipples, yclept her two youngest, Zama and Skaga, a girl and a boy, that too.

Neither did she clepe him Toothy because it sounded a little like the name Mani-Balam, better known as Jester Jaguar, her much older, long estranged husband, and his pan-aboriginal fanatic of a foster father Lamechlan gave him at birth. Which was Teo-tihuacan, Teoti for short. She called him thus because of what he was once and, against all sanity, was yet again.

Toothy-Teoti was a vampire.

========

The Hidden Continent of Sedon's Head contained numberless wonders.

Those who found a way to the Inner Earth from the Outer Earth could be forgiven when they spoke of entering a dream world, even if it was sometimes more of a nightmare. For some, if not all, of these outsiders, perhaps the most marvellous thing about the Head was that everyone on it spoke the same language: Sedon Speak; pre-Babel babble, as some wags' wagging tongues would have it.

Outsiders didn't have to learn Sedon Speak; once they were inside, beneath the Sedon Sphere and therefore under its influence, they automatically spoke it. So long as they stayed insiders, that is. So long as they weren't already mutes, equally so. Come from China, speaking only Chinese, whatever dialect, meet someone from Arabia, speaking only Arabic, dialect-ditto, and suddenly you were speaking the same language. Were even though you knew damn well you were still speaking Chinese or Arabic.

About the only exception, besides Time-Retarded Dukkha – where Janna St Peche-Montressor was born and raised, where Yataghan Sentalli, also Montressor, was raised, and where Sabreur Somata, Andaemyn's missing squeeze, came from – were the mantels of Subcranial Temporis, until the 6th of Tantalar also known as the Thousand Caverns of Dand Tariqartha, Lazareme now self-cathonitized Persian or Earth Magician.

For the most part they were just earthborn replicates that the Dand, when he was around, pre-programmed for a specific time and place, complete with the appropriate language. (Her being so recently elevated to its rulership, it still wasn't clear if Lakshmi Artha, the current Kronokronos Supreme, had acquired the same Persian abilities of her devic half-father when she took over Temporis.)

Nonetheless, if you weren't a replicate and you entered a cavern populated by Incans or Cossacks or anybody else, you'd understand them as well as they'd understand you. The same held true when it came to writing. Say, more than three thousand years ago, you came in here from Moses-Akhenaton's Egypt, possibly through the still visible door between the legs of the Giza He-Sphinx, though there were many other ways through the Dome in that remote era: remarkably prevalent, bee-hive-shaped Tholoi with Gypsium hearthstones, for the most part.

Came through, that is, and met someone from contemporaneous Sumer or Babylon. That happened, you could read, if – depending on its subject matter – perhaps not understand, his cuneiform as easily as he could your hieroglyphics. A thousand years later, you were a Greek mercenary marching ever-eastward with Alexander's Macedonian armies and somehow slipped through a howsoever-temporary opening between-space to the Hidden Continent.

Maybe a volcano had torn a trans-dimensional rift that wandered like the SAG Gap, for Sodom and Gomorrah, yet did. Or a Brainrock-laden meteor had crashed comparatively nearby. You had copies of Aristotle's treatises with you, Aristotle having been Alexander's most renowned teacher. You could trade them with a similarly recent arrival from India for a copy of his Vedas and neither of you would need dictionaries to read either/or.

Similarly, you've lived all your life beneath the Dome. You write a letter in the language of modern Samarand, what was once Sedon's Tongue, but was now on the far east coast of the Head's occipital regions. You mail it across the Inner Earth to a distant cousin, or maybe even a faerie, living in Twilight, Sedon's Outer Nose, what was once Daybreak and situated roughly where Samarand was now. Even if he'd responded in Druidic runes, you'd reckon he wrote it in Samarandin because that's how you'd read it.

Magical symbols? There being no such thing as magic on the Head, you'd nevertheless understand them — so long as they didn't purport to be magical, it went without writing. Although there were faerie types, the Headworld wasn't populated by masses of mush-men and mush-women. Far from it.

There were easily recognizable races on it and most of those races had its own homeland. Once had its own homeland, better make that, since freedom of movement had never been restricted; not by devic fiat anyhow.

That said, while it was true not all of even the human races were represented on the Outer Earth – for example, there were no Bandradins, they with skin that was both orange-coloured and orange-textured, found out there – equally so there were often vast territories largely populated by distinctively Semitic, Caucasian, far eastern Asiatic, African, Australian aborigine and American aboriginal types.

Just as there were noticeable differences among racial types on the Outer Earth, there were marked differences among racial types in here. However, presumably because of the sameness of language spoken and/or written throughout the Head, what might be called either racial intolerance or racial exclusivity was rarely an issue. Then there was the, mostly amongst themselves, perceived plight of the Headworld's American aboriginal types.

Homogenously referred to as Iraches, they no longer had an uncontested homeland to call their own. Had one once, for multiple centuries on end. It, territorially one of the biggest on the entire Inner Earth, was Iraxas; what was nowadays known as Hadd, the Land of the Dead. Iraches only got what they deserved, Godbadians, and not just Godbadians, would have it. They worshipped their ancestors, not proper devil-gods like nearly everyone else on the Head.

Fed them, too, Iraches countered. Nice to have Dead Aunt Pocahontas over for supper once in awhile; stopped her from having you for supper, didn't it.

The ambulatory Dead had always been a factor of life in Iraxas, especially in the dry season. When there was a dry season, that is, and not a forever cloud-covered, but rain-free, de facto devic protectorate. Which is what it became once Nergal Vetala took over old Iraxas, the shaft of Sedon's Muttonchop, during the expansion of the Lathakran Empire in the Dome's 48th Century; today's 5900s constituting its 60th Century.

Byronics, its onetime 'overlords', in a land whose populace didn't acknowledge devic overlords until Vetala came along, never had protectorates as such; just spheres of influence. Then came the First War between the Living and the Dead, most of five hundred years gone now.

At that point in time Dead-numbers got seriously out of whack. In fact on All Death Day there were more Dead Things animate than there were sentient beings moving anywhere anyone went on the whole Headworld. However, as the tide of triumph turned after Midsummer 5495 and the First War wound down, an impressive percentage, perhaps even the majority, of the losing Dead fleeing the winning Living congregated in Hadd.

Whereupon, for the most part, they just stayed there. Piled up there, too, when their food, such as it was – rot, compost, the era's equivalent of road kill and, yes, once in awhile each other – got scarce. Hence the heights of Dustmound, Vetala's middle finger salute to the Sedon Sphere, before Mithrada-Monday's Diluvia-worthy rains hit.

Illuminaries of Weir, for reasons non-whimsical, dated the beginning of the First War between the Living and the Dead to the Year of the Dome 5480. They declared it over in YD 5538. All Death Day, Maruta 1, 5494, the equivalent of All Souls Day 1494 beyond the Dome, occurred almost exactly two years after the beginning of what Illuminaries termed the Thousand Days of Disbelief.

For almost all of those thousand days, a Mithradite moon goddess, Nergal Vetala – whose most distinguishing characteristic, besides her fangs and unless she remembered to change them round, was that her thumbs were seemingly on the wrong hands – was the only devil worshipped on the Head. And it wasn't just the Iraches who worshipped her, either. Virtually everyone, living or dead, who worshipped anyone in those devastating days worshipped her.

A very minor part of the reason for that was because, in order to gain her independence from older, mostly male devils from any of the three tribes, she'd voluntarily become a wholly infertile vamp. Did so mostly to show them who was boss ... and it wasn't them. No point trying to make her pregnant when it wasn't possible anymore. No point attempting to boss her around, which she'd always figured only Grandfather Sedon should be allowed to do anyway.

Indeed, as a vamp, even the Mighty Moloch couldn't do that any longer. She liked that. Her adherents, in their impotent hatred for what the two remaining Unities were doing to the Head, liked it even more. Hidden or otherwise, it was the only world they had. If sentient beings are genetically disposed to having a need to worship someone, then her being godless made her the perfect god to have during the Thousand Days of Disbelief.

No one was too sure how she pulled it off. Allowed herself to be bitten by the first recorded devic vamp, Faustus Vladuca, aka the Fop, perhaps; he being a decathonitized, as of the Thirtieth, Lazaremist Black Godling. Or went to the Domination of Satanwyck, Hell on Earth, like not yet First Fangs had after Janna Somata, before she became Second Fangs, jilted him.

Whereupon, once there, she did as the Fop did. Gave herself over to a Black King, a vampire maker like Count Molech purported to be and his uncle, Azrael Sangati, definitely was when he tried to put the bite on a young Celestine D'Angelo near the tail end of the Outer Earth's 19th Century in London England.

Or just possibly she didn't mean to lose her fecundity at all. Had simply gone to Satanwyck to visit her favourite elder sister, Bouncing Belle, Beguiling Belialma, Lady Lust, its then Prime Sinistral. Seduced or got seduced by a succubus who turned out to be haemogoblin, a demon-type that carried the infection much like rats carried fleas who carried the plague, small case. Maybe it made a meal of her and she instead emerged vampiric.

Howsoever she pulled it off, Vetala went from being a lunar temptress commonly addressed a Fecundity, a fairly typical – if, as her nickname implied, astonishingly fruitful – fertility goddess along the lines of highborn Lazaremists such as Flowery Anthea, Vishnuvita and Vanalal, or Djerrid Ruin, Byron's Bowman, the dryadic Green Man who actually had more to do with trees than crops, to the blood-drinking, death-lusting Vampire Queen of the Dead.

========

Teoti-Toothy left Hadd shortly after dark the night of Sedonda, the 7th of Tantalar, 5980 Year of the Dome. Left on a self-imposed mission of recruitment.

========

Hadd's Blood Goddess, Nergal Vetala herself, was back. Although it was highly unlikely she either knew who he was or who his parents were, she'd nevertheless put the bite on him, on Sapienda-Thursday, at the abattoir Hadd-side of the Diluvia mountains. (That was where she'd bathed herself back into the fullness of vampiric vigour after thirty-five years in the Forbidden Forest of Kala Tal, her brood sister's protectorate, Sedon's Moustache.)

Put the bite on him, yes; sucked him nearly dry, yes as well. But then kindly, or at least considerately, regurgitated then spat some of it back into his throat, thereby returning him to what he considered the divine state of vampirism; one of a very few Iraches so honoured. (Most vamps were Marutian or Godbadian. Their leader in Vetala's absence, Second Fangs, Janna Fangfingers, herself being Marutian-Utopian, bore Iraches no great love, not even for feeding purposes.)

Consequently, after emerging from the standard 3-day gestation period, he was as full of determination as he was freshly supped blood.

(Come to think of it, maybe she did know who he was; who his parents were, more like. Vetala had come back in a human Summoning Child, Barsine Mandam, reputedly a fabulous photographer who eventually married Holgat Anvilson, the Irache-hated Sraddhites' High Priest in the late Thirties, early Forties.

(She did so, came back, beyond the Dome in Tantalar 5920; the same year, maybe even on the same day, that his maternal grandmother was born in the Weirdom of Cabalarkon, Sedon's Devic Eye-Land. They'd become friends, this Barsine and Grandma Morgianna on the Outer Earth, so his Mama Tsishah used to tell him, a friendship that continued in here.

(She'd also told him her demon was born human; even had a proper name once, Shahiyeda, usually shortened to Shah. Astonishingly Shah's mother, whom she called Solace or Sorciere, was definitely born on Mithramas Day 5920, the same as Grandma. What she didn't tell him, until it was too late to stop her, was that her Shah-demon retained a unique deviant talent despite debraining, one that allowed her to bite back vampirism.)

Many might characterize his intentions as evil evangelicalism. But he meant to do much more than just rally the troops, as it were, by spreading the good news of Vetala's reappearance eastwards, beyond the confines of Hadd. He had no misapprehensions with respect to her omnipotence. More vampire than Master Deva, which was how she could get away with chomping folks without being cathonitized, she wasn't anywhere near all-powerful. However, she was pro-Irache in a world he was hardly alone in perceiving as anything but.

Teoti may not have been the brightest of Tsishah's four children. Nonetheless, even he could see that, notwithstanding the return of the Iraches' Goddess, all was definitely not well in the Land of the Dead. Hadd was under attack. It was by far the largest assault the Living had mounted on the Dead in many generations.

Godbadians spearheaded it from the west, formerly friendly Krachlans were coming up from the southern tip of the Penile Peninsula, Sedon's Muttonchop, and the hated Marutians of Lake Sedona, which was sometimes called Sedon's Teardrop, were being reinforced from the north and east, from their settlements Hadd-side of the Diluvian Mountains.

As dreadful as all that anti-Irache vitriol, too often become violence, in 'civilized' quarters was, there was more, much more. There was the greening of New Iraxas, the oil-rich Godbadian province across the Gulf of Aka, to consider. Iraches zombies worked there. Its endemic pollution was so foul-smelling, so eyes-watering smoggy, so coughing cancerous, so overwhelmingly brumous, the Outer Earth North American slang term smaze (smog + haze) bespoke a good day, they were about all that could.

The Godbucks they earned, sent back to tribesmen in Hadd, was so very useful; in particular when it came to purchasing howsoever-primitive weaponry in order to defend the land, its hunting grounds and its crops from the miserable, ever-encroaching Sraddhites. Yet from the day its backers won the Godbadian Civil War, twenty years ago now, Centauri Enterprises – why Godbad was properly considered a Corporate State – has been trying to clean up the air and thereby drive out its Haddit workforce by robbing them of their right to, ahem, earn a living.

So yes, imperialistic, Byronics-worshipping Godbadians – they with their huge, next-to-unstoppable, Outer Earth inspired and at least partially equipped, modern day military – were behind it. As formidable as they were, the seafaring, always mercantile Panis of Krachla (the head of the Penile Peninsula, of which Iraxas was its shaft) and the despicable Sraddhites, as Hadd's become-indigenous Marutians were known (after Sraddha Somata, whom they'd as-good-as-deified), were hardly their only allies.

There were, among others, CE-paid mercenaries hailing from all over the Hidden Headworld, Trinondev Warriors of Weir from the faraway Weirdom of Cabalarkon, as well as 30-years' exiled ones from the not all that much closer, south-eastern Cattail's Zebranid Leper Colony; they and their highland neighbours, the orange-skinned, and orange-textured Bandradins whose transplanted dynasty once ruled the subcontinent.

There were also amphibious Piscines, water-breathing Akans and, to his mind most appallingly, Athenan War Witches. At least nominally these last were mother Tsishah's very own subjects; ones additionally who addressed Grandma Morg as Superior Sarpedon. Clearly the Dead needed reinforcements of their own.

Yama Nergal's Inglorious Dead were reputedly on the march south from the radioactive Ghostlands, in the Hidden Continent's forehead regions. Their touch could kill, which would make them very formidable friends to have in a fight; all the more so when most of your forces, and all of its vanguard, were dead already.

Unfortunately, as the pessimists were quick to point out, Death's Angels were as vulnerable as Hadd's mostly Vetalazur-animated zombies were to running and/or falling water, so it was unlikely very many of them would make it this far. Wasn't like they had their own portable warren to shelter them all that way, was it.

The optimists weren't very optimistic, either. As they noted, even if the long-lasting drought afflicting the north and Sedon's Cheeklands held – and even if, relatively intact in terms of numbers, they made it through the tunnel system in the Diluvian Mountains, over top of which it seemingly never stopped raining – the distance they had to travel was immense; the intervening dozen or more devic protectorates formidable.

So it was no one he spoke to in Necropolis – once the Gleaming City of Manoa – before leaving it had high expectations of imminent assistance from that quarter.

Then there were the Sangazur-animated Warrior Dead from the Bloodlands (New Valhalla, Sedon's Inner Nose). Thus far they'd only been supplying minimal and, to his mind, suspiciously inadequate tactical support rather than truly modern weapons and manpower. It was almost as if the Godbadians had got to the Sangs, bought out or co-opted their leadership, notably Guardian Angel Tyrtod, which they might have.

Similarly, although the so-called Indescribables, almost all of whom were man-eating demon-types, often did take their side, they were more interested in coming out of their homeland, the Forbidden Forest, Sedon's Moustache, to forage for food than to fight. And hey, spoiler alert, demons ate Dead Things, too. Indeed, because of their indiscriminateness Kala Tal's hungry horrors weren't very popular among anyone alive, including native Iraches.

Simply wasn't good enough, not an ounce of it; wouldn't be even if it was an ounce, 1/16th of a pint or roughly 30-milliliters of Human Type O Premium. Which those deep-pocketed few could occasionally buy in Manoa-Necropolis. Hadd's Dead, wherever they more like resided than lived, needed immediate support; Teoti reckoned he knew where to find it. In his Free Iraxas birthplace, across the narrow strip of water from Hadd on the Cattail Peninsula.

Flying between-space, which only bats turned by Janna Fangfingers, Hadd's regent in Vetala's absence, and self-evidently Vetala herself, could do, Teoti arrived at Ire, their chieftain's bursting-at-the-seams, coastal stronghold. In part because the High Chief was his father – Jester being a title meaning, funnily enough, chief; Jaguar being the honorific he'd acquired during his youth when he was a celebrated ballplayer – Teoti anticipated a sympathetic ear and an enthusiastic response.

Expected it especially from the young buck warriors Jaguar surrounded himself with as a chieftain's right. So it was, upon arrival, Teoti was delighted to discover his father's stronghold, which was justifiably called Ire, meaning anger, was teeming with impressively armed warriors. No slings and arrows, atlatls, spears and suchlike. These were guns; big guns that shot fast and often, with real bullets. Had big other things as well — except in pictures he'd never seen bazookas before.

Free Iraches the locked and loaded lot of them, they were already preparing to mount an invasion of Hadd. Then, to his shock and dismay, his father, whom he visited in his single-room wigwam before dawn the morning of the 9th, told him where they got their advanced weaponry from and what he and his army intended to do with it.

They were returning to Hadd in order to join the fight against the Dead. And he wasn't jesting.

=========

Prior to becoming a vampire, devils referred to Nergal Vetala as Fecundity.

=========

Over the almost six millennia since the Moloch Sedon raised the Cathonic Zone out of his own essence, thereby protecting Pacifica, the Places of Peace, and for most practical purposes separating the Inner from the Outer Earth, no devil had ever given birth to more azura spirit beings than she had. (A few male devils, notably Thrygragos Varuna Mithras and Tantal Thanatos, may have sired almost as many, but they never gave birth to anything.)

Azuras were as immortal as their parents but, absent shells, could never become individually solid entities. Even then they couldn't dominate much of anything with a brain of its own. They were also the only kind of offspring Master Devas could have by themselves. Which was to say when they weren't possessing any otherwise ordinary sentient shell. In which case, if they were at the time of conception, then their consequentially only half-offspring were the usually long-lived, but invariably mortal deviants.

Her thousands, even hundreds of thousands of azuras – call them Vetalazurs – were divided into two main groups. Likely the eldest, but certainly the most numerous, were the Nergalazurs. Their sires were the two male Nergalids: Zuvem, whose star no longer shone in the night's sky for some reason, and Yama, King Harvest, the Mithradite Grim Reaper and overlord of the Inglorious Dead, who were mostly animated by Vetala's offspring as well. Nergalazurs could have been born anywhere on the Head whereas the other main group of Vetala's azuras were invariably born in Hadd; hence their most common appellation, 'Haddazurs'.

Between them, the Nergalazurs and Haddazurs were responsible for animating the vast majority of the Head's yet Walking Dead. The therefore biggest reason for Vetala's status as the only devil left with worshippers after All-Death Day was self-preservation, pure and simple. For any fully alive sentient still inclined to look for assistance from higher powers during the First War between the Living and the Dead, it made religious sense to worship the devic mother of the azura spirit beings who largely kept the zombies going.

As a fertility goddess Nergal Vetala long made a point of leaving Iraxas from roughly the equivalent of the Outer Earth's Halloween, after the harvest was in and the fields turned over again, until her triumphant return on the Spring Equinox or thereabouts. That she chose to do so, that she could do so, was of course because she was a Master Deva, a third generational devil. However, an ever-so-ironic consequence of her becoming a vamp during the First War between the Living and the Dead was she'd perhaps inadvertently traded her devic immortality for a vampire's immortality. Which was a far more tenuous state of affairs, to say the least.

The lone female Nergalid was killed, thought killed anyhow – really killed, by Sraddha Somata no less – long before Illuminaries declared the First War officially concluded. She nevertheless managed to come back, time after time. While her absences now lasted decades, even hundreds of years in the first instance, she would eventually reappear – recur might be a better word for what she did – and when she did, when she in effect arose anew, Irache nationalism reawakened with her.

Vetala's most recent disappearance lasted something like 35 years, from 5945 until only a few days gone. During that time, as had been the case for most of her absences going back to her first death, during the First War, Hadd was ruled by one of Vetala's herself-made surrogates, a female vampire commonly known as Fang-fingers or, more simply, Fangs. She was no Irache, however; came originally from the vast plains of Marutia, Sedon's Cheek, north of Hadd-Iraxas beyond the Diluvian Mountains, the rainiest region of the Whole Earth. Had in fact a Utopian ancestry, which meant her forbearers were unearthly, extraterrestrial.

In life her name was Janna Somata. Her father was Zalman, the Master of the Weirdom of Kanin City, while her mother, whose name was Melina, premarital surname Tethys, though she never became a Legendarian, was that Weirdom's High Illuminary during her husband's reign. (Both later became howsoever short term Masters of the still extant Weirdom of Cabalarkon.)

Kanin City bordered the Gregarian Fields, which was then, as it was now, by Sedonic Decree, a violence-free hump of raised land on Sedon's Upper Cheek, hence Sedon's Mole. Her twin brother was the selfsame Sraddha deified by the Sraddhite Warrior Monks of Lake Sedona and the southern Diluvia Range.

Neither Zalman nor Melina were pureblood Utopians. That meant they could be, and were, possessed by devils. Reputedly Zal's father had been possessed by Lord Yajur, a firstborn Lazaremist, the Unity of Order, when he was conceived. When the truly terrible twins were conceived in 5456 YD, Mother Mel was possessed by none other than Order's immediate sister, the exquisite Harmony, the Unity of

Balance. To most minds much more significantly, Zal was apparently occupied by Thrygragos Lazareme, Thrygragos Everyman himself, whom everyone that beheld him believed embodied their ideal God.

Although, some of their best friends and relatives having become one, they had nothing against vamps per se, many Iraches took exception to being ruled by a Marutian vamp. So it was, and had been for the better part of two hundred years, there were now three territories occupied by a majority of Iraches.

These were Free Iraxas, in the upper, north-westernmost corner of the Cattail Peninsula centred on the township of Ire (anger); New Iraxas, the upper north-easternmost province of Godbad; and old Iraxas itself, what comparatively ancient, as in pre-Vetala, Godbadian usurpers called El Dorado and modern-day Sraddhites sometimes still did.

The biggest settlement in New Iraxas was the port city of Petrograd whereas the Byronics' Gleaming City of Manoa, not all that far north of the Circumcision Canal that separated the Mutton Chop's shaft from its head, remained old Iraxas's capital city. Only now it was most commonly referred to as Necropolis since that was where Second Fangs (Janna Fangfingers) and her vampire elite dwelt.

Those on the Cattail fled there to avoid being subject to Janna and her vamps. They, those Jester Jaguar was banding together in order to fight against Hadd's Dead Things, had never really abandoned their hunter-gatherer ways; still considered themselves warriors. So did many of those who stayed where they were, in old Iraxas, though many of them had over the centuries become domesticated farming folk, the same as the Marutians, whose settlers had to be kept driven back to Hadd's wettest periphery regions.

(While it never rained there, it was thoroughly irrigated by under- and overground streams and canals, big and small, fed by the lofty barrier mountains of Diluvia, where it never stopped raining. For a land of the Dead then, Hadd was fairly lush. But for its rain think Mexico's Yucatan Peninsula, with its plenitude of cenotes, and you wouldn't be far wrong.)

As for those in New Iraxas, they initially went there to work at the start of the Subcontinent of Aka Godbad's equivalent of the Outer Earth's Industrial Revolution nearly two centuries earlier. Took many of their ambulatory ancestors with them and these are the ones who not only stayed but whose numbers continued to increase dramatically until relatively recently.

The province of New Iraxas was the only place in the sub-continental landmass – in most of the known Head, actually – where petroleum could be found in any abundance. Unchecked extraction, on the spot refining, ancillary production and manufacturing factories rendered it so polluted only Living Iraches, in the short term, and Haddit Zombies, for the long term, would work there. Also until recently most of the Iraches, living and dead, working there were overseen, overruled put better, by Janna Fangfingers' vampires.

Although a decent percentage of them were Iraches, many more were Marutian or Godbadian. However, as an Outer Earthling who was also popular in Godbad once famously sang, the times they were a-changing. Centauri Enterprises, in addition to greening-up New Iraxas, now paid a bounty on vampires. It was payable in Godbucks and calculable strictly by weight.

The weight was made up of bagged, vampiric dust.

========

Jester Jaguar protested he was being just as duplicitous as Godbadians always were.

========

Sure, he was going to Hadd to fight against the Dead, but he was only doing so in exchange for armaments vastly superior to anything the hated Marutians had. Once the Godbadian navy finished ferrying his army of Free Iraches to eastern Hadd they'd find a way to slow their march inland. The idea was to allow Marutians in particular ample opportunity to suffer most of the casualties. Then, when he judged the moment right, the slaughter would truly begin. Haddazurs would have plenty of Marutian corpses to replace the zombies they'd lost.

That was what his father said, but Teoti was unwilling to accept his assertions at face value. He convinced himself his father was actually teetering on the brink. He could go either way: the way of his ancestors or the way of fools. Jaguar, he argued, appealing to his father's ego, hadn't lasted so long, hadn't risen so high in the ranks of the Free Iraches, by being a fool, a 'Nagamal' to use a word he'd learned when he was growing up. It referred to just that, a fool.

He, a Summoning Child the same as Teoti's grandmother Morgianna and grandfather Tammuz Rhymer before he was transformed into the Tom-Tiddly faerie sort, wasn't stupid. He – Mani-Balam further claimed he was in part named after his grandfather, an Outer Earthling – wasn't brain-damaged like his youngest son, Skaga, became. (Now 14, he'd reverted to crawling about on all-fours after being saved from drowning by Teoti himself most of 7-years gone.)

Jaguar, Teoti argued, had to know the Godbadians would never give him weapons equal, let alone superior, to their own. Had to have figured they would expect him to turn on the Marutian zealots and try to reclaim Hadd-Iraxas for his people. It was probably exactly what they wanted him to do.

Attrition worked as well on one side as it did on the other, daddy dearest. When they judged the time right, the Godbadians would turn the tables on him as surely and as ruthlessly as he intended to turn them on the Marutians. That being the case, Hadd-Iraxas would be theirs, not his. Much more honourable would be to march his armies alongside Vetala's Dead Things right from the onset.

Evidently at the end of his tolerance-tether, Jester Jaguar dismissed him. Toothy-Teoti obeyed. It wasn't just because he was a dutiful son. His father had as good as disowned him after Skaga's near-drowning. Had in fact given him over to the Blood Priest (Molech) Xibalba a couple of years later, to become a Blood Priest himself, and quite clearly no longer considered him his son.

No, he left because he didn't have much choice in the matter. Even though Iraches living there had already identified Manoa-Necropolis and its vamps as their primary target, they wouldn't get all of them. Consequently his father was armed with silver blades as well as flash grenades and a Godbadian-supplied pistol that fired silver bullets.

Teoti knew where his next stop would be, after resting out the coming daylight: Shenon, Witch Isle. Could have saved himself the between-space journey because, at just about the same instant Dad the Jag, his father, was dismissing him, Sea-saw, Mama Tsishah, was nearby, hidden from sight in a tipi within her own personal

Shelter. True, she was occupied by the ever-impressive Klannit, the Thanatoids of Lathakra's Haunted Angel, but azura-possession, like devic possession, often proved beneficial to mortals.

Going to see his mother that night, after darkness returned, proved anything except beneficial to a certain toothy vampire.

========

Hadd-Iraxas, the shaft of the Penile Peninsula, Sedon's Mutton Chop, remained by far the largest Irache homeland in terms of both area and population. Therein both hunter-gatherers and ply-the-ground peasants lived much as they always had, with one eye looking for their next meal and the other looking over their shoulders hoping to spot and thereafter evade anyone sneaking up on their behinds to count coup. Or make them their next meal, as the case may be.

Hunter-gatherers were the more adventurous. So long as they felt strong enough to make it back home to tell the tale, they went wherever they pleased and took whatever they wanted. Which was often Marutian scalps; something that had likely led the Sraddhite priesthood, male and female, to shave themselves bald. Not that that ever did them much good.

(Actually the Brown Robes shaved themselves because, after a disfiguring assassination attempt, Sraddha Somata had. Presumably he liked the contrast between a big black beard and a bald, not quite as black, head since he never went back to his former look even after he healed.)

Although they still considered themselves warriors, it wasn't members of different Irache tribes they fought anymore. When they didn't run, that is. By comparison, the stay-at-home soil-toilers continued to raise and cultivate whatever they could on the edges of natural cisterns, homemade reservoirs, rivers and ancient canals fed by runoff from Diluvia. Over the centuries, though, these more domesticated types, who would only fight to defend what they had, and then not very well, had lost whatever tribal identity they once claimed.

Nowadays they did what they'd always done in communities whose only commonality, besides the fact they were located in the vicinity of precious, too often hard-to-reach waterholes, was that those settling them were Irache. Non-Iraches were generally killed on sight. So were Iraches who came, entered freely, albeit only after accepting certain conditions, then, for whatever reason, subsequently attempted to move on.

The inhabitants of these hideaways were very picky about that; brain-extracting-picky with respect to suchlike ingrates. With considerable justification they reckoned their isolation from one another was about all that ensured their survival. That and the multitude of Dead Things plodding the wastelands between settlements of course.

Water for these not so much so few as far-between communities percolated, bubbled up, into ponds, oases, wadi, cenotes, billabongs, call them what you will, from underground rivulets running throughout the perpetually cloud-covered but, for nearly five hundred years, rainless midlands of Hadd-Iraxas.

No matter where you were, on either side of the Dome, water was precious. In old Iraxas, as in either New Iraxas or Free Iraxas, it was a commodity deeply desired by not just Iraches. Which was why Hadd-Iraxas could no longer be considered the uncontested homeland of a communalized Irache Nation.

Hunter-gatherers skulked and subsistence farmers made do in secluded settlements for the same reason: the seemingly eradicable curse of insatiable Marutian marauders originally from beyond Diluvia. By strength of arms as well as, just as importantly, their ability to live sociably behind skilfully constructed fortifications, these always unwelcome occupiers controlled the most arable area of Hadd's heartland. Which lay in and around Lake Sedona, Sedon's Teardrop; it also with its multitude of eminently habitable islands.

The Sraddhites ongoing advantage in terms of arms derived from the Marutians' ages-old mastery of metallurgy. At the time of their arrival in Iraxas during the late 55th Century of the Dome, they were led by their then fully alive, patron saint, Sraddha Somata, who'd already invented the fireboxes and hoses Sraddhites wore on their backs when fighting Dead Things.

Back then they mostly manufactured comparatively lightweight armour, heavy-duty, Imperial Roman-style pikes, long and short-bladed swords, knives that were next to unbreakable, crossbows and the medieval like. However, all but simultaneously with what was going on in Europe, Asia and the Americas during the same era beyond Dome, they slowly, painstakingly – emphasis on pain – learned how to make single-charged muskets and handheld pistols, cannon and hard-to-come-by rocket-propelled explosives.

Their expertise grew quickly thereafter. As it did so they made more and more sophisticated firearms; handheld grenades, crank-controlled Gatling guns they called 'woodpeckers' due to the tok-tok sound they made, repeater rifles and revolvers, to name only the most lethal examples.

The Cheeklands were subject to infrequent, but devastating Time Quakes; had been since Thrygragon, Mithramas 4376 YD. Such was their ferocity that most everything post Stone Age that Marutians wrought could be reduced to nearly naught in a matter of moments. Still, their oral tradition being highly accurate, what they worked once they never forgot how to do again; after the Quake subsided.

Not surprisingly they refused to share their developing technologies in not just weapons-making with by-then-Hadd's Irache natives, who in the 55th Century were still relying on sticks and stones, flint and obsidian, the same as their Palaeolithic ancestors had been for multiple millennia pre-Genesea. (Time Quakes never hit Hadd-side of the Diluvian Mountains. Which was why Sraddhites built their foundries in their foothills, where to this day it never stopped raining.)

Such remained the situation until the early 59th Century of the Dome. That was when neighbouring Godbad (Sedon's Mouth, Lower Lip, Lower Jaw and Beard or Goatee) needed a reliable source of willing workers for the rapidly expanding, yet thoroughly vile, smoke-belching, coal and oil-fed factories an emerging class of Godbadian capitalists, more often than not members of its Bandradin or hybrid aristocracy, were establishing in the subcontinent's north-easternmost province.

Even though they wouldn't worship him or his, Iraches responded in such numbers its Dand or devic overlord, a lesser Byronic Illuminaries called Tzihk-Rzrui, but general consensus had as Petrogod, decided to declare it – his territory, if not strictly speaking his protectorate – a new Iraxas. Unlike, as of Devauray-Saturday, his second generational father, Bodiless Byron, and his elder, second-born siblings, Vayu Maelstrom, Chimaera Glimmenmare and Sedona Spellbinder, this Tzihk-Ezrui Petrogod was not shining out of the Sedon Sphere right that moment.

As for where he was, or what his name meant, Teoti-Toothy could care less.

========

Neither his presence in Ire, anger, how his father treated him, angrily, nor his mother's between-space presence there, let alone what she was about to release her demon to do, went unnoticed. No matter what their names meant – Zama was Mayan for 'dawn' while Skaga was an Outer Earth, Northwest Native term for a shaman – they were Trouble Incipient.

As for their ghost, he was just waiting for the Samarandins to fashion him a new homo; make that, to quote Jordan 'Q for Quill' Tethys, a new homun being. Preferably a really hideous one to match the rabble-rousing earlier one, he whose name really was Reilly Haddeus.

========

Consistent with the viciously antipathetic nature of the contest for domination of Hadd-Iraxas, neither side intermarried with the other side. Far more significantly, the Marutians burned their dead whereas the Iraches, once barrow builders, took to leaving theirs exposed deep in the wasteland. Whereupon they promptly, or not so promptly, got up and walked anew. Not so promptly if the already Walking Dead decided to bury them themselves, for themselves, as reserves, like stashing money in a Godbadian bank or gold dust in a Krachlan's pillow case, for purposes of future occupation.

Irache Dead Things liked nothing better than to feast on Marutians. Fresh kills, preferably ones still twitching, were the best, but still warm corpses were an acceptable alternative. And it wasn't as if Marutian firearms, as opposed to fire, were much good against Dead Things. They kept going even after their heads were blown away. As for dismemberment, that wasn't very effective either. More than a few bald-headed, Sraddhite priests and priestesses had died of strangulation at the hands of a zombie's otherwise severed forearm.

Another thing, besides immolation, Hadd's Dead could not abide was running water. Sraddhites, to call Marutians as Iraches called them, therefore stuck close to Lake Sedona and the rivers and creeks that fed into it. They fortified their settlements on what they called El Dorado's mainland with moats filled with diverted streams and, in addition, dug shallow trenches between the moats and settlements proper that they filled with pitch and other easily ignitable substances.

Whenever they ventured inland, which they rarely did anymore, and then usually only to conduct slash-and-burn retaliatory raids, it was always in small groups, the members of whom had received special training in clandestine military techniques. Night time marches, daytime camouflage, wigs and body paint; they may not be illusionists, shape-shifters or self-teleporters, but sometimes when they attacked it seemed like they came out of nowhere.

Even if, in the early years after their invasion especially, Marutians firearms were handmade and, by Godbadian standards at the time, any time, comparatively rudimentary – they misfired almost as often as they worked properly – living Iraches quickly learned to stay well away from them. Nonetheless, there was then, as there was now, never any shortage of man-eating zombies and the occasional Indescribable to oppose the expansion of Marutian territory beyond their easily defensible areas in and around Sedon's Teardrop.

Slash and burn as they may their way through swarms of zombies, a kind of you-stay-away-from-me and I'll-stay-away-from-you attitude had evolved between the two conflicting camps. Over the course of centuries the Sraddhites even adopted a leaf out of the Irache notebook and took to leaving carcasses outside their compounds for the zombies to feed on instead of attempting raids of their own.

That remained the case even after Iraches began to acquire firearms of their own, mostly supplied by southern Panis and paid for in Godbucks sent by Iraches, living and dead, working in New Iraxas. As slow-witted as they were slow-moving, zombies with guns would shoot anyone, themselves as well as Marutians and/or Iraches. Sooth said, zombies came to think of lead-poisoning as a particularly pleasant, even desirable, speckle of spice.

As primitive as they were – and some still may be – Iraches had many other ways to maintain a balance of power; had lots of other things going for them, put better. One was that the presence of a common enemy in their homeland meant Irache-infighting long ago became a thing of the past. Another was they were hardier than outsiders; had a natural resistance to their native diseases, including those carried by their Haddazur-occupied zombies. Irache offspring were nowhere near as prone to succumbing to the occasional plague or common childhood illnesses as those of the Marutians.

They also had literally thousands of years worth of ancestral assets buried in barrow mounds throughout their homeland. These mounds, some of which predated the Genesea, going back well into the time of the Pacifica archipelago, amounted to storehouses. They supplied an approaching endless supply of cadaverous shells for the Nergalids' Spirit Beings to use as immediate reinforcements should the corpses they'd been possessing become inoperable due to a lack of sufficient limbs or an unavoidable immolation.

Even with the fancy hacking weapons and the heavy, unwieldy and hardly reliable – because of what they contained: ignitable fluids – fire canisters that Sraddhite fighters and raiding parties wore on their backs, they could only destroy Haddit zombies, not the Haddazurs motivating them.

As well, Haddazurs would congenially animate any corpse they didn't help wholly devour. Marutians who died in battle would rise up fighting for the very foe they died fighting against: the Iraches and their zombies. Onetime brothers-in-arms in life not only became instantaneous enemies in death, they continued to wield the howsoever-superior weaponry they had when they were killed.

Haddit zombies also had what amounted to an air force; two of them, as it happened. Second Fangs' bats-of-burden handled night flights. Often these were Irache vamps Fangs herself chose, some said bred, presumably for size, then turned specifically to do her carryall work after dark. Enormous, semi-sentient and altogether mortal Vultyrie, vulturous bird-things native more to the Bloodlands than to Hadd, took over zombie-transportation duties by day.

The Vultyrie's latest cloud-general was known as Kronar. For decades he or his predecessors doubled as Nergal Vetala's majordomo during her latest lengthy absence from Hadd; her go-to guy in the sky, as it were, in Sedon's Moustache. Had done, make that, until the 8th of Tantalar, when, between them, John Sundown and Raven's Head proved just how far from omnipotent Teoti's great hope goddess, Nergal Vetala, was; just how more like impotent the Vampire Queen of the Dead was to prevent her own eradication.

Not that, having left Hadd the night before, Teoti-Toothy was aware of any of that as yet. Might not last long enough become aware of it, either.

=========

"Holy fuck!" she screamed out loud the moment the cold touch of his lifeless hand awakened her and she realized who was in her bedroom. Far-screamed, in addition, mentally, for fishy, goatish and Alt-healer friends to hear loud and clear one Quarter Queenship away: 'Toothy's back. And I mean back. Only I've no Shah-demon to put the bite on him this time.'

"Only thing holey about me, woman," Teoti countered, upon clamping an iron grip on the bluish-skinned stranger's neck, "Is what I can do to you, should I so chose." He said holey, meaning puncture wounds, deliberately, thinking himself humourous. "Now tell me what you've done to my mother, Tsishah Twilight?"

In his seventeen years of life, unlife or undeath (dependent on one's perspective), life again, then not a second time, he'd never seen his mother without her Shah-demon.

****

There is a sequence in "Decimation Damnation", the first mini-novel extracted from the open-ended saga of '*Wilderwitch's Babies*', wherein Lakshmi of Lemuria demonstrates that she has indeed inherited Persian or Earth Magician abilities from her devic half-father, Dand Tariqartha.

As might be expected she's also inherited the mantel replicates (half-lifers) who populate the vast majority of Temporis's Thousand Caverns. As the saga continues more of these half-lifers will come to play perhaps significant, as well as unexpected roles.

Phantacea Six, which was largely reprinted in the graphic novel entitled "Phantacea Revisited 2 — Cataclysm Catalyst", presented a shortened version of the final battle for Dustmound. Therein, somewhat incorrectly, one apparent survivor is depicted moments prior to disintegration.

The complete version of what the Living winners had already declared D-Day Dustmound appeared in "Goddess Gambit", albeit with an only slightly significant addendum found toward the middle of "Helios on Moon". It was inspired by a **Phantacea Mythos** web-serial entitled '*The Trigregos Gambit*'.

Reilly Haddeus, albeit probably not the Molech Xibalba, showed up in "Janna Fangfingers", the third mini-novel extracted from '*The Thousand Days of Disbelief*'. It was also where we (sort of) met Night Owl, Lamechlan, the Irache vamp who so plagued Second Fangs earlier this century, for the first time in the 5980 timeframe.

Games 14: **Begin Problem Pyrame Once Again**

========

Demetray, 9 Tantalar 5980

Tsishah Twilight hadn't meant to send out the far-cry of distress heard via their witch-stones by Fisherwoman, Pusan Wanderlust and Telepassa of Godbad, who wasn't just Telepassa of Godbad, in once-Europa Heliopolis's Ventricle. Her psychic scream, between-space-loud as it was, was purely reflexive. It resulted from a combination of rapidly deteriorating health, alarmingly debilitating exhaustion and immediately stunned-stupid shock.

Teoti had been sorted. Her Shah-demon (born Shahiyeda Sunrise, arguably as well as, given what became of her, ironically, in 5934) saw to that when she bit him back to normalcy … what? Most of two years gone. Now he'd have to be sorted again, she without Shahiyeda transformed and he about to rip out her throat.

Had she already taken her last gasp?

========

Sedonda the Seventh Tsishah had done her best to expel Pyrame Silverstar from All of Incain. Either she was nowhere near as strong, mentally or physically, as she once was, or the Pauper Priestess was quite simply too much for her. Whatever the case, short of overly weakening herself in the attempt, Pusan Wanderlust could only do what she did for her.

Yet the slight jolts of their life-force she transferred into her from the sand crabs wouldn't keep her going for long. The Traveller knew that; also knew that until the Dual Entities resolved their business on the Moon, one way or another, Tsishah was about the lone hope anyone in the Panharmonium Project had to get Pyrame out of the She-Sphinx.

Of course Tsishah was also her friend; her Shah-demon had been too, when she was altogether Shahiyeda, the daughter of latterly Blind Sundown and long late Sorciere. She, both of them, the two Shahs, deserved a chance at survival and in order to get that chance she, they, had to be hidden somewhere safe; somewhere even Pyrame, decathonitized as she was, would never be mad enough to ride All. Always assuming she, Silverstar, could find her, them, the two Shahs.

Not only that, Tsishah had to be bolstered; rendered ready, if that wasn't too impersonal a notion, to take on Pyrame again as soon as possible. All in all then, even if it was Pyrame in All, Pusan felt she had no choice in the matter. She had to take her, them, the other two-in-one, to the Frozen Isle of Lathakra, the devic protectorate of Tantal Thanatos, King Cold as he was common coldly known as amongst his own devilish kind.

A firstborn of Thrygragos Varuna Mithras, he was Pyrame's elder by a considerable margin and, short of becoming a vampire herself, devils were genetically incapable of disobeying their elders; their superiors in almost every way. Except … maybe that didn't hold true anymore, her being decathonitized. Were she otherwise, a never-cathonitized Master Deva, he told her to get lost, she'd have to get herself lost. Not so now; rather, presumably not so now.

Then again she disobeyed him, well, it was still his protectorate. He had this double-headed war-axe, his Brainrock Labrys, his Tvasitar talisman. Were he so inclined he could recathonitize her with a single swing; probably could recathonitize her with little more than a thought, truth told. Plus maybe a snap of fingers, if he was feeling the need for some physical flare.

Pyrame being inside All wouldn't make much difference. Beyond Incain the She-Sphinx was little more than a mandroid psychopomp, a howsoever-oversized version of Fish's psycho-bicycle. All only contained devils, the demons that made them whole and, in some cases, the talismans that made them special. While that (probably) meant she couldn't be cathonitized, if the Thanatoid sensed her trying her to sneak into his protectorate between-space, he could easily block her entry.

Could just as easily send her packing once he discovered her within his sphere of influence.

Came down to power of the people — and the entire population of Lathakra, thousands upon thousands of them, worshipped King Cold devoutly. So, no, All definitely couldn't devour him, not in his own protectorate. Hadn't been able to during the roughly eleven hundred years he and immediate sister, Heat to his Cold, lay asleep after the Idiot Twins (Tammuz and Osiraq, Equinoctial Spring and Equinoctial Autumn) blew up in their face, thus the Ghostlands.

Couldn't do so then; not for lack of trying either. Couldn't do so now; not even if he was unconscious or passed out drunk as he often was these last nearly fifty years. Ever since the Byronic Nucleus effectively eliminated his ten fourth generational offspring in Antheal 5933 (April 1933). Indeed, given they were partially powering All while one of her prisoners – one of the Atomic Twins – was often outside charging the nuclear dragons Crystallion and Hell's Horsemen rode as one of the more unsettling aspects of the Panharmonium Project, All was actually dependent on the Thanatoids these days.

Knowing this, knowing him (as the Traveller did, much to her occasional regret), Tantal did detect All, chances were he wouldn't bother with such niceties. All could be chopped apart and his Labrys had wickedly sharp edges. So Pusan took Tsishah to Lathakra.

Didn't linger; left her with Klannit, ice statue that she was then ambulating. Pusan Wanderlust could be chopped apart, too.

========

Comparatively speaking, Toothy Teoti was one up on Klannit Thanatos.

========

Although he was quick to dismiss him, Jester Jaguar did at least deign to talk to him whereas Klannit's father, King Cold, didn't even acknowledge her existence. By contrast, his sister-wife, another of Mithras's firstborn, Klannit's mother, Tantal's Crimson Queen, did. When it suited her. Once in awhile she even deigned to talk to her. Consequently Klannit usually took direction solely from Mama Methandra (Miss Myth, Mediterranean Athena, Heat to husband and triplet-brother's Cold).

Ego sometimes got the better of the Thanatoids' Haunted Angel. Because of her affinity for mirrors, Klannit reckoned herself a power to be reckoned with; one worthy of being considered a full devil. She wasn't; was an everlasting azura. Had a strong life-force, though; went into Tsishah late that afternoon, the 7th. Did so not just to make her, the Aortic, livelier. She had a plan. They both did; one supported by Pusan Wanderlust. Sort of worked, too.

Mama Shah's demon Shah was as talented in its (her) own way as Klannit Thanatos. In addition to be a vampire biter-backer, she (it) could get about on witch-stones and Pusan knew the perfect place to dispose of Pyrame — Minius, also Absudyl, the Subterranean Land of the Mandroids, which largely lay beneath Sedon's Devic Eye-Land at the western edge of the Hell Well of the World.

The best laid plans of witches, goats and tough-stuff azuras notwithstanding, Klannit's life-force didn't do her any good. Instead, it kick-started, kick-restarted, that of the Shah-demon.

And demons ate azuras as readily as they did devils.

========

Demetray the Ninth, the day after John Lennon was murdered on the Outer Earth, Teoti-Toothy wasn't paying attention to the propped-up mirror beside this deathly ill, disgustingly bluish-skinned impostor's bedside when Klannit physically came through it. Acting reflexively, rather than holding off reflectively as he perhaps should have – not that being a vampire he could be reflected in a mirror – he released his clamp on Tsishah's neck and went for Klannit's instead.

Was rewarded by this suddenly growing huge statue being flung into his face. He mystified, turned into mist, as vamps were wont to do. The statue passed right through him, crashing, though not smashing, only chipping, on the lushly carpeted stone floor of Tsishah's Anthill of a bedroom.

It wasn't the only thing chipping. So too did his claws as soon as he reformed and tried to rip out her throat. Then he cracked a fang trying to put the bite on her. Undeterred – vamps healed quickly – he got behind the ice woman, gripped his hands together underneath her breasts and began to squeeze. Vampires, even a teenage vamp only a few days turned, for a second time, really were very strong. Klannit wasn't; didn't need to be, at least in theory.

She was a spirit being, an azura not all that different from any other azura. Bodies for her were nothing more than a way station, something to wear, and discard, as the mood, or the need, struck. Only trouble was, as an azura she could never hope to dominate a sentient being; not even a simpleton like the Sraddhites' long-serving High Priest, Thartarre Holgatson's Nanny Klanny had been before Nergal Vetala disposed of her.

She got careless, the host became aware of her presence, or even if she didn't, she risked being taken in so quickly she'd cease being able to think for herself, if not permanently, then at least until said host got sick or died. Consciously or otherwise, that was exactly what was happening to her when a suddenly Shah-less Tsishah got All to fly her back to her Atrium in Shenon.

Fortunately, upon her arrival back home the Aortic looked into a mirror, perhaps to see how diminished she'd become without her demon, and Klannit escaped through it to Lathakra. Not all that long thereafter she'd come back, on her own again thanks to a new ice statue made specifically for her by Sedunihas, her age-retarded, fourth generational devic brother-Thanatoid.

Had returned as per usual following mother Methandra's latest instructions. Wasn't to know Tsishah had acquired the attention of a vampire. Didn't have time to avoid him going for and catching her unawares. Both the others in the room were sentient beings; last resort outlets. Ill-advisedly once again fearing inescapable assimilation, she, icy-she, struggled against him physically. Did so futilely.

He heard a satisfying crack as something in the ambulatory ice statue – its spine, he hoped – snapped. Looked up, triumphantly, at the impostor's bed. Had enough time to realize she was now sitting up in it when something came out of her. It was blazing very brightly indeed and, just as Klannit was no different than any other azura, other than he could traverse between-space Teoti-Toothy was no different than any other vamp; not even one turned by Nergal Vetala herself. He couldn't abide dazzling light.

The three who just then came through the Weird, came through it glowing as brightly as Tsishah had been; brighter. For Pusan Wanderlust, who really should have been off chasing the Untouchable Diver, thief of the Trigregos Talismans, her brightness emitted from her shepherd's crook, a Tvasitar talisman made out of Brainrock-Godstuff, like all devic power foci.

For Telepassa of Godbad, and not just Godbad – for Europa Heliopolis then, she born on the Outer Earth island of Aegean Trigon in 1941; mother: Human Memory; father: Agenor, the first Olympian – her glow came from a prolonged blaze of eyefire emanating from her suddenly apparent third eye. Make that Althea Brand's third eye, nothing apparent about it. (When she transferred Althea to Telepassa, Melina then still Zeross kept the devil's power focus, her caduceus, masquerading it as her stunted eye-stave's equivalent of a Trinondev's 'gargoyle'.)

Fish (Fisherwoman, Scylla Nereid, Lady Achigan, the onetime marital Queen of Godbad) had three talismans: a fishhook, a fishnet and a fish-bladder, which came in the form of a clam-shaped gem imbedded in her navel. All three gleamed marginally more blindingly than anything Telepassa or Pusan could conjure.

Fish's last, her Vesica Piscis, a term that did indeed mean fish bladder, but actually referred to an artistic device – a sort of halo drawn around holy people in renaissance paintings on the Outer Earth – was a splendiferous spotlight, a belly-button blast of brilliance, a veritable miniature sun that nevertheless didn't burn her oft-times baby belly.

(When used as a protective force shield about her body – thereby reminiscent of a Trinondev's expandable, and altogether physical, thought-projection – it glowed golden then as well. Proof, some said, that it came from Mandorla Auricaura, Lazareme's often annoying Enlightenment, who hadn't been seen pretty much as long as Fish had been alive. Then again neither had the winged Byronic, Pyçonja Volant, and the Mithradite, cloud-headed Diluvia Ran.)

Toothy couldn't take it. He withered, dried up, became akin to desiccated parchment and ignited; burnt unto ash, vanished into so much acrid smoke.

"Goddamn you, Fish, That was my son!" cried Tsishah, propping herself up on her elbows atop her close-to-deathbed. "He just wanted to give me a kiss."

"A vamp's slash-splash-kiss of death, Twilight. I didn't save you from fin-fantastic forever-fairyhood for that to bat-happen."

"Oh, do shut the fay-saying fuck up, Fish," admonished the azura-animated ice statue, from the floor where she'd fallen not far from the now very much oversized and minutely chipped statue meant to replicate the Morrigan's chrysalis. Which wasn't in the room anymore. (So long as it wasn't into or out of another devil's protectorate, Klannit's Mama Methandra could teleport stuff, too.) "And help me get the fuck up."

As the others glared at her in bemusement, not doing anything to help her do just that, Klannit tried to do it herself. Tried and failed; tried again, failed again. Wasn't succeeding, was she. Was made of ice after all, partially melted ice as well. All that brilliance these witches had been radiating had to have had some degree of warmth to it. But there was another reason she kept slipping onto her face. She couldn't coordinate her movements because her back – her ice statue's back anyhow – was broken.

"Hurry up," said Fish, unable to resist. "One of you slap me silly with a seahorse filly." All eyes turned to her. The exotic was grinning so broadly she looked about to split her piscine puss. "Too late, I'm going to say it anyway." Which she proceeded to do. "Take it from me, Klannit, a fish out of water, you're flopping about like a ..."

"Don't you dare finish," groaned Telepassa.

Fish didn't; didn't stop grinning, though. And her grinning, with her double row of shark-sharp teeth, was never a pleasant sight. Made everyone there wonder if they were on the menu.

"I'll look after her," volunteered Pusan. "Looking after folks, any kind of folks, that's what I do second best."

She went into Tsishah's bathroom. By the time she came back, having ripped down the Aortic's plastic shower curtain, imported from Godbad as it was, Telepassa was bending over Morg's oddly oversized chrysalis. Amal-Althea's third eye was once again open in her forehead; was softly bathing the cocoon in its resultant eyefire.

"Something's wrong, Fish," she said. "Morg's demon-coated, the way she should be. Except I can't detect anything of her flesh left inside it. Either she's well and truly dead or ..."

"What have you done to my mother, azura?" With an obvious effort, the living wraith, as Fish had thought of her, got out of bed and half-walked, half-staggered, over to where the others were gathered. Klannit was making a regular puddle of herself. It would take some work to get the stain out her carpet, the Aortic couldn't help mentally observing as she did so.

"Get me home, Goat," gurgled the Thanatoids' Haunted Angel. "And Great-Grandfather Sedon curse you to grated feta if you tell my mother about this."

"Should have brought a bait bucket, Wanderer," said Fish.

"I'll get you for this, Nereid," were Klannit's last words before Pusan shoved the slush that was left of her onto the shower curtain.

"Not if I drink you first, Frosty Femazur," Fish responded. (Frosty Manazur was an icy general who hardly ever left Lathakra for fear of exactly what was happening to Mirrors.)

Ignoring her, Pusan wrapped the curtain as best she could. Gathered it up, trying to avoid dripping too much in the way of the Mirror Mentalist out of it. Waving her shepherd's crook like a torch-bearer in a lantern parade, then took herself and presumably Klannit's still viable spirit self between-space to the Frozen Isle of Lathakra.

As soon as she was gone Fish and Telepassa frog-marched Tsishah back to bed. Whereupon, third eye again open, the Althean Ventricular proceeded to eye-fire-examine the sad excuse for an Aortic in the same way she'd examined Morg's supposedly subtle-matter-crusted cocoon moments earlier. As she did so, Fish checked out the chrysalis hands-on-probingly. She was forming an idea. Which worried her. Ideas often caused more trouble than they were worth.

Had Klannit's spirit-self, as next-to-useless as azura spirit-selves usually were, gone into her instead of back to Lathakra with Wanderlust? For years, make that decades, her Vesica Piscis protected her from devic possession the same as the others' witch-stones did. All that changed when Nowadays Nihila got hold of her on Sedonda-Sunday. The onetime Unity of Balance had been too much for it; unless it had lost too much of its Gypsium due to Nihila's proximity or, as she'd presumed at the time it happened, the Diver at least partially consuming it.

"Kelp-help me haul it back to Dustmound, Ventricular," she requested of Telepassa as soon as the latter finished her ministrations and Tsishah was resting quietly. "It's tanker-tonnage-heftier than it was when I brought it here."

(They never called her Europa due to the fact a hastily-made, mandroid facsimile of her, along with similar facsimiles – call them fairy stocks, because that's what they amounted to – of her then only three daughters, the terrifying triplets, lay dead and buried on the Outer Earth's Centauri Island. Had done since 1965. And who knew who might be listening between-space.)

"That's because it isn't it, Fish. I told you that. Or weren't you listening?"

"Oh, I was glistening. Heft with the left, I'll right whale it with the right. There may yet be a faint grouper-grope-hope, left or right, left for Panharmonium."

"She's a hollow woman," Telepassa warned, referring to Tsishah.

"Nothing new about that. Morg's Shah fillet-filled Sorry's Shah."

"A more hollow woman then. She's lost her soul-self."

"Ahoy the Great White Dyck; that explains that. I was driftwood-wondering what's with all the Illinois River illusions she was fly-casting about when we arrived."

"So was I actually. Still haven't figure it out, though."

"A-hi, the Hawaiian tuna-fish, but you have. Krill-kill the fresh kills; fillet-fill fresh krill with your salty soul-self. Tsishah Twilight's textbook-made a psychopomp of her own salivating son. She'll be fine. Let's go."

"Whoa, Fish. Now you're starting to worry me."

"How so, Amal-eyes?"

"You just made it through most of three sentences without fishifying."

========

"Oh, just go away, you two" muttered Tsishah, from her not-as-yet-deathbed. Given the state she was in, she sounded almost perky. "Leave me to my mourning. And, even if it's not my mother, take that thing with you. She's who needs saving; who at least needs a monument to her passing, if you take my meaning."

Fish did. Telepassa didn't. Was, approaching her 40th year on this or any other planet, still somewhat naïve, was Telepassa of Godbad, and not just of Godbad. They both went away. Carried with them her mother's chrysalis; if it was her mother's chrysalis and not an oversized semblance of such, as they did so.

Once they were gone, Tsishah Twilight recalled her soul-self. It came back in the form of a big, toothy bat. One that talked.

"Who are you, witch?"

"Your mother, Teoti."

"My mother's an Irache. You're a fucking faerie."

"That, too. Sort of. Go to sleep, boy. We'll start sorting things out tomorrow."

"You can't order me about. I'm no Dead Thing given gratuitous animation by your fucking soul-self."

"So you say."

Tsishah Twilight was born on or about the Autumnal Equinox (Harmony's Feast Day) of 5934. She came out of Morgianna then Somata in an Anthean Shelter outside the township of Ire, but within the confines of Free Iraxas, not far from the border differentiating it from that of the Barrings' homeland.

Barrings, yet another product of old Eden's failed genetic manipulations from many centuries pre-Dome, when Pacifica was its zoo, were anthropomorphic bear-men who came to worship a Lazaremist Inner Earth Illuminaries called Ursine Bardol for reasons obvious— his most common likeness was that of a were-bear, an enormous Kermode Spirit Bear in fact.

One time the teddy-bear her Auntie-Ants – the ones Mama Morg left her with while she attended training, this before the fucking faeries kidnapped her – gave her transmogrified into an actual Barring; one that they'd used Mariamnic trickery into fairifying (not be confused with either fairing or ferrying).

It didn't munch on her, though it did wake her up. It munched on an Irache teenager named Xibalba, thus perhaps prematurely activating the Summoning Child's ghostly, even (non-bloodsucking) vampiric talents.

Tonight, the 9th into the 10th of Tantalar, Tsishah didn't sleep with a fairified (not to be confused with ferried, farcified, gasified or even aerified) teddy-bear.

She slept with a teddy-bat.

========

If Wanderlust had gone after the Diver instead of coming to Tsishah's assistance in her Aorta (Atrium?), she wouldn't have had to go far to catch up to him. That's because he really had no idea how to get to this Sedon's Peak he'd heard Fish, the fauna and the too pretty to be handsome healer talking about, howsoever at odds with each other.

So he did the sensible thing. He decided to ask for directions.

========

"Your parents were brother and sister? How very Pharaonic of them. Surprised you aren't moronic."

The youngest of his dark-haired hostesses giggled at that. "Pharaonic, moronic, that's fairly fabulous a fay-say."

Around midnight, on the cusp of Tantalar the 9th, UD, Yehudi Cohen, the Untouchable Diver, celebrated the start of his fourth full day on the hidden continent having late night tea with four delightful young women. These were Semele, who was barely budding, and her triplet sisters, Autonoe, Ino and Agave, who had thoroughly blossomed already. Probably any number of times by then.

They were on Shenon, they told him; Witch Isle, they added, hearteningly. Because it was a heart-shaped island off the west coast of the Cattail Peninsula, Sedon's Ponytail. Shenon was in the Head's Caribbean-warm Interior Ocean of Akadan. More specifically, they further heartened him, they were in their lovely mother's Ventricle, her Quarter Queenship; their mother being one of Shenon's two Ventriculars, Telepassa of Godbad.

Among other places they also told him, dishearteningly. Even more specifically, they were sipping tea in Pretty's triangular-shaped wooden fortress, what the girls called Wooden Trigon for more than just the watchtowers at the fort's three corners. It did resemble a landform the Diver well-recalled from pre-Limbo.

Except, they said, it, Aegean Trigon as they referred to it, sank in 1968. Except again, it hadn't; not really. Had more like been blown into the time stream.

Each was enchanting in her own way. The triplets, however, were well beyond merely enchanting. Were, in their nightgowns and woollen bathrobes, exquisite — not that the Diver was easily eroticized. A month shy of their twentieth birthdays they were still kids in many respects. Given the unabashed way they spoke, though, it was simpler to think of them as lovely ladies rather than as beautiful children.

Which is what they were; in both senses of the term. Were Lovely Lady Afrites; the closest thing there was to Temple Prostitutes in this day, this age and this Head. Semele on the other hand was just that, a truly beautiful, big-eyed child, but definitely just a kid. Would not turn twelve, she told him, until this coming Kamor, the first month in the Byronic Ternary, July on the Outer Earth.

All four said they were conceived on the outside; as was their mother, the Althean as well as Afrite Ventricular. Except this time, she was not only born there, she spent the first half of her life there. Telepassa, which was not her given name, had been born in 1941 on, yes, the Aegean Island of Trigon he recalled with such mixed feelings, hence the shape and appellation of their fortress. They said their surname was Heliosophos, after the Male Entity who seemed to be their god, but a bit of prying extracted an even more startling admission.

Although the Diver did not realize his supranormal attributes until he was seventeen, being a German Jew – part German Jew, anyhow, on his mother's side – growing up in Hamburg in the Twenties and Thirties; being as well a Summoning Child, with all its concomitant baggage; he had been around strangeness, very little of it good, most of his recently extended life. Nonetheless, their story was one of the strangest he had ever heard.

"Be that as it may," said the Diver, then attempted to recap, mostly for his own benefit, what they'd told him so far. "So, your mother's Europa Heliopolis, the daughter of Agenor Heliopolis and Mnemosyne D'Angelo. And your father's her half-brother, Argiope Bright Face's boy, also by Agenor, Kadmon Heliopolis."

"Maybe," offered Agave helpfully. "Mother may not have just been mother when she conceived us. She may have been some one, some thing, called Strife."

The Diver had hoped he would never hear that discordant name again. Secretive, for reasons now obvious, yet undeniably knowledgeable witches – and recent events indicated he'd met more than a few of them pre-Limbo – considered Strife a virus; an infectious spirit that took over unlucky 'sisters' travelling through the Weird, as he'd learn to call the dark grey between-space of Samsara, the Universal Substance; the Grey, as witches perhaps understandably preferred.

As well as rendering them faceless and red-skinned, she maddened them; made them, for want of a better term, heartless killers. Wilderwitch, for one, was terrified of catching this Strife virus. The Morrigan, Superior Sarpedon by the time D-Brig was thrust into Limbo in late '55, had even set up a phalanx of half-life hard-cases, as she sometimes referred to her also-called Stopstone sentinels, between-space for much the same reason.

Did so more in hopes of capturing and thereafter destroying Strife than of catching her, like the common cold, true. Which, even if the Witch hadn't approved of her authoritarian ways pre-Limbo, didn't make Morgianna Somata, then Sarpedon, a bad person. Far from it, since it was now clear to the Diver that Strife was a devil. Morg's performance over the last couple of days did, though.

He ever got around to writing his memoirs, he'd do two. They wouldn't necessarily be called 'Pre-Limbo' and 'Post-Limbo' but, whatever he ultimately decided to call them, she'd definitely be featured most prominently in his bad book. Truth was, as perhaps inappropriate as it was for someone of his oft-proclaimed lofty sensibilities, he couldn't help hoping Superior Sarpedon was now Morg in a morgue.

Sicking her barfed-up demons on them earlier today – even if it was yesterday, or two days ago by now – albeit in an effort to regain control of the devil-killing Trigregos Talismans, that was what was inappropriate. Still, 'Barfed-Up Demons and More Serious Strangeness' might make a decent title for a memoir.

"And daddy," added Ino, equally helpfully, "Well, daddy may well have been God, capitalized; before he became God of course." (Master Devas were gods, small case; hence devils, meaning little gods.)

Autonoe was even more helpful, in an unhelpful way. "Then again, mother and the three of us may have been killed on the Outer Earth's Centauri Island back in '65, four years before Semen came along."

Semen, Semele, topped her sisters. "My daddy may have been their daddy and my mommy may have been their mommy. But my daddy might have just become God when he made love to my mommy and, by making me inside her, may have not only made her alive again as made me an angel."

The Diver would have thought the four young ladies completely crackers except for the fact he had finally placed Telepassa mentally and, yes, she may well have been Europa Heliopolis, one of the most strikingly pretty little girls and young teens he had ever come across. Only her cousin, Laodice born Atreides Hent, who may or may not be still alive, came close. Other than his own wife and pair of darling daughters at their age, it went without saying.

Cousin? Oh, probably. Seemed like all the Minoan Maniacs – Etocretan Extremists, equally so – who fought alongside, rather than for, Agenor Heliopolis (the first Olympian) and his original Black Rose of Anarchy were interrelated. Or if they weren't, within a generation or two, they were without going too far back in time.

Even Melina and Demios Sarpedon qualified, at least honorarily, because Sarpedon was the name of one of Ancient Crete's founding Europa's three sons by Zeus, according to tradition. (The other two, Minos and Rhadamanthys, became Judges of the Dead, the Diver recalled, apropos of nothing.)

As for the shockingly beautiful Laodice, aka Electrocretan, among other codenames, her mother Clymene was the first witch he could remember who identified herself as a Hellion. ('Shockingly' wasn't even his play on words. Given the distractions of the moment he couldn't instantly identify who coined it first, but recollected that it didn't take long before everyone who knew about Lao's startling electrical abilities was using it.)

As an infant and toddler both, Europa was a charge of Headmistress Virginia Mannering on Aegean Trigon at the same time as a number of other young kids, including Harry Zeross ('Kid Ringo' in 1955, 'Ringleader' now), and Gloriella D'Angelo, now Dark, Memory's niece, were in the mid to late Forties. Gloriel – D-Brig's Rainbow, its codenamed Radiant Rider – was eight years older than Euro and ten years older than Harry. Despite Gloriel's prepubescence, the Diver recalled her acting as Ginny's unofficial assistant.

He recalled much more than that. Recalled that during the earliest, bleakest, deep-darkest days of WWII, Aegean Trigon had somehow remained a relatively safe haven for he and his fellow supras, on both sides of the conflict. Not that the D'Angelos, who were Italian born and bred, ever were on the other side of the conflict. In fact, the whole family had fled Italy for Scotland before actual fighting broke out.

(That he was a German Jew didn't disqualify him from entry, this despite the Minoans hatred of Germans in general. Being half-Jewish helped in that regard, but both Lao and Ginny were close to a couple of other German Summoning Children, actual cousins, including his maybe half-sister Brunhild von Alptraum, and he vaguely recalled both of them – the other being Tanith von Blut – being on Aegean Trigon for a time.)

There had always been something eerie, verging on the magical, about the place. For one thing, make that three things, its three spiral peaks, its Dragon's Teeth, had always struck him as unnatural. What were their names again? Cadmus, Telepassa and Harmonia, he recollected, surprising himself yet again.

But who were Cadmus, Telepassa and Harmonia? Something to do with Greek Mythology, he felt sure. So were the girls' names: Semele, Autonoe, Ino and Agave. So was their mother's; a whole continent was named after that Europa. Indeed, going back to the 19th Century Godling Guild, mythology had significant influence on the backgrounds of not just Europeans like himself, but also New World suprasorts like the Sundowns and Rynes.

He would put it all together eventually. Said so, too. Albeit in nowhere near as many words. "Look, I'm going to have to get back to you on a lot of this. Show me this Sedon's Peak," he requested, "On that map of the Headworld Lady Achigan helped the Godbadians make after that Civil War of theirs."

"We could do better than that," claimed Agave. "We could take you there on our Afrite Bulbs."

"Afrite Bulbs!" The Diver shook involuntarily. Non-Lao shockingly, he'd coined the term.

More than forty years past, at the first Academy of Man in Amsterdam, not long after he met Slipper, Roxanne Heliopolis already Kinesis – a Summoning Child like him and the four girls' paternal great aunt, if he could believe them – she told him about her attitude toward matters sexual. Told then showed him, he vividly remembered, somewhat nonplussed in the presence of Hot Rox's grandnieces, thus earning her nickname of just that, Hot Rox.

Back then he had jokingly – and quite cleverly, he felt – referred to her tiny stepping stones as dinky Afrite Bulbs. The term had clearly stuck.

"Love beads," said Ino. "That's what Daddy Kad called them when we met him in '68."

"Of course," said Autonoe, "Semen couldn't take you there. Love beads don't work for her. She's still a virgin."

"Only for a couple more years, Car-Nose. Mommy says she might start teaching me some tricks when I turn twelve."

"Hang on a sec," pleaded the Diver. Again thinking of his two daughters – he also had three sons, one by none other than Fish (Fisherwoman, given name Scylla Nereid, evident title Lady Achigan these days) – he winced at the word 'tricks'. "Isn't there any way you could set your witch-stones so I could go there myself? Sedon's Peak's an active volcano from what you told me. Bubbles and burbles like one, too."

"Buckle my shoes," the triplets giggled simultaneously.

The Diver sighed dutifully, then finished making his point: "It's dangerous."

"So was Mt Maenalus on Apple Isle," said Agave. "But mommy was going to let us swim in its lava river, the stinky-Styx, when we turned seven."

"But Great-Grandaunt Pandora Mannering wouldn't let us," pointed out Ino. "She said there wasn't any point anymore. The Moloch Sedon was already dead. Except, ten years later, he wasn't and by then it was too late for us to become Great Goddesses." The Diver had already figured out the Moloch was Dark Sedon, this Hidden Continent of theirs being at least nominally his Headworld.

"Great Grand-Ant Pandora's Superior Sarpedon's mother," provided Auto-Nose, who must have been feeling left out of the conversation. "We call her Hush; most everyone does," she further said. Then, just in case the Diver was starting to understand anything, added a truly astonishing detail: "She's only seven."

"Not quite," objected Agave.

"She was bewitched," insisted Ino.

"Stop!" demanded the Diver.

"I guess so," said Autonoe.

"I don't guess," said Ino. "I know."

"Just do it," insisted the Diver.

"What, here? In front of Semen!"

The Diver didn't need the aggravation. Agave-vation?

========

Demetray, 9 Tantalar 5980

Being a faun, a fauna as some preferred, a female satyr, looking after folks, any kind of folks, was indeed what Pusan Wanderlust did second best. After all, satyriasis – as

========

Frequenting Lathakra was hardly the best way to look after herself.

Her transportation service to Klannit came with a price, one the onetime Mirror Mentalist gladly paid. She told the goat-woman what had happened before she scarpered back to Lathakra in part to report to mother Methandra, but also out of fear Tsishah, with her formidable willpower, would subsume her inescapably.

It was almost exactly the same story Tsishah told her, albeit with one addition. Mirrors got Pyrame out of All by in effect reflecting her into Tsishah, covered as she was by the Shah-demon. After that, well, who knows what happened for sure. It seemed to her, Klannit, that the Shah-demon somehow reactivated, hardened Pyrame inside her chthonic crust then buggered off, the one still in the other, via one of the Aortic's Hellstones or agates, to wherever.

Unless Shah was a self-psychopomp of course, which Klannit couldn't say because she didn't know. (Pusan did, but didn't say.)

As for that addition, that Klannit-specific insight, it had to do with that wherever. Seems Klannit had a thought; one, it had to be admitted, initially given to her by her Methandra of a mother, that she dutifully passed onto Tsishah-Shahiyeda after she came back with her marching orders. Want a hint as to what that thought was, a hint as to where Shah took herself and Pyrame? A hint's better than lint, you bint, fay-said Pusan.

Where was the one place on the Whole Head even devils dread to tread, Mirrors fay-questioned. The Weirdom of Cabalarkon, the traveller non-fay-answered. Check that, she caught herself, eyeorbs didn't work on Pyrame. Primarily because they didn't work on Miracle Memory, who had a long history – her-story? – of using the Pauper Priestess to humanize herself.

Had done pre-Earth too, she'd heard; perhaps even from the goatfish's mouth, as it were; not that the Goatfish, Deneb Makara, her devic mother, had been humanizing the Mnemosyne Machine when she was conceived; not unless Memory happened to be a fauna at the time. That being the case, Klannit teased, better make that … where was the one place on the Whole Head even the Devil Himself dreads to tread?

Old buggery, said Pusan Wanderlust, knowing the answer. As well as the futility of trying to find anyone there.

========

========

In that regard he was like father, like son. Except his father Godfrey – one of those, Ringleader amongst them, who helped Fish draw up a modern map of the Hidden Headworld – was dead. Crom wasn't; hence didn't need a Sangazur to keep on serving Alpha Centauri. Or Alfredo Sentalli, as far as that went, on the Outer Earth, its Centauri Island, launch site of the Cosmic Express, where he and his men had been serving him only a few days passed.

Today's mission was also to headman the Godbadian air force – a select part of it, rather – in a series of bombing raids over the so-called Prison Beach of Incain; so-called because All the self-proclaimed Invincible kept her prisoners, demons and devils reputedly exclusively, within herself between-space.

Crom was just an ordinary man; an altogether mortal, albeit thoroughly and multi-variously trained professional soldier. Within the Godbadian military, to whom he was more like seconded than belonged, he was not so jokingly referred to as a one-man army unit. As such, what he did first, second and third best was kill. Wasn't much to kill on Incain, though.

The not-just-windswept beach looked to him, he looking down on it from his bomber, empty, pristine, untouched by human intrusion. Looked just as lifeless, though hardly untouched, when he finished his last go-over, dropped his last load of maximum-grade, for the Hidden Headworld, explosives, by the time day turned to dusk above it.

Who'd have thought all that was underneath it? The Fatman answered that. Maybe the scuttlebutt was right; maybe he was devil-possessed after all.

Duty for the day done, he flew back to Pear Port. Was past time for a vacation.

==========

Even though she hunkered down between-space throughout the bombardment, what was originally designated Ginny the Gynosphinx quickly discovered she was All the not-so-invincible.

==========

Caught completely by surprise; not so much helpless as directionless to do anything about it; the dozens of devils for so long dozing quietly inside her suddenly woke up; gave her the Mandroid Maker Mother equivalent of gastric indigestion. Consequently the She-Sphinx did mean to send out, again and again, far-cries of alarm, ones heard by apparently no one. Certainly no one came to her rescue; especially not with a dose of anything approximating monstrous bicarbonate of soda.

Not the Dual Entities, her five years returned fabricators, as much as creators, of more than seven millennia earlier; the ones who used to nickname her Ginny, because they couldn't come up with a better appellation. (Lacking any sense of moderation, any sense at all in most respects, she named herself All the Invincible.)

Not the Thanatoids of Lathakra, of late her devic rechargers; not that mass of darkness with a pink face and three eyes that she occasionally remembered to call 'Judge', but whom the name Rhadamanthys also fit (in what passed for her mind anyhow); and especially not much-missed Pyrame Silverstar, whom All regarded as her last best-chance at salvation.

All not only acquired a severe headache to match her barely quelled bellyache; she was thoroughly distracted from what was going on beyond the Dome. Most critically the mandroid functionaries she semi-controlled remarkably close by in terms of miles, albeit on the other side, shut down rather than try to defend the appropriately dubbed Phantom Freighter against the Outer Earth's version of Centauri Island's imported Silver Signallers.

Although it probably didn't matter in any way whatsoever, that their way back inside was thereby lost, more All-built monstrosities failed abysmally to accomplish their anointed tasks out there. Failed in particular, that lot – Crystallion, Hell's Horsemen and their atomic firedrakes, as powered by one of the Idiot Twins, either Tammuz or Osiraq, Mithras's millennia-plus, imprisoned torchbearers – to obliterate said selfsame Centauri Island.

In the end, their end, about all they successfully blew apart were themselves.

========

Hours later, on what was by then Demetray, the 9th of Tantalar, the trailblazing fauna finally gave up tracking Pyrame-Shah down in Absudyl-Minius, (Definitely the ass-end of the Hell Well, as she kept cursing it in mounting frustration at the sheer senselessness of her efforts.) It was situated deep beneath Cabalarkon, the Weirdom thereof, in what was an absolutely massive but, with one anomalous exception, notably flat, weather and plant-free cranial cavity.

There was nothing else for it. She went over to said anomaly, Trans-Time Trigon, and looked for a door to knock on. Why shouldn't she? They were related, after a fashion.

Her deviant father, Chrysaor Attis, was the time-tumbling Dual Entities' half-son.

========

Two that did hear All's far-cry of deepest distress, but perhaps lacked any sense of the immediacy of her need, or the ability to do anything to help her, eventually did respond to it. Did in fact show up, separately, on her no-longer-pristine, now foliage and debris-strewn Prison Beach after dark that very day, Tuesday the 9th of December 1980 on the Outer Earth. By then, though, All feared herself dying.

"You shouldn't be out of bed, Tsishah," Wanderlust told Shenon's stricken, non-Lemurian Aortic, who'd arrived some time before her.

The bleary-eyed, increasingly bluish-skinned cyanotic barely looked up at the newcomer. She was sitting on what might have been a log, though the Traveller was pretty sure it was the shell-shattered leftovers of part of All's equivalent of a fallopian tube; how she, in her role of Monster Maker Mom, whelped mandroid guard-bodies for Lemurians and 'special orders' for those behind the Panharmonium Project.

"It's a disaster, Pusan. Had to have been the Godbadians. Somehow or other the Fatman must have realized we were using All to get Crystallion, Sharky, the Horsemen and their nuclear technopomps beyond the Dome. We are, and we aren't, of course. Shenon's very own, transplanted technomages designed the mandroids, and All built them to specs for us, sure, but it's the load of Gypsium we found in the Krachlan freighter's hold that sank off Incain's coast a few years back that allows us to take it, them in it, back and forth through the Dome."

The Fatman was Alpha Centauri in here, Alfredo Sentalli out there. As Cromwell Necator had heard from his now dead, but still functional, father, among others, for over three decades he was the sometimes host-shell of Thrygragos Byron. Wasn't that anymore, obviously. The Great God was now the brightest star in the Byronic Quadrant of the Sedon Sphere. But Centauri, as he preferred to Fatman, whom both Tsishah and Pusan knew passably well, had always been a bright light in his own right.

He founded Centauri Enterprises before he turned twenty. Even named it after himself (his chosen alter ego, rather), the name he gave himself when Bodiless Byron first brought him inside and he, a fan of Edgar Rice Burroughs' Barsoom series of heroic story sequences, thought he was on another world; one of the comparatively nearby star's planets, perhaps. Then, with the Unmoving One's tacit, though invaluable support, ensured that CE became the corporation that made 'Corporate State of Greater Godbad' a reality, as well as a military powerhouse.

He also, by being there, adrift in the Pacific the same terrible day in August 1945 that the Nagasaki Atomic Bomb went off in Japan, very likely saved Byron's life. Did so by providing him with an emergency shell; this after he, the Great God, had become afflicted with the A-bomb's residual radiation long distance.

To say the least, the (not yet) Fatman and the (by then six thousand years) Unmoving One had a mutually beneficial relationship from their days one together.

(The Great God had ventured beyond the Dome to investigate what had ripped it a new rift, so to speak; what, once it settled in place, became the Nag Gap between Aka Godbad City and the Outer Earth's Centauri Island. Despite there being an impressive distance between Japan and Hawaii, where he came out, he'd almost immediately become deathly ill, presumably poisoned by its far-flung radiant emissions between-space.

(Quite clearly devils and atomics don't mix. Then again, atomics don't mix with anyone, not even within shielded, power-producing reactors in geologically stable areas.)

"All that's neither here nor there, no pun intended," said Pusan, who probably didn't intend to pun; just couldn't help herself. Punning for her was akin to Fisherwoman fishifying or faerie tricksters fay-saying. Came as a condition of conversation with her. At least she wasn't cursing inordinately; something else she was prawn-prone to do.

"Point is he sent in Godbad's bombers to blast the beach to kingdom come. I would have too, if I didn't have a slew of today healthy daughters that I don't want to come back in the moment the first starts dying. Which could be years from now. Not that All looks to be in any condition to go anywhere and retaliate any time soon. My only real question is which of you is going to die first: you or your dog?"

Tsishah was petting a patchy, pathetic-looking, lap-rat-doggish thing that looked far beyond the whimpering stage. It was so mangy or flea-bitten it had scratched, chewed or otherwise worried away most of what was left of its evidently already severely singed fur. Pusan wouldn't have touched it even if she had first transformed her shepherd's crook into a ten foot pike. Which she could have, devic power foci being transmutable shape-wise.

What was only moderately more disturbing and, for a healer who'd put so much of herself into averting it, empathetically sickening, Tsishah appeared as if she could barely manage the petting stage. "Hey, you could cremate me. If I'm as much a faerie fart as my father became once he got dusted – and I was too, once, as you'd know – maybe you sprinkle my ashes over one of my children, maybe I'll come back, three."

"I was just about to get to that. You are aware you have a bitty bat perched on your shoulder? To look at you, it was much bigger, it'd snap it off under its weight."

"That's Toothy. I made him my personal psychopomp. He doesn't like it and neither do I. Had I my Shah-demon I might be able to chomp him human again."

"Why bother? He'd just go off and have Fangs, if she's still around, turn him into a vamp again. Ask me he's better off as a psychopomp."

Fish had reported that Second Fangs, Janna Fangfingers, had been dusted – vampire-dusted, as opposed to faerie-dusted – by Vetala and her soldier last Devauray night. Apparently that event had been recorded by the Legendarian, Jordan Tethys, whose deviancy was so similar to Pusan's many thought them brother and sister.

Pusan always came back as a faun, whereas who Tethys came back as depended on what, albeit usually humanoid race, his children had been. So that wasn't too likely. Nevertheless, it may be Fangs was no longer an issue. Or maybe she was laying low until all sorts of other dust settled and she could make a comeback.

"I am not," asserted the bitty bat perched on Tsishah's shoulder.

"A talking psychopomp," Pusan remarked, unperturbed.

When you'd been coming back, in living daughter after dying daughter, for more than three thousand years – ever since the Attis, Mithras's deviant son by Marut Kanin, sired the first her on the Byronic Goatfish during the height of the Mediterranean Goddess Cult – not much could perturb her anymore.

"Elder Ants recommend against talking psychos; them talking makes them seem more like slaves than properly devoted familiars."

"No slave neither," insisted the bat, flashing his fangs. Pusan was becoming perturbed. "Only thing I'm devoted to is having you for supper, if she'd let me."

"See what I'm dealing with?" said Tsishah, who no doubt felt she deserved better than a mouthy, pompous pomp for all her efforts to preserve his life; or non-life, as the case may be. "Is it any wonder I'm so despondent. All thinks Pyrame Silverstar could be her redemption, I think Shah could be Toothy's, and look what we've got besides neither of them."

She pointed out towards Tempestuous Psychron, the Headworld's eastern ocean. Fish's incubative whale, Island Leviathan, was nowhere to be seen. However, the charred remnants of All's formerly underground, and undersea, factory-like complex wherein and whereby the Gynosphinx manufactured her mandroid monstrosities – integral aspects of Crystallion, Sharkczar and Hell's Horsemen most predominantly – either poked grotesquely out of the foaming waves or bobbed on them like so much flotsam or jetsam. Wasn't so much of an oil spill as a huge ichors spill, but still … there was nothing organic about it.

"It's all destroyed, her reproductive system, our link to the Outer Earth and, any moment now I'm afraid, All's capacity to hold onto the devils within her. She does, they do, they'll come out mean and probably in need of a power-boost. Any sentient being in the vicinity, no matter how well warded, better not be here then."

The look she gave her wasn't desperation; was more like resignation. "Meaning us," she added, just in case the fauna somehow missed what she was implying.

"Maybe not," said Pusan. "From what Klannit told me before I dropped her off on a Lathakran glacier, it sounds like Shah took the Priestess to Absudyl-Minius. Only thing is, finding a needle in a haystack's infinitely easier than finding a demon in the Subterranean Land of the Mandroids. Hell's Teeth, demons and mandroids are made of the same infernal Godcrud. And there's no one home in Trans-Time Trigon. I know, it's there and I checked."

All perked up at hearing that. Could talk as well, after a fashion. "All Stopstone stuff, too. All's monsters all mandroids. Hell Well end in Minius, All mine Minius. Hell, All made Magnus Minus. All Minotaurus mom. All go. All knows Shahdemon. All knows Pauper. Minotaurus my demon, not priestess's demon. All smell them out; All dig them out."

(The lead-headed, but mostly malevolent Magnus Minus, who coated the supranormal known as Mr Miniature during the Suprawar, was actually a demontype from in here. He, a daemonic demiurge who fancied himself Daemonicus Reborn, named Absudyl Minius after himself, millennia earlier.

(Thereafter self-proclaimed the Mighty Minotaurus of just that, Minius, Pyrame revived him circa 4825 YD in order to help the Unities of Lazareme, and their Thrygragos Everyman of a father, wreak her revenge on the Death's Head Hellion. Revived him with vats of pilsner beer produced in the Dinq Doinq Danq Cavern Tavern, which not just Jordan Tethys, the 30-Year Man, aka 30-Beers, regarded as the best brew on the planet, either side of it. Which it was, for thousands of years.

(To this day Wanderlust often both stayed and worked at the DDD whereas, prior to the 1000 Days of Disbelief, it belonged to none other than Datong Harmonia, the Illuminary-named Unity of Balance as well as, for 500 years, the Unity of Panharmonium, her version of it. As for whether All actually made Magnus Minius, even whether she made him on Pyrame's instructions, that could be debated. If anyone felt so inclined, that is.)

"I've a nose too," said Pusan. "And I've eyes, with better night vision than even Toothy there. I'm telling you, it's flat-out hopeless. There isn't an irregular pimple in the place."

"You know what toothless folks say, Traveller," said Tsishah, getting to her feet with difficulty, yet nonetheless re-enkindled enthusiasm. She and said Legendarian, 'Q for Quill' Tethys, went way back, so she wasn't averse to quoting him. "Nothing dentured, nothing chewed. Time to show your subtle matter stuff, Toothy."

Bitty bat to behemoth bat took next to no time. Expanding to take in Pusan Wanderlust and Tsishah Twilight, the latter cradling All, still in canine form, under her arm, was something else psychopomps, even freshly minted psychos, could do with ease. Subtle matter was the stuff of between-space, as expansive as it could be oppositely so, hence Mr Miniature's capabilities during the Suprawar. Flying through the Weird was a dot-ditto; a dick-dildo in his case, as Pusan would say, being a faun.

It took awhile to get there. Toothy didn't know the way but Pusan did. Taking herself out of the self-important bat-psycho, she walked them through the dark-grey universal substance of between-space to their destination. Her shepherd crook made for a decent beacon and, yes, All had a worthy nose. Proved a good, dirty dog digger, ditto.

Had as well a nose for trouble and an urgent compulsion to strike back in kind for slights far more real than imagined. That, though, might not have been entirely her idea. After thirty years of, to her mind, unwarranted punishment in the night's sky; not to mention another week and a half of being bounced around like a billiard ball in need of a pocket to fall into and rest; All wasn't the only one looking for payback.

Begin again problem-Pyrame.

========

Eggs were eminently edible. Baaloch Hellblob was only egg-shaped; was also Sinistral Sloth of Satanwyck. Then again the Highchair of Hell shouldn't have been akin to a griddle either. It was hot; too hot for sitting. Demons were notoriously flammable. Lord Lazy had never moved so fast. Recovered, uneaten. Look up at said Highchair.

"Now what?" he demanded of its occupant, a mass of darkness in a female shape.

"Ass-end of Hell?" said occupant wondered. "Does that make this its Hell-Mouth?"

****

Andy and Ginny devoured the King and Queen of Demons not long after the Dual Entities, mostly Miracle Maenad, made the male and female sphinxes. As told in "Helios on the Moon", this happened during the Male Entity's 61st Lifetime when he was golden-apple-eating Alorus Ptah (the second biblical Adam according to **the Phantacea Mythos**) and she was Trishtar Thrae (Ptah's Eve, mother of Abel, but not Anti-Patriarch Cain). How Daemonicus got out of one or the other, Ginny or Andy, was provided, in smelly detail, early on during "Feeling Theocidal".

The Heliosophos killed during Oriartes Ma's patriarchy, as depicted in "Forever & Days — the Genesis of *PHANTACEA*", also came about during the time Miracle Memory had hold of Pyrame's demon. How Thrygragos Lazareme, aka Thrygragos Everyman, came to be made using 'raw material' taken from Helios has never been told in any detail.

Neither was it ever confirmed that Thrygragos Lazareme was on the Moon at the end of HELMOON. As also per "Hidden Headgames", that was when, ably assisted by the UNES Liberty bombarding it from planetoid orbit, Lunar Trigon came tumbling down.

In all likelihood he was, however. Unless he made it onto the cosmicar Mik Starrus piloted with Rom Kinesis and OJ Maxwell on it, that is; hence why no one can find him on the Inner Earth anymore.

Games 15: **Downwards Onwards Upwards**

========

<u>Birhym, 10 Tantalar 5980</u>

They say God works in manners mysterious. The same could be, and often was, said about the miraculous Godstuff, Brainrock-Gypsium. It was, at least theoretically, often self-replenishing remnants of the original Godhead whence exploded the Big Bang. Whence the Universe; whence also, according to even more tenuous cosmology, Adam Kadmon and the Cosmic Woman.

Not that the Dual Entities accepted they'd been around since the beginning of time; not unless it was in one of Heliosophos's lifetimes that they'd yet to experience.

========

Also on what was Tuesday out there, on the lone planetoid circling the Whole Earth, more specifically in a big old hole clearly not just full of moon dust anymore, Miracle Memory – Moon's Angel, the Female Entity, the Mnemosyne Machine, Lunar as well as Trans-Time Trigon's innards – survived faceless, bloody-minded, as well as bloody red-skinned, Strife's attempt to take her over. Prison-podded then expelled her, aka Fitna Marutia, Marut Kanin, Kore-Eris, Kore-Discord, with relative ease, hadn't she.

Felt good about it. Did not feel so good about sticking Strife in Sophia born St Synne, become D'Angelo ... but what else could she do? Strife had been podded before; ring-gotten, too. Neither stuck, hence the sticking. Would get her out of her maybe original self's nearly eighty year old sister-in-law eventually, she promised herself conscientiously.

(Strife had been stuck in before — during the Simultaneous Summonings of 19/5920. The then recipient was none other than Cybele born St Synne, Mama Sofa's nominal sister. Nowadays Miracle Maenad, the Korant Sisterhood's long-serving Mother Superior, Cybele's mind-over-mind abilities were even more acute than those of prayer-powerful Sophia. At least they were in their youth. Strife eluding her in 1938 Rome, after nearly eighteen years of Cybele holding onto her, proved an instigative moment in the ensuing Secret War of Supranormals.)

Had no time to rest on her laurels. The next day, Wednesday the 10th – yclept Birhym, after Bodiless Byron, on the Head – her Herr Hel Heliosophos should have died and she, Miracle Memory, along with Trans-Time Trigon, should have been dragged back into the time stream with him. Memory took it as proof the Maestro of Confusion, or whoever was really conducting this no doubt ultimately Fatal Symphony, must have still had parts for them to play.

Even though Cosmicaptain Mikelangelo Starrus did manage to cut off Kadmon's head with his aural-generated astral blade, unwanted time-tumbling did not ensue. Would have, had not Helios by that time become possessed by and of

Thunder and Lightning Lord Yajur, the decathonitized, onetime Unity of Order, whom Freespirit Nihila retroactively hated. Would anyhow, should he become dispossessed. Devas could pull themselves together again, but mortals couldn't, at least never altogether as themselves; not in Memory's experience anyhow.

How that came about Memory – one-third of the most advanced, nevertheless ever-evolving computer system in the cosmos – hadn't as yet had time to compute. (She, though not Helios himself, figured a future version of Yajur, one known as Vajra in their 99th Lifetime, already occupied him. For some reason, she further reckoned she was humanized by Nita Night, a future Erebe Thanatos. She was wrong in both cases, thus showing how fallible tripartite-she could be even after so many eventful existences.)

Yajur escaped Cathonia in Mik Starrus on Sedonda-Sunday, the 30th of Maruta. Two days later, after being thrust back inside the Sedon Sphere from an uncountable distance, he engaged the Mighty Eye-Mouth in the Sky in a classic Theomachy (War of the Gods), already deemed the Bright Battle, that was seen above the Head on that week's Demetray and Birhym nights. (Witches, and not just witches, had also started to refer to it as the day the Gypsium stopped.)

This time he didn't escape. His grandfather of a Moloch ejected him; he still holding onto Starrus. Eventually he/they ended up in Lunar Trigon. There they separated, or were separated, and he, courtesy of his most recently erstwhile shell, not only lost his head, he cost the Male Entity his, two-in-one.

Decapitated or otherwise, Yajur occupying their all-of-a-sudden bifurcated joint being meant the Male Entity was not about to die for a hundredth time; was not about to die quite yet, make that. It also meant she, Moon's Angel, his female counterpart, could stay in this devil-infested time-space-present without him bossing her about, at least for the time being. Which was fine with her. Was, sooth said, very nearly how she planned it.

There was only one way to preserve the situation.

As the tri-towered lunar citadel, and her systems built within it, disintegrated under the barrage coming from the orbiting UNES Liberty, Miracle Memory sent a teleportive beam of Gypsium to the cosmicar Starrus and his two middle-aged companions – O'Ryan James 'Big Max' Maxwell and Professor Romaine Kinesis – commandeered in order to get off the Moon. She thereupon latched onto and sent the Yajur-Head, which on the spur of the fleeing moment Big Max had decided to take with them, to their home base, Trans-Time Trigon.

This Trigon, arguably the first of many like-named, tri-peaked landforms, currently sat in Absudyl, the Subterranean Land of the Mandroids. For reasons crud-credible (shit-sensible?), they habitually situated it there – the westernmost terminus of the Head's subsurface Hell Well, lying as it did deep below the Weirdom of Cabalarkon on the Inner Earth of Sedon's Head – whenever they plummeted out of the continuum onto the Whole Earth.

The underside of the Upper Head was honeycombed with eminently habitable caverns. Neighbouring Temporis reputedly had a thousand of them while Pandemonium, the capital of Satanwyck, where Nehrini Purandar's Cosmicar Six ended up on the 30th, had at last count seventeen layers to it, most of them underground and a few in a near constant state of flux.

The Dual Entities chose Absudyl because it was full of mandroid-making muck in its raw, controlling-mind-awaiting form. Some said demons could swim in it but, other than via extraordinary means, humans and most other sentient beings couldn't get into it. Witches didn't frequent it either, because the Stopstone-Solidium Godcrud absorbed – seemed to suck in and swallow – their Gypsium-centred stepping stones upon contact; thus rendering them useless for just about everything, even glitter.

As for devils, unless they were Mithraic-style 'Persians' or Earth Magicians like Dand Tariqartha, the now self-cathonitized Devalord of Temporis, or Yama 'Miners' Nergal's fellow 'Earthlings', Gibran 'Mines' Nimiki and Shal 'Minerals' Ereshkigal, both of whom Lord Yajur ill-starred almost exactly a thousand years earlier, they generally stayed away from tellurian half-lifers, regardless of whether it was no more than merely mundane material.

Feared they'd be immobilized within the chthonic quicksand; as some of them had been a number of times in the past. As Pyrame, Shahiyeda-coated as she was, had been until All dug her out and once again gave her a home to call her own. For a great flat surface of purest crap, as Pusan put it, Absudyl-Minius had quite a history. A her-story as well, since somewhere down here was where the Death's Head Hellion found her life-train's terminus hundreds of years before a different Unity saw off Mines and Minerals.

(Until the Shah-Demon brought her here – and Machine-Memory left them both sunk in – Pyrame had fancied herself something of an Earth Magician in her own right. Now, though, considering how long she'd been immured herein, it seemed apparent her primordial demon, the one she'd fused with in Ginny and Andy's shared digestive tract, had the Persian knack, not her. Something else to pay somebody back for, she figured. For a change, she further figured, that somebody else was Miracle Memory, not Grandfather Eye-Mouth.)

All that Stopstone in Absudyl was why he, the Devil Himself, the Moloch Sedon, never ventured there. Potentially it could engulf and hold even him, a fact never lost on those involved in the Panharmonium Project. The difficulty was either getting him down there or it up there, into the Sedon Sphere. Even before the Dual Entities returned for the start of his 100th lifetime, they'd had thoughts on how to do just that. With the Dual Entities around, realizing those thoughts became that much more attainable.

In terms of salvaging the situation on the Moon, the Female Entity reacted just in time. Seconds after she sent the Yajur-Head to Trans-Time Trigon, James Aremar, captain of the United Nations of Earth Ship Liberty, ordered rocket-torpedoes fired at the cosmicar. As Aremar said when congratulating his gunners moments later, the Liberty's aim was bang on.

(The UNES Liberty had been built and sent into lunar orbit by SPACE, an anagram coined by Loxus Abraham Ryne, Cerebrus and Psycho's father via Eden Nightingale, Fish and Wilderwitch's sister in more than just Flowery Anthea, to counter the perceived Menace on the Moon. It meant, rather niftily, 'the Society for the Prevention of Alien Control of Earth'.

(The born with the century Great Man, the long-serving patriarch of the still extant Illuminated Faith of Xuthros Hor was quite clever when it came to anagrams.

One he denied coining, however, was WORLD, the Worldwide Order with the Right to Life and Death. Its most recent iteration bore responsibility for the kamikaze craft that blew the Cosmic Express into the Sedon Sphere on Sedonda the 30th of last month.

(First WORLD, apparently corrupted by Faceless Strife, was to blame for the death of Aristotle Zeross's wife for a day, Belificent D'Angelo, in 1960. Its denouement resulted in Harry, the second Ringleader, the King Crimefighters' Kid Ringo, re-realizing his supranormal inheritance and, due in part to both Fisherwoman and Morgianna Sarpedon, coming to the Hidden Headworld shortly thereafter.

(Which was where he renewed acquaintanceship with Melina until then always Sarpedon — whom, despite an age difference of over twenty years, he eventually married.)

Miracle Memory – more like Machine-Memory now that she had neither demon nor devil to humanize her – did not waste any time weeping for the three humans aboard the cosmicar. This despite the fact that, except for maybe Mik Starrus, who wasn't born until '43 (the same as Aristotle Zeross and Aremar himself, as it happened), her conceivable template Memory of the Angels – 'of the Devils' according to eldest, still-surviving sibling Raphael, Sainted Sophia's husband – would have known them quite well.

Make that very well, carnally in the case of Big Max, whereas Rom was her nephew by marriage. (His mother, Human Memory's protégé with respect to the Outer Earth's version of the love-loving Afrite Sisterhood, was Roxanne Kinesis, the Gypsium-gifted supra codenamed Slipper. Hot Rox, as she was ever-so-appropriately nicknamed, was Agenor Heliopolis's twenty years younger sister. And Agenor was Memory's husband, Kadmon Heliopolis's father via first wife, Argiope 'Bright Face' born Zeross, Ringleader's aunt, who died having him.)

She still had to find the rest of Helios's body and transport it back to Trans-Time Trigon. Succeeded too, in the proverbial Old Nick of time; found it and one other, a three-eyed 'Nick'. That this could transpire was in turn also largely due to All, as revitalized by Pyrame Silverstar and her absorptive session digging a hellhole in Absudyl to unearth and thereupon reacquire her; Pyrame and a certain little trickster, a Tralalorn-fairified, perpetual seven year old born and bred to be a Trigregos mother, who thought up the stratagem in the first place.

(Human Memory's eldest, long-dead sibling Celestine had at least one probable daughter. When she, Human Memory, was altogether alive, she may or may not have known this explicitly, let alone implicitly. She would have known the trickster, though, under a plethora of different names and guises; Young Life being more of a title than a name. In parts of the mid to late Thirties they even stayed in the same massive mansion: the Family D'Angelos' Roman villa just up the street, and under it, from Vatican City.)

Did so admittedly – Pyrame, All and Hush – mostly to get Freespirit Nihila out of their hair and into Memory's, such as it was when mostly just a machine.

What goes around, comes around, howsoever-haphazardly.

========

"Have you forgotten me, little Lord Lazy?" asked the mass of darkness in a female shape from her perch atop his Highchair in Pandemonium, the domain of all demons.

(The one Hieronymus Bosch rendered, albeit as more of a toilet seat than a baby chair, and its monstrous, man-eating, man-defecating occupant having a bird's head and a slop pot for a helmet. Which, eye squinted, this one might have had. Only two bright yellow eyes shone out of the obscuration, but there was a hint of a beak, or a lizard's snout, beneath the murk.)

"Not you; it's who you remind me of ... a male shape, not a painting. Did your Morrigan die, the other Shah? Have you come back to raise, as you put it, Holy Hell?"

"Male shape, painting, other Shah, Morrigan ... who do you think I am?"

"Shahiyeda Sunrise of course. Not who you're pretending to be, so unimaginatively double-dipping in the same Hell Well of spent ploys, twenty years later. This is my protectorate. I may be a devil, but these are my demons; to them I am a god; to them you'd just be a sod in need of flushing. You need to be gone. As in never come."

"How dare you! This is my domain, has been since time immemorial. I am its queen. Why is there only one throne? Where is my king? Where is Daemonicus?"

"Same place I told you last time you tried this nonsense. Melted out of existence by the true King of Hell, the Moloch Sedon, well over six thousand years ago."

She leapt, attacking him, Baaloch Hellblob. In his own protectorate. She, not Shahiyeda equally Sundown. She — Primeval Lilith, Demon Queen of the Night.

And yes, that was a reptile's snout; an alligator's. She looked an anthropomorphic alligator with wings.

========

Going to an underworld cavity full of replacement Stopstone, which All could absorb as if she was the sponge and it a healing balm – or the self-sought-after relief for excessive stomach acid of the devic variety – was the main reason the She-Sphinx revived so quickly. Was, however, undeniably Pyrame's presence inside her, again, that motivated her such that, also on Birhym the 10th, All took herself between-space to Aka Godbad City.

There she, All, though Pyrame enjoyed it almost as much, proceeded to gain a literally devastating degree of payback for the Godbadians bombing her beach. Literally because the She-Sphinx started a very good day out in Alpha Centauri's private quarters off Aka Godbad City's unofficial headquarters of Centauri Enterprises. Which she derived tremendous pleasure in trashing whilst making a very satisfying meal out of a gaggle of Byronic Master Devas, ones who just happened to be already gathered there for some reason.

Aphropsyche Morningstar – APM All-Eyes, Byron's Venus, whom Telepassa of not just Godbad worshipped – and her immediate brother Damon Goldenrod, who once plated Manoa in gold, were among the heartiest courses in her welcome, if unexpected feast. They, along with as many as ten of their lower born siblings, more than made up for her loss, by Byron-dictated release, a week earlier of two of their higher born siblings, firstborn Umashakti Silvercloud and the other third born, Nevair Neverknight, whose star was already upstairs for its second shine in his lifetime as an individually solid being.

The void left by the absent, and probably lost for good, Atomic Idiot, either Tammuz or Osiraq, hadn't been adequately filled by inhuming Trawl the Taskmaster shortly before the Byronic Nucleus came calling. However, downing so many Byronics all at once – including an aforementioned couple of last week's then constituent Nucleoids – proved almost as efficacious a constitutional boost as reacquiring the Pauper Priestess after vacuuming up all that Solidium-Stopstone Godcrud.

(Something Primeval Lilith would have done as well; thereby refreshing herself before she walked, unless she swan, from one end of the Hell Well to the other.)

Thus even more energized, All went on to stomp dozens of planes on Aka Godbad's air field then, for good measure, took herself to Godbad City itself, the Corporate State's capital and a onetime Utopian Weirdom like Manoa, Kanin City and Shenon's non-Lemurian Aorta (Atrium?) of a Quarter Queenship, to do a ditto on its huge Air Force base. Might have even totalled Cromwell Necator' bomber in the process. (Not Crom, though; he'd gone on vacation.)

Had enough get up and go left to start cleaning up Incain once she returned home. Only rested because she had a pair of unexpected visitors, ones who'd escaped the Fatman's domicile, along with the Fatman himself and Jordan Q Tethys, moments before she began her morning and well into the afternoon's sport.

Mostly because of Pyrame's influence All resisted the temptation to greet the three-eyed, golden-gorgeous stunner with a hearty: 'Hi, mom. How fares the sanity?' She nevertheless did as they requested; transported unsaid mom via her between-space, cross-Dome digestive track to the moribund Male Sphinx in Egypt.

Did so without once hinting non-pal Pyrame was back in charge of her, of All.

========

Lunar Trigon was ruined, but the headless remains of her onetime lover from nearly thirty-five hundred years earlier were not.

========

The gods, devils that they were, that she was and continued to be, celebrated their wedding three and a half millennia earlier. Celebrated his death as well, years later, after he and his atheistic Xuthrodite followers caused Strongyne – in the Aegean Sea, northeast of Crete; the remnants of which, in modern times, was known as Santorini or Thira – to erupt ever so catastrophically for the Minoan and, to a lesser extent, Achaean societies of the eastern Mediterranean Basin.

The same cataclysm may well have been the basis for what found its way into the Bible as the ten plagues of Mosaic Egypt. Likely also forced the famously as yet unidentified, if not necessarily unidentifiable, Sea Peoples who eventually invaded Egypt into their wooden vessels of cruel conquest.

But it definitely, as well as incidentally, caused the end – or at least the beginning of the end – of the Goddess Culture that had thrived in the region, the crucible of western civilization, for hundreds of years. Moreover, and this was intentional, it sealed a rent in the Cathonic Dome that allowed demon-devils like her to come and go outside, where they'd reigned as worship-rewarding gods. Now though, other than her, they were nowhere in evidence.

"Why didn't you truly die then?" she cried to the non-devic stars visible from the Earth's Moon. They gave no answer, but someone else did.

"Because he couldn't then and won't now. I won't let him."

The voice came from a dark, barely perceptible presence in the somehow broadcast semblance of a human woman. (Both Helios and Miracle Memory loved dressing up. While showing off on the UNES Liberty the previous Sapienda-Thursday, he introduced one of his alter egos as the Hologram Houdini. So maybe that's how she did it, used his Holocaster to project her insubstantial shade.)

The semblance was hers — minus the third eye, butterscotch hair replaced by Nita Night darkness of same (Nita Night being the supra-nickname achieved by Human Memory's niece, Anita D'Angelo, once she attained her Summoning Heritage as, briefly, Madame Midnight), her broken chains, the talismanic torc around her neck and the golden glow of Gypsium that some said made her up.

(Just as Hellenic Athenians believed their Athena was a virgin, her adherents, who numbered most of those living on the Hidden Headworld during her heyday, didn't believe she needed anything as tainted, as corrupt, as a debrained demon in order to solidify herself, their vision of loveliness, of female perfection. Were probably right as well. She wasn't just godly; she was living Godstuff.)

"Memory?"

"Harmony!"

=========

This much, and perhaps this much alone, could be said of Sinister Sloth of Satanwyck, the Lord Laziest Master Deva on the planet. He was very good at self-preservation. Couldn't be bothered moving to avoid Alligator Ally's assault on his personage. It wasn't that he was too stunned to move. He didn't even need to blink, though he did.

It really was his protectorate.

=========

Might have shrugged slightly when the Evil Eye, which was actually former Viceroy Ibal's power focus, appeared between them. Had already informed her Dark Sedon, not her fabled Daemonicus, was the real Demon King. Perhaps hadn't said 'since Ragnarok', but might have, given the opportunity. Which she, Crocodile Kate, didn't give him.

Taking inspiration from said (Sed?) Mighty Eye-Mouth in the Sky, he happily let Ibal's Brainrock-rendered-mutable, Mightily Much More Massive Mouth-ball (mouth + eyeball) swallow her; her, Cayman Carmen, not her Hellblob-him. He might be adorable, but he wasn't about to become edible.

Next issue was what to do with her, whoever she was — was awfully impolite to seek suicide without a proper introduction, be she a Surrogate Shahiyeda or a seriously silly 60's she-thing wanting to be redubbed Second Shot Shah. Easy to answer that, what to do with her. Couldn't keep her in Hell. He'd made that mistake with either her or her predecessor in 5960 and look what he ended up with, Paradise for the Damned.

Had as well mentioned Grandfather melted his – Sedon's – only known predecessor out of existence centuries pre-Flood. Maybe she'd enjoy sharing the same fate; infatuated with infatuate, soft 'a' at end. Unless 'infatuatee' was a word. Which it would be, if he wanted it to be, at least here in Satanwyck. Knew just the place for it, submerged in the lava lake of Sedon's Peak. Could the Evil-Eye Mouth-Ball spit-ball that far between-space?

Only one way to find out.

Vaguely hoped the obdurate obelisk Tvasitar Smithmonger habitually made of himself overlooking it wasn't standing in the way. That he didn't get a splat instead of she getting a splash and, evident shape-shifters never counting as lesser beings, melting away in short order thereafter, just as the incomparable Harmony always claimed she'd forced Kore-Discord to in the aftermath of Phantast-Dream's Crimson Conspiracy most of two thousand years earlier.

Could care less if he missed. Sooth said, which devils always did, so long as she didn't come back any time soon, it didn't matter to him if he hit the target, large as it was, or not. Wasn't like he was ever going to check. Would be too much effort. Still, a far cry to its devic Dand just to confirm plop wouldn't be amiss.

You never knew when you might need a new power focus.

========

Lazam, 12 Tantalar 5980

Two days later (Friday on the Outer Earth), a mostly recovered Demios Sarpedon finally convinced Nanny Klanny's son, General Quentin Anvil, to assign some men, including a couple of fully-equipped, Dead Things fighting, Sraddhite veterans, to drive him to the pimple of land they called Desecrated Dustmound in the Godbadian equivalent of an ATV (All-Terrain Vehicle).

Once there he was stunned to discover that, in place of his wife's body, an oversized, stone – presumably Stopstone – sculpture of her stood.

Had to be a bizarre joke.

========

The woman who'd been described as a walking statue on the Outer Earth had been replaced by actual statuary of non-ambulant alabaster. How it got there was a puzzlement wrapped in an imaginary newspaper like an English takeout of fantasy fish and chips. Which suggested it was the work of one or other of the two tricksters, Young Life or Young Death, who claimed to be her Tralalorn-fairified parents.

Whoever was actually responsible – Hush more likely than Aug the Dog, since she was so good with fairy stocks, ensorcelled illusory wood or, in this case, hardened mandroid mush – Demios vowed that before he died it would be erected in the enormous central square of Cabalarkon, the City.

He'd place it there – yes, after a parade worthy of marking her heroism – in front of those two splendid, millennia-old piles, the Citadel of the Sleepers, where many of twin sister Melina's Illuminaries and the Weirdom's scientocrats toiled away on a daily basis, and the tri-towered Cathedral of the Thinkers, what was effectively Devic Eye-Land's museum.

He'd be sure to place it within sight of her brother, Saladin Devason's abhorrent Skyrise. Which, true enough, he'd only seen in pictures sent to him, via her intermediary 'spies', by Mel herself, its High Illuminary. And that, it went without saying, just before he had it demolished and the ground it stood upon salted.

Of course none that couldn't happen until he was Master of Weir. More to the immediate point, it definitely went without saying that the statue was too big to fit in the back of an ATV. He'd be back, though, he promised the veteran Sraddhites he left behind to guard it. With a helicopter so big and powerful it could heft it into its cargo hold without any need for him to bust his brain trying to do a ditto via his eye-stave, no matter how pre-Earth it was.

Some things, vengeance not included, were best left to modern technology.

========

Devauray, 13 Tantalar 5980

When she wasn't being leontocephalic, like a standard Shekmet-sphinx or, in male devic terms, Djinn Domitian, once Mithras's Herald, Heliodromus, sun-runner or messenger of the gods, All sported the head of a usually two-eyed human female. Which in turn would have reminded Outer Earth demonologists of a manticore. Not inexplicably did remind many Inner Earth manticores of looking in a mirror

(The Hidden Headworld's prides of manticores mostly ranged in the Forever Forest of Wildwyck, an untamed, Lazaremist land in its occipital region.)

Sometimes her hair was dark, like Human Memory; sometimes it was golden, like Datong Harmonia, before Abe Chaos all but killed her with the Susasword. And sometimes it was silvery, like Gloriel D'Angelo, D-Brig's Radiant Rider when she wasn't using her rainbow attributes, or her long late aunt, the Celestial Superior born Celestine D'Angelo out there, who was murdered a decade before Glory's birth.

In here the arguably most renowned Anthean of the late 59th, early 60th Century of the Dome, was known as Celeste Mannering — her surname meaning, peculiarly to many, nothing more than she was sired by a man. Seeing All wearing that face, the face of her putative mother, did not encourage the little trickster.

Because it wasn't of her mother; it was that of Celestine-Celeste's devic half-mother. The third eye gave that away.

========

There were those on the Inner Earth who called Hush (believed born Pandora Mannering) Young Life. True to her word she bopped over and down to Incain on what she assumed were Anthean Agates or their equivalent, left behind by Tsishah Twilight, Fisherwoman or Amphitrite of Lemuria, all known associates of All the self-proclaimed Invincible She-Sphinx.

By then, two weeks after the launching of the Cosmic Express, which she clandestinely witnessed on the Outer Earth's Centauri Island, she'd heard from Centauri's daughter-in-law, Janna St Peche-Montressor, who hadn't left Hadd until the 9th, of the death of her believed daughter by Augustus Nauroz (Auguste Moirnoir – the Black Death – on the Outer Earth; Young Death in here.)

There wasn't much she could do about it except mourn Morg. Hadn't even gone to the Sraddhite Monastery, on Lake Sedona, in order to commiserate with son-in-law Demios and granddaughter Andaemyn. According to Janna, both were doing poorly, Andy in particular, but that wasn't the main reason she avoided the monastery. Aug the Dog was the Sraddhites' chief revenant and Young Life did not get along with Young Death.

She'd considered going to Shenon in order to be with her other granddaughter on Morg's side – she had stacks of grandchildren on Sal's side, all of them born out of wedlock – but didn't like what she'd heard about the radical witches' latest Panharmonium Project. When you're dealing with devils, chances are you're going to get burned, albeit probably not before you burn an inflammable bag full of folks caught in the resultant wildfire.

Can't trick a trickster, she always said, and Morg hadn't been the only one dissembling about it when asked for details. Besides, had it been altogether on the up and up, as in approved by life-loving Antheans' Nightingale hierarchy, they'd have invited her to join them — she was, after all, bred to be the Great Goddesses' mother-in-waiting pre-Summoning and, to the surprise of many, remained in the Superior Sisterhood's good books.

Plus, Hush shared her Daddy Alpha's suspicions – more like dead certainty – that all the bad boogie befallen since the launching of the Cosmic Express and its interception by WORLD's kamikaze craft could be traced to All, and therefore to the witches' machinations intended to bring the Trigregos Sisters to earth, one way or another, gone tragically awry.

So she gave into Janna's insistent 'reminding' (read nagging) and finally got up the nerve to go back to Incain. Ostensibly it was an effort to do as Janna wanted, for her to persuade All to release the unfortunate Byronics she'd eaten earlier in the week, as presumed payback for what their Godbadian 'subjects' did to her, Incain itself and its then buried, now reburied, mandroid manufactory.

(The Byronics amounted to accidental casualties in the witches' Panharmonium Project. They shouldn't have been there, in the Fatman's now ruined private domicile, atop and to the side of CE's Aka Godbadian subsidiary headquarters. That they were was mostly due to Hush herself. She'd captured them in Utopian Prison Pods on the Outer Earth and only released them to deal with ... well, faced with golden-whom she was suddenly faced with, it seemed like the thing to do at the time.)

Janna did miss the fullness of her occasional APM occupancy. So did the Fatman. Ever since All consumed almost all of All-Eyes three days earlier, something had been lacking when it came to Janna getting him out of bed in the mornings. A lot of that had to do with her entire family having to live together under the same roof, even if it was a luxurious hotel. To say she was distracted by them didn't account for all of her, to his mind, negligence.

(Entire family for Janna included, foremost, her formerly Outer Earth based husband Yataghan raised Montressor, father of their 4-year old daughter Cholorain Gudrun, and the Fatman's son by long gone Emeralda Plantagenet, but also Hush herself and said 4-year, who was jealous of the trickster's access to her grandfather. The Fatman's other offspring, by none other than Sister Jordan, Kirin hence Tethys, remained confined to the nunnery she was born in 27 years earlier.)

Exhaustion and the early stages of her second pregnancy affecting Janna's enthusiasm for early morning duties wasn't all of it. The kernel of APM left in her, what All-Eyes referred to as one of her little angels, really missed her siblings. Sooth said, her incessant banging on and on about getting All to release the Byronics was mostly just an excuse for getting Hush out of there. Cholorain Gudrun was a real pest and, as much as she could be just that herself, both Hush and Janna felt her a bad influence on the 4-year-old.

The trickster was also acting as a howsoever-reluctant emissary for Centauri Enterprises and therefore the Corporate State of Greater Godbad. Above everything else the Fatman was a highly successful businessman and worrying about an enraged, practically unstoppable monstrosity going on another rampage wasn't good for just that, business. It behoved him to oblige Hush to sort out the She-Sphinx, no matter what it took.

Hush got along fine with All; didn't with Pyrame Silverstar, whom she still hadn't figured out had helped motivate All a few days ago. No surprise there. The devil or demon child Tralalorn – generally conceded to be Pyrame's brood sister and not her daemonic daughter – was why she was a perpetual seven year old, this after she'd already had two children of her own. And Trala had done the dastardly deed – devolved, reduced, reversed, both her and Pandora's husband at the time, Augustus Nauroz – under Pyrame's direction some sixty years previously.

"The answer's no," said Pyrame's humanoid head atop the Shekmet-sphinx. Warded against possession as she was, Hush nevertheless couldn't prevent her reading her mind.

"Nothing to do with you, Priestess," she disagreed, dangerously dismissively.

Hush realized whom she was dealing with at once, but not how sensitive – call it fragile, thin-skinned, temperamental, retaliatory – Pyrame had become to slights, real or imagine. In petty-petulance-particular, after thirty years a silver star glaring out of Cathonia, Pyrame was decidedly no longer anyone's 'Priestess', least of all the Moloch Sedon's.

"It's All I'm here to see. Let her speak for herself."

"How about I gob on you, instead?"

"What? You wouldn't dare!"

"Hey, I'm decathonitized. I can do whatever I want; get away with it, too. Besides, I'm not going to kill you. I'll leave that to Trala. She's rough on her toys."

========

Multi-Horns, the Bull of Mithras, Kind, Cruel or Indifferent, as the case may be, couldn't believe his three eyes. That immense, seemingly impossibly flying gargoyle had to be All of Incain taken to the air over Apple Isle for the first time Plathon could recall in years, maybe decades. Surely she (it?) didn't plan to violate the sanctuary of Theopolis Hill in search of devils to munch or, speculatively, even hopefully, ones who'd escaped her?

The conurbation of Corona City was his protectorate. Strictly speaking Theopolis Hill lay outside it. Did she know that? Did it matter? More to the immediate point, even if she flew into Corona, would she leave if he ordered her to? The Thrygragon Compact only applied to devils. Dare he even approach her to demand it? Her appetite was bebrained daemonic, either spelling, when it came to his sometimes unkind kind.

After All circled the city and neighbouring countryside – a good percentage of which was overgrown jungle – a few times, as if just to make sure everybody noticed her, he had his answer. The She-Sphinx came to ground in front of the Mithradium atop Theopolis Hill; where any devil was, by Sedonic decree, allowed to dally without concern for recrimination. Shortly thereafter the Devil Child's latest chimera, Tralalorn riding it, trotted out of the Weird and All's head went from leonine to tetrahedral.

So, he realized, the Pauper Priestess, once as much of a Perpetual Presence on the Hidden Headworld as Trala and the Moloch Sedon, was back from her stellar exile and in control of the She-Sphinx. Pyrame Silverstar, his much younger sister in Mithras, who never had a power focus to call her own, had simply come by to say hello to her brood sister, unless she was her daemonic daughter.

Then she vomited and Plathon had a supplemental answer. Maybe-mommy had brought maybe-daughter a new dolly.

****

How Strife got away from Cybele still (as far as anyone knew) St Synne was told in "Heliodyssey I — The Moloch Manoeuvres". The two-part opening of these story sequences was set almost entirely in Rome, Italy, in January 1938. Anita D'Angelo played a prominent role in that lengthy web-serial. So did Human Memory and Hush Mannering.

The Miracle Memory who made off with, yes, Primeval Lilith, the Demon Queen of the Night, in 19/5950 did so at the end of Heliosophos's 11th Lifetime. As per the second *'Heliodyssey'* web-serial entitled "Helioddity", set in the same lifetime, albeit a dozen years earlier, in 19/5938, it wasn't the first time she'd done so.

It may be that Pyrame Silverstar wasn't always in denial as to the identity of her demon. However, she certainly has been since being decathonitized, if not for the first time this century, then definitely this time, which may or may not be the second time overall. Being ill-starred is, as one might expect, a traumatic, mind-jarring experience for devils.

Being stuck with Pyrame inside All's shared digestive tract, Lethal Lily wouldn't have been conscious during Ragnarok. Which, as per the graphic novel "Forever & 40 Days — the Genesis of ***PHANTACEA***", occurred in the year 230 PD (Pre-Dome).

Even though Baaloch Hellblob knew the Smiling (Forgettable) Fiend fused with Daemonicus at some point after Ragnarok, he wouldn't be able to recall that since Smiler wasn't there with them in Satanwyck on the Tenth.

Couldn't have been, as per the endgame of "Goddess Gambit".

Games 16: Unchain My Demon

========

<u>**Devauray, 13 Tantalar 5980**</u>

Some philosophers called Life Itself, chock-a-block as it was with high and low notes, a Fatal Symphony.

========

If so, it's conducted by a Maestro of Confusion with everybody who ever lived playing in the orchestra pit. Even a Fatal Symphony had to have a score, though perhaps not a composer; especially not a solitary one, one that would make not just Christians want to capitalize Composer. Most games had scores. Scores are how one determines who wins and who loses. This particular game was still afoot. So far all it had were losers.

It also had many names. If the Moloch Sedon was behind it, which he wouldn't be given he, often thought the Devil Himself, was its main, targeted fatality, it might have been called a Sedonplay. If the Conquering Christ, Wiccan Warlock in here, Jesus Mandam out there, was still around – which he wasn't, thanks be to Celestial Christ; thanks be to John Sundown and Raven's Head, more like – the game of 'Kill Sedon' might have been better known as 'Kill-All-Sedons' since that was his strategy.

It might even been called bowling, because that was what would happen if anyone managed to inject all or even most of the Stopstone stuff in Absudyl-Minius into the Sedon Sphere. Certainly they'd have a resultant bowling ball, a baby black hole, with which to play it. (As opposed to the faux black hole, actually the once again Wandering SAG Gap, that Miracle Memory hooked between-space near the Moon in order to link this microcosm with that of New Weir's macrocosm, to use her terms.)

A few of the Panharmonium Project players and losers – notably Nergal Vetala, the Blood Queen of Hadd, her Soldier, Cosmicaptain Dmetri Diomad, Akbarartha's despised quarter-brother in Dand Tariqartha, Kronokronos Susano Mikoto, the two remaining Tethys Triplets, Katatribe and Yomikuni, and Tsishah's mom, Morgianna died Sarpedon, the turncoat Morrigan – called their version of this game the Trigregos Gambit.

Freespirit Nihila got caught up in it, too; make that three, since fellow first-borns Umashakti 'Lunar Gravity' Silvercloud and Methandra 'Hotstuff' Thanatos had as well. If they gave their version of it a name it would likely be the Goddess Gambit. This because that was their aim, to become the Three Great Goddesses, in effect their own mothers, re-embodied here on Earth. That would make them superior to their own siblings and cousins; brood brothers and husbands in Uma and the Thanatoid's case.

Howsoever anyone called it, it was just a variation of the Panharmonium Project. Indeed, had they been successful, the firstborn goddesses wouldn't have wanted to kill Sedon so much as bring him to ground, quite literally. Unfortunately for those, mostly witches, still foolhardy enough to persist with it, their version of 'Kill Sedon' needed the three Sacred Objects in order to win it and the Diver must have destroyed them by now.

Which, as Wanderlust told Twilight – reunited with the other Shah, her demon, as she was – really was a shame. All the more so since quite clearly Telepassa's three eldest daughters, Ino, Agave and Autonoe, were incarnations of the Trigregos Sisters. While, given their parentage, combined with the infrequency of triplet births, there'd always been suspicions of same, there wasn't much doubt anymore.

The terrible talismans Tvasitar Smithmonger crafted specifically for third generational Master Devas' three-in-one – except at birth – second generational mothers wouldn't have adhered to them all the way between-space from Diminished Dustmound if they weren't, would they have. (It wasn't a question.)

Of course, as Pusan told Pyrame Silverstar, she in All, fay-saying typically, when they both came to see her on the Prison Beach of Incain upon her return from Ap Isle on Devauray the 13th, what could be made once could be remade thrice. All it would take, in their view, Wanderlust's and Twilight's, was for Silverstar to get laid. And they had a Subtle-Matter-coated body tailor-made for doing just that.

Both remarkably and resiliently healthy again, Tsishah was feeling as feisty as Pusan, who sometimes disappointingly for her wasn't a shape-shifter; always was horny, however.

To which Pyrame, out of All, responded: "Get laid, or get screwed again?"

========

Something else often said was that the best marriages were made in heaven whilst the worst ones were made in hell.

========

In some respects, their Mnemosyne-forced marriage to each other – not that in 5980 females generally married other females; union, put better then – was made in the heavens, on the Whole Earth's moon. In other respects, Sedon's Head was Hell on Earth; Seventh Sinistral Sloth's Domination of Satanwyck being proof of that.

Demons, not even Primeval Lilith, whom she must have held onto for something like ninety of Herr Hel's lifetimes, never providing her much in the way of oomph, Machine-Memory preferred having a devil humanize her. Happenstance, rarely a reliable friend, presented Nowadays Nihila as that devil. Needing meaning for her renewed existence, the latter had come to the Moon in search of her Great God of a father, Thrygragos Lazareme.

In a way she'd been drawn there – as in seduced, not transported – by Q's quill (once Rumour's power focus) somehow etching Cadmus Agenorid (the Male Entity in his second life) in lieu of Lazareme, on the Moon of all places. Shouldn't have happened. If in here (which it was), it couldn't locate (via artwork) anyone, or anything, beyond the Dome; not even between-space beneath it. Yet it did.

Aka Thrygragos Everyman, the Great God had been good at using Rumour's, then the Legendarian's, talisman back in the day — notably on the Mithramas Day of 4376 YD, ever after recalled as Thrygragon. But long-distance, from the Moon?

Alarm bells should have gone off, and perhaps they did, but Harmony had always regarded her Lackland sire as her bedrock and she hadn't been able to find him anywhere she'd looked since her comeback, albeit as Freespirit Nihila.

She (formerly also Datong Harmonia to Illuminaries) was so desperate to reconnect with her father, she was even willing to chance going through All, Ginny the Gynosphinx, to her millennia-moribund male counterpart on the Outer Earth, Andy the Androsphinx. Despite her butterscotch-blonde or golden hair, All mistook her for her mother-maker and felt obliged to oblige her, minus the masticating.

Once through the Dome it was comparatively easy for a godly someone who really was mostly Brainrock-Gypsium Godstuff herself, to leap to the Moon — where she did indeed find the headless remains of Cadmus Agenorid, ninety-eight lifetimes later. Or was it? Could Miracle Memory have drawn her there herself?

Memory had no known history of familiarity with the workings of Rumour's quill and, besides, she could have ported Nihila up there any day of the week. Had no need to ask first, either. By contrast, the Legendarian had to first gain acquiescence for his astonishing quill to work properly on behalf of anyone. Memory wanted her up there, why bother with subterfuge?

No, it had to have been Father Lazareme; there was no other explanation. So how – and why – had he got to the Moon in the first place? More to the point, where had he gone by the time she got there? It was irrelevant now that they were united, two-in-one. Still, unanswered questions had a way of lingering, very much annoyingly, long past their due date.

Better make that reunited, since they often had been thus, howsoever short term, in the past. Short term because neither was debrained, both had always had exceedingly strong personalities and were used to getting their own ways, so long as the main males in their lives, Heliosophos and his Great God lookalike – who was built using Helios's cells, just as Sedon was using Cabalarkon's – didn't object.

(Actually Lazareme only looked like a blue-skinned, sun-blond Heliosophos when he was looking at himself in a mirror. To anyone else he looked like their idea of God the Singular.)

Plus, the onetime Unity of Balance or Harmony was a self-pronounced free spirit these days; determined to remain so as well. To top it off, ex-Balance really, really, wanted to embrace her new name for herself – as opposed to the bordering on defamatory Nemesis designation others assigned her when being harmonious wasn't working very well – and annihilate her triplet-brother, Lord Order.

She wanted his head, colloquially speaking, for abandoning her to their equally hated, though apparently unreachable, at least for the time being, brood brother Abe Chaos, Unholy Abaddon, a week before her traditional, Autumnal Equinox, feast day in 5492. That, howsoever-ironically, she sort of got his head – half-got it anyhow, both literally speaking and severed from his shoulders – accounted for the immediate awkwardness of the moment.

(According to Jordan Tethys on Birhym-Wednesday, the third former Unity was trapped in much younger sister Antagone "Perfection" Negaura's Land of Nothingness on the Cattail Peninsula, where everything was reversed as if a photographic negative; not that such a thing existed in 1492 out there. Might have in here, in

5492, but if it did it was probably in a Weirdom like Cabby's or even Kanin City, which other brood brother Chaos hadn't got around to destroying as yet.

(Unless you could figure out how to alter your constituency from matter to antimatter – which apparently Chaos could once, but couldn't or wouldn't again – there was no way into or out of it anymore. Of course that didn't mean she, Nihila, couldn't pull it off; just hadn't got around to it as yet.)

Said awkwardness worked both ways. Since annihilating Yajur would consequently kill, if not precisely annihilate, her already headless, Herr Hel of a Heliosophos, the Female Entity was presented with a distinct dilemma. Nihila was good to keep her whole again for a while … but might it not be time to make use of Pyrame Silverstar again? Generally speaking she was paper bags more docile, even compliant, than the always wilful, but never before quite so challenging, ex-Unity.

She decided it was. Was a shame she couldn't find her. Or was it even worse … make that, for Pyrame, terminal? She was decathonitized. Had the mandroid muck she'd left her subsided within last week abolished her, the same as it had the Celestial Superior – her spirit self – in 5938? Further to that, would Nihila, so transparently locked into her own avenging angel agenda, even let her far-look for Pyrame?

More pertinently, she did, she found her, would Nihila let her ditch her?

========

Above Sedon's Peak flew Aortic Tsishah. She, a devil within her and a demon without her, was riding a creature of nightmare.

========

This would be All of Incain in her most common form, that of a winged, female sphinx with a lion's head – one that glowed with nuclear might. All had effectively turned herself into a technopomp; one powered by an Atomic Twin, one Tammuz by Illuminary-given name. Unless it was one Osiraq by dot-ditto. One of Mithras's equinoctial torchbearers; the one not lost on the Outer Earth.

Technopomp – not to be confused with renegade Utopian technomages, many of whom now lived and worked in the land area of the Lemurians' Aorta (Atrium?) on Shenon – was a term coined by Crystallion, born Crystal St Synne, in one of her more lucid moments. It referred not so much to Hell's Horsemen, all of whom were mandroids and, as such, creatures of All, as it did to their Nuclear Dragons, the lot of them Monster Maker Mother-moulded firedrakes powered by the other Atomic Idiot, Osiraq; unless it was Tammuz.

Which meant it was very unlikely Silverstar could fulfill her vow of almost two weeks past to King Harvest (Underlord Yama Nergal) up in Pettivisaya in return for deliverance to All on Incain. When two made the enduringly radioactive wasteland of the present day Ghostlands, chances were poor only one, of what had once been three, could clean it up all by his lonesome.

Then again the third – Solstitial Summer to devils, Novadev to antique Illuminaries – hadn't been shining out of the Sedon Sphere for the same couple of weeks by now. He might be able to duplicate what the missing Equinoctial, and whichever Atomic Idiot wasn't lost, might have accomplished in that regard.

Trouble was, how could anyone anywhere find him? None of the decathonitized devils ended up where they were supposed to — on the Prison Beach of Incain, as a matter of abjectly failed design. Indeed, Purandar's cosmicar was the only one that ended up on the Inner Earth as far as anyone knew.

(Weirdly, all seven of the 'alphabet' bunch who started out on the not exactly empty cosmicar containing the Apocalyptics et al, the one that ended up on the Outer Earth's Damnation Isle, did reappear beneath the Dome. These were cosmi-companions A, B & C on the far northeast down-slope of Diluvia near the DDD; cosmicompanions E, F & G on the far southwest side of Diluvia, bordering on Hadd, and 'D', Cosmicaptain Dmetri Diomad, well west of Hadd-Diluvia in the Forbidden Forest of Kala Tal.

(Blame the unknowable qualities of Brainrock-Gypsium for how they got any-where without a cosmicar. Everyone who knew anything about the launching of Cosmic Express did.)

While her trans-Dome link to the Male Sphinx, via a shared, between-space digestive track, wasn't required – except by Nowadays Nihila, on Birhym the 10th – All's abilities to make use of the absolutely amazing Godstuff found in the sunken, then raised, Krachlan freighter proved invaluable. All the more so when massively assisted by the worship-bolstered Parents Thanatos long distance from Lathakra via Klannit, their azura-daughter's mirrors.

That was how the She-Sphinx sent Crystallion and her tellurian terrors, Hell's Horsemen and their technopomps, to the surprisingly near Hawaiian side of the Dome, aboard the selfsame Phantom Freighter, starting the previous Mithra-da-Monday, the 1st of December 1980. Their initial instructions were, when the time came, to blast Centauri Island's Nag Gap out of existence by the compara-tive expedient of sinking the island. What man makes, mandroid breaks. So they claimed; should have had little difficulty proving it either.

This NAG Gap, a long-lasting rent in the Cathonic Dome, came into being when the Americans dropped an A-Bomb atop the Japanese City of Nagasaki in August 1945 out there, Hektoris 5945 in here. The resultant gateway to the Inner Earth had been exploited by Byronic Master Devas and the Great God, their second generational father, ever since.

Subsequently some of their number, most likely Sharkczar, Sheba-Strife and Solomon-Daemonicus, determined that while sinking the Outer Earth's largely manmade islet wasn't too likely, obliterating it in much the same way the Elysian Fields were when they became the Ghostlands was entirely feasible. (There was a Centauri Island on the Inner Earth as well. Part of the Panic Isles that dribbled south-westward across the Gulf of Aka from Krachla toward Godbad proper, Alpha Centauri – Alfredo Sentalli beyond the Dome – owned it.)

Neither were to be. Neither anymore were Crystallion, Hell's Horsemen, the atomic firedrakes (Nuclear Dragons) they rode, nor, as near as anyone in here could make out anyhow, either Tammuz or Osiraq; one or the other. Enter their names, those that had them, on the never-shrinking list of the not-to-be-anymore; losers the lot of them.

Crystal was the illegitimate, perhaps foredoomed, undeniably bitterness-filled daughter of Sedon St Synne and Corona Power, OMP-Akbar's still living ex-wife. Born in 1946 and never very stable; like Harry, Europa, Gloriella and, among the aforementioned many others, a succession of twins born to Loxus Abraham Ryne by a succession of his wives, Cerebrus David Ryne being only one of them; she was yet another former charge or student of Headmistress Virginia Mannering.

(Ginny to many; for – as far as anyone knew – a non-supra, she was one of the most accomplished of the myriad Summoning Children. Not being Morgianna's twin she definitely wasn't Hush's daughter. She was, however, quite possibly her Summoning Aged sister by Celestine D'Angelo, aka Celeste Mannering, whose Living Agate aspect Ginny housed for a while. Proving her claim to being the Celestial Superior, it seemingly survived her murder in 1923, albeit initially inside a D'Angelo family pet, a daemonic black cat named Bast.)

A good percentage of Crystal's instability was due to the fact Strife started messing with her mind in 1960, twenty years gone now. Her mental and physical condition thereafter deteriorated so badly it was considered something of a mercy when All helped to transform her into a mostly mandroid, hybrid human a few years earlier. That was when she began calling herself Crystallion.

Was still calling herself such when she self-destructed trying to take Sea Goddess (Thalassa either D'Angelo or Thanatos, or both) with her into the endless night on the 9th. That act was both her last and likely her least lucid moment in a life and half-life consumed by bad moments.

All of that was, as far as both All and Pyrame were concerned, not so much water already run under the proverbial bridge, as so much radioactive ocean-current currently turning seawater surrounding the Outer Earth's Centauri Island into a fish-free zone. Was a case of the best laid plans of witches, devils, machines, mice and men *'gang aft agley'*.

There'd been a lot of that going round since the launching of the Cosmic Express. Tsishah-Sandwich, as she, the meat between the devil within and the demon without, thought of herself, hoped their effort to seduce Tvasitar Smithmonger into remaking the Trigregos Talismans wasn't another.

True, as a still active Afrite, Telepassa of not just Godbad would have been a better choice. (The story, apparently not at all apocryphal, of how her aunt, Hot Rox, Slipper, seduced the devic Smithy in order to get back outside was well-known amongst members of the various Sisterhoods.) Ex-Europa couldn't be relied upon, though; especially now that All and, more importantly, Pyrame had refused to release the rest of All-Eyes, her devic goddess.

Besides, she'd have had to first dispossess herself of Amal-Althea (aka Althea Brand, Lazareme's goatish nurse-slash-healer) and, even if the Traveller would happily take her on again, which she probably would – and Althea would go back to her, dot-ditto – that might not be advisable. Although it had never been confirmed unequivocally, theirs may well be a super-symbiotic relationship; meaning, maybe, one couldn't survive without the other anymore.

True also, as a fauna, Pusan Wanderlust would have loved to take on Tvasitar unabashedly, as in concupiscently – wouldn't be the first time – but she wasn't about to let Pyrame take her over first. And Pyrame was key to their scheme. The devic Prometheus, as the Smithy was often thought of, hence his Prometheum of a domicile, owed her a power focus. Why not call it interest and make three?

All in all then, albeit with none of them in All, Tsishah – insulated by, and in firm control of her Shah-demon – was probably their best choice. Of all the things she'd done in the name of Panharmonium, this had to be the wildest. She just hoped it would be the most enjoyable. Or, just as much so, not the dumbest but the numbest. Just hoped as well that her Shah-demon didn't reawaken, again, and try to eat him whole.

Tvasitar was no devic Spirit Being. Indeed, when volcanism was among your attributes, chances of a made-demon digesting him were Nihila-nil.

========

Sometimes obelisks were much more than phallic symbols on the Hidden Continent of Sedon's Head.

========

That was especially true of the dented obelisk standing immovably in front of the magnificently megalithic, not to mention massive, manor house, the afore-mentioned Prometheum. It overlooked his, by default, for roughly four thousand years, devic demesne, the huge caldera and distant shore of Sedon's Peak, a lava lake filled with molten Brainrock. Its three cliff faces, in the right light, looked like devic goddesses — none other than the Trigregos Sisters, according to many.

(The Prometheum sat atop the middle cliff, yclept Demeter, whose likeness reminded some of Datong Harmonia, the Unity of Balance, in the fullness of her unmatched prime.)

It, he, the obelisk, was a devil, a third-born Lazaremist. His immediate broth-ers were the physician, Askeezyoos, whose Great God of a father, long before Fisher-woman came along, used to call him Surgeon the Sturgeon for fun, and Dand Tariqartha, aka the Chronocollector or Time-Space Displacer. The impressively powerful Dand was Lazareme's Persian or Earth Magician. Very few, if any, other Master Devas could equal his abilities when it came to controlling the vaguely man-droid-like, tellurian mantels, sometimes capitalized, or half-lifers.

(Lakshmi of Lemuria, just turned 18, had officially ruled Subcranial Temporis in his stead since the 6th. That she was the eldest surviving Kronokronos offspring of its Trigregos-poisoned, and thereafter self-cathonitized, former overlord had every-thing to do with the War of the Apocalyptics. That and the fact she gave the rightful Kronokronos Supreme, OMP-Akbar, the boot as soon as what was left of his D-Brig drove the Quadrang Nucleus upstairs into Sisert, the Silent Sands of Cathune, that exceedingly eventful Devauray at the beginning of Tantalar.)

His Illuminary-given name was Tvasitar Smithmonger. He was, after Pyrame Silverstar, the second for sure Master Deva to become an independently solid indi-vidual. (The 'Tralalorn is a Demon Child' school of thought didn't consider her a 9th born Mithradite, whereas highborn females who attained solidity, even pre-Earth, always did so as amalgamations; conglomerate devils. During the Zodiacal Age of Taurus, for example, Mithras's Boss Cow, later dubbed Divine Coueranna, wasn't as yet Kore of the Many Names. She was Kore of the Many Kores.)

Tvasitar was the only devil who could fashion devic power foci such that every other third generational devil that made it to the Inner Earth after the Genesea, the Great Flood of Genesis, welled up – and down – could become solid. (His was the first, an anvil; hence why devils often called him Anvil the Artificer.)

That it took him two thousand years to figure it out was mostly down to being in the right place at the right time. In other words, it was a fluke.

Ask Klannit Thanatos, who was inside her demon, a reflective glass creature akin to a mobile mirror of the sort known as Klannits, whence her name, whilst he was inside his, a Gobble Stone Rockhead. She was with him, her demonic lover, on Sedon's Peak when it erupted. Or ask Pyrame almost always Silverstar. She was there as well, momentarily thereafter.

Sooth perhaps surprising said, even for devils, she air-walked out of the yet-erupting volcano hand in hand with her paramour of not just that time. Only then she was Queen Gomorrah and he, presumably Sedon, though she tended to call him Judge, was King Sodom. They'd just survived the Dual Entities attempt to assassinate him, more so than her, via an asteroid. (Unless it was a Utopian generational ship that had run out of oomph.)

Their survival was quite an inordinately convoluted, his and her story; his and her stories, better make that, since Klannit and Tvasitar were hardly bystanders. Plus, there were a Pusan and a Jordan involved; a pair of ill-starred human lovers, as it happened. (Happened in the traditional sense of ill-starring; humans couldn't be cathonitized, catasterized, the same as devils.)

The first power foci he made after his own – after his Rockhead demon lost its mind due to pervasive Gypsium particles in the air, not just the lava flow, dot-ditto – were replacements for Queen Gomorrah's very much, even then ancient regalia. And, yes, they were a mutable crown, a mirror and a sword. (The second set, which he dedicated to devic fathers, not mothers, consisted of a just as mutable mask, cloak and cruciform. The were the Judge-King Sodom's regalia, also lost in the eruption.)

If today's gambit worked, then it wouldn't be first time Tvasitar Smithmonger remade the Trigregos Talismans.

========

The She-Sphinx landed next to the howsoever chipped, self-calcified devil.

========

Tsishah Twilight, Pyrame Silverstar inside her, her Shahiyeda of a Shah-demon outside her, clambered off All. Shyly, also slyly, claiming a preference for privacy – what she really wanted was to remove the Mandroid Monster Maker from temptation, just in case she had hunger pangs whilst they were otherwise too occupied to prevent her devouring them – she instructed the She-Sphinx to come back when psychically called.

After All, whose brain was artificial, not daemonic and therefore vulnerable to too much ambient Gypsium, flew off to forage, or at least explore what for her amounted to either a new realm or one she hadn't visited for a very long time, Tsishah approached the stone monolith that was the devic smithy. As she did so, she pumped herself psychologically for the assignation ahead. Antheans used to do this sort of thing all the time, the Aortic tried to persuade herself.

It was one of main methods they used to get through the Dome after Harmony shut down the Tholoi Gateways she'd inadvertently generated not just during her era of Panharmonium, but for centuries prior to then and the NAG Gap opening up. And she was an Ant — one now closer to fifty than forty, true; one who had her children already and had never particularly wanted to go to the Outer Earth anyhow, equally so.

(The Smith's 'Sheen' protected those who wished to swim across the lava lake far below, and over which All had flown, and thereafter dive into the grotto off it. Known to some as the Wishing Hell or, less frequently the Totem Pool, that was where the Stationary SAG Gap, so long as it wasn't wandering off again, could generally be found.)

(Another potential exit, the so-called Kore Gap on Apple Isle, belonged to the Korant Sisterhood. Tsishah was on good terms with its Mother Superior, Miracle Maenad, but it may not be open anymore. Certainly Sheba Faerieflight, their ally in the Panharmonium Project, couldn't access it and she was Miracle Maenad's granddaughter. As for the so-called Hir Gap, named after the Hiroshima Cavern in Temporis, it collapsed in on itself moments after opening in 19/5945.)

If only to quell appreciable trepidations, Tsishah cheered herself that it was not altogether her who was about to have sex with a Rockhead (Rock-cock?), presuming that was the price Anvil demanded. And it usually was for favours soon to be rendered. Or not, as the case may be. He, like she, could always say no.

After first ensuring her Shah-demon wouldn't reflexively eat her again, she allowed Silverstar to come to their joint forefront. Materialist that Pyrame was – like Strife, albeit only on the Outer Earth, since Sedon would cathonitize her the second he detected her within Cathonia, she was an excellent Etherealist; could manipulate her aura proximately as well as tangibly – the devil brought her own clothes. Virtually none of it went much higher than her waistband. Brought her own head too; tetrahedron that it was.

"Wake up, big fellah. Time to get hard a different way. I've a favour to ask."

"Been a while, priestess," Tvasitar yawned, once he sucked back, visibly painfully, rather than shucked off his stone semblance and realized who awaited him.

"Been a while for me, too. Over a week."

"That's not what I meant. You missed her, by the way," he said, massaging the bruising on his upper chest and left shoulder where the dented area had been on his obeliskoid form.

"Missed who?"

"Your demon. Hellblob long distance swore he wasn't trying to hit me, just wanted to get her out of his domain and into mine, as in melted out of existence."

"Hellblob again," she all but cursed. "Why'd he think it was mine?"

"He didn't. She did. Once we got to talking."

"I.C.," she said, making a joke. "What'd you do with her?"

"Funny you should ask …"

========

Pusan Wanderlust didn't have to track down the Untouchable Diver, though he, UD, Yehudi Cohen, no more found her than she found him.

He rolled over, as if in a nice warm bed – which he wasn't, though the ground was appreciably bordering on hot – and found something entirely non-pillowy staring down at him: an impressively large Gynosphinx. True, it was comparatively tiny by comparison with the Giza plateau's moribund equivalent, what not just Illuminaries of Weir still sometimes referred to as the Osiris Sphinx, but it dwarfed him.

Was it salivating and, if so, why did its drool resemble liquid mercury?

========

After WWII ended, and rather than return to war-ravaged Germany, where Jews, even half-Jews like him, still weren't welcome, he moved to Israel. (Back then it was still ruled by the British as the awkwardly identified Mandatory Palestine.) Thereafter, officially, the Diver became a legitimate university lecturer, amateur mythologist, not overly religious biblical scholar and field archaeologist.

So he knew that, being wingless, the Giza Sphinx was male; an Androsphinx then — Andy the Androsphinx, he fancied characteristically whimsically, without realizing that was precisely how its fabricators, more so than creators, originally, not to mention unimaginatively, designated it. (Or, if he once knew otherwise, which he may have, he no longer did.)

This one might have passed for a manticore of legend. Had a lioness's only vaguely human, Shekmet-style head (meaning no mane), folded demon-wings and disturbingly humanoid, hopefully motherly-milk-filled, very-much woman-ly-shaped breasts; as opposed animal dugs. That made it female, the same as the one that riddled Oedipus before he went off to diddle his mother, howsoever-unwitting-ly, though no less enthusiastically.

(There were many different types of sphinxes. As far as he knew the lion's body was a constant, but Oedipus's Sphinx had a woman's head, so this wasn't it.)

He'd been taking in Gypsium ever since his arrival, thanks to instructions more so than directions given to him by Telepassa's troubling daughters — he'd have called them enchanting but, being on the Head, the word might have a different meaning; one that involved induced memories. They'd showed him Sedon's Peak on a map of the Hidden Headworld, told him to visualize it mentally, then in effect think himself there. Which he did; worked too.

Turned out it was on the enormous Cattail Peninsula's mainland, east and not very far inland across from Shenon as the crow flew, or the Diver dove, albeit between-space. Was just on the other side of the Land of Nothingness, which on their advice he didn't try to cross, and the renegade Irache Nations' home away from home, which he did, also on their recommendation. (A passage that did not go unremarked by a currently bodiless spectre who believed himself the epitome – couldn't say embodiment, since he didn't have one – of the Irache underworld.)

Inhuming so much Gypsium after melting the Trigregos Talismans out of existence in the lava lake caused him to blip. Might have come out of it a couple of times, very briefly. Couldn't say yay or nay to that, not for certain, but had, however, probably dreamed the bit about coming to with a winged alligator-demon clamped to his head and thereby (presumably) reading his mind.

Had always been prone to nightmares, had the Diver. When your putative conceptive father was a von Alptraum – meaning just that, nightmare – that per-haps wasn't surprising. (During the war years he was active in, the old baron, Tyrtod von Alptraum, earned the justifiable sobriquet of the Nazi Nightmare. Even today, as Cerebrus confirmed the first few days they were on the Outer Earth at the be-ginning of the month, his son Günter, who therefore might have been the Diver's howsoever-legitimate brother, was known as Prince Nightmare.)

Having only de-blipped moments ago, he had no idea what day it was; let alone, other than it was daylight, what time it was. Didn't really have a chance to worry about it. Had on his gorgon goggles, which he only suspected were a devic talisman. (They were, though whether Neith and Lathe, Count Molech's Lamiae, were either/or Stheno and Euryale, he wouldn't know.) And as per always wore his sponge rubber, sleeveless, homemade sealskin and hood, which he never took off for fear of disassembling.

(The Diver, a Summoning Child, had his abilities-triggering run-in with an undersea slab of Brainrock after pushing an explosives-laden raft out to a German freighter he not just hoped to sink to the bottom of Hamburg Harbour in early 1938. It did, blow up and sink; though before he could get far enough away from it to be unaffected. January 1938 was some fifteen years before proper wetsuits were invented and even more years before they became available commercially.)

That old saw about curiosity and the cat? How about getting along like cats and dogs? Well, whatever else he was, the Outer Earth supranormal wasn't a cat. All, however, was rather fond of taking on dog-like semblances. If the Diver realized how brightly he was glowing after absorbing all that the Gypsium, he might have forgiven All for mistaking him for a devil and having him for lunch.

Forgiveness was something else he didn't have a chance to contemplate.

========

The term 'nihilism' had been around long before the Russian philosophical and literary movement of the mid-Nineteenth Century on the Outer Earth capitalized it.

========

Sure, the Russian Nihilists questioned and protested against conventional and established values, but a nihilist already was considered a proponent of just about any negativistic philosophy. Darwinians, also of the Nineteenth Century, albeit more so in the English-speaking world, were often called nihilists simply because they tended to believe in the survival of the fittest.

All it really referred to was a 'me-first, screw-you' attitude. Consequently, lugubrious Libertarians, frustrated by rejection of their, to them, perfectly Utopian ideals by the conservative mainstream, were nihilists. So was the considered incomparable Harmony, the already failed Unity of Panharmonium. Once Thrygragos Lazareme's Unity of Balance, she was now a determined, as well as self-determined, Nihila.

She wasn't consciously around in the 19th Century beyond the Dome, the 59th underneath it. Was nailed immovably to a boulder of Brainrock and left for dead in an Stopstone-sheathed cave within the desolate Crystal Mountains of the Head's easternmost, occipital regions. Had been ever since the Year of the Dome 5492.

She'd been pinned to it, with the Susasword, by brood-brother Chaos, not other brood-brother Thunder and Lightning Lord Order. Nevertheless, Order, whom the Illuminaries of Weir named Yajur after an Outer Earth Vedic God (rather, his bolts of Vajra-lightning), knew exactly what Chaos – Unholy Abaddon, whom the Illuminaries named after the angel who lived in the Bottomless Pit of Apollyon, from the Biblical Book of Revelations – was intent upon doing and hadn't made the slightest effort to prevent it.

His lapse of filial loyalty had nothing to do with laziness, fear or ignorance. Yajur wanted her out of the way so he could go after Abaddon full-bore. And that's exactly what he did. Except, he was the one who ended up cathonitized; Chaos merely ended up committing devic suicide. And suicide for devils had yet to prove more than just third eye fatal.

Extreme, make that absolute, payback was definitely due both; overdue both. Wasn't most of half a millennium overdue for her. She'd had her punishment, and eaten it too, for five hundred years. Without Harmony around, Order and Chaos went at each other as unrelentingly as they did so unremittingly; no quarter asked, none given and with no thought whatsoever to whomever or whatever they trampled beneath their often superhumanly enormous feet.

Which, on All Death Day, the 1ˢᵗ of Maruta 5494 (1 Nov 1494, beyond the Dome), actually amounted to more than half the Headworld's sentient population. 'Actually' because on that date, the Ambulatory Dead outnumbered the Ambulatory Alive. Thus once again proving azuras were such indiscriminate whores they'd animate anyone.

That her immediate brothers were doing exactly what Grandfather Sedon commanded them to do still hadn't percolated through to her. The Headworld needed purging from the poxes and plagues she involuntarily brought inside from beyond the Dome. Involuntarily does not mean innocently of course. Manslaughter's still murder, just a matter of degree is all.

She wasn't the only hence contagion collector; however, she was the main Master Deva involved. Although some of the others were bebrained demons holding onto devils such as Sinistral Envy of Satanwyck, the rest were wholly human conscripts chosen by then Morrigan, then also High Illuminary of Weir, Quoits Tethys and her lackeys. Which explained how the likes of Hieronymus Bosch, Albrecht Durer and Tomas de Torquemada ended up in here for a few, thereafter thoroughly forgotten, as in memory-wiped, weeks or months as the Outer Earth's 15ᵗʰ Century wound down.

(The Moloch must have known no one else could, or would, do what the male Unities did — and even they wouldn't have done anything of the sort if she, Nowadays Nihila, was around to 'balance' them off against each other. And if that meant Sedon played a Trigregos Gambit all those centuries ago then, perhaps arguably, he was its only ever winner.)

Ex-Harmony came altogether alive again the moment Kronokronos Susano Mikoto, a 30-years' banished headman of one of the so-called 'living' caverns within Subcranial Temporis, yanked the Susasword out of her chest, and out of the slab of Godstuff, on Devauray the 6ᵗʰ. Too bad for him, Vetala's Soldier having blasted him into a candidate for immediate resurrection, he didn't stay alive long after in effect liberating her.

Too good for her, she immediately realized the Unity of Balance had not been resurrected. Out of Harmony's nothingness had come … She needed a name. Two words related to nihilism occurred to her foremost: a seldom used noun, nihility, meaning nothingness; and a verb, annihilate, meaning to destroy utterly. Which was what she – the always around, but usually suppressed, Nemesis aspect of her complex personality – wanted to do to both Chaos and Order, if either/or remained extant in whatever age it was now.

Mere moments later, she chased Vetala's soldier – who'd machine-gunned Mikoto and made off with the Susasword – through the Weird to the Faerie Garden of her two broods' younger brother in Lazareme's Temporis. There she encountered, and recognized as such, her own incarnation, Wilderwitch, no other name, and her companion, Dand Tariqartha's deviant faerie half-son Akbarartha, the rightful Kronokronos Supreme of same, the Thousand Caverns of Subcranial Temporis.

They'd vanquished Vetala's soldier by then. Somehow got rid of Vetala too, who'd only been a ghost. Hadn't killed him, though. Especially given how things turned out, probably should have. Be that as it may, even if she'd been able to stick around, she was still too much of a thoroughly inculcated Master Deva to do it – kill Vetala's soldier – for them. This despite her having already decided to christen her new self Freespirit Nihila.

(That she hadn't been able to stick around, well, as she now knew, due to humanizing Miracle Memory, that was down to a former friend of theirs, OMP and the Witch: namely Aristotle 'Kid Ringo' Zeross, Ringleader. Ironically, he was the very person, now in his late thirties, who abandoned the then King's Own Crime-fighters, plus Sundown, Raven and said Witch, to their fate, what they'd thought of as Limbo, a quarter century earlier.)

Had, on balance, all things considered, done rather well for herself, for Freespirit Nihila, in the intervening week and a day. Certainly her fleshy bits, de-brained demonic as they undeniably were at first, had knitted up physically perfect-ly. Her headaches, non-physical as they likely were, she attributed to her constant battle of minds for body supremacy with the Female Entity, whom she'd united with on the Moon. Her frustration level, though, was approaching unbearable.

Bifurcated Yajur was just there, right in front of her, should she look in the proper place. His head was in one transparent Tantalus, his body in glassine other one. Both display cases were filled with preservative Cathonic Fluid identical to that used upstairs, in the Weirdom of Cabalarkon, for the likes of the Undying Utopian, Sedon's Daddy Cabby, and D-Brig's nominal leader, David Ryne, Cyborg Cerebrus.

Identical because guess who invented them all those multiple millennia ago in the first Weir System? No guessing required. She was humanizing the answer.

Should she look in the proper place within the partially hollowed-out, hence waffle-holey hive of Trans-Time Trigon, that is. Which was Machine-Memory's ter-ritory and which she could only do when she was winning her battle for individual dominance of their joint being with selfsame Memory. And thus far their battles had only provided her the briefest of victories.

Was it any wonder she had a sore bum?

=========

The Diver's digestion meant Pyrame-Tsishah didn't need a favour from Tvasitar Smithmonger. Nonetheless, she, they, enjoyed herself, themselves, immensely. Quite lit-erally immensely. Tsishah in particular was sore for days. At least she wasn't recathon-itized. Not that, being part faerie, part Utopian, yet nonetheless mostly human, she could have been.

Or needed a response, other than 'no' to the whole notion of playing a Trigregos Gambit with new talismans.

At least she wasn't killed.

=========

Sedonda, the 14th of Tantalar, 5980 YD

It took a tad less than two days for Godbadian General Quentin Anvil to get per-mission to reassign a huge, armament-transporting helicopter and its crew to Demios

Sarpedon. Took the personal intervention of Alpha Centauri to get it given. Regardless of how it came about, it easily met Sarpedon's needs; was perfectly capable of lifting the massive sculpture someone had made, and somehow transported to Desecrated Dustmound, of wife Morgianna, the Hecate-Hellions' missing Morrigan.

He was under no illusions; presumed her dead and buried when Drenched Dustmound began collapsing in on itself on the Ninth. Unless, that is, her not quite dead corpse was inside it.

Which would make it a cocoon, not a coffin.

========

Be she in it or not – and, if she was, be she alive or otherwise – he figured it'd look tree-tremendous, as Young Death put it, in Cabalarkon's central square. Figured further that's where he'd erect it, this long-before-then as good as surgically opened effigy (husk, if it was cocoon). He'd do so as soon as he could after succeeding her brother, his brother-in-law, as Master of Weir. Reckoned, with the appropriate assistance, that shouldn't take much more than a year.

Why shouldn't the most modern civilization on the Head add the most ancient one – long pre-Earth ancient as it was – to its list of satellite states? No reason, agreed the Godbadian general, who had Sraddhite blood, as well as Sraddha for a middle name. Quentin consequently Sraddha Anvil, a Summoning Child, like both Demios and Morgianna, was already anticipating his next big assignment from the Corporate State.

Two weeks to the day after almost dying in the same spot – albeit late at night, not early in the morning, which it now was – Sarpedon noticed an attractively built, if perhaps somewhat skinny, though hardly skeletal, darkly dressed woman sifting soil through a boxed screen on the largest hump of ground in the near-area.

Even though it was still a mere pimple of its former self, the Sraddhites and their living allies, possibly even native Iraches – who couldn't be considered the Brown Robes' friends, just the vampires' foes – no longer dubbed it Diminished Dustmound. Now they referred to it as Desecrated Dustmound. (They couldn't very well call it Desiccated Dustmound because it rained there now, a lot.) Weren't to know, but should have called it Demon Mound.

The Sraddhite veterans he'd left here to guard his wife's whatever had kept in radio contact with the Lake Sedona monastery, where he and daughter Andaemyn, who had finally begun showing signs of making a full recovery, were staying. So had the nonetheless heavily-armed Godbadian salvage crews General Anvil bivouacked in the vicinity, just in case more weirdness presented itself. It had, but she was most of it, so he'd been expecting to see her.

Was shapely but, as he was about to find out himself, spookily pale. Dressed exactly as they'd reported: like a widow, caped and cowled, veiled and all in black. Even though it wasn't raining, for a change, it – if she wasn't human – couldn't be a Haddit Zombie since those that hadn't rotted away had mostly dug themselves deep underground, apparently to await a new master or mistress. Possibly one of Hidden Headworld's two notably supernatural Iraches, the Molech Xibalba or his acknowledged father, Lamechlan Night Owl.

(The former, not so jokingly once aka Reilly Haddeus, an Irache rabble-rouser obliterated by Janna Fangfingers, may have been reborn; had in fact been seen, syinx in hand, pied-piping the rat-attack into the Headworld Museum on the 28th of last month. By contrast, the latter, another of that Janna's enemies, was something of an anomaly, an Irache vamp; one that, thanks to the support and patronage of Metisophia, Jordan Tethys's bodiless, devic half-mother, took the form of her totem, an owl, rather than the traditional bat, when on the prowl.)

Neither the Sraddhites nor the Godbadians who radioed in about her reckoned she (it?) was any other kind of Dead Thing; nor a daemonic Indescribable, all of whom seemed incapable of flawlessly masquerading as a human being. Besides, having lost Hadd, those riding vultures or Vultyrie had already fled westward into the Forbidden Forest of Kala Tal, Vetala's brood sister, or maybe just to the north of it, to the Bloodlands, New Valhalla.

Those still on foot most of a week later were doing a ditto, heading west in perhaps forlorn hope of finding refuge within the arachnid devil's still inviolable protectorate, the southernmost of any Mithradite Master Deva. (The Bloodlands, also Sedon's Inner Nose, was no longer a devic protectorate. However, Battle Babe, the Morrigu Badhbh, had been making moves to its west; her Godbad-financed forces massing on its border with Twilight, Sedon's Outer Nose. Which was a devic protectorate, that of Krepusyl Evenstar, Lazareme's Venus.)

Finally, this time because it was broad daylight, hence quite cold for the latitude, but with nary a cloud in the sky, she couldn't be a vampire. That didn't mean she couldn't be Nergal Vetala, somehow reverted to her devic self and suppressing her third eye as she searched for her lost moon-sickle. Though why she'd need a sand-sifter for something that big, who could say?

Was of course one way to find out. And they'd done that too, the Sraddhites and Godbadians who'd been watching her these last couple of days. They'd gone over to speak with her, the Black Widow, as they thought of the night-shrouded madwoman who had been as good as haunting Diminished Dustmound. Learned, much to their added bewilderment, that she was trying to piece together a mirror broken during the decisive battle for Hadd.

Which suggested she was an Athenan War Witch. Except, when they asked her directly, she insisted the term meant nothing to her. Besides, why would anyone carry a mirror into battle? It defied logic. Not really, explained Thartarre Holgatson. Oversized mirrored eggs and amulets were among the Sraddhites' most sacred objects. And, being their High Priest, he should know

Along with General Anvil, Demios often went over the reports coming in from Dustmound with him. Unless it was the other way round, as they – the island's big shots – would have it. Occasionally went over them with Young Death, the Sraddhites' Chief Revenant, as well. That would be the male trickster once known as Auguste Moirnoir, the Black Death, beyond the Dome.

In here's arguably fairified Augustus Nauroz also denied having anything to do with (supposed) daughter's statuary remains, as he called the hence still largely inexplicable coffin-cocoon. Said it didn't sound like something Hush, Young Life, would do. Suspected it was devil-doings, but the witches behind this Panharmonium Project of theirs couldn't be ruled out either; not with their link to All of Incain, the Mandroid Monster Maker.

Demios speculated out loud that this Black Widow of theirs might well be looking for the Amateramirror. It was one of the Three Sacred Objects; he, his wife, both her daughters, her brother Saladin Devason, the rest of Andaemyn and War-lord Mikoto's Good Companions, Ringleader and many another had been trying to find it for decades now. Had to be, insisted the High Priest, who it turned out had unwittingly had it for most of those selfsame years.

Masters of call-me-Cabby's Weirdom brandished a replica of it on important occasions, but Vetala's Soldier, Trigregos Incarnate (aka the Trigregos Titan, to recall an earlier Melina, Tethys become Somata, not Demios's sister, whom Illuminary records had as the Trigregos Titaness for her rebelliousness), had been wielding the long lost original, along with OMP-Akbar's Homeworld Sceptre, when he attacked Sraddha Isle a week ago.

By all accounts it, the original, was as obliterated as Reilly Haddeus was sup-posed to be. Almost as soon as he, Akbarartha, the rightful Kronokronos Supreme of Temporis, recovered his equivalent of a devic power focus — thought the source of much of his undoubted might — the next day, he destroyed it and its two sister objects, the Susasword and the Crimson Corona.

The head of his Homeworld Sceptre could blow up anything, including itself, albeit only to re-form almost immediately. Still, Thartarre had a nagging notion that her soldier had shattered it, the mirror, before Akbar destroyed what was left of it minutes later. Did so with someone looking out of it; the same as D-Brig 4 – Akbar, Furie, Sundown and Raven – had been until the Diver got them out most of a day after the Trigregos Titan trapped them in its reflection.

Presumably that explained the need for the sifter even though, if so, then sure-ly whoever was stuck inside it would have been just as thoroughly destroyed. Vetala's Soldier, due to his ill-advisedly tangling with the amazingly alive and apparently unaged membership of the newly christened Damnation Brigade was; that the High Priest could clearly recall.

He, once Cosmicaptain Dmetri Diomad – a finally lifeless, eyeless crust of pre-maturely decrepit humanity at the end – was definitely buried beneath Dustmound as it collapsed in on itself.

Something else to chalk up to OMP-Akbar, Young Death verified. He then added, typically ghoulishly, that so wrecked was he, the soldier, even he couldn't have got him moving again. Not all that significantly, he further added, he shared with Thartarre a tinge or tingle of something else about the whole episode; some-thing besides Vetala's death, atomization or cathonitization and her soldier's disin-tegration; something before the Nihila Nereid enormity of Freespirit Fisherwoman showed up and brought her Borealis Brolly into play above Dustmound.

That hardly surprised Thartarre. Everyone who'd been there that he subse-quently queried as to what took place conceded much the same uncertainty. This Diomad might have shattered the mirror before Akbar got to him; then again he might not have. Was a great deal going on for most of them simultaneously; trying not to get killed primarily. Worse for him, the High Priest, was the dread his own muddled memories of what they actually witnessed left him. They, his recollections, were so imperfect and so fast-fading he feared the onset of dementia.

Young Death, who was there initially inside Garcia Dis L'Orca, another of those born in midsummer 19/5953, and who was still out there somewhere, a Dead Thing Walking, had a similar, personally disquieting sensation of premature senility. His was more understandable than Thartarre's of course. Fairified or not, he was well into his seventies.

He did say that, whatever Dustmound's Black Widow was looking for, he doubted it would be, could be, Vetala's moon-sickle. As admittedly unknowable as Brainrock-Gypsium Godstuff was, he knew what became of it and so did they. Dead Garcia had smacked it into the head of yet another Dead Thing, the one he'd taken over after vacating her, none other than Alastor Molorchus, Morg's ringer.

It re-empowered him as if he, the otherwise deceased Outer Earthling, was some kind of rechargeable Brainrock battery. Which was probably as good a description for Molorchus as any. And not just him either. Would tend to confirm the theory that the astonishing glow Vetala's soldier was emitting last Sedonda night was due to him inhuming a superfluity of Godstuff just before he all-but-singlehandedly attacked the monastery to such devastating effect.

He, Young Death, had gone on to use him, Morg's ringer, to send D-Brig only-4-left back to the Weirdom of Cabalarkon, where they presumably still were.

========

Prior to arriving on, at least partially because of her, Haunted Dustmound that morning, Demios had already decided to interview this oddly unidentified Black Widow. In some respects he could care less who she was; just wanted to determine for himself if there was any connection between the mirror whose remnant shards she was single-mindedly sifting around in the dirt looking for and the Amateramirror. Might even use the coercive capabilities of his eyeorb to ensure her soothsaying.

So, once again armed with his pre-Earth eye-stave, the oldest on the planet, what still manufactured its own eyeorbs and provided some degree of support as well as levitation, should he need it, he limped over to where she was ever so diligently digging away in order to have a few words with her himself.

And so they did. She seemed friendly enough. Told him her name was Olivia Tenebrous and that she hailed from Tenebrife, the capital of Crepuscule, the Grey Lady's devic protectorate on the Hidden Headworld's far west coast. Which, the sun hardly ever shining in the Land of (hence) Twilight, Sedon's Outer Nose, accounted for her paleness. She even allowed him to scan her for devic possession. Which he did; no devil she.

Turned out she was an Athenan War Witch; one with Mariamnic training, too. Which was how she could hide herself when she didn't want to be seen; like at night when she slept. Didn't want that bruited about, though; unsure as she was about how the guards and soldiers would react to witches in their presence.

She had indeed broken a mirror during the final battle for by then Drenched Dustmound; a keepsake from her long time, but now dead, Sraddhite mate. If he had to know, which he didn't. (Every Sraddhite carried a mirrored pendant or two, often moulded into something akin to one of those disco balls so tiresomely found in Outer Earth dancehalls these days. Often cleverly housing flash grenades, Brown Robes used them to detect and, if triggered, defend themselves against Janna Fang-fingers' mostly non-Irache vampires.)

This self-professed widow claimed she was simply trying to find its pieces so she didn't have any more bad luck. Not that there could be any worse luck than losing a lover, she added dolefully. As a fighter himself, one who'd lost more than a few of his Zebranid comrades and friends recently, he appreciated how badly combat unsettled people, no matter how well trained they might be.

As logical as it sounded, as consequently unhinged as she also might be, her explanation nevertheless struck him as too facile; like she'd come up with it after testing out a variety of flagpoles on her previous interrogators, be they Godbadian, Sraddhite or, perhaps, Irache.

He felt obliged to point out that, on the evidence of her meshed box and the piles of bits and bobs she'd left dotting the area, she hadn't been having any luck finding pieces of anything resembling glass as yet; just, as one might expect given where they were, buckets of bone fragments.

Perhaps she should let him mentally fashion a proper sifter. Showed her he could do it too, visibly telekinetically. Silently entertained notions of showing her a whole lot more of what he could do, once they got to know each other better. She really was very attractive under all those layers of darkness. Plus, her skin was almost as white as Morg's had been; looked a whole lot more pliable, though.

After thirty years of marriage to a very white witch, a Goth — as her type and their favourite bands had recently started being called on the Outer Earth — would make for an appealing change. He wondered if he could use his eye-stave to fashion them a comfortable bed, assuming she didn't have one already in what must have been her personal Shelter.

Assuming also that War Witches could conjure up such things as Shelters. His wife and the likes of Sorciere and Fisherwoman certainly could, but they were also Mariamnic trickster-witches like Hush, Morg's little mother. She did say she was from their homeland. Didn't fay-say it, though. Did Mariamnics always far-say? Why was he thinking nonsense?

Much to his disappointment — muted delight also, as if he'd just been released from her spell — she declined his offer. Said it kept her busy; that she had all eternity.

Feeling a distinct chill he left her, seriously strange creature that she was. Shaking his head in amazement at what he'd just been contemplating, he made his way back to the Sraddhites and Godbadians in order to supervise them finish lifting the, abruptly to his mind, even more singular statue representing Morgianna aboard the carrier copter.

Had an instant sense of profound relief once he got back to his men, who neither wanted nor needed his supervision. Couldn't help himself; looked back. Shockingly, even at that distance, and as if out of the corner of his eye, he spotted someone new speaking to her, the Black Widow. Where had he come from?

The man, if man it was, manlike shape anyhow, wasn't in uniform. Nor was he wearing a hooded brown robe like all the shaved-bald, Sraddhite warrior monks, male or female, did. Was hooded, though; was in fact dressed similarly to her, entirely in black. Only it, his clothes, if clothes they were — it really was hard to see from this far away, distracted as he was; all the more so, by the copter's crew yelling at him that they were done — had spotlight-sparkles glinting off what Demios took to be his all-covering cloak and cowl.

Reminded him of someone … but who? An Outer Earth supranormal from its long concluded Suprawar? If so, why did he inspire such an eerie impression of the night's sky? More instantly disconcerting, why was his eye-stave suddenly heating up? Couldn't hold it; let it drop. Watched as it … What? Fattened like a plugged hose about to burst, yes.

Its interior, nanoscale devices manufactured its own eyeorbs, yes again. Wits like Quill Tethys sometimes called eyeorbs eye-eggs. Was it pregnant, a python about to have puppies? Absurd. He looked over towards them again; made to look over towards them again, make that. Both had vanished. Of course they had. She'd stepped on an agate and gone away, holding hands with whoever had been with her. If someone had been with her, besides himself. Or maybe it was him who led her away. Couldn't Jesus Mandam teleport?

She'd affected his mind, whoever she was. Almost made him cream his jeans, as Outer Earth kids sometimes put it, fay-saying amusingly. As Andy sometimes did, too, when she was growing up. What was it about dads and daughters, he wondered, horrifying himself. She couldn't have been Hell's Belle, Bouncing Belialma, who got hold of Morgianna the night they'd jointly conceived her, Andaemyn. Not unless Lady Lust found a way to, first of all, get out of the night's sky while leaving her star up there and, second of all, gained an immunity to eyeorbs.

A name came to him, a memorable one; one almost as equally terrifying as base ones about his not unexpectedly – un-expectantly? – born-striped daughter; one from, most recently, WORLD's phony fish packer last week on the Outer Earth near its Centauri Island. But what had Daemonicus got to with anything? Besides, hadn't Lady Guillotine, Ramona nee Avar Ryne, taken him out once she got hold of a couple his eye-stave-manufactured prison pods?

Then another one did a nominal ditto. Wasn't Strife, whom Ray also took out last week. In the same way as well, in one of his own eyeorbs. (He hadn't been in very good shape by the time he got to the fish packer. Too close an encounter with what was left of the Magnificent Psycho and his temporary bodyguards, Blind Sundown and Raven's Head, accounted for that.)

Came from legend this time, not any Suprawar he'd experienced. At least not one that he'd been allowed to recall. (White Witch wife was a great one for redactional mind-reaming or, put moderately less clinically, memory-editing.) Was that who she was, the Black Widow? Had she in fact more like toyed with than straight out told him her actual identity? Olivia Tenebrous from Tenebrife, Land of Twilight, indeed!

Had she really been Primeval Lilith, the Demon Queen of the Night?

========

On the equivalent of Sunday, the 14ᵗʰ of December 1980, UD, Yehudi Cohen, the Summoning Child who, in 1938 on the Outer Earth codenamed himself the Untouchable Diver, wasn't too sure where he was. This was explicable. His last memory, after being brain-sucked by an oversexed alligator with wings, was of being eaten alive. Or what passed for alive in his case; he who only breathed when he remembered to breathe.

By a Gynosphinx … unless it was a manticore.

========

He had the Crimson Corona wrapped around his rubber-hooded forehead, like some sort of malevolent, but non-penetrative boa constrictor; the Amateramirror strapped onto his left arm as a shield; and was brandishing the Susasword in his right hand. Ergo, he hadn't destroyed the terrible talismans – the Thrice-Cursed Godly Glories, so called – at all. Had only been made to think he had. This possibly by Telepassa's, um, glorious daughters; more likely, if far harder to wrap his mind around, the notion of it, by the Crimson Corona itself.

Had, to his knowledge anyhow, only been in the Weirdom of Cabalarkon ever so briefly and that was on the 6th, a week and a day ago. Sooth said, as he suddenly thought – or someone (some thing?) thought for him – he wasn't altogether in the Weirdom right now, either.

Was on its outskirts, on top of or just beyond the Slopes of the Sleepers. In what he had until then no idea was called the Ghostlands due to the rampant radio-activity that had rendered it, a vast territory in the Upper Head south of the Mystic Mountains, Sedon's Crown, virtually uninhabitable for anyone, or anything, alive for well over a thousand years.

A quick glance to either side of him did not make him feel any better. To his left was, well, Death, in the stereotypical guise of a tall, but hunched skeleton in a dark, hooded cloak and carrying – what else? – a scythe. (Also wasn't to know it, but this was Underlord Yama Nergal, King Harvest, the Mithradite Grim Reaper.)

To his right was, hmm ... a nicely shaped woman, that was for sure. Brazen, too. Wasn't a traditional amazon in that she had both her (bared) breasts. Except, to his mind detrimental to the attractiveness quotient, she had a tetrahedron for a head; out of which, trebly disconcertingly, a solitary eye blinked on each of its three upper sides. Her he'd been introduced to, albeit as All's mistress, Tsishah Thrae. Until, that is, she transformed into this extraordinary looking but, just as much so, highly self-important devil who answered to Pyrame Silverstar.

If he'd looked behind him he'd have seen Death's Angels, the Inglorious Dead, whose touch, he'd been forewarned, could kill. Most of what was left of them any-how; this after two weeks ago next Demetray-Tuesday's quite literal debacle in the Flood and Lake borderlands. Each of them glowed radioactively.

Which could also be (sort of) said of Death's scythe, though not identically. If its telltale golden-glow indicated what it was made of ... could he eat it? Would he have to ask permission first? He certainly hoped he wouldn't be tempted. Didn't appear at all appetizing. Still, if Death said 'eat this, mother fucker', should he duck or open his mouth?

Many of the wraith-like horrors – could call them ghosts, though not all of them were transparent – not only could and did levitate, they had varying degrees of flesh left. For better or worse, probably worse, that meant they weren't entirely emu-lating their skeletal leader, whose bony feet seemed firmly planted on the ground (if not in it), at least for the time being.

Unlike the unspeakable spooks, who looked uniformly two-eyed anthropo-morphic, as if they were once human or humanoid bipedal, Death's skull had a third eyehole. Presumably he presented as much considerately, just in case the Diver had any doubts about his race. If devils could be considered a race, that is, and not a biomorphic, entirely inhuman lifeform.

Looking about, he would have also seen a certain, not quite so invincible She-Sphinx, one who mistook him for a devil a few day earlier due to his own glow of the moment, but whose digestive system couldn't quite handle a human being. Thanks be to Miracle Memory for that, Tsishah told him prior to going so fetching-ly devilish on him.

(Did Sundown know he had a daughter with Solace-Sorciere before they had their three ill-fated boys and the never-named girl she died having? Would he be allowed to remember everything he'd been told should he survive this march – invasion? – of theirs?)

To either side of this All stood a twosome familiar to him from looking in on them from between-space back on … Where and When? On one of Shenon's Ventricles answered the first; still wasn't too sure of the answer to the second … the Eighth, the Ninth, the Tenth? Was almost certain today was the Fourteenth; knew that almost for sure because that's what the Pretty told him and she wouldn't lie to him. They were buddies, almost uncle and niece; had a shared past. Depending how things went, might well wipe his mind afterwards but, hey, he was (probably) used to that by now.

As for the who, they were the goatish fauna and said Pretty, mother of the absent pretties, of whom he should really count only the triplets as pretty. Semele, at twelve, or near enough, should only count as cute; even budding might be considered rude in this sensitive day and age. Top-of-the-line healers the pair of them, Pusan Wanderlust and Telepassa of Godbad, who had been Europa Heliopolis for her first couple of decades plus a bit.

Could well be they'd be needed, since they were preparing to proceed – Pyrame-progress, as Pusan put it; battling all the way if necessary – to Cabalarkon City, the pupil of Sedon's Devic Eye-Land. Would do, if this Hidden Headworld's Dark Sedon of theirs didn't accede to their demand that he clear up the Ghostlands right smartly.

He didn't, they were going to play Blue Belly Yankee Northerners to the Southern Grey Coats' Confederacy (at the end of the American Civil War), and lay to waste his Weirdom, his thought-father and anyone else who dared try to stop them.

So where was he, aka the Mighty Eye-Mouth (usually) in the Sky? Would they really have to get down and dirty just to get his attention?

At which point, as if on cue, came into view, well, not a massive earth-striding man-god as such, but something out of Outer Earth iconography. A winged globe or oddly-dim sun, ancient symbol of divinity, flapped over the horizon in front of them, in front of him. Flew out of the Weirdom proper at speed to face them, to face him. Was that him; was that how this Sedon chose to manifest himself down here; on the Outer Earth as well, in days of (very) long gone yore? Had to be.

The Diver felt himself torn as if asunder. Now he was the ghost, barely there, mostly between-space. Rising in his place – he being their conduit, their in effect through and through, Gypsium-imbued teleportal – rose three sisters times two, the Trigregos Sisters in the form of their teenage incarnations, Telepassa's triplets: Ino, Agave and Autonoe. Each carried one of the three sacred objects. Make that, he'd been promised, the three deadly objects.

Deadly to Sedon, that is. Who, seeing them, promptly exploded.

Out of this winged globe of his came hundreds of levitating Utopians, Trinondevs of Weir. To a man, interspersed with a couple of women, they appeared armed with the same sort of eye-staves Black Skull-Face (Golgotha Nauroz) and his Warriors Elite had in Hadd less than a week earlier.

So, not Sedon: ordinary mortals, albeit ones capable of manifesting gargoyles (grotesques) off their eye-staves, daring to take on Death's Angels and those who'd come up here with the Diver via All of Incain.

Among them, much to his shock and queasy knees, were five members of what was left of his very own Damnation Brigade, including the wondrous Gloriel, Radiant Rider, arguably their most singly powerful member. Why were they involved? Were they actually joining forces with Sed's men? What no doubt possessive madness was making them willing to die in a futile effort to fight them off?

Then Blind Sundown and Raven's Head split in two ... dozens of times!

========

Humanized by Nihila, she, two-in-one, in what properly was her Trans-Time Trigon, not anyone else's, her equivalent of a devic protectorate, Machine-Memory shared the ex-Unity's pain in the butt. Decided, convincingly, she, jointly they, needed a break from all their internal squabbling re annihilating Lord Yajur by killing Helios.

Fortunately, mostly because she was part-computer, Freespirit Nihila was no good at reading her data banks.

========

A break for humanized Memory, Miracle Memory, was a nice hot bath.

In her many millennia as the incomparable Harmony, her current other half was no shrinking violet, as the saying went; though, being a shape-shifter, she could be if she put her mind to it. Unfortunately, given how busy she'd been since her re-emergence – how bloody-minded she was when it came to what had become of ex-Order – Nihila wasn't one for shirking violence either.

She did have an oddly incomplete, comparatively recent memory indicating she wasn't averse to the pleasures of the flesh, demonic as hers (presumably) was and, as a result, that of Machine-Memory as well. As one might expect from someone with a name like hers, Miracle Memory was good at extracting memories.

Nevertheless, she couldn't quite get at the fullness of Nihila's regarding her latest rumpy-pumpy-romp in the Gypsium Wall, Sedon's (and for a time Harmony's) Hairband, what separated the Head's southernmost occipital regions and the Cattail Peninsula, Sedon's Ponytail.

Think sexy thoughts, start playing with yourself. Memory did both, on Nihila's behalf, on both of their behalf. Seemed to be working. Blackness, pink face, pink hands, too many pink fingers on said pink hands ... what's that about a Judge? And the sound of what ... reed-syrinxes, as opposed to ordinary syrinxes (a bird's vocal organ), or panpipes playing?

Memory liked her water astonishingly hot; apparently liked it astonishingly murky, too. Which at first sort of bothered her, Nihila; just not enough. Still, she was a great believer in cleanliness. Was so very harmonious; next to godliness even. Felt good. Was even better with extra fingers. Thrygragos Sedon. VAM Entity. First-borns had a thing for firstborns. Huh?

Relaxation came too quickly, addled her defences. By the time her mind wrapped around the notion that entering the bath had been more like dipping herself wholly in a slurry of quickly hardening concrete, Memory was a digitized face grinning out the computer walls of Trans-Time Trigon admiring her latest Stopstone statue.

Grinning? Smiling? Smiler? Panpipes? Firstborn A in VAM? No matter.

"Old buggery, eh, Nihila the Nihility," she couldn't help but gloat. "Serves you right for wanting to carve my Kadmon, your Cadmus, a hundredth headstone."

The Female Entity wasn't just good with memories. She was good with mind workings; mental manipulations, put even more specifically. Was quite chuffed she'd managed to keep her intentions secret from Nowadays Nihila. Wasn't concerned about the identity of Nihila's first, and for the time being last, sexual co-conspirator. Did file her oddly disturbing ruminations away for future reference, however. Couldn't help it; filing was second nature to her.

Had a more immediate concern. Still hadn't found Pyrame Silverstar, and that did bother her a tad. Oh well, she consoled herself, there were plenty of devils around. Being, perhaps unlike Nihila – pink face, darkness, Judge – exceptionally fond of the pleasures of the flesh, her first choice was Aphropsyche Morningstar, APM, All-Eyes, Byron's Venus. As with Pyrame, she couldn't locate her. Couldn't locate a single one of the dots of herself, a single 'little angel', secreted anywhere.

Lazareme's Venus, once Mariamne Dawnstar, she of Daybreak, now and for over twelve hundred years the Grey Lady, Miss Mist, Krepusyl Evenstar, she of Twilight, was another of her favourites. She was occupying her when she had Wilderwitch around this time of year in 5927, during Helios's 11th Lifetime. Irony of ironing boards, to quote her Herr Hel himself, given what she'd just done to Nihila, it seemed the Witch, as even she preferred to refer to herself, turned out to be an incarnation of none other Harmony herself.

Best stay away from Miss Mist then. Wouldn't want, first of all, to whelp yet another Harmony. Second, and much more likely, wouldn't want her to find a way to release her eldest sister in the Libertine. Or any of the other Stop-stoned statuary she kept in her gallery, Master Devas all: more than a few she'd acquired during hers and Herr Hel Heliosophos's lifetimes of time-tumbling off-planet.

(Hadn't kept the three she'd given the Medusa touch to after she/they had Fisherwoman, instead of she becoming a solitary Trigregos Sister in 5918, though. Them she'd kindly – more like unkindly – stuck in the night's sky, such that they could look down on the Hidden Headworld and watch their joint daughter grow up into such a fine specimen of Piscine deviancy.)

Where was APM anyhow? What with her father's star shining so brightly out of the heavenly Sedon Sphere for a week now, maybe she'd gone undercover more so than usual.

(Heavenly as opposed to earthly, as in the Outer Earth's demon, Shedd or Shedim-made Sedon Sphere; near, maybe even in, what's now the Middle East's Dead Sea. That Sedon Sphere was a huge geodesic dome that lasted nearly two thousand years; until they, Helios and her, destroyed it at the start of his Seventh Lifetime, ca 2000 YD, in an attempted assassination by an asteroid that wasn't an asteroid.)

Could be anywhere on the Head in that case. Or even beyond it if the Fatman (Alpha Centauri) still had access to the so-called Nag Gap that, due to an atomic bomb blast, formed in August 1945. Was a self-psychopomp; rather, all those eyes of hers were her collective power focus. Of if they weren't her one out of many, they did a damn good job masquerading as it. Plus, she had an amazing knack.

It wasn't bifurcation per se. That was difficult task for even top of the line Master Devas to master; required an overarching mind presumably kept between-space, as if in a witch's Shelter, but nevertheless in close proximity to both aspects of the same devil. Was more like fragmentation. All those eyes of hers weren't just pieces of herself; they were all of herself.

So maybe she was hiding out in someone. Maybe she was hiding out in a bagelry-bundle of some-ones; the better to keep herself from suffering the same fate as her siblings now in the night's sky. Would someone in her Lovely Lady Sisterhood know? Was there anyone better than the Afrites' Sister Superior to ask?

Tricky business that. Ventricular Telepassa was her howsoever-speculatively original self's daughter — Machine-Memory wasn't omniscient, so she still wasn't convinced that Mnemosyne born D'Angelo, become Heliopolis by the time of her death in '45, was her original self; her template, as it were. That she, born Europa Heliopolis, was that Mnemosyne's daughter was well-known amongst certain circles, and one of them was the biggest, brightest, sometimes even circular, though it was more usually ovular, star in the night's sky above his Headworld.

Did the Moloch Sedon realize she, they, the Dual Entities, made it through the mostly Liberty-caused destruction of their Lunar Trigon in somewhat manageable pieces last Birhym-Wednesday? Probably not. He did, he might risk the dangers of the Subterranean Land of the Mandroids and come after Trans-Time Trigon anyhow. Especially now that both Helios and Thunder and Lightning Theomachy foe Yajur had effectively neutralized each other, he might find seizing the opportunity to ensure Heliosophos went onto his 101st Lifetime irresistible.

Someone else best to stay away from then. Who else? One of the dozy dozens of devils imprisoned within All of Incain? Dark Sedon tended to avoid All almost as much as he did Absudyl. Shouldn't hurt to do an inventory of whom the She-Sphinx currently contained. So she did, she being All's creator more so than her Herr Hell Helios.

Was yet another '*old buggery*' moment. All wasn't on Incain; not even in her usual state of being altogether between-space off the Prison Beach. Nay probs. A few mental twiddles of her computer-self's buttons and she could find All anywhere. Proceeded to twaddle just that.

Double Old Buggery! Make that Treble Old Buggery! How the fuck did they get those ungodly things?

========

Some Time Later

Not so very long ago, in the Zebranid Leper Colony high up in the Whiplash Mountain Range overlooking Incain, Pusan Wanderlust openly speculated about setting up an art gallery on Witch Isle. It wasn't a fanciful notion. Broken statuary found in museums throughout the Outer Earth was testament to just how effective mandroids were at encasing devils.

That the statues were broken was mostly due to other devils, or their followers, smashing them in order to release the ones trapped inside.

Impermanence had many a nickname. One of them was Sledgehammer.

========

Despite all that broken statuary, some of those behind the 'jailbreak' of Maruta the 30th considered the so-called Greek solution to be the most sensible way they could deal with the dozens of suddenly decathonitized devils they anticipated arriving on the Inner Earth that day inside the 60-plus Outer Earth crew members of the Cosmic Express.

Nothing of the sort materialized then. However, after their very much (they'd decided) miraculous escape from Dark Sedon's wrath the morning of the 14th of Tantalar, a solitary some *thing* of the sort did materialize, ever so mysteriously, that night in Tsishah's residence, her so-called Anthill, in Shenon's Anthean Atrium. They'd been trying to decide what to do with it ever since.

First, though, they had to identify which devil it contained.

(Having lost Pyrame Silverstar – though not All, who made it back to Incain – on the Slopes of the Sleepers; having lost much more than that there: Telepassa and her daughters, they with the Trigregos Talismans, vanished; as did the Untouchable Diver, whereas King Harvest's star now shone out of the night's sky; well, only the teleportive intervention of the Female Entity could explain any of it.)

Who it looked like was easy; at least it was easy for Pusan, who'd been coming back in the bodies of her terminally-ill daughters or granddaughters, female fauns or faunas the lotus lot of them, for the better part of four thousand years. The torc depicted around her neck, the chain mail gown, the chains depending from her wrist-bracelets, and the scales-of-justice earrings pretty much gave her away.

And Harmony, the Unity of Balance, had been seen back in circulation again during that first fateful week of last Tantalar.

Teoti, now bitten back to wholly human again, said he spotted her in Hadd, on Dustmound in fact, not long before he left for Free Iraxas the night of the 7th. Said her name wasn't Harmony; claimed it was Nihila. Which was something else Pusan verified after she made inquiries, notably on Tympani, Sedon's Eardrum, the Isle of the Undying One in the Aural Sea, Sedon's Ear, where Nihila had been seen as late as the 10th.

Of course that still didn't mean it was Harmony, call her Nihila if you must, inside the Stopstone statue of her that appeared the night of the 14th. Didn't mean it even encased a devil, sooth said. Could just be a statue; though Stopstone wasn't exactly readily available on the Head's surface. It was in its subsurface; particularly in the upper parts of the Hidden Continent, its Hell Well of the World; no more so, especially in its raw form, than in Absudyl.

And Stopstone statues didn't just appear on their own; they had to have been teleported. Ergo …

"You reckon it's a parting gift from Machine-Memory, Jordy?" wondered Tsishah, feeling her normal self again now that she'd repatriated her soul-self.

She was in the big, otherwise empty room within her Anthill where the statue appeared almost as if it knew where it would be best displayed. With her were a number of others including, oddly for Shenon, a few men. One of these last was the man – recurring male deviant, more correctly – she'd just addressed.

Tsishah had known him all her life. So had Fish; so too had Pusan Wanderlust. In fact, even though she was always a faun and he was usually a human, albeit not necessarily a man, there were those who said they were not just devic suicides, they were two/thirds of a set of triplets born to Thrygragos Lazareme in a much later litter than that of the firstborn Unities.

Jordan Tethys was myrionymous, multiple-named. Sometimes he was called Storyteller. More times he was the Legendarian. Just as often, he was the Thirty Year Man — because that was as long as he ever lasted in a single incarnation. There were probably almost as many tales told about him as he told tales about others. He was here not just because he was their friend or that he was another who had seen Harmony post-becoming Nihila.

He was here because, short of busting the statue apart, he alone could determine if Nihila was inside it. "If it is then, well, let's just see if it is before we start speculating."

Devils called him Artist. There was a reason for that. Like Fish, with her three, and Pusan, with her shepherd's crook, he had a Tvasitar-talisman; one that, like his maybe-triplet-sister's crook, seemingly followed him from one lifetime to the next. It was a Brainrock quill. It generated its own ink. Did a few other neat-trick-things as well.

He sat down on a stool provided by one of the other men there, an erstwhile, long-exiled, Trinondev Warrior of Weir, one of a number, male and female, Tsishah brought in from the Zebranid Leper Colony because of the prison pod capacity of their eyeorbs on the 14th of Tantalar last.

Always somewhat of a showman, Tethys waved his quill in a box pattern, as if drawing on nothing but the empty air, and thereby materialized an ordinary pad of paper. This in lap, Tsishah among those looking over his shoulder, he licked the quill's tip with his tongue and proceeded to draw Freespirit Nihila as he'd last seen her, in Aka Godbad City on the 10th of that moth.

It was a good likeness. Had to be for the rest of his quill's arguable magic to work. He had the torc, the chain mail, the chains, the scales-of-justice earrings, the long, crinkly, butterscotch hair, the body now beautiful again, the Melanochroic skin complexion, had it all down pat.

Let go of the quill; let it fill in the background. Which it did. Did so, not from the perspective of the Stopstone statue representing her in the middle of the room.

Did so as if from the perspective of someone looking over his shoulder.

========

Jordan Tethys looked over his own shoulder; looked directly at Tsishah Twilight. Looked right into her face; right into her eyes. He said: "Now what?"
She said: "What the fuck!" Probably should have said: 'Old buggery!'
It wasn't the first time she had three eyes.

****

WILDERWITCH'S BABIES 5980/1

– "HIDDEN HEADGAMES" –

=========

Character Companion

(Extracted and adapted specifically for this mini-novel from a capsulated character companion for the open-ended saga of *'Wilderwitch's Babies'*)

INDEX

1. **The Damnation Brigade**: Blind Sundown, OMP-Akbar, Radiant Rider, Raven's Head, Untouchable Diver, Wilderwitch
2. **The Dual Entities**: Heliosophos, Miracle Memory
3. **The Shining Ones:** First, Second, Third and Fourth Generation Devakind

- **The Moloch Sedon**
- **The Six Great Gods and Goddesses**: Thrygragos Brothers (Lazareme, Byron & Varuna Mithras); Trigregos Sisters (Demeter, Devaura & Sapiendev)
- The Forgotten Fiend, also Smiler; hypothetically one-third of the VAM Entity: Varuna **Ahriman** Mithras (making Sedon a Great God or Thrygragos)
- **Master Devas**
  - The Firstborn Unities of Lazareme: Freespirit Nihila, claims she was once Datong Harmonia, the Unity of Balance as well as Panharmonium
  - Thanatoids of Lathakra: Tantal, Methandra, Klannit
  - More Mithradites: Silverstar, King Harvest, White Dwarf, Taskmaster, Leontocephalic Trumpeter, Sinistral Sloth, Cathead, Chroma Chameleon, Fiery Mildoth, Saurlord,
  - More Lazaremists: Amal-Althea Brand, Unholy Abaddon, Lord Order, Anvil the Artificer, Battle Babe, Rumour of Lazareme, Bright Enlightenment of Lazareme, Perfection/Antigen, Icy Miros, Ursine Bardol
  - Byronics: Firstborn Silverclouds, Primary and Secondary Nucleoids, 'Flying Fish' Volant, 'Goatfish' Makara, 'Beautiful Butterfly' Tzigame, Flying Carpeteer, Elephantine, Monk-Eye, Byron's Dragon, Byron's Babbler, Byron's Paladin, Petrogod

4. **Deviants, Demons, Faeries and a Mandroid Mother Machine**
   - **Demons** (Hell-Queen, Hell-King, Shahiyeda Sunrise)
   - **Definite Deviants** (Fisherwoman, Pusan Wanderlust, Tsishah Twilight, Lakshmi Arthadot, the Legendarian)
   - **Probable Deviants** (The Molech Xibalba, Jester Jaguar)
   - **Mandroids** (All of Incain)
   - **Outer Earth Supranormals other than the Damnation Brigade** (Sorciere, Saul 'Psycho' Ryne, Lady Lemurian, Faceless Strife)
5. **Mortal Descendants of Original Extraterrestrials**
   - **Utopians of Weir** on Earth (Capputis Masterson)
   - **Pure U-Bloods** (Cabby the Daddy, Melina born Sarpedon become Zeross, Demios Sarpedon, Ubris and Augustus Nauroz)
   - **Hybrid Utopians** (Saladin called Devason Nauroz, Morgianna born Nauroz become Somata then Sarpedon, Andaemyn 'Andy' Sarpedon)
   - **Utopian clones** (Golgotha and Gethsemane Nauroz)
6. **Norman & Norma Notables**
   - Pandora 'Hush' Mannering become Nauroz, Alpha Centauri, Janna St Peche-Montressor, Godbadian Ambassador-at-Large Gomez Niarchos, Governor Ferdinand Niarchos, Sraddhite High Priest Thartarre Sraddha Holgatson, Godbadian General Quentin Sraddha Anvil, Senator Sophiscient Barson, Telepassa of Godbad, her four daughters, Toothy Teoti, Godfrey & Cromwell Necator

========

1. The Damnation Brigade in Cabalarkon

- **Blind Sundown:**
  - real name: John Sundown, most of his fellow D-Brig members seem to call him Johnny;
  - father of Shahiyeda, long nowadays Tsishah's demon;
- **OMP-Akbar:**
  - Obadiah Melvin (Old Man) Power, who on the Inner Earth of Sedon's Head proved to be Akbarartha; in the midst of "The War of the Apocalyptics" (WAR-POX), became revealed as the eldest half-son of Dand (Devalord) Tariqartha, Lazareme's Persian or Earth Magician and, therefore, the rightful Kronokronos Supreme of Temporis;
  - father, by Takeda Mikoto (Corona Power) of Senator Sophiscient Barson, once Lakshmi of Lemuria's betrothed;
- **Radiant Rider:**
  - birth name: Gloriella D'Angelo; married surname: Dark; codename Radiant Rider; also known as Rainbow, Gloriel, Glory of the Angels;
  - a materialist or etherealist (as in 'make ether real'); flies on rainbow hair and casts solid rainbows;
- **Raven's Head:**
  - inhuman, possibly ageless, hybrid creature akin to something out of native Indian mythology or trickster folklore, albeit after the arrival of Wasichus (the White Man) and his horses;

- considers herself a Creature of the Cosmos like her usual rider, Blind Sundown; also calls herself a Wakinyah Thunder Being or, sometimes, a Thundercloud Creature;
- **Untouchable Diver**:
  - real name: Yehudi Cohen;
  - German born, probably only half-Jewish Summoning Child whose father may have been the old Baron Tyrtod von Alptraum (Nazi Nghtmare, Shark-czar, Steltsar);
  - gained the ability to make himself untouchable at will while dressed in a rubber wetsuit of his own making in 1938; can also render those he's in contact with just as intangible;
  - he found his Gorgon Goggles – what allow him a degree of far-sight and the ability to see through the ground while soil-swimming – in the Roman Colosseum a few weeks prior to becoming the Diver;
  - discovers he's not only Brainrock-blessed but can feed off the miraculous substance also called Gypsium-Godstuff during "Goddess Gambit" (GAMBIT);
  - as such has become a self-psychopomp (spirit-carrier), meaning he can travel between-space by himself, without using the equivalent of a devil's Tvasitar talisman, Ringleader's rings or witch stones;
  - unfortunately, when he does so he tends to 'blip' (become unconscious, sometimes for long periods of time — hours, even days)
  - seems he also had a son by Fisherwoman (Scylla Nereid) in the late Thirties, early Forties, who grew up to become Chthlonius 'Tiger' Tiecher, one of Kadmon Heliopolis's Trigon Spartae, all of whom apparently died on Aegean Trigon in 1968;
- **Wilderwitch**:
  - born around the Winter Solstice or Mithramas Day, Tantalar 5927, purportedly of the Dual Entities, though who was humanizing Miracle Memory is unclear;
  - devic half-mother might have been Krepusyl Evenstar, Twilight's Grey Lady, which would make her Tsishah Twilight's quarter-sister as Miss Mist was occupying Morgianna not yet Sarpedon when she conceived her a few years later, in 5933;
  - the Witch, capitalized, had one child pre-Limbo, a daughter (nowadays Fey Woman), born in 1946, but keeps the identity of her father secret;
  - Freespirit Nihila once claimed she was her Harmony-self reincarnated;

========

2. The Dual Entities

- **Heliosophos**:
  - Helios called Sophos the Wise, the Male Entity;
  - Brainrock-blessed time-tumbler ('controlled' time travellers do not exist in **the Phantacea Mythos** due to contextual impossibility);
  - believed decapitated and killed (for the 100th time) on the Moon in early-to-mid December 1980;
  - actually survived HELMOON; currently in a bifurcated state deep beneath the Weirdom of Cabalarkon in Absudyl/Minius within Trans-Time Trigon;

- thinks he was Kadmon Heliopolis in his first lifetime;
- many others reckon he was originally Anti-Patriarch Cain, Slayer of Abel, and therefore the son of Primeval Lilith and the second Biblical Adam (the golden-apple-eating first patriarch Alorus Ptah, who had blue skin and golden hair, the same look Helios and Thrygragos Lazareme often affect);

- **Miracle Memory**:
  - the Mnemosyne Machine, Machine-Memory, the Mnemosyne 3-Thing, the Female Entity;
  - believed thrust back into the time-stream along with Trans-Time Trigon when the Male Entity was killed on the Moon in mid December 1980;
  - since Thunder and Lightning Lord Yajur, the former Unity of Order, is currently keeping Helios alive, she's still a part of Trans-Time Trigon deep beneath the Weirdom of Cabalarkon in Absudyl/Minius;
  - believes she's an amalgamation of First Weirworld's original Mother Machine, Mnemosyne D'Angelo (Human Memory, Kadmon Heliopolis's long dead stepmom from his first lifetime), and Datong Harmonia (Harmony), the Unity of Balance, from his second lifetime;
  - can only be fully humanized by Master Devas (devils), prominently Pyrame Silverstar, the Harmony Unity or Methandra Thanatos;
  - demons seem to have much the same solidifying effect on her, but are dull-witted and weak compared to devils; evidently she can't conceive when solely solidified by demons;

========

3. Shining Ones: First, Second and Third Generation Devils

- **The Moloch Sedon**:
  - seemingly immortal, tremendously powerful, but nowhere-near-almighty All-Father of Devazurkind; likes to appear to Westerners in particular as the Devil Himself, capitalized;
  - the sames as it did the Sedonshem on its multimillennia journey throughout the cosmos, his essence makes up Cathonia (the Cathonic Zone or Dome, also the Sedon Sphere);
  - a dark star above the Hidden Headworld during the day, hence Dark Sedon;
  - there, as seen as early as 1977's **Phantacea One**, his star takes the form of the Mighty Eye-Mouth in the Sky, a fact devils, Illuminaries of Weir and a number of witches seem to know;
  - as per 4Ever40, believes the Undying Utopian Cabalarkon is his father/creator, thus denying any contribution from the time-tumbling Dual Entities in Helios's Fifth Lifetime on the first Weirworld some two hundred light years earlier;
- **The Six Great Gods and Goddesses**:
  - the Thrygragos Brothers and Trigregos Sisters comprise the entirety of the second generation of devakind;
  - the Three Great Gods are:
  » **Thrygragos Lazareme** (aka sometimes the Lackland Libertine, but most commonly Thrygragos Everyman), who sees himself as having blue skin and

golden hair; in other words, a three-eyed version of Alorus Ptah (the Male Entity in his 61ˢᵗ lifetime); those who behold him think they're seeing their idea of what God looks like;

» **Thrygragos Byron** (aka both Bodiless Byron and the Unmoving One due to that fact that he's all head, with his facial features frozen in the same expression, not because he can't transport himself wherever he wants on the Inner Earth); and

» **Thrygragos Varuna Mithras**, who, as per Feel Theo, may well have also been Uranus, Kronos and Zeus, in that order, as well as many another pantheon's God the Father prior to circa 1500 BC (2500 YD, Year of the Dome);

- circa 2000 YD (2000 BC) Anvil the Artificer (Tvasitar Smithmonger, the devic smithy) crafted the Thrygragos Talismans for the Thrygragos Brothers; they are (or were): the Mask of Byron, the mutable Spear of Mithras and Lazareme's Cloak of Many Colours;

» the often three-in-one Great Goddesses are Trigregos **Devaura** (the Spirit or Soul), Trigregos **Demeter** (the Body), and Trigregos **Sapiendev** (the Mind or Individual Consciousness);

- they appeared in 4Ever40 and, much more prominently, throughout Helmoon, but do not appear in Games;

- their terrible talismans do, however; the devic smithy crafted them for the Master Devas' simultaneous mothers; they are (or were): the Amateramirror, the Crimson Corona and the Susasword; OMP-Akbar (Akbarartha, the righful Kronokronos Supreme of Temporis) believes he captured them on Diminished Dustmound whereas the Untouchable Diver reckons he'll destroy them in the Brainrock caldera (lava lake) of Sedon's Peak;

- may yet prove both of them are wrong and that, thanks to Miracle Maenad, who believes them Human Memory's grandchildren, Telepassa's Triplets (Ino, Autonoe and Agave) made off with them to the Outer Earth on the 14ᵗʰ of Tantalar 5980;

» **Ahriman-Daemonicus**, even according to he himself he isn't a Great God, just the fusion of the middle third of the VAM Entity and Daemonicus, the King of Daemons, until Ragnarok, circa 234 Pre-Dome (4234 BC);

- the never-remembered Smiling Fiend is myrionymous; among his many names include Smiler, Rhadamanthys (from the **PHANTACEA** comic book series) and Judge Druj; Druj means 'the Lie';

• **Master Devas**

- dictionaries often define '*devas*' or '*daevas*' as '*the shining ones*'; hence also the English word '*devils*', meaning '*little gods*';

- Master Devas compose the third generation of devazurkind; the Trigregos Sisters always bore them simultaneously, in threesomes;

- they believe their fathers are one or another of the Thrygragos Brothers; hence why it's accepted that there are only three devic tribes: the Lazaremists, the Byronics and the Mithradites;

- when Master Devas, whose bodies are debrained daemons, interact sexually, without possessing anyone, all they can produce are azura spirit beings;

- a fourth generation of devakind (as opposed to devazurkind) began coming into existence during the second, third and fifth decade of the Dome's 60th Century; as of late Maruta 5980 YD, every known member of the 4th Generation has been born as a twin instead of a triplet;
- thereafter, on the 5th of Tantalar 5980, the Quadrang or, less accurately, Apocalyptic Nucleoids (Jah Dreadlock, Hatchethands, Mandragora Gallows Ghoul and Flying Doltaur), whom Matare had in the Calvary Cavern of Temporis, were born a foursome, not as either a twosome or threesome;
- the Byronic Nucleus and the hence Apocalyptic Nucleus cathonitized each other the next day, the 6th of Tantalar, an event that brought to an end the war of the Apocalyptics and also resulted in what was left of D-Brig's expulsion from Temporis by Lakshmi Arthadot;
- when Sedon, Great Gods and/or Master Devas possess sentient beings for procreative purposes, their resultant offspring are often long-lived and, once in a while, unnaturally gifted mortals known as deviants;
- it seems likely that many of the Outer Earth's so-called supranormals or supras also had devic half-parents; this is especially true of supras born as a result of the Simultaneous Summonings of 59/1920;
- controversially, the myrionymous Smiling Fiend claims he is the middle third of the VAM Entity (Varuna Ahriman Mithras), the firstborn brood or litter of Thrygragos Sedon; making himself and his two brood brothers Master Devas and the Mighty Eye-Mouth (usually) in the Sky a Great God, not the Moloch (King) of devazurkind

- **Significant Lazaremists**
  - » **Harmony**, called Datong Harmonia by bygone Illuminaries of Weir;
    - the Unity of Balance as well as Panharmonium (her pet project, a planetary panacea for beneficial devils and their worshipful multitudes alike; as per "The 1000 Days of Disbelief" {DAZE}, actually existed from roughly 5000 to 5500 Year of the Dome);
    - reputedly, by a matter of a few seconds, the first Master Deva ever born; beauty incarnate as well as loveliness personified;
    - her power focus or Tvasitar talisman is a golden torc, the so-called Necklace of, as you might expect, Harmony; from it she conjures her golden, chain-mail gowns and the broken chains often manifested manacled to her wrists; from them she sometimes shoots… what else? Chain lightning;
    - also associated with auroras such as the Northern Lights, hence her Borealis Brolly at the conclusion of ENDGAME-GAMBIT;
    - folklore has it that Harmony is incomparable because she is mostly Gypsium and, therefore, not humanized by demons; probably isn't true, however;
    - those who beheld her thought they were seeing their ideal female;
  - » **Freespirit Nihila**, from WAR-POX, GAMBIT and HELMOON, claims she was once Harmony (from FEEL THEO and DAZE);
    - told Kronokronos Akbar and Wilderwitch in the Faerie Garden of Temporis, on the 6th of Tantalar, that she believed the Witch was her incarnation;
- **Significant Mithradites**

» **Pyrame Silverstar**, the Pauper Priestess, the fabulously female (adult) Perpetual Presence; formerly (sometimes) called Providence, among many another name or title;

- decathonitized, on the 30th of Maruta 5980, possessing Cosmicaptain Nehrini Purandar in the cosmicar that crash-landed in the Domination of Satanwyck (Sedon's Temple, Hell on Earth, then currently the domain of Sinistral Sloth);

- unless programmed otherwise, All of Incain obeys her; hence why she can often be found occupying the She-Sphinx on the Prison Beach of Incain, at the bottom of the Cattail Peninsula (Sedon's Ponytail on a map of the Hidden Headworld), about as far south as one can go on the Head without having to swim or ride in a boat;

- had no need of a devic power and daemonic body in 2000 YD (because she was already a solid entity, having been fused with her daemon while imprisoned pre-Dome in the Sphinxes and becoming Sed-mom shortly after her release ca 0 YD) when Anvil the Artificer first discovered how to render Master Deva individually solid and powerful entities;

- due to her lack of a power focus, for centuries after Anvil began making them Pyrame relied on her relationship with the recurring Attis to get hold of always mutable power foci anyone can use (he would give the foci of vanquished foes to her as tokens of his affection);

- as per Feel Theo she had to give them up on Thrygragon (Mithramas Day 4376 YD); thereafter relied on Sedon, All or a variety of psychopomp demons to get about beneath the Dome;

- for reasons not fully explained in Games, cathonitized in 5950; that suggests she lost her formerly (and perhaps still, at least partially) bebrained, daemonic body, disputably that of Primeval Lilith, the Demon Queen of the Night, much like she did in 4824 YD when, as per Hellion, they were jointly occupying Morgan Abyss, the Melusine Master of Weir;

- devic half-mother of Saladin born Nauroz Devason, the Master of the Weirdom of Cabalarkon since 5950; (half-father: the Moloch Sedon — it may therefore be that Saladin is the last Sed-son or sedon, small case, left alive beneath the Cathonic Dome);

- some believe she was the devic half-mother of Meroudys and Akbar Artha near the beginning of the Cathonic Dome's 59th Century (it's now late in the Dome's 60th Century), though that was more likely Byron's Butterfly;

» **King Harvest**, Underlord Yama Nergal, a fifth-born, so-called Earthling;

- when the Lathakran Empire conquered the Penile Peninsula (better known as Iraxas, Sedon's Mutton Chop on a map of the Hidden Headworld), he helped cathonitize Vanthysces Vastness (Scarecrow), the Byronics' Reaper;

- he thereafter fused the latter's power focus, a scythe, with his own, a miner's pickaxe; hence King Harvest, the Mithradites' Grim Reaper or Harvester;

- for millennia alternated, on a lunar basis, impregnating duties of much younger sister Fecundity (Nergal Vetala) with brood-older brother Gravedigger (Zuvem Nergalis);

- unchallenged devic ruler of the radioactive Ghostlands since circa 4825 YD;

- Death's Angels, whose touch can kill but, being predominantly animated by Nergalazurs, bodily dissolve in rain or running water, are his to command;
- more so than the first-born Thanatoids of Lathakra or the eighth-born Primary Apocalyptics' Mother Murder (the Medusa, Mater Matare, who wasn't born until, at the earliest, Mithras's Twelfth), he's considered the devils' primary Death God;
- in Sedon's Sweat Glands (the Flood and Lake Lands on a map of Sedon's Head), during the first week of Tantalar 5980, suffered a severe setback to his efforts to march his Inglorious Dead from the Ghostlands to Hadd; thus failing to bring much needed reinforcements to Janna Fangfingers in Hadd;
- forced to retreat to his usual domicile Pettivisaya (Wailing Souls), which was Dark Sedon and Pyrame Silverstar's power base prior to events described in 2010's "The Death's Head Hellion" (HELLION); as such, and for most of the Hidden Headworld's history, Pettivisaya was known as Grand Elysium;

» **Klannit Thanatos**, the world's first azura; presumably the entire cosmos's first azura as well;
- Thanatoid parents were subsumed by demons, one of whom was a glassine Klannit, when she was conceived pre-Dome;
- aspires to becoming a Master Deva in her own right, but can't dominate sentient beings unless they're either simpletons or else dead;
- nevertheless has a near-devic affinity for mirrors; so much so she can both far-see and communicate either verbally or mentally through them;
- when they were both strictly spirit beings she and Anvil the Artificer, the Lazaremist master craftsman eventually named Tvasitar Smithmonger, were lovers; he has been striving for nearly four thousand years to craft her a functional shell such that they can be lovers again;
- appeared a number of times throughout **the Phantacea Mythos**, most notably in GAMBIT, wherein she occupied Nanny Klanny, the brain-damaged Sraddhite who looked after Thartarre Holgatson once his parents disappeared in the 5940s;

» **Sinistral Sloth**, Illuminary given name: Baaloch Hellblob, also known as known as Lord Lazy;
- succeeded to the throne of Satanwyck after predecessor, Sinistral Envy (Bobby Badboy, Robin Goodfellow, from CONTAGION), insisted on possessing Marie Antoinette's executioner;
- seems to have acquired Chancellor Ibal's power focus, the Evil Eye, in 5950 when the latter was cathonitized; his own Tvasitar Talisman: a glowing fan or frond;

» **Domdaniel-Pride** and most of the other former or eventual Prime Sinistrals of Satanwyck, as well as their Viceroy or Grand Vizier, **Chancellor Ibal**, are mentioned, usually by name, during the course of GAMES;

- **Moderately Significant Byronics**
  » **APM All-Eyes**, as she is most commonly known, is the lone daughter born in Bodiless Byron's third brood;
  - as such, a member of his secondary Nucleus (along with her triplet brothers, **Damon Goldenrod** and **Nevair Neverknight**);

- a love goddess, Byron's Venus, bygone Illuminaries of Weir named her Aphropsyche Morningstar, hence APM;
- likes to appear as if composed entirely of eyes, hence All-Eyes;
- her witch-followers, who aren't just confined to the Byronics' territory of Aka Godbad, are known as love-loving Afrites;
- as per HELMOON, an aspect of APM survived the attack on Godbad by an outraged All of Incain;
- it, a dinky, winged eyeball akin to Gloriel's little angels, did so inside of Janna St Peche-Montressor (q.v.), a love-loving Afrite as well as an Athenan War Witch, who was APM's most frequent host-shell in 5980;
- her primary host on the Outer Earth's Centauri Island was Connie Lindquist, the Fatman's doctor as well as that of the pre-Launch cosmi-companions; Connie's parents were the supranomals known as Soanso and Prince Translav;

» **Rufous Rudra Silvercloud**, Bodiless Byron's only firstborn son, his Beast Master, also his Storm Lord;
- as per HELLION, a onetime friend and ally of the Thanatoids of Lathakra who, along with sister-wife Umashakti, led Byronic forces during the First War between the Living and the Dead;
- as of the 6th of Tantalar, along with Uma, the eldest surviving Byronic on the Hidden Headworld;
- after events detailed in HELMOON one of the last three highborn Byronics, the others being Umashakti and what little is left of APM All-Eyes;

» **Umashakti Silvercloud**, Byron's only remaining firstborn daughter;
- a Moon Goddess, she waxes and wanes with its phases; consequently sometimes called Lunar Uma;
- her attribute is gravity; hence why devils usually address her as just that, Gravity;
- as per HELLION, a onetime friend and ally of the Thanatoids of Lathakra who, along with brother-husband Rudra, led Byronic forces during the First War between the Living and the Dead;
- in the absence of Devil Wind (**Vayu Maelstrom**, one of Byron's Primary Nucleoids) freed from All of Incain at the beginning of Tantalar 5980;
- immediately thereafter became involved in the Byronic ploy that saw Apple Isle's Devil Child Tralalorn, the Ghostlands' King Harvest, and, among others, the Flood Lands' Klizarod Rex humiliated and nearly ill-starred (cathonitized);
- like Methandra Thanatos and Freespirit Nihila barely survived GAMBIT;
- as of the 6th of Tantalar, along with triplet-husband Rufous Rudra, the eldest surviving Byronic on the Hidden Headworld;

» **Deneb Makara**, one of Great Byron's Winder Zodiacals, Capricorn the Goatfish;
- the recurring deviant, Pusan Wanderlust, who always comes back in one of her daughters or granddaughters, claims Makara was her devic half-mother;
- others argue that Goatfish committed devic suicide by cutting out her third eye during the time of the Goddess Culture on the Outer Earth ca 2000

to 2500 YD (2000 to 1500 BC) and that therefore Pusan is what's become of her (in much the same way Rumour of Lazareme became Jordan 'Q for Quill' Tethys circa 4000 YD);

- Makara's Tvasitar talisman or power focus is a pedum, which is akin to a bishop's crosier or a fairy godmother's shepherd's crook; it comes back to Pusan whenever and wherever she reincarnates;

» **Malar Tzigame**, Byron's Butterfly;

- odds on favourite to be the devic half-mother of Akbar and Meroudys Artha while being possessed by the Temporis Faerie Queen known as Cabala (Dand Tariqartha would have be occupying Faerie King Archon);

- in early Tantalar 5980 among those involved in the Byronic ploy in the borderlands between the Flood and Lakelands (Sedon's Sweat Glands) that almost led to the cathonitization of the Ghostlands' King Harvest and also saw the Devil Child Tralalorn devolve the Floodlands' Kilizarod Rex;

» **Pyçonja Volant**, another of Great Byron's Winter Zodiacals, Pisces the Flying Fish;

- odds on favourite to have been Fisherwoman's devic half-mother because when the newborn Fish (Scylla Nereid, Lady Achigan now, but once the marital Queen of Godbad) was found by Aortic Merthetis, Volant's Tvasitar talisman or power focus, a Fisher's Gaffe, was found beside her;

- prior to and during Fish's Godbadian Queenship, its air force was known as the Royal Byronic Volant in her honour;

- if she was Fish's devic half-mother then she must have been humanizing Miracle Memory, the Female Entity, when Fish was conceived in 5917/18;

- • **More Lazaremists**
  » **Amal-Althea Brand**, Lazareme's long missing, goatish Female Healer; previously seen in FEEL THEO;

  - Mel-Illuminatus appears to have her power focus, a caduceus, which Mel pretends is actually akin to the gargoyles (more correctly known as grotesques) Utopian Trinondevs manifest off their eye-staves in the Weirdom of Cabalarkon;

  - Mel claims she acquired it from the Olympian Tantalus in the Forties on the Outer Earth, which is possible, but there's plenty of speculation that while, as a pureblood Utopian she can't be possessed, as a Summoning Child she may have been born with Althea Brand inside her, the same as Barsine Mandam was born with Nergal Vetala inside her;

  - previous hosts of Amal-Althea include the Traveller (Pusan Wanderlust); current host believed to be Telepassa of not just Godbad;

  » Thunder and Lightning **Lord Yajur** (the Unity of Order);

  - survived HELMOON, albeit in a bifurcated state; currently keeping the Male Entity alive in Trans-Time Trigon;

  » **Tvasitar Smithmonger**, the devic Prometheus (Anvil the Artificer, the Master Craftsman), whose effective protectorate is Sedon's Peak;

  - it's possible. if unlikely, that he can remake devic talismans such as the (now destoyed?) Trigregos Talisman, which he dedicated to the Trigregos Sisters, the simultaneous mothers of devazurkind; and Pretty Parsis's flying carpet, which Methandra Thanatos may have;

- **More Byronics**
  » **Chimaera Glimmenmare** (Byron's Stallion), along with triplet siblings, (Smoky) **Sedona Spellbinder** and **Devil Wind** (the Whirling Deva, aka Vayu Maelstrom), are Byron's Primary Nucleoids; **Draconic Yati,** Byron's Dragon (beware his burps), was last seen in HELMOON devouring Sharkczar; **Babbar Ninkuray** is known as Byron's Babbler because, even though he is among the most knowledgeable and perceptive member of the tribe, he seems to speak nonsense that only Sedona and APM can interpret; **Tau 'Monk-Eye' Hanuman**, Byron's Monkey Man, a trickster whose power focus is the Bazooka Banana; **Parsis 'Flying Carpeteer' Urartu**, burqa-clad Byronic who may have lost her flying carpet to Methandra Thanatos during expansion of Empire of Lathakra; in which case she either uses someone else's power focus in the form of her own or had Tvasitar make her a replacement;

- **More Mithradites**
  » **Methandra Thanatos**, a firstborn Mithradite also known, accurately, if perhaps somewhat disrespectfully, as Hot Stuff;
  - a red-skinned, flame-haired giantess; almost always masked and thoroughly covered in fabrics invariably coloured different shades of red, pink or purple;
  - power focus is a firebrand or matchstick (cane);
  - the mother, while being subsumed by a bebrained, glassine daemon or demon pre-Genesea (the Great Flood of Genesis) of Klannit, the first azura;
  - considered the devic patron of the Athenan War Witch sisterhood (to which Janna St Peche-Montressor, Fisherwoman, Superior Sarpedon, dangerous daughter Andaemyn and Garcia 'Dead' Dis L'Orca, among others, belong in the mid-to-late 60th Century of the Dome; Dustmound's Black Widow, Olivia Tenebrous, claims she does too, though that probably isn't true);
  - for thousands of years known as Mithras's Virgin; shunned the attentions of both her grandfather, Dark Sedon, and her father, Thrygragos Varuna Mithras, while in turn being ignored by true love and triplet-brother Tantal (King Cold);
  - self-proclaimed death goddess, that of heat and fire, who became the conceptive and birthmother of the first members of a fourth generation of devakind (not to be confused with devazurkind) starting about ten years after waking up from a thousand year sleep in 5908 Year of the Dome;
  - her ten, fourth generational offspring from when she was possessing Miracle Memory and Tantal Heliosophos were Day and Night (Castella and Ereba), the Four Elements (Antaeor-Earth, Acheron-Fire, Thalassa-Water and Aires-Air) and the Four Seasons (Veronas-Summer, Auraura-Winter, Constantin-Spring, and Orinth-Autumn);
  - was pregnant with Sedunihas (who has yellow skin & only ages one year in five) and Motan (who was stillborn) when hit by Sedona's Spell of Disproportionment on Antheal 14, 5933, on the downward slopes of Sedon's Peak;
  » **Tantal Thanatos**, firstborn Mithradite commonly known as King Cold;

- a gigantic, blue-skinned, icicle-bearded, archetypal-Viking whose power focus or Tvasitar talisman is a labrys (a double-headed war axe);
- pre-Dome father, while being subsumed by a bebrained ice daemon or demon pre-Genesea (the Great Flood of Genesis) of Klannit, the world's first azura;
   - besides his thought-father, Thrygragos Varuna Mithras, probably the most prolific male Master Deva in terms of having azura offspring;
- self-proclaimed death god, that of cold and ice, who nonetheless became the conceptive and birthfather of the first members of a fourth generation of devakind (not to be confused with devazurkind) sometime after waking up from a thousand year sleep in 5908 Year of the Dome;
- his ten, fourth generational offspring from when he was possessing Heliosophos and Methandra Miracle Memory were Day and Night (Castella and Ereba), the Four Elements (Antaeor-Earth, Acheron-Fire, Thalassa-Water and Aires-Air) and the Four Seasons (Veronas-Summer, Auraura-Winter, Constantin-Spring, and Orinth-Autumn);
- hit by Smoky Sedona Spellbinder's Spell of Disproportionment on Antheal 14, 5933, while coming down from Sedon's Peak with sister-wife and ten fourth generation children;
- also father of yellow-skinned Sedunihas the Artist who came along in 5955 and only ages one year in five; (Motan, Sedunihas's twin, was stillborn);
» **Tralalorn** (White Dwarf, the child devil who along with Pyrame Silverstar and the Moloch counts herself one of the Hidden Headworld's three Perpetual Presences); her brood sisters are Pyrame Silverstar and Cathune called Cathead '**Apocalyptic of Drought**' Bubastis, who may or may not appear in the book;
» **Trawl the Taskmaster**, a devic Cyclops like Satanwyck's Viceroy Ibal, once Mithras's Punisher; **Djinn Domitian**, the Heliodromus of Mithras, his Leontocephalic Trumpeter; **Chroma Chameleon**, colourful (huge as well as hue-imbued) Emperor of the Lake Lands; **Fiery Mildoth**, Mithras's bordering on brainless firedrake, and **Klizarod Rex**, Saurlord of the Floodlands, all appear in "The Forgettable Fiend"

========

4. Demons, Faeries, Deviants and Mandroid Monstrosities

- **Demons**

   Soulless, often nearly brainless, chthonic creatures also known as eldritch earthborn and Indescribables. (Similarly spelled **daemons** {meaning 'spirit' or 'deity'} are generally less antagonistic to humans.) The Mantel replicates of Temporis are related to demons, as are the capricious, but much more intelligent faeries of Crepuscule, the Land of Twilight (Sedon's Outer Nose), and those of Subcranial Temporis (notably Archon and Cabala, their king and queen).

   To this day (5980), certain highly skilled witches and rogue Utopian biomages can manufacture demons by using tellurian raw material found in the Hell Well of the World, which underlies most of the Upper Head. (Some of these rogue Utopians, usually hailing from the former Weirdom of Samarand, once Sedon's Tongue Stud, nowadays dwell on Shenon, Witch Isle, where they are protected by the Panharmonium-supporting Aortics Amphitrite of Lemuria and Tsishah Twilight.)

Although mostly confined to Satanwyck and the Forbidden Forest of Kala Tal (whence Hadd's Indescribables), they can be found throughout the Hidden Headworld. Much feared, omnivorous walking appetites, contrary to many traditions they are notoriously flammable. As the Morrigan, Morgianna born Nauroz (Morg, Superior Sarpedon) was able to compel them to do as she desired.

Demons come in all shapes and sizes, with a wide of variety of so-called magical or supernatural abilities. Morrigan Morg wore a teleportive demon she brought back from Satanwyck prior to the final battle for by then Diminished Dustmound. Psychopomps are likewise empowered and therefore may be at least part demon.

» **Primeval Lilith**
- earthborn seductress, the Demon Queen of the Night, the lovely but often lethal Lily;
- ageless, apparently both immortal and unkillable, partial mother of the Sedsons (sedons, small case) on both sides of the Dome;
- even though Pyrame Silverstar denies she's her demon, arguably the source of Pyrame's Earth-long hold over the Moloch Sedon;
- apparently Machine-Memory got hold of her during the events of 5950 (the Challenge of Weir, also the Siege of Cabalarkon) but expelled her on the Moon (thirty years and ninety odd lifetimes later) while thinking she was Erebe Thanatos (Dame Darkness) from a future lifetime;
- now that she's free, attempts to regain the Throne of Satanwyck; when that doesn't work, and (presumably) after reading the Diver's mind beside the Brainrock lava lake of Sedon's Peak, becomes the Black Widow haunting diminished Dustmound; in that capacity identifies herself as Olivia Tenebrous, an Athenan War Witch;
- this before she goes off with the Night's Sky Alive (King Gomorrah?, more likely the Moloch Sedon come to ground);
- during DecDam, becomes Wilderwitch's saviour & Saladin Devason's White Goddess once she settles in the Weirdom of Cabalarkon;
» **Daemonicus**, the long time, pre-Flood King of Demons (Dark Sedon is the current King of Demons; has been for well over six thousand years);
- evidently as ageless, indestructible, and immortal as forever mate Lilith;
- seems to be just a wearable body these days, with no mind left;
- when last seen, during NUKE, Solomon 'Boom-Boom' Mandam was wearing him;
- people who wear Daemonicus, such as Judge Warlock in the '40s and '50s, tend to speak **like this**;
» **Faceless Strife**
- probably not a demon; more likely what's left of Marut Kanin (Fitna Marutia, Kore-Discord), a second-born Apple Goddess, known in legend (as

well as, most notably, FEEL THEO) as Mithras's Ewe for Aries, meaning she was with him from roughly 2000 to 4000 Years of the Dome;
- Balkis (Sheba Faerieflight) Mandam, Solomon's twin sister and one of Shenon's two Ventriculars (the other being Telepassa of not just Godbad), was occupied by Faceless Strife throughout much of NUKE;
- witches regard Strife as a sentient virus; as per WAR-POX, she's why Wilderwitch refused to carry anyone through the Weird in the aftermath of Damnation Isle on the 30th of November 1980;
- Harmony thought she'd disposed of her, Strife, ca 4000 YD in the Brainrock cauldron of Sedon's Peak;
- as per HELMOON, Miracle Maenad reckons she disposed of her inside Sainted Sophia (born St Synne, Cybele's presumed sister, D-Brig's Gloriel D'Angelo Dark's Mama Sofa) at least temporarily on the 9th of December 1980;
» **Shahiyeda**, the first child born of Solace born Sunrise (Sorciere); father: D-Brig's John (Blind) Sundown;
- born in 5934 on the Hidden Continent, Blind Sundown may not know of her existence (let alone of her 'survival') until 5980, if then;
- an apparent Outer Earth supranormal turned into a demon at some point; all indications are that, even as a demon, she retains some of her brain and her main supra talent, an ability to bite back vampirism;
» **Tsishah Twilight**, born Thrae, currently wears said Shah-Demon; seems to have since events that took place in 5960 of the Dome;
- daughter of Morgianna born Nauroz, become Somata, then Sarpedon, and Tammuz Rhymer of Dukkha, rather his faerie aspect, Tom-Tiddly Taddletale, who looks much like Thrygragos Lazareme does when he looks in a mirror;
- has four children by **Mani-Balam** ('Jester Jaguar'): Makhta ('Brave Woman'), **Teotihuacan** ('Place Where Gods Born'), Zama ('Dawn'), and Skaga ('Magician'); the last two of whom seem to be connected to the Molect Xibalba, who is only a shade in late 5980;
- **Deviants**
     When Great Gods and/or Master Devas possess sentient beings for procreative purposes, their resultant offspring are often long-lived and occasionally unnaturally gifted mortals known as deviants.
» **Fisherwoman** (Fish), amphibious Piscine born sometime in 5918;
- as a newborn, found in the Belly of the Beast (Island Leviathan) by Aortic Merthetis who gave her the name Scylla Nereid;
- tends to fishify, a form of not always rhyming or alliterative fay-saying that often makes her difficult to understand;
- something of a breeder, first child (Wave or Winifred) born in 5934 and raised by Godbadian Royal Family (the House of the Crimson Gold) because they believe her father was **Achigan Auranja**, a Summoning Child;
- Achigan, 5980-nowadays the sitting Duke of Achigon (sic), Sedon's Lower Lip-tip, in the north-westernmost corner of the subcontinent of Aka Godbad, was therefore only 13 when Fish conceived Wave-Winifred, but already the nominal King of Godbad;

- because of their child, Fish married King Achigan prior to Master Kyprian, the then Master of Weir and Whole Earth's Anthean Superior, taking over her training when she was sixteen;
- eventually learns her parents were Ulysses Heliopolis and Miracle Maenad, who, at the time of her conception, seemingly possesed three Master Devas simultaneously (Pyçonja Volant, Diluvia Ran and Mandorla Auricaura);
- if so, then this explains the three devic power foci Merthetis found beside her in the Belly of the Beast: a fisher's gaffe (Byron's Pisces), a gillnet (Mithras's Apocalyptic of Flood) and her bellybutton bauble (a Vesica Piscis formerly belonging to Lazareme's Bright Light Enlightenment);
- in 5950 became Master Kyprian's champion such that she could compete in that year's Challenge of Weir on her behalf; resigned her role when Kyprian died under the usual mysterious circumstances;
- despite their former enmity, seemingly became 'involved' with Saladin Devason in 5960; may have had a son as a result, someone she called, typically fishily, 'Sal-man' (as in salmon);
- in 5980 known as Lady Achigan since she and her husband, Godbad's reigning King and marital Queen, were deposed during the Godbadian Civil War in the vicinity of twenty years earlier;
- briefly fused with Freespirit Nihila during GAMBIT;
- in DECDAM has a daemonic psychopomp (spirit carrier) she calls Ronnie Ray-Bum, after the incoming POTUS; others call it Eagle Ray Revenant;

» **Saladin** born Nauroz called Devason;
- Master of the Weirdom of Cabalarkon as of 5950 YD, when he beat Golgotha Nauroz (a clone), Demios Sarpedon (disqualified for being a year too young) and Fisherwoman (Scylla Nereid) in that year's Challenge of Weir;
- as per GAMBIT, humiliated on not-yet-diminished Dustmound in Hadd on the 7th of Tantalar by niece Andaemyn ('Without Demon') Sarpedon; rescued by Jordan 'Q for Quill' Tethys (the Legendarian, conceivably once Rumour of Lazareme);
- first depicted in 1980's **Phantacea Six**; mother: Pandora 'Hush' Mannering, father: Augustus Nauroz (as the devil-transformed faerie tricksters, Young Life & Young Death) appeared in Sister-Grandmother, a short story published in 4EVER40;
- has an abiding hatred of witches;
- presumed devic half-mother: Pyrame Silverstar; presumed devic half-father: none other than the Moloch Sedon himself;
- (arguably) the last Sed-son or sedon, small case, alive beneath the Cathonic Dome (equally arguably, Sedon St Synne is the last living sedon beyond it);

» **Morgianna 'Morg' Sarpedon** (born Nauroz become Somata, an Inner Earth Summoning Child, Saladin Devason's year-younger sister;
- apparently killed in Hadd by John Sundown during the final battle between the Living and the Dead on by then Drenched Dustmound; when last seen in HELMOON was somehow forming a cocoon around her evident corpse;
- probable devic half-mother: Pyrame Silverstar;

- mother Pandora 'Hush' Mannering and father Augustus Nauroz (as the devil-transformed faerie tricksters, Young Life & Young Death) appeared in Sister-Grandmother, a short story published in 4Ever40;
- husband: Demios; mother of Andaemyn by Demios; mother of Tsishah Twilight by the blue-skinned, faerie-human hybrid, Tom-Tiddly Tattletale (think Lazareme and the Male Entity) born Tammuz Rhymer of Dukkha;
- codenamed the White Witch on the Outer Earth; called Superior Sarpedon by Wilderwitch (who distrusts her intensely) during War-Pox;
- the Hecate-Hellion's Morrigan, disgraced Anthean Superior on Outer Earth, became an Ant Nightingale then the Athenan War Witches' acting Mother Superior after daughter Tsishah left Shenon on the Spring Equinox of 5980;

» **Pusan Wanderlust**, the trail-blazing Traveller;
- the fauna or female satyr who runs the DDD (the Dinq, Doinq, Danq Cavern Tavern) on the far, north-eastern slopes of the Diluvia Mountain Range;
- a recurring deviant who's been coming back as one of her daughters or granddaughters since the time of the Outer Earth's Goddess Culture ca 2000 to 1500 BC (2000 to 2500 YD);
- some claim the long missing Byronic Goatfish (Deneb Makara, a Winter Zodiacal) was her devic half-mother;
- others argue that Goatfish committed devic suicide by cutting out her third eye and that therefore Pusan is what's become of her since;
- Makara's Tvasitar talisman or power focus is a pedum, which is akin to a bishop's crosier or a fairy godmother's shepherd's crook; it comes back to Pusan whenever and wherever she reincarnates;
- nevertheless, many – including Pusan herself – hold that her devic half-mom was Amal-Althea, the notoriously randy Lazaremist healer associated with Mel-Illuminatus;
- in this scenario the earliest recurring deviant Taurus Chrysaor Attis (last seen in Feel Theo) was her father and that he gave her Makara's power focus as a birthday gift;
- a long time associate of Tsishah Twilight and her mother, Superior Sarpedon;
- as such, heavily involved in the witches' Panharmonium project that resulted, on the Outer Earth, in Kamikaze Kaligula and the apparent destruction of the Cosmic Express on the 30th of November 1980 (story mostly told in Nuke);

» **Lakshmi of Lemuria**, called Arthadot due to the fact she's Dand Tariqartha's half-daughter;
- born on the 5th of Tantalar, Year of the Dome 5962, in Goddess Culture Temporis, wherein her crabby mother, long time Aortic Amphitrite (Lady Lemurian), was masquerading as her namesake, the demigod Amphitrite, and Dand Tariqartha was playing at being trident-wielding Poseidon;
- was scheduled to be married to her quarter cousin, eventual Senator Sophiscient, Akbarartha's son by the Lady Takeda Mikoto, on the 6th;
- once the Awesome Akbar (OMP, Old Man Power, an Outer Earth supra), still thinking himself Obadiah Melvin Power, a high level Outer Earth

Xuthrodite, showed up on her 18th birthday, she peremptorily dumped his son and, on Tariqartha's insistence, became engaged to marry him instead;
- when their half-father self-cathonitized on the 6th, Lakshmi gained his mutable power focus (Power Sceptre, similar in appearance to Akbar's Homeworld Sceptre) and expelled what was left of the Damnation Brigade, including betrothed Akbarartha, its by then rightful Kronokronos Supreme, from Temporis;
- secretly in love with someone other than Sophiscient or Akbar;
- because of Tariqartha's genetic strength looks more human than Lemurian, though still has gills behind her ears and slightly scaly skin;
- wears a shape-shifting guard body and carries Tariqartha's Power Sceptre while acting as Temporis's Kronokronos Supreme;
» **Eden Nightingale**, believed dead since 5955; declared dead on Outer Earth in 1939;
- Fish and the Witch's sister in the Dual Entities, born in 5909; as such, one of the Trigon Triplets, who were believed to be incarnations of the three Great Goddesses (Trigregos Demeter, Sapiendev and Devaura);
- mother, by her then husband Loxus Abraham Ryne (the Great Man, the Outer Earth Xuthrodites' now 80-year old patriarch), of Aranyani Nightingale (who was born on the same day as Gloriella D'Angelo, Good Friday, April 14, 1933) and her older brothers, the twins David (D-Brig's Cyborg Cerebrus) and Saul (Magnifico, the Magnificent Psycho), who were born four years earlier, in 1929;
» **Tsishah Twilight**, born Rudar 5934 (September 1934);
- devic half-mother: Krepusyl Evenstar, presumed therefore to be Wilderwitch's quarter-sister;
- mother: Morgianna then Somata, eventually Sarpedon; father: Tammuz Rhymer of Dukkha, by then a blue-skinned faerie type known as Tom-Tiddly Tattletale;
- mother of a number of children by Jester Jaguar (Mani-Balam, probably Solace Sunrise's twin brother by Shaman Manitoulin and Lamia Louise St Synne, which technically should make him Miracle Maenad's half-brother);
- in Tantalar 5980 the still acting, non-Lemurian Aortic or Quarter Queen of Shenon (Witch Isle); due to (finally) retire come the Spring Equinox, which in many parts of the Hidden Headworld is celebrated as its New Years Day;
» **Jesus 'Jesse' Mandam**, the King Conqueror, the Conquering Christ, but probably not the otherwise never identified ('Bolder-Brain') Conqueror;
- believed to be, by a matter of seconds, the first Summoning Child born on either side of the Cathonic Dome (just after midnight Christmas Day 1920 on the Outer Earth, Mithramas on the Hidden Continent of Sedon's Head);
- acknowledged son of Magister Joseph 'Old Joe' Mandam and Mary Magdalene born Ryne; brought up as the twin brother of Barsine (Vetala) eventually Holgat-wife even though he didn't look like her;
- early on (in the late 1930s) declared himself the Christ-like Saviour of Supranormalkind;

- known as Wiccan Warlock on the Inner Earth; as such, incorrectly assumed to be the son of Judge Warlock (Sedon St Synne) who wore the Daemonicus shell while on the Hidden Headworld);
- a great friend of Saladin Devason during the late Thirties and throughout the Forties; evidently stole all his advanced technology from the Weirdom of Cabalarkon during this time;
- unstated in Nuke, but strongly suggested in both Helmoon and DecDam, much of the tech used by New Century Enterprises, to build the Cosmic Express, and by WORLD, to counter it with Kamikaze Kaligula, Crystal-lion, Hell's Horsemen and their Nuclear Dragons, was derived from Jesse's notes, as kept in the Soviet Supracity throughout the Fifties, Sixties and Seventies;
- killed when Blind Sundown and Raven's Head dropped a prototype Soviet Hydrogen Bomb atop him on Salvation Island on his 33rd birthday in 1953;

» **Legendarian** (Jordan 'Q for Quill' Tethys, devic half-father: Rumour of Lazareme, devic half-mother: Metisophia, Wisdom of Lazareme), **Miracle Maenad** (Cybele St Synne, born 5909, a Trigon Triplet, grandmother of Solomon and Balkis Mandam), **Human Memory** (Mnemosyne D'Angelo Heliopolis, the third Trigon Triplet, might be Ventricular Telepassa of God-bad's mother), the truly Terrible Twins (**Solomon 'Boom-Boom'** and Ventricular **Balkis 'Sheba Faerieflight' Mandam** are among the deviants mentioned in Games

- **Probable Deviants**

  » **The Molech Xibalba**, a Black King or Vampire Maker born as a result of the Simultaneous Summonings of 59/1920 who seems to have vampiric abilities without being a blood-sucker;
  - a long-thought dead Irache shaman believed thoroughly sliced and diced (killed both decisively and irretrievably) by Second Fangs (Janna Fang-fingers) sometime prior to 5980 YD;
  - possibly has a twin brother or sister who became an Outer Earth supra-normal during its Secret War or Wars thereof;
  - as per the "Janna Fangfingers" (Fangers) mini-novel, in the subcontinent of Aka Godbad (starting in the province of New Iraxas, Godbad's huge but thoroughly polluted oil field) for a time went by the name Reilly Haddeus, an Irache rabble-rouser, before true identity revealed;

  » **Night Owl**, otherwise unnamed (Lamechlan?), presumed Inner Earth Irache who became a vampire during the Simultaneous Summonings of 59/1920;
  - most likely Xibalba's father;
  - somehow associated with Metisophia (Titanic Metis, Wisdom of Lazareme, devic half-mother of the Legendarian);
  - as such, becomes an owl rather than a bat when he transforms into anything non-human other than smoke;

- **Mandroids**

  » **All** the (self-proclaimed) Invincible She-Sphinx of Incain; as per Feel Theo, once Ginny the Gynosphinx;

- based on Weir's original Mother Machine and made, long pre-Dome, by Machine-Memory to capture daemons, can also eat and therefore imprison Master Devas;
- Mandroid Mother Machine as well as occasional monster maker;
- more often than not appears as a huge and winged griffin type; a therefore perhaps surprisingly mobile psychopomp;
- as such, can travel at will through the Weird (between-space, the dark-grey universal substance of Samsara, mundane reality), though always leaves a root of herself behind on the Prison Beach of Incain;
- used by devils, especially Unmoving Byron and the Unities of Lazareme, as a temporary holding cell or a long-term prison for their transgressing fellows;
- in addition to highborn devils, though not to the Moloch Sedon, whom she's designed to eat, All tends to be responsive to Pyrame Silverstar (q.v.);
- All, whose human head resembles the Female Entity (think Harmony), tongue-tugs Pyrame and non-devils she favours (notably Chrysaor Attis, from FEEL THEO, and the Legendarian) through the Dome to her otherwise moribund male equivalent out there, the Egyptian or Giza Sphinx, whose head resembles the Male Entity (think Lazareme);
- although possessed of a modicum of sentience, if not much in the way of actual intelligence, still a machine; as per HELLION, can be turned off and on as well as reprogrammed;
» **Demogorgon**, the much-feared conglomerate devil, a version of whom may have appeared in FEEL THEO speaking *like this*;
- comes out of All, Incain's (self-proclaimed) Invincible Mandroid Monster Maker (q.v.);
- composed of the multitude of Master Devas still imprisoned within All either FANGERS-recently or over the course of her millennia-long existence.

=========

5. Mortal Descendants of Original Extraterrestrials

- **Utopians of Weir on Earth**
  » **Utopians** living in the Weirdom of Cabalarkon are brought up to hate the Moloch Sedon and his devic progeny;
  - oddly, as if to prove their non-Earth heritage, pureblood U-men are always black whereas pureblood U-women are invariably white;
  - pure U-bloods can't be possessed;
  - the be-all and end-all of most completely cognizant U-bloods, pure or hybrid, stuck on the Whole Earth (either beneath the Cathonic Dome or, due only in part to an absence of functional spacecraft, beyond it) remains the destruction of their ancient enemies;
  » **Illuminaries** of Weir, Utopian polymaths, supposedly learned in a wide variety of not-necessarily-related matters;
  - the highest educated class in Cabalarkon, Illuminaries could also be found in former or decrepit Weirdoms like Godbad City, Samarand (Sedon's Tongue Stud), the Gleaming City of Manoa (Hadd's Necropolis, Fangfingers' cap-

ital), and the five hundred years ruined Kanin City, in the vast Plains of Marutia near the Gregarian Fields (Sedon's Mole);
- often act as advisors to the reigning Master, many of whom were elevated from their ranks (Quoits Tethys, Melina born Tethys Somata and Kyprian Somata were once High Illuminaries of Weir); seldom not pure U-bloods;
- Melina nee Sarpedon Zeross, an Inner Earth Summoning Child codenamed Illuminatus in the Thirties, Forties and Fifties, became the High Illuminary of Cabalarkon during the reign of by-then brother-in-law Saladin Devason (which began in 5950);

» **Imbeciles** of Weir, also the idiots of Weir; inbred and therefore very much low functioning Utopians; almost always purebloods, hence the inbreeding;

» **Trinondevs** of Weir, Weir's Warrior Elite, nowadays mostly clones but formerly almost always purebloods who managed to overcome inbreeding in order to function as soldiers;
- their main weapons operate by willpower channelled though extraterrestrial devices such as Mother Machines and eye-staves;
- eyeorbs placed atop eye-staves double as prison pods in that they can suck devic and azura spirit being out of the shells they're occupying and into them, thus incarcerating them;
- eyeorbs supposedly work on demons, too, though being so flammable they're easier to kill;
- once an eyeorb is full it ceases to function as anything except a prison pod; if it's not replaced, the eye-stave becomes useless;
- eye-staves, like all their other anti-devil weaponry, never functioned in the Weirdom of Kanin City during the reigns of Zalman then Melina, Sraddha or Janna Somata;
- since Saladin Devason began his reign as Master in the Weirdom of Cabal-arkon in 5950, its Trinondevs are exclusively male;

» **Utopian Development Teams**, surrogate parents charged with raising non-born clones as well as difficult, natural born children like the Master's felt-entitled kids and those born of Outer Earth 'imports';

» **Cabalarkon**, Cabby the Daddy, the Undying Utopian; a biogeneticist when he lived and worked on, or travelled off of, the First Weirworld ca 200,000 light years earlier;
- when he was a wholly alive and ambulatory Utopian Scientocrat, the Dual Entities used his right eye to jumpstart the process that resulted in the Moloch Sedon, hence Cabby the Daddy;
- currently subsists in a tub of life-preserving, but animation-suspending, Cathonic Fluid beneath the Citadel of the Thinkers in Cabalarkon City; as such is probably the oldest, continuously alive mortal in the entire cosmos;
- it, like the rest of the territory composing the Weirdom of Cabalarkon (Sedon's Devic Eye-Land on a map of the Hidden Continent of Sedon's Head), is named after him;

» **Melina born Sarpedon** become Zeross, twin sister of Demios; may have been named after the Trigregos Titaness of the Dome's 55th Century (Melina born Tethys become Somata from "Contagion Collectors" {CONTAGION});

- a Utopian pureblood, an Inner Earth Summoning Child like twin brother Demios and Morgianna by then Somata, who first came to the Outer Earth in 1938 and attended the first Amsterdam Academy of Man until it closed with the outbreak of war;
- there, on the Outer Earth during its Secret War (or Wars) in the Thirties, Forties and Fifties, codenamed Illuminatus;
- became the High Illuminary of Weir (Cabalarkon) during the reign of (deeply disapproving) brother-in-law Saladin (born Nauroz but called Devason), which began in 5950; Sal, who hates Demios, seems to have been enamoured of her, but she rejected him for reasons as yet only implied;
- the mother by much younger Aristotle (Ringleader) Zeross (born in 1943) of three daughters: Persephone, Helen and Athena, all of whom appear in GAMBIT, HELMOON and DECDAM);
- directly descended from the Sarpedon underclass who, as revealed in HELLION, are inclined to worship Thrygragos Lazareme since they see him as the Male Entity;

» **Demios Sarpedon**, twin brother of Melina become Zeross;
- pure U-Blood Summoning Child who first came to the Outer Earth in 1938, along with twin sister Melina; there served under the clone Golgotha Nauroz as a bodyguard for eventual wife Morgianna;
- there also, during its Suprawar (or Wars) in the Thirties, Forties and Fifties, codenamed Blackguard then the Ace of Spades;
- exiled, along with wife Morgianna, from the Weirdom of Cabalarkon once Saladin (born Nauroz but called Devason) won the Challenge of Weir in 5950 and became its Master;
- considered Saladin Devason's chief rival for what passes as Cabalarkon's throne and the Weirdom's Mastery;
- reputedly possesses the oldest eye-stave in the world (Morgan Abyss, the Death's Head Hellion, had it in HELLION);
- directly descended from the Sarpedon underclass who, as revealed in HELLION, are inclined to worship Thrygragos Lazareme since they see him as the Male Entity;

» **Capputis Masterson**, teenage, apparent clone with an overlarge head (hydrocephalic), scaly skin and gills behind his ears
- claims to have been bred amphibious deliberately so as to become Weir's ambassador to the Hidden Headworld's mostly Akadan-based, undersea realms, who tend to be anti-Godbadian;

========

6. Norman & Norma Notables

- **Inner Earthlings**
  » **Alpha Centauri**, called the Fatman for reasons immediately apparent to anyone who sees him;
  - founder, in 5945, and to-this-day head of Centauri Enterprises, the de facto corporate government of supposedly democratic Godbad;

- CE, as it's often called, is why the subcontinent and territories neighbouring it in Goatwood, the Gulf of Aka and Sedon's Underlip, as well as Krachla, at the tip of the Penile Peninsula, and on the coast of the Inner Ocean of Akadan of the near-western Cattail Peninsula, is best known as the Corporate State of Greater Godbad;
- an obese Outer Earthling born **Alfredo Sentalli,** he's so grotesquely fat he's confined to an automated wheelchair for most of his waking hours;
- reputedly the only way he survived being so massively overweight for so long is because he was often the very willing shell of none other than Thrygragos Byron himself — proof, as he, despite his Roman Catholic background and persistent faith, very much begrudgingly acknowledges, that devic possession can be beneficial;
- since Bodiless Byron is now a (very bright) star in the night's sky above the Hidden Headworld this is no longer possible;

» **Janna St Peche-Montressor**, wife of Yataghan raised Montressor, daughter-in-law of Alpha Centauri, evidently the most common host of APM All-Eyes in 5980 YD;
- a Lovely Lady Afrite as well as an Athenan War Witch;
- effectively the Fatman's nursemaid as well as his chief bodyguard in Aka Godbad City, where – until All of Incain destroyed his living quarters – he lived in the same Outer-Earth-modern building that houses the ancillary headquarters of Centauri Enterprises.

» **Gomez Niarchos**, Godbad's dead, but Sangazur-animated ambassador to the Bloodlands (New, Valhalla, Sedon's Inner Nose);
- a friend of the Legendarian, albeit from earlier incarnations, Gomez is charged with negotiating the neutrality of Bloodlanders (Valhallans, the Glorious Dead of FEEL THEO), all of whom are dead and, after the elimination of both Guardian Angel Tyrtod and an imbecilic Apocalyptic of War, leaderless;

» **Telepassa of Godbad** & her four daughters (**Ino**, **Agave** + **Autonoe**, who are triplets, and the youngest **Semele**);
- the Female Entity (Miracle Memory also Machine-Memory) is very protective of Telepassa and her daughters;
- she regards them as her Human Memory template's daughter and grand-daughters, which they may be (Human Memory, one the Trigon Triplets, was Mnemosyne born D'Angelo Heliopolis; her daughter was Europa Heliopolis, who vanished {along with uncle, Alexandros 'Pluman' Kinesis, and his wife, her aunt, Roxanne 'Slipper' born Heliopolis} from the Outer Earth in 1960, whereas her stepson was Kadmon Heliopolis, who supposedly died in 1968);
- it appears Ino, Agave & Autonoe are the long-awaited incarnations of the Trigregos Sisters and thus essential to the Panharmonium Project;
- it further appears that after she realized, on the 14th of Tantalar 5980, that they had somehow got hold of the Terrible Talismans (the Susasword, the Crimson Corona, and what's left of the Amateramirror), Miracle Maenad teleported them to safety elsewhere, presumably to the Outer Earth, along

with their mother, Ventricular Telepassa, and their baby sister, Semele, who's not quite 12;

» Among the Hidden Headworld's other notable, presumed mortals mentioned in the mini-novel include **Holgat Sraddha Anvilson** and **Barsine born Mandam Holgat-wife** (both of whom were Summoning Children) as well as their son, **Thartarre Sraddha Holgatson**, the current High Priest of the Brown-Robed Sraddhites, Godbadian General **Quentin Anvil**, Senator **Sophiscient Barson**, Teotihuacan 'Toothy Teoti' Balam

****

DAEMONIC DESPERATION

— Winter Solstice 5980 – Autumnal Equinox 5981 —

Jim McPherson

A *PHANTACEA* Mythos Print Publication
James H McPherson, Publisher

Coming in 2018
(6018 Year of the Dome, assuming the Hidden Headworld is still around)

Daemonic Desperation

Two-Demon: **HALF-MAMA MEMORY**

========

Toward the Spring Equinox, 5981

"You killed Cynthia?" disbelieved Saladin Devason.

"Don't need her anymore," Gomorrah-Lilith answered.

Somewhat earlier that same day, in early Yamana 5980, Sal's Cynthia Masterwife wasn't dreaming of dying.

========

John Sundown and Raven's Head gone, if not necessarily dead, and the un-loaded, then reloaded, Pani Merchant ship sent on its way south, its skipper carrying Gomez Niarchos's head in a box, the High Illuminary of Weir fulfilled her promise to Wilderwitch. Gathering up her girls, the Witch and their attendants, including a few hand-picked Trinondev guardsmen, she headed out to the coast for some over-due rest and relaxation.

Not even two weeks after leaving the metropolis proper, a blinding snowstorm blew in from Fearsome Fobbiat and it was winter wonderland time. A day or two thereafter the Witch, in her wheelchair, was rolling toward the edge of the raised, snow and ice-covered, concrete patio outside her bedroom. She was wearing a parka and mukluks, with lots of other clothes underneath. Her metallic marigold was in her chair's side pocket. It was cold as the deepest depths of Hell, Dante-version. What she was doing out there, in those conditions, was responding to someone calling her name — her real name; arguably her only name besides Wilderwitch.

It was her mother. Half of her mother anyhow. The other half couldn't be the same other half her mother had when she was conceived. Nor could it be the same half that shared her birth pangs with Machine-Memory. Even for the Headworld, given the timeframe of her birth, late Tantalar 5927, both scenarios were quite im-possible. What was far less certain was whether she should have celebrated her 53rd birthday or her 28th around Zmas Day.

She chose, instead, not to celebrate anything even resembling a birthday. Was too preoccupied trying to stay alive for her next one.

========

"Cynthemis Dyana?"

========

Wilderwitch was exchanging wary glances with the Female Entity, Miracle Memory as she was known in human form. Which, being otherwise a machine, the Mnemosyne Machine, the innards of Trans-Time Trigon, she could only be when possessing a Master Deva. Unless it was the other way around. And that was a possibility.

Other than possessing or being possessed by a devil who was pinned to a slab of Brainrock in the Crystal Mountains by a Trigregos Talisman, the Susasword, in 1927, 5927 in here, and still was until early Tantalar 5980, December 1980 out there, most anything was when it came to dealing with her.

"Why ask when you already know, Nihila?"

Freespirit Nihila was the devil she and Akbarartha (the Outer Earth's Obadiah Melvin Power, Old Man Power or just plain OMP) encountered in the Faerie Garden of Temporis a little more than a month earlier. As Datong Harmonia, the Unity of Balance, her breed brother, Unholy Abaddon, the Unity of Chaos, pinned her to the aforementioned slab of Brainrock.

Did so with the aforementioned talisman (the other two being the Crimson Corona and the Amateramirror) toward the end of 55th Century, Year of the Dome. Utopians of Weir called the Trigregos Talismans, replicates of which Saladin Devason wore on special days, the three Sacred Objects. They called them thus because they were anything except sacred to devils.

Datong Harmonia (or just plain Harmony, as she preferred) changed her name to Nihila, as in nihilism, she told them in the Faerie Garden, because, unless it was nothingness, as a result of her humiliation she no longer cared about anything, especially harmony. Newly named Nihila, albeit with longer, crinkly butterscotch hair, rather than straight black same, also minus the third eye and broken Brainrock chains on her wrists, looked like Humanized Memory.

Of course, with thick, shoulder-length, dark hair, rather than much longer yet stringy, partially scalp-baring dark-ditto, a toque, fur gloves, pants, boots and a warm-looking winter overcoat, Wilderwitch also looked much like Human Memory. That'd be Gloriel's aunt, Mnemosyne nee D'Angelo Heliopolis.

Who died in 1945. Who was once the supra codenamed both Circean and the Queen of Spades. Who, as one or the other, had fought both with and against SOS, the Society of Saints. Whom the Witch knew, unfortunately all too briefly. And who never had a third eye that the Witch knew about, let alone could recall.

No surprise there. As the High Illuminary of Weir, Melina nee Sarpedon Zeross, once explained to her, the Female Entity's humanized form was derived from either/or. The first, Harmonia-Nihila, was likely if the Male Entity, Heliosophos, was originally semi-legendary King Cadmus of Thebes, who lived circa 1,500 years before Christ. The second, Memory of the Angels, was conceivable if the Male Entity, Helios called Sophos the Wise, started out as Kadmon Heliopolis, Human Memory's stepson, who was born in 1940 and died in 1968.

Mind you, Mel cautioned her at the time, if he began his existence as Anti-Patriarch Cain, Slayer of Abel, or some unknown other, then all bets were off.

"Not Nihila who knows, Witch. No matter how high up the totem pole she, ex-Harmony, may be in terms of early born Lazaremists, in terms of Master Devas period, her spirit self, her true being, along with her daemonic, subtle matter body, would be automatically imprisoned the moment she entered Cabalarkon's territory.

I was just curious if you'd answer to it. You see, it's a new one on me. I was happy with Witch."

"So was I. Who's humanizing you, Memory … Pyrame or Irisiel?"

"Obviously not Lazareme's female Heliodromus, Witch. Wouldn't be standing here so calmly if I was. The messenger, Angelus, enters Cabalarkon solely at the Master's sufferance. And then not for very long. She slows down, seeks to linger, at her own peril. Myself, I need no one's permission, not even that of the Moloch Himself, to come here.

"The Mnemosyne Machine made eye-staves on New Weirworld, in case you were unaware of that, and I've long since made certain they can't capture me any more than All can or does. Consequently, I go where I please in the Weirdom and, with me holding onto her, so does she, Miracle Memory. We're old companions, her and I. Like Siamese twins in one body."

Wilderwitch was about to demand Pyrame – definitely the Master as well as, according to some, Akbarartha's devic half-mother, and an historic enemy of the Weirdom – manifest herself as she most commonly appeared instead of hiding behind Memory's lovely likeness. Was about to, that is, until uncontrollable convulsions began wracking her.

The only other time in living (sorry) memory that she felt anything approximating the sensation was on Damnation Isle, the 30th of November (Maruta) last. She wasn't alone then. Six of the ten members of the comparatively momentarily reconstituted Damnation Brigade, as they'd been freshly deemed by the now, ever-so-regrettably, and relatively recently late Cerebrus David Ryne, were occupied by demon-devils.

Except for Memory-Pyrame she was alone right now and, to judge from the look of astonishment on Memory's face, it wasn't Pyrame trying to possess her. Which was about it for her memories until she found herself hurtling out of the sky toward the snow-covered forest, way, way below her, howsoever many minutes or hours later.

This was no time to even think 'disconcerting', let alone how to spell it.

========

Toward the end of Balek, February on the Outer Earth, Capputis Masterson, as he was now known, collected Melina born Sarpedon Zeross from her own lower down domicile and brought her to the top floor of a by-then thoroughly restored Skyrise. The hydrocephalic non-clone with the gills behind his ears he'd inherited from his Fish of a deviated mother, the Witch's nine years older sister via the Dual Entities, was clearly unhappy about something, but he wouldn't tell her what it was.

All he would say was his father, the Master of Weir, required the immediate presence of his High Illuminary. She was to bring nightclothes. Or not, as she pleased.

She would, however, be staying the night regardless.

========

Quite literally after putting on her stoniest face, Mel packed a small overnight bag then went upstairs with Capputis via the matter transducer the non-clone activated for the first time since the stone gnomes completed their repairs. In addition to her nightgown she filled her bag with some carefully selected medical supplies, including a few, very selectively preloaded syringes, if only for self-protection.

Not quite black-as-midnight Saladin Devason (his mother and grandmother hadn't been purebloods) met them once they arrived. He promptly dismissed his eldest acknowledged offspring and, as she'd been dreading, took her into his bedroom. Wilderwitch and her hadn't been getting on at all well of late. It started about six weeks earlier when middle daughter Helen, following freshly covered tracks in the snow towards the edge of the patio balcony outside the Witch's room, spotted her wheelchair toppled-over. No Witch, though.

Had she jumped to her death, parka and mukluks, metallic marigold and all? Had she braked, slid off it, then skidded over the edge to her just as terminal end? Maybe yes, but more likely no. They searched everywhere. Still no body. Still no metallic marigold. The Witch couldn't fly, but with it she could air-walk. So that was a hopeful non-discovery.

Finally Melina used her caduceus, her equivalent of the Witch's stunted eye-stave, her oversexed lollipop, and tried to contact the Master in Cabalarkon in order to tell him the bad news. Wasn't him she got hold of, however; was her, the Witch. Only it was: 'Don't call me Witch, High Illuminary; don't even call me Wilderwitch; I am, as you keep deliberately neglecting to recall, Cynthia Masterwife and, as such, I will be accorded the respect due me, from you, and from now on.'

Matters only went downhill from there; so much so Melina caught herself wishing, against her training, the Witch had gone off the balcony, body and all traces of her swept away in Fearsome Fobbiat, that day in mid-Yamana instead of (presumably) using her metallic marigold to levitate herself back to Cabalarkon.

Not only was she no longer answering to Wilderwitch or Witch, she had begun wearing the White Goddess glamour all the time now; what she first put on that distressful Zmas Night, when they laid her Harry in his tub of animation-suspending, but life-preserving, Cathonic Fluid. Had changed her hair colour, though. Straightened it, too. Was now the Master's All-White Goddess in actuality rather than artifice.

(Supposedly most personalized witch-seemings were nothing more than auric – as in body aura, not golden colouration – manipulations. Casting them was something else Mel, despite years of howsoever half-hearted, witchy training, on both sides of the Dome, had never come close to mastering.

(Aside from what the Master thought of her, she wasn't much of a witch at all. Certainly not an old-time Anthean like the Witch was born to, hence her being classed a supranormal, as opposed to learning the tricks of the trade, the craft, the same as every other Ant Mel had come across in her sixty years of life.)

Then there was the 2-week tour of the countryside the Master sent her and her daughters on earlier in the month. Although Melina enjoyed being outside the city, she couldn't help but reckon she'd been sent away not so much to show the flag, as it were, and to show off her three wonderful daughters – they were Weir's first family after all – as to get her away from seriously sanity-losing Cynthia. (Some women gorged themselves during pregnancy. The Witch was evidently more into gouging others, starting with their pride.)

They were not only not seeing eye-to-eye by then, the Master must have figured they'd soon be going at each other, stunted eye-stave to stunted eye-stave. Which they might have done. With uncertain results. Melina was good with the things. And she'd had her caduceus for something like forty years longer than the Witch had her metallic marigold. Her gargoyle, not that it was a gargoyle as such (or even a grotesque, as gargoyle were more properly known), may have been the emblem of her medical profession but sometimes its two snakeheads had fangs that dripped poison.

Although pleasant enough, it wasn't just her and her daughters, with a huge retinue of her Illuminaries and his Trinondevs, including two of Master Kyprian's loyal leftovers, Golgotha Nauroz, who must be 81 by now, or close to it, and Thobruk Grudal, a Summoning Child like Melina, who went on tour. Three others were the cosmicompanions Harry brought back from the Dinq, Doinq, Danq Cavern Tavern the previous Tantalar.

Two of them were Demonites, his long dead brother's children: Angelica, which didn't sound very Greek or even German (Dem's still living wife Hiliarti was one of those Schroffs), and the even more oddly named Baalbek Schroff Zeross. Which was also pleasant, particularly for her daughters, who enjoyed their cousins' companionship. The third, though, even if she had a pleasant enough personality, wasn't so much so to be around.

Cosmicompanion Carmine Carmichael turned out to be a nymphomaniac; no nicer way to put it. Unless it was 'swinger', although that had the ring of a hangman's noose. Had a tongue on her, too. Which was what might get her hung someday; albeit not in the Weirdom, which didn't do Capital Punishment, never had.

Liked to tell tales out of bed, did the Outer Earthling, and some of the tales she told, fortunately without her daughters being around to hear them, were about Cynthia Masterwife. According to Carmine, who swung both ways – as (apparently) did the Witch – when the Master was away, the Masterwife would play.

And tie knots; to bedposts, among other places.

========

Mel was a bit of a prude anyhow.

Harry would have called her a bit of a prude anytime. And often did. But, hearing 'C', as she was nicknamed, go on and on about sinful Cynthia – her word, not Melina's – and in such titillating, deliberately tantalizingly lurid detail, almost made her glad she couldn't blush in public. Or even in private, no matter how hard she tried to tint her face pink.

Wilderwitch, she knew, had always been wild. Probably should have been called Wildest Witch. Monogamy, as someone like the Diver might put it – were he here, could anyone locate and then get him, draw him, back here – and Wilderwitch were divorced long before they even tied the knot. Which was only one reason, her total distain for Christianity's Holy Sacraments, almost everyone was as surprised as Mel was the Witch agreed to marry the Master.

Her own reasons for refusing to marry him, which she'd enunciated well before she became a closet Christian – and not just because of the Fatman's abiding faith in a Celestial God, this despite him being a Thrygragos Brother's shell for by then howsoever long – made a lot more sense.

As she told Kyprian Somata in 5950, she finally on her deathbed, after years of ill-health, her attending the then-Master with a consciously, if unconscionably, pre-prepared syringe at the ready: 'Loyalty to the State does not have to translate into love for it; especially not love when the state's Master is about to become a son of a devil; the son of the Devil.'

Mercy-killings, she rationalized then, as they may well prove again this night, might well prove, well, merciful.

========

It was with huge relief she realized the Master hadn't brought her into their bedroom, as she'd initially feared, for any sickeningly kinky sex. It was with shameful relief she realized he'd brought her here to be Dr Melina Zeross. There, in the bed with its mirrored-sidewalls and roof that they had shared since mid-Tantalar last, lay Cynthia Masterwife. She was naked. She was wasted. She was, as the famous Outer Earth song had it, a whiter shade of pale.

"You saved her before," said Sal. "Save her again."

"I saved her leg, not her."

"Sleep with her." On second thought, maybe it was.

Quick thinker that she was, though, she thought thirdly and gasped in horror as much due to outrage as revulsion. Not that her facial expression reflected anything other than outward beneficence.

(Pureblood Utopian women like her put on their face, as it were, before they entered the company of others. This because they couldn't crinkle or wrinkle in front of anyone normally. Proof, one of them, of their extraterrestrial origins — another being that they were as white-as-light whereas Utopian men were the opposite, as black-as-night.)

"What!"

"You're an Althean Witch, a healer," Saladin told her, desperate. "Lay on some hands. Lay on more than just hands if you have to. Save her baby at least."

Relief did not wash over her face only because it couldn't. She did speak much more calmly, however. "A foetus barely 2 months in uterus does not constitute a baby, Master. Other than potentially I'm not even sure it constitutes an intelligent being. At this point in its existence I don't see how I can save what's inside without saving what's outside first. We'll have to immerse your Cynthia Masterwife in Cathonic Fluid until we can figure out what's killing her."

"Cathonic Fluid's at least partially made up of distilled Brainrock, isn't it? That'd kill her for sure," he added, without explanation.

(Melina didn't ask for one. She'd had her suspicious about the Witch for a couple of months now. She'd recovered from the injuries she suffered in Temporis on the Sixth of Tantalar beyond even supranormally quickly, Mel reckoned. And, with a very few exceptions, neither devils, nor their azuras, proven lifesavers both, could last long in Cabalarkon without being detected and automatically captured in myriad Trinondev eyeorbs.)

"Can you transplant the pre-baby? Have someone else bear it? I heard stories about something like that happening when I was growing up."

"You're referring to the Trigon Triplets," she said, knowing he'd probably heard it at the same time she did, and probably from the same person, Kanin Nauroz (Granny Garuda), one of his proper aunts, also once Kyprian's High Illuminary, "Eden Nightingale, Cybele St Synne and Human Memory, Mnemosyne D'Angelo later Heliopolis. I suppose it'd be possible, if the Witch was a three-thing like her maybe-mother, a machine, a devil and a human, but she isn't."

"Cut it out of her then. Stick pre-baby in a Development Tank so we can bring it to infancy as a clone and have it raised the same way."

"Now you're asking me to do something that's never been tried before. Not that I've ever heard of anyhow. Let me consult with my Illuminaries, scientocrats and fellow physicians. I'll advise you what we can do in the morning." (Cloning was an ages-old technique perfected by extraterrestrial Trinondevs in order to avoid inbreeding. Did so prior to leaving Second Weirworld for the multiple millennia they pursued the Sedonshem in their generation ships, it was that old.)

"Give me a list of those you want to consult and I'll have Capputis fetch them. In the meantime the least you can do is hold her hand."

=========

"And she probably did have kids, little Sed-sons if Pyrame was involved," Mel-Il-luminatus told Wilderwitch the night (Yamana the 1ˢᵗ) they counted themselves exceedingly lucky to survive the Master trying to kill Blind Sundown, with all-too-predicable results. "That's her gift; her hold over Sedon. For some reason, heaven and hell come together when she beds Sed on both sides of the Dome. Only she can half-have the deviant little buggers."

"One-third-have … and she didn't."

"No, and how might you know that? You weren't there." The two exchanged glances. The Witch didn't say 'boo' and Mel, who was anything except stupid, didn't say 'oh'.

=========

That night atop Skyrise in late Balek 5980 (already 5981 in Satanwyck, where Baaloch Hellblob, the month's namesake, ruled as its Prime Sinistral), the High Illuminary of Weir fell asleep considering why the Master reckoned sticking Cynthia-Wilderwitch in a tub of Cathonic Fluid would kill her for sure.

Had to have something – make that everything – to do with the conversation she and the Witch had at the beginning of Yamana, what would have been New Years Day in most places on the Outer Earth, but in here was just the start of the third month in the Mithraic Ternary. (Balek was its fourth and final month. The Lazaremist Ternary started on the first of Surma, the equivalent of March beyond the Dome.)

The Witch couldn't have been there since the events they were discussing took place in 4825 YD. Neither could Master Morgan Abyss, the Death's Head Hellion, who died under the usual mysterious circumstances that same year. However, someone else could have – someone who could get one-third pregnant – and, if it wasn't Pyrame Silverstar, it could only be her biomorphic, presumed, but ever-unacknowledged daemon, Primeval Lilith, the just as immortal, or at least undying as well as unaging, Demon Queen of the Night.

Plus, according to seemingly eternal speculation by not just Illuminaries like her, lascivious, also lethal, Lily was the third maternal aspect of Sedon's Dome-preserving Sed-sons. Was she, more so than Pyrame, who'd long denied Lilith was her daemon, the one earthborn constant the mighty, as well as mightily masculine, Moloch needed to maintain Cathonia? Had she survived all this time not only to find herself inside Wilderwitch today, but helping to preserve her life since at least early Tantalar?

When she woke up, not all that long later she reckoned, it was no longer an issue. Ding-dong, the wildest, if hardly the wickedest, of witches was dead.

========

"Burn her," commanded the Master, when roused and come as called by attendants he'd grudgingly allowed stay nearby after his trusted, eldest acknowledged son summoned them. His voice no longer sounded desperate. Now he sounded disgusted, though whether it was with the Witch for dying or her for failing to save her, Melina didn't feel qualified to determine.

"At least let's have a proper ceremony, sire," pleaded Capputis Masterson, who came with Fish-Mommy's Daddy. "She was Cynthia Masterwife after all."

"And I'd like to do an autopsy before we do anything else," she insisted in her capacity as a Dr Zeross. "If only to find out what happened to her."

"Do as you please, Illuminary. Just make sure you bring me all of their ashes."

****

Launch 1980

This is how they should have ended

Finally a fitting finale

to the PHANTACEA comic book series

The War of the
Apocalyptics

Nuclear Dragons

Helios on the Moon

PHANTACEA

www.phantacea.com

Paradise for the Damned

A lone woman walked into the throne room of Pandemonium. Sloth, the reigning Prime Sinistral of Satanwyck, regarded her curiously. He reasoned she was from the Outer Earth but, ordinarily, there would be nothing special about that. What was so special about her was her spirit, her soul, still seemed housed in an apparently healthy body. In other words, she was alive.

That was the only reason he had agreed to give her an audience. She could not possibly be here. And otherwise inexplicable things intrigued even Lord Lazy, as his mostly demonic subjects often referred to him when they were just talking amongst themselves in private, rather than when they were out and about attempting to slaughter each other as painfully as possible.

Why wasn't she being digested?

"Welcome to Hell," he shrugged, obligatorily.

... from "The Forgettable Fiend — Hellsent to a Pauper's Grave"

========

Hours later, she sensed a presence, opened Purandar's two human eyes and beheld the Grim Reaper. Must be time to do her witch-glamour trick again.

"About time you showed up, Nergalid. Where've you been: Sowing the seeds of your own destruction as usual?"

"Priestess?" he queried, seemingly recognizing her voice and sounding shocked, though being skinless, not showing it.

"Know anyone else with three eyes, one on each triangular side of her uppermost head? I definitely don't know anyone else who looks like you. What's with all the blood? Don't tell me Devil Deaths have lowered themselves to death-dealing while I've been away?"

... from "Pyrame's Progress — Sorrowful City"

========

Some philosophers called Life Itself, chock-a-block as it was with high and low notes, a Fatal Symphony.

If so, it's conducted by a Maestro of Confusion with everybody who ever lived playing in the orchestra pit. Even a Fatal Symphony had to have a score, though perhaps not a composer; especially not a solitary one, one that would make not just Christians want to capitalize Composer. Most games had scores. Scores are how one determines who wins and who loses. This particular game was still afoot.

So far all it had were losers.

... from "Acquiring Nihila — Unchain my Demon"

========

This is a work of fiction. All the characters portrayed in this book are either fictitious or used fictitiously.

HIDDEN HEADGAMES

VIGNETTES, VERISIMILITUDES AND AT LEAST ONE VAMPIRE LEADING INTO, AND CARRYING ON, '*WILDERWITCH'S BABIES*'

Copyright © James H McPherson

A *PHANTACEA* MYTHOS PRINT PUBLICATION

Conceived, written and produced by Jim McPherson
Interior Collages, Front and Back Covers by Jim McPherson

Phantacea Publications

(James H McPherson, Publisher)
74689 Kitsilano RPO
2768 West Broadway
Vancouver BC
V6K 4P4 Canada

Phantacea Publications featuring

Jim McPherson's

PHANTACEA Mythos

- ***PHANTACEA* One to Six**

(1977-80, a series of comic books with artwork by various artists)

- **Forever & 40 Days – The Genesis of *PHANTACEA***

(1990, a graphic novel with artwork by Ian Fry, background material and a short story featuring the Damnation Brigade, the Death Dodgers & Signal System)

- **Feeling Theocidal**

(2008, Book One of *'The Thrice-Cursed Godly Glories'* trilogy*)

- **The War of the Apocalyptics**

(2009, the first full-length entry in the *'Launch 1980'* story cycle*)

- **The 1000 Days of Disbelief**

(2010-11, Book Two of *'The Thrice Cursed Godly Glories'* trilogy, consisting of three mini-novels: 'The Death's Head Hellion'*, 'Contagion Collectors'* and 'Janna Fangfingers'*)

- **Goddess Gambit**

(2012, Book Three of *'The Thrice Cursed Godly Glories'* trilogy*)

- **Phantacea Revisited 1: The Damnation Brigade**

(2013, graphic novel featuring a complete story sequence primarily excerpted from Phantacea One to Five, various artists*)

- **Nuclear Dragons**

(2013, the second full-length entry in the *'Launch 1980'* story cycle*)

- **Phantacea Revisited 2: Cataclysm Catalyst**

(2014, graphic novel featuring a complete story sequence excerpted from Phantacea One to Seven and Phantacea Phase One #1, various artists*)

- **Helios on the Moon**

(2014, the third and final full-length entry in the *'Launch 1980'* story cycle*)

- **Wilderwitch's Babies**

(2016, 'Decimation Damnation'*; 2017, 'Hidden Headgames')

**E-versions also available*

The
Forgettable
Fiend
Pyrame's
Progress
Acquiring
Nihil